KW-223-119

Max Handley was born in Blackpool, Lancashire, on 23 December, 1945, and was educated at Arnold School and the University of Sussex. He has worked as a magazine editor, a singer/songwriter (his album *Max* has been released on the Virgin Records label), and a composer of film music. He has travelled extensively in Asia, Russia and the USA. At present he lives in Notting Hill Gate, London, and edits *International Times*.

Max Handley

Meanwhile

with decorations by the author

published by Pan Books

First published 1977 by Arlington Books (Publishers) Ltd
This edition published 1978 by Pan Books Ltd,
Cavaye Place, London SW10 9PG
© Max Handley 1977
ISBN 0 330 25572 X
Printed and bound in Great Britain by
Cox & Wyman Ltd, London, Reading and Fakenham

This book is sold subject to the condition that it
shall not, by way of trade or otherwise, be lent, re-sold,
hired out or otherwise circulated without the publisher's prior
consent in any form of binding or cover other than that in which
it is published and without a similar condition including this
condition being imposed on the subsequent purchaser

Of course, the most striking example of this in our own history was The Copyright Wars.

The esoteric group calling itself The Mark of Cain Club secretly acquired exclusive copyright in all existing religious texts and thereupon demanded enormous sums for permission to reprint even a single copy.

War inevitably followed.

The male population was decimated and the female of the species, weary of needless suffering on behalf of a male God, drove the few survivors from the land, forcing them to establish the small and scattered submarine *civilizations with which we are all so familiar today.*

The males survived by cloning, the females by virgin birth and, as centuries passed, their memory of each other faded.

from *The History of Man with a Big M*
by Andrew (what me forget?) Bathurst

This book is dedicated to
Alexander, Stephanie, Helen
and to
Oliver Max Handley
Wherever or Whoever he is

1

I spent the Summer months near a little village called, no, wait a minute, if I give the name the place will be flooded with tourists. The severest warnings are never adequate. People still go to goggle through high-powered binoculars and end up being ambushed. Eaten there and then.

Alfresco, as it were.

It was on the coast, that's all you need to know, and I still had a pair of revolveroids which I put to near-magical use to clear out a pack of Orphachins holed up in a fortified boathouse.

'Hardy har!' I shouted, busting up through a patch of floorboards I had spent several stealthy hours easing loose.

'And hardy har har!' I roared, flecking my tee-shirt with spittle and spinning the revolveroids deftly on my index fingers.

'Hubba hubba,' they responded unconvincingly, their nasty sharp little teeth rattling together with nervous excitement.

'Hubba, Hubba, Hubba.'

It was a rout.

They had nailed up the door, and naturally, ran round and round until they disappeared one by one through my hole in the floorboards (their worst little nightmares come true). It took but a few moments to nail down the floor and batten myself good and snug in my new home. Later, when I heard them furtively scrabbling under the floor, I simply crept over, put my mouth close to a crack and shouted,

'Byoff!' at the top of my voice.

They ran away like hailstones.

'Gobbly, Gobbly,' one of them squeaked in his unbroken little voice, but it didn't frighten me.

I'd been threatened by nasties four times his size.

'Byoff!' I yelled again and gave a hearty laugh for good measure.

It's the laugh that really upsets them.

The filthy swines had been cooking something in a broken old cauldron, but after I found an arm I backed off in disgust. But it gave me food for thought.

Cannibals in heaven?

Then I swiftly checked out the defences: mostly ancient, rotting vehicle tyres cut in strips and woven into massive peek-proof tapestries by smaller, nimbler hands than my wrinkled sodden forelimbs. A labour of love. No – fear. Mad, blue-eyed panic. Strip, knot, pull, hang, until the curtains must have been bone-breaking burdens for the dirty little scavengers.

Smart little punks.

An impenetrable armour nailed on to the walls and roof. The place could have survived a good old-fashioned shelling and just bounced back into shape.

But they were too young to know about the floorboards. That was a stroke of luck for me. Too young to know that *things* could come up out of the water waving revolveroids and shouting 'Hardy har har' and 'Byoff'. Alright. So they learned something. They should thank me. They learned something and they didn't get eaten.

That's not a bad deal these days.

They came back, of course, they always do for a while. But after a couple of days they began to realize they had made the place so trim and tight inside that outside was where they were going to stay.

That's always the way, I suppose.

Then, on the third night, they began to fall out with each other.

At first it was just the odd cuffing sound on the roof or a quick scuffle under the floorboards and then something nasty and screaming happened on the dark side by the water's edge and I couldn't help feeling a bit of a wince for some stinking Orphachin that was getting his from his little buddies.

I risked a look outside after a week, scanned both banks, upstream and down. It was all quiet. I'd never expected it to be so easy and took it as a sign that my luck was beginning to turn.

I was wrong.

Had I known what I was swimming into I would have stayed in the water another year.

But that's me, I suppose. Impulsive. Others have used a less flattering word but, significantly enough, they're the ones who never came up from the sea at all.

*

After a while, despite the injuries of that nightmare journey from the bottom of the sea, I ventured out for short daylight swims in the river and would sometimes pull myself out on to the bank to exercise my back and legs, although one day, having crawled too far, I was nearly ambushed by two large Orphachins lying in wait among the branches of a tree and thereafter never really relaxed except in the water or in the security of the boat house unless I had my revolveroids with me. But I used my time to the full, exercising and meditating over the manuscripts I had brought up from the sea-bed, slowly bringing back muscles that were all but defunct, learning again how to function without the resistant buoyancy of water around me and waiting for the physical damage of the submarine ascent to heal.

I was constantly amazed at how well I could re-adapt myself to dry land.

After only four or five days it was hard to believe I hadn't been born there.

Even my pattern of sleeping and waking changed; instead of sleeping for fifteen minutes each hour I found myself staying awake for sixteen hours at a stretch and then falling completely unconscious for seven or eight. But this was a change that I found very disturbing.

And I must confess that the hours of darkness were difficult for me. I didn't sleep much at first. I would stare round nervously at the woven tyres in the light of my fish-scale phosphorescence lantern, wondering if the cunning Orphachins might not have left some secret entrance through which to ambush me. Each night I would check every inch of the rubber tapestry, curl up in a corner trying to doze, then jerk horribly awake, already halfway to my feet, hairs rising on my spine, peering into the darkness, hallucinating their horrible little eyes gleaming through the walls.

Nightmares of booby traps.

Daydreams of unexpected attack.

A time of pain, fear and hunger.

And disgust.

For as the days passed, their grisly cooking-pot began to stink and fester, filling the boathouse with its distinctive ammoniac stench, and I dared not throw it into the river for fear of attracting some other prowler of this unknown world, some beast strong and smart enough to smash through my defences.

But it was all worth it. Behind my pain and fear I was still confident. You can call me crazy. Perhaps I was. Perhaps anyone who had a dream is crazy – reaching out from one reality to another may strain the muscles of the mind.

I didn't care.

I was in too deep by then anyway.

If I was crazy then I was going to stay crazy until I'd done what I set out to do from the beginning.

'It's his Father's madness,' they used to say. 'He's going to end up just the same way.'

I resented that.

I had always felt especially fortunate to have come from such an adventurous cloning. And now *I* was here, fulfilling *my* dreams and *my* ambitions. With every nerve at my disposal I was willing *myself* on to the fulfilment of The Dream: I was going to be the first human male to mate in a thousand years!

No doubt about it.

I had decided.

2

Over the years a lot of myth and legend grew up around this 'mating' business. Some thought it a figment of disordered minds; others felt that the ability to mate, at one time real enough, had atrophied from disuse; a few, usually those of a fanciful disposition, allowed it to dominate their conversation and consciousness to the exclusion of almost everything else.

from *The Sociobiology of Submarine Civilizations*

It was about four weeks before they found me.

Bump.

Against the central pillar. I thought maybe it was just some low-brained Orphachin pottering about for scraps but then it hit again.

Bump.

Against the next pillar. I broke out in a sweat of fear.

Bump.

Moving heavily underneath the boathouse with a long, deep scraping that shuddered the floorboards and shivered through my knees.

'That's no Orphachin,' I thought, hanging on tight to my adrenalin pumps.

Squinting down at the river through a knot-hole, I glimpsed something silent and enormous moving below me.

'That *is* no Orphachin!' I muttered, drawing back in terror, 'That thing isn't even *alive!*'

I peered down another knot-hole and saw the thing in its entirety. It was a boat!

An old drifter. A faded, pink, press-moulded, shiny-tight cork of a river-bum, freckled with age and crackled by weather, it smiled up at my eye like an ancient, cosmetic kiss.

'Wow!' I murmured in delight. 'A boat!'

I hurried to the trap-door and dropped eagerly through, picking my way along a structural crossbeam.

What a find! What a gift!

But, about to reach out for the neat coil of rope on her bow, I saw a tell-tale white flicker in the water almost too late from the corner of my eye and blacked out, momentarily, as animal panic stiffened me rigid and, with a massive burst of glandular activity, spun me round and hurled me back through a trapdoor that I had closed and battened even before fully realizing the import of those trailing legs.

I crawled over to the peephole and watched for a long time.

It was a trap.

Boat-bait.

An old River-people's trick. I must have been getting idle-minded. Nearly stepped into it. My skin crawled to think how close I had come. I stared down with a whirling mind.

There must be a breathing-hole somewhere. Whatever was fishing for me had to be an air-beather and almost certainly a mammal, for no other species would be driven to the use of such elaborate cunning.

For long moments the boat swung lazily in the current and then, with the smooth slowness of an entirely natural event, it turned and was plucked gently away by the river. I scurried frantically from peephole to peephole, fearful that the creature might still be hiding beneath the boathouse. But it seemed to have tired of its sport and taken its boat.

I lay until dark that day, motionless, the side of my head against the boards, analysing out the tiny sounds of the river and my boathouse planted in it from the eerie echoes of the distant mountains mewing in the sinking sun: sniffing the air, separating the rough dust of plank floors from the molecular droppings of the ripped rubber trellises and the light Spring sauce of running river with its water-breathing life crawling up my pillars, dying, bleaching and being crept upon. But in all that roaring stink there was no trace of the floating pink pucker-up and its hunter captain.

I slept.

Exhausted.

And then.

Bump.

In the darkness.

And again. Directly beneath me.

Bump.

The same lingering tremor of grazed, bleached greenery.

It was back.

By night.

It knew I was there.

I was trapped like a mollusc in a shell.

It remained only to see whether the predator could break me open.

Bump.

It had passed under the boathouse to rest against the downstream pillar. No scraping this time. Purposive. It had stopped. Torn between screaming and silence, I held my breath for too long and then gasped for air, muffling my mouth in my hands. My heartbeat was as ragged as my respiration in the waiting agonies of anxiety.

Tons of soundless water moved slowly past that night as I breathed and listened. Listened and breathed. But at first light, soon after the mountain tops had turned from orange to silver as the sun slid from the hostile peaks to the softer soils of the lowlands, I squinted through my holes and found that whatever it was had slipped away unheard in the darkness, leaving me to grind myself gaga, listening for something that was gone.

Another old trick.

'I'm up against a mastermind,' I told myself. 'Or else I'm getting paranoid.'

But thought, 'Or perhaps it was just a log.'

Then realized, 'That's what I'm supposed to think, but I'm not falling for it. I *know* it was a boat.'

And then, 'It was hoping to confuse me, unable to decide whether it was a log or a boat.'

And then, 'No, it damn well knew I'd realize it had come back and it *wants* me to go through this log fantasy to wear me down.'

I put my face in my hands in despair.

'I'm up against a mastermind,' I told myself.

'Or else I'm getting paranoid.'

I shut myself in securely all that day and night and all the next day. Uneasy. Listening. Hearing everything except what I least wanted to hear and feeling worse for it. Wondering whether to run now, run later, or hope it wouldn't come back at all. Torn with indecision I exhausted myself without moving a muscle. Then, on the third morning it *did* come back.

Bump.

I roared with rage, unthinking. Fear, really, raging against my own terror. Ferociously I dragged a disgusting lump from the Orphachins' stinking cauldron and, kicking open the hatch in frightened fury, flung the abominated flesh into the boat.

'You want food?' I yelled. 'So *eat*!' and slammed down the hatch with shaking hands. Trembling like a punished puppy, I crept to a peep hole and looked down. There it was alright. Gleaming like wrinkled, moistened lips in the submarine shadows, bobbing, idle and innocent, on the unruffled waters, the wheel shifting softly into the current.

Not a living thing to be seen.

And the meat was gone.

I didn't know what else to do.

I began to clean my revolveroids.

3

Aint no hesitatin',
Had my fill of waitin',
I'm anticipatin'
Matin'.

A popular traditional hymn.
(Hymns like this were sung at clandestine religious
gatherings until the turn of the present century)

This is the scene. The mountains run like a stickleback's double spine down the centre of the scarab-shaped island. A high altitude spring, swollen by melting snows in the Summer and filled with crushed ice in the Winter, trickles down the glass-bound rock faces, leaping a step or two by way of short cuts to the lowlands where it warms up, broadens out, takes on a cargo of mineral salts and microscopic life dissolved from the soil, dead creatures and vegetables that have stumbled from the banks, and winds towards the sea, licking at the pillars of my boathouse on the way and, in this case, bumping against them a gloss-pink speedboat upon her broad liquid bosom. Then, rounding a self-induced bend, she spills out into the sea between stone jetties built for long-vanished fishing fleets whose crews had strolled the cobbled streets of the bright, white village looking for taverns, trinkets and tarts and finding only a wineshop and a launderess who, between them, somehow managed to handle all the business.

I do not speak, of course, from personal experience. All my knowledge of the village comes from old travellers' notebooks in the history libraries, except for one peek from the river that I couldn't resist shortly after I first arrived.

It's a small place. Seemingly deserted. But appearances are almost certainly deceptive. (And the boat must have come from somewhere.)

The river runs from East to West and across the water from me the land flows Northward in a broad strip to round a shoulder of the mountains several miles away. Behind me the view is lost in patches of gnarled and stunted trees climbing thickly along the gentle sides of the valley. And below the planks where I watch through chinks of my hands and knees is the damnable polyester coracle with its monstrous white plastic, button-backed engine-cover, its wafer-thin, contour-moulded bendibenches and its furtive carnivorous, air-breathing pilot clinging, eyeless, to the underside of the hull like some megalomaniac scorpion-shark or a man-eating swordfish. More deadly than a million starving Orphachins. More single-minded than a fly-trap. And worse, as events had already shown, probably more intelligent than me.

'Well,' I thought, enjoying the irony of it, 'this is what I came for.'

But I hadn't expected to tremble quite so much. When I had thrust myself out of the tubes of the submarine city to seek the heaven 'up there' of which the ancient manuscripts foretold, I had hardly expected to find a world so bleak and hostile. I had looked forward to what the teachings described as the 'thrill of the chase' or the 'waiting game', but I had not foreseen being so easily and edibly cornered. I realized it had been a mistake to throw out the cooked meat. The creature would just hang around waiting for more until it grew hungry and decided to come for the last, coincidentally living, morsel.

'Ya rotten fink,' I muttered. 'Ya dirty rotten fink.'

For as long as it stayed out of sight in the water the now gleaming revolveroids were useless, so we waited, it and I, for each other's first false move. And I consoled myself with the thought that the longer it kept me boxed up, the less of me there would be to eat when it finally bust in.

I crept over to my back-pack and opened the waterproof seals on the map compartment. It seemed the right time to check through the literature on the subject. I scanned the pictures and diagrams – anatomy, physiology, biology – I already knew them better than the reflection of my own face and body. I stirred up the light of the phosphorescence-lamp against the gathering gloom and meditated over them. What I didn't know from the literature now I would never know. All the rest simply had to be culled from experience.

Bump.

Experiences like this one, I thought, already on my startled feet, backing into the farthest corner to leave my options open. I heard movements in the water, strenuous splashings and a tiny tapping like fingernails on a mirror then, sickeningly sudden, a massive muscled assault on my battened hatch.

'The thing knows how to get in!' I marvelled, almost vomiting with the notion. The hatch bounced and splintered but the battens held and, abruptly, all fell still and silent. I listened to the creature covering the floor from beneath, inch by inch, and pause, breathing, at one of my spyholes. The lamp was glowing softly. It was looking at the lamp. It moved on, coming towards me in my corner. I stepped on the spyhole at my feet and held my breath. I heard it scratch across the floor then felt something press my sole with an inquisitive claw, feeler or finger. And it sniffed and scraped at it through the boards.

'Get lost, ya horrible, slimy, rotten monster,' I whispered into my teeth, feeling sweat run down my back and legs.

And then with a curious moaning sound it was gone.

Bump.

I clung to the walls to keep from crumpling up on the floor.

'Could be a trick,' I thought.

Then, 'But that's what I'm supposed to think and stand here like a fool till I'm too exhausted to defend myself.'

I marvelled once more at the fiendish intelligence of my adversary. 'But that's another cunning trick,' I thought, 'to impress me so much with the weakness of my position that I fail to take counter-measures.' I smiled bitterly to myself.

And went to work fast. I strengthened the hatch, built a shelf halfway up the wall on which I could take cover with my pack if the thing got in but couldn't climb well out of water. And cut a fist-sized hole in the corner over deepest water, a hole just big enough to take a revolveroid-wielding hand or the lunging-gaffe I had sharpened to a needle-point.

'Come on baby,' I whispered as I lay down on my shelf to sleep, 'Let's see what you're made of.'

And then, as an afterthought,

'Or at least what you are.'

I spent a restless night. Tangled dreams. Hideously interlocked episodes of the real and the unreal. Flesh-eating night-predators turning this way and that in the throes of mating behaviour (symptoms of what they called my sickness) and red plastic apertures shuttered with pointed teeth flashing closed at speeds exceeding that of light itself.

As nightmares go they were fairly enjoyable. At least twice as enjoyable as the waking day that preceded them, but savage enough to make me think as I lay in the darkness, having just woken myself up by screaming too loudly, that if I didn't dispose of the creature the next day I would have to make a break for the mountains.

Even as I turned this over in my mind the thing came back.

Bump.

'So soon?' I thought, 'It must be ravenous.'

. Bump.

4

Meanwhile, high in the mountains, sat the father of the besieged boathouse dweller, he who had been thought lost in the crushing sea-pressures outside the walls of the submarine city. Now he sat in the snow staring at the frozen shackles on his knees.

There was an old saying in the Snowcamp that went, 'Six Full Moons and your lower legs fall off', snap in two like icicles, and you

don't notice until you try to stand up. That's why he stared at his knee-shackles as he sat restless during the noon snowbreak, keeping an eye on shins and ankles, chains and shackles, in a shallow valley between the twin spines of the island's snow-filled mountains.

They were twelve.
They were always twelve.
Prisoners came, prisoners vanished and they were still twelve. Each new arrival meant that somewhere up on the shovelling-slopes some poor bastard's Sixth Full Moon was hanging in the sky and his lower legs were lying in the snow. At least that was what they muttered to each other over the evening pots. That was the myth that had grown up around the regular Full Moon disappearances.

No one ever blamed a new arrival directly for the oldest prisoner's death, he was just shown how the mathematics worked and left to draw his own conclusions. He invariably said, 'I didn't *ask* to be brought here, you know,' with a trace of anger in his trembling voice. And the others invariably replied, '*Everyone* says that.'

When The Father first stumbled into the Snowcamp, blundering down the slopes, blankly amnesiac and bewildered, as all the prisoners had come, he had ridiculed this placid acceptance of Life's cyclic determinism and tried to disturb it with irrational responses.

'Hardy har!' he had shouted gleefully. 'And hardy har har!'
But the other prisoners smiled gently and said,
'That's exactly what *we* said when we first found out how things were going to be.'

'Byoff!' retorted The Father.
'*And* that,' replied the other prisoners.
'Well you're not going to get me to play along with this ridiculous charade,' The Father declared with waning confidence.

'We said that too.'
'You're lying! It's not possible! We're all different. *Nobody* does exactly what's been done before. Things can't happen twice!'

'More than twice,' they answered.
'Does that mean you already know what I'm going to say or do next?' cried The Father in bewilderment.

'Yes,' replied the other prisoners, mingled pity and cruelty in their eyes.

'What?' demanded The Father tremulously. 'What am I going to do next?'

'You're going to cry,' replied his fellow-prisoners. 'We *all* did.' And they munched dispassionately as he burst into tears.

Now he munched on the crisp snow with studious resignation. It was tasteless, tedious eating but kept one alive until pot-time. A more recent captive sat against his shovel further down the slope and tossed a handful of lunch aside to squint up at the sun.

'What do you reckon?' he yelled, his voice floating faintly up the white, motionless cascade.

'Nah! Not yet!' shouted back The Father, shaking his head. He knew what the lad was feeling. He too could remember becoming restive at snowtime, wanting to get back to his shovel for the sake of activity.

'Nah! Not yet!' the older prisoner had shouted back, shaking his head. Then, throwing a snowball, added, 'Try this, it's tastier the higher up you get.'

Now, today, his last day, The Father threw his own snowball and shouted too.

Ridiculous really.

He knew the ball would roll down the slope, picking up weight and momentum, until it smashed against the younger man's back and shovel, dividing into a hundred pieces and careering in a small, escalating avalanche down the slopes it had taken all morning to smooth.

Dreamlike, he saw the young man stagger to his feet with a bellow of rage, seize his shovel and try to mince up the slope in his knee-shackles shouting, 'You bloody swine!' and other such profanities.

'You won't make it,' muttered The Father, remembering how, in his own red-eyed fury, he had cut his knees against the shackles and tumbled bleeding and raggedly panting into the soft fresh snow, his tormentor perched unconcerned a hundred feet above him. Looking down now he knew the tiny struggling figure would try to crack open his skull at pot-time and knew that he would forget, be taken by surprise and suffer a savage blow to the head that would lay him out and that tonight, damaged, disillusioned and empty he would trudge up to the highest slopes in the light of the Full Moon, and lay himself down to die. He smiled grimly at the prospect, fingering the deep red scar on the back of his right hand.

The young prisoner would receive one of these in that fight.

He shook his head sadly again.

If there was one thing he had learned in the Snowcamp it was resignation.

'Hardy har har,' he muttered under his breath, resigned to the knowledge that men must have sat up on this slope and muttered 'Hardy har har' under their breath every month since this nightmare place had first been built.

Whenever that was.

Or by whom.

For whatever purpose.

In what spot.

He tried to think about these questions, but the bright dazzling light of the snows filled his head with a blinding *Now* that burned out memory and desire alike.

Come from?

Been?

Am?

Going to?

The questions set up no resonance in his head.

They were almost meaningless.

And yet sometimes he sensed a fleeting intuition, a vanishing impression of something familiar. It was always quickly gone.

It always made his head hurt.

He glanced at the sun. Snowtime was over.

'Okay!' he yelled to the tiny crumpled form downslope. It lifted its tiny snow-fringed head, mouth moving, and fractionally later the words floated up to him as he started his afternoon smoothing.

'I'm going to bash your bloody skull in,' it said.

'Yes,' said The Father softly to himself. 'I know you are.'

5

Later that evening he sat at the Pot-table waiting for the others to come. It was traditional for a man to have some time alone on his last night.

The months he had lived in the amnesiac community came back to him slowly, filling him with an even greater bitterness than usual.

'Listen,' he had protested when he first came. 'You don't understand. I shouldn't *be* here.'

'Here's your smoother,' they said. 'If you want to eat you work.'

'But of course I want to eat!' he complained 'I'm human aren't I. But it's all a mistake!'

'You can say that again,' they replied. 'Now work.'

They put him on the newcomer slopes where the job was hardest.

'You walk the length of the valley pulling the smoother behind you, making sure you don't miss any marks.'

'Why?' he asked.

'So the snow will be smooth, of course.'

'But the snow is smooth *now*,' he pointed out.

They looked at each other as though he were mentally defective.

'How can it be smooth when you've just walked on it?' they enquired with heavy sarcasm.

'But what if I don't walk on it?'

They looked at each other again and shook their heads.

'How can you smooth the bloody stuff if you don't walk on it, you dummy?' they replied. 'Now here's your smoother. Get to work.'

In the end it had seemed easier to smooth snow than to argue, so he smoothed snow, getting up each morning, going to work, coming back to the huts exhausted, eating frugally and falling into bed to wake up and repeat the cycle the next day.

Before long he forgot who he was in the hypnotic white sameness of one day to the next.

Sometimes he tried to argue, but learned that it didn't pay.

And he learned it the hard way.

It was at pot-time, the only occasion when one could hold a conversation without shouting across great distances of snow.

It seemed a simple enough question.

He said,

'What are we all doing here?'

There was a long silence and everyone stopped eating.

Then, one by one, without looking up, they began to eat again.

He turned to his neighbour, who studiously examined each mouthful of food before shovelling it into his face, and whispered,

'What did I say wrong?'

'Nothing,' the man replied, without breaking his rhythmic spooning. 'Now shut up.'

The Father ate in puzzled silence for a while then, partly out of embarrassment, said,

'I didn't mean to offend anybody.'

One of the older prisoners replied,

'You didn't son. It's just that your question didn't need answering.'

'Why not?'

Everybody's spoon came to an abrupt halt and he looked round, but no one met his gaze.

'It's like this,' the man replied again. 'We just don't ask questions like that here. Okay? We're here. We work. We eat. We sleep. And we don't bother our heads about questions that don't concern us.'

And all the spoons began to move again.

'Well, wow!' said The Father, nettled, 'I think it jolly well *does* concern us if we're stuck here in this place smoothing snow for no good reason until the day we disappear. I think it's very *relevant* to ask why we're here and what's going to happen to us all and who is running this show.'

The only reply was silent spooning. He looked around wildly.

'Well don't just sit there eating and ignoring me! Is it relevant or isn't it?'

Another man responded without raising his eyes.

'Have *you* got any answers to these so-called "relevant" questions you're asking?'

'Of course I haven't.'

'Well then,' he replied and seemed satisfied.

'Well then?' cried The Father. 'Is that all you can say? Look!' He rapped on the table with his spoon for emphasis. 'I'm asking some extremely important questions here and you're all making out that I'm some kind of dodo. Doesn't it *concern* you that we're all stuck here and don't know why? Doesn't it even *involve* you? Are you just content to sit there without the answers and pretend there aren't any questions?'

'Look, buddy,' said the man on his left. 'Let's clear this up once and for all. I'll answer any questions you got. You want to ask me a question? You *ask* me a question. I'll give you an absolutely clear and straightforward answer.'

'You will?' cried The Father, delighted to have finally broken through to them.

'I surely will,' was the reply.

'Okay then, for starters answer me this one.'

The Father thought carefully to frame a good question.

'Okay I've got one. Why do we spend all day working out on the snow instead of sitting in here talking or playing tag outside or something along those lines?'

The man looked at his plate for a long moment, nodding slightly to himself and then, faster than The Father's reactions could handle, swung an explosive left fist into his unguarded face.

Other blows followed, some from the table as he fell forward, others from the floor as he was punched backwards, others still from various boots that swung in slow pendulous arcs across his field of vision to lay their separate pains upon his person.

'Enough!' his cortex declared and darkness fell.

It seemed like hours.

Then he stared round. In the unfamiliar lights. Wondering why he wasn't sitting at the table with the others.

'I must have fallen over,' he thought naïvely. Until the discomforts of his body recalled many a specific blow.

'Any more questions?' a voice rasped and another voice, his own, close by, through thick lips, unfamiliar, weak and wobbly, said,

'Pardon?'

'Ah shutup,' came the reply. 'That should solve *his* bloody dilemmas for a bit anyway.'

He lay back peaceably on the floor beneath the flickering oil-lamps while they finished their meal, wondering if it wasn't a strange position to adopt at pot-time.

'So many puzzling things,' he muttered to himself in bewilderment. 'One minute I'm eating a meal, the next I'm lying on my back on the floor.'

Then he remembered what had happened and became angry;

quietly angry, of course, in the face of such overwhelming odds, and crawled with some difficulty to the door.

He wasn't going to stay somewhere he wasn't welcome, he thought, and prised open the latch with his as yet unhurt fingers.

'Yar boo sucks,' he whispered belligerently. 'I'll fix all of you for this, just see if I don't.'

And crawled defiantly out into the mud.

'That showed them,' he muttered, dragging himself to the bunk-house.

'Har har, they'll think twice before they try to strongarm *me* again.'

He crawled across the board floors to his cot and dragged himself painfully up to his pillow.

'Why did they do that?' he thought.

And fell unconscious.

Now he sat alone in the pot-house and shook his head sadly to recall the misery he had suffered in this place.

He had often wondered what it would feel like when time-to-go drew near, when it was his turn to wander up the slopes and lie down in the snow to die.

Now he knew.

All emotion had been bleached out of him, no hope, no desire, no surprise, no joy, he sought only respite from weariness, absence of hunger and freedom from pain. He felt inexorably drawn to the legless sleep of the six-moon snows. But he had feared that easy fatalism. Day by day he saw it grow even in himself. Simpler to pat the heads reliving a well-known past than bash against bolted trap-doors to the future with one's own skull. One comes to persuade oneself, 'if I am not free to choose, then why make the vain pretence of choosing?' As though being held captive and giving up one's freedom were the same thing. (Although, certainly, a damnably seductive idea when your knees are shackled together.)

But something rankled, some fleeting glimmer of reluctance tugged at his mind.

He tried to concentrate.

'Think,' he told himself angrily. 'This is your last chance. Tonight you die!'

He tried to shut away the bleak, blank brilliance of his sterilized world and sink in to the blackness of his injured and fermenting unconscious.

'I *must* know where I came from, he muttered. 'I must at least remember something.'

It was at this moment that the first tremors came.

At first he thought it was blood pounding in his ears and felt his heart with a nervous hand. But as the structure of the huts began to wobble and creak faintly he realized what was happening, jumped up in alarm, only to lose his balance as the ground beneath his feet trembled almost imperceptibly. The lanterns swung gently on their hooks and the air shivered with unheard vibrations. Paralysed by fright, he clung motionless to the wooden boards until, gradually, the earth grew silent and the tremors subsided.

'An earthquake,' he muttered anxiously. 'Thank God I'm not under the sea now!'

He picked himself up and was about to sit down again when realization struck him with even greater force than the terrifying earth shudder.

'Under the sea?' he exclaimed aloud. 'Under the sea?'

Then it came back to him, crashing into consciousness with the force of a great mass of water squeezing through a tiny fissure in a dam, changing from a trickle to a mighty torrent as it burst the retaining walls asunder.

He remembered it all. The City on the sea-bed. The Trial. The Barbans making out their fraudulent charges. The Arbitrator pronouncing him guilty.

'But double-cloning was never a crime *before*!' The Father had cried as the death sentence was passed. 'You've changed the law!'

'You cloned two sons from the same cells,' The Arbitrator had wheezed in his ancient voice. 'That is against the law now, even if it wasn't when you did it. In this community you are allowed only one clone. And since your twins are still alive then I find you guilty as charged.' And then The Tubes. The dreadful airlocks, the inner door closing, the outer door opening and the black sea crashing in!

He remembered it all with renewed anger and bitterness.

'Legal murder!' he hissed angrily. 'The Barbans were trying to murder me with the law and they had The Arbitrator in their pocket!'

He remembered recovering consciousness in bright sunlight on a sandy beach, the pain of a crushed body, the agony of thirst and hunger and then the Devils! He shuddered as he recalled The Devils! Hideous in form, mutant creatures, appalling travesties of life! And they had carried him up from the sands to a caged waggon and thrust him into the mouth of a river bursting from a cliff-face, forcing him to climb up against the rushing water by releasing humanoid dogs upon him, with their hideous childlike cry of hate,

'Gobbly, Gobbly. Gobbly, Gobbly.'

He ran trembling fingers over his face and felt the perspiration running off on to his palms. That was how he came to be here! That river mouth widening into a crevasse and at the end of it, looking down, he had seen the lights of the Snowcamp huts gleaming invitingly at the bottom of a deepsnow-filled bowl and had stumbled gladly towards them, floundering and tumbling, slowly transformed by some natural magic of the mountain whiteness into a mindless amnesiac.

'There *is* an outside world,' he thought wildly. 'Why should I just lie down and die when I can *escape*? I've remembered the past! I can tell the others! It will change everything! It will release us all!' He heard footsteps behind him and turned in jubilation to break the news.

But for that the blow would have split his skull like a coconut instead of grazing his temple, spattering blood on the table as he wheeled drunkenly from the bench and lashed out at the assailant with his knife, noticing with secret satisfaction, as he sank faintly to his knees, that the young man leaped back with a scream of pain, all the fight carved out of him and a savage tear opening up on the back of his right hand.

'Destiny preserve me,' said The Father, muttering the long-forgotten prayer without thinking as blackness overwhelmed him in billowing red-edged clouds, washing away the image of eternal snows that afflicted all their imprisoned, ice-bound souls.

Slipping from consciousness he heard a young one say,

'I think he's dead.'

No one replied. Someone always said 'I think he's dead' when this happened and no one ever replied.

And the one who spoke would now be noticing that every right hand save his own bore a livid red scar and he would sit suddenly silent with terror as the machined nightmare into which he had stumbled became ever-clearer to him.

6

'He's not bleeding!' The Father heard a voice exclaim and felt himself lowered on to the bed.

'He must be! All the others were soaked in it when it was time-to-go.'

'He's not, I tell you. Here, give me that lamp. Look. What colour is his hair?'

'It's white.'

'Alright then. So don't tell me he's bleeding. He's not shed a drop! That's the way it is.'

A third voice said,

'It *can't* be,' and there was a snort of anger and the sound of a scuffle.

A chill draught razored across the bunkhouse as the door banged open and he heard the old man's voice shouting,

'What the hell's going on?' with fear and horror in his questioning.

'Look at this,' came the reply. And as he slowly rose to consciousness he became aware of lamplight swaying crazily across his orange-veined eyelids.

'Is he bleeding, or isn't he?'

There was a long silence of mixed breathing, the sounds that men make when they stumble upon an ancient mummified catacomb corpse or a carelessly cloned cast-out.

'I don't know,' answered the old man finally, barely able to speak above a whisper.

'Well bloody look at him!' The lamp came closer. 'Just bloody look at him! What colour is his head? Blue? Green?'

'I can't tell,' the old man stammered. 'The light, it plays tricks. Hard to tell. Should be red. Should be covered in blood. Can't be white because it was white before.'

'Oh, sod this. Alright. It's not what. It *looks* white, but it's *not* white. It just *seems* to be white. Just like that snow out there *seems* to be white. In actual fact, in the right light, you'll see that the mountains are really *brunette* with a *centre-parting* and a *cow-lick*! You're absolutely right. And not the slightest bit out of your bloody minds!'

Wind-razors scoured the room again as he banged out into the darkness, yelling off into the night.

The silence his shouting left behind was treacle-thick and sweat-flavoured.

'I don't remember, that is, I can't actually recall this happening before,' the old man said reflectively, almost to himself. 'Funny how the memory plays tricks.'

'Maybe he's got white blood,' suggested another. 'You never know. It's possible, isn't it? I mean that would account for it not showing.'

'Yes,' said the old man, 'that's probably it,' and then, slowly, 'but it's best if we don't mention this to the others.'

'Absolutely!' a third voice replied. 'No one ever mentioned it to us when it happened before so why should we?'

'What about his hair being dry?' said the second voice.

'Trick of the light,' the old man broke in firmly. 'Either that or white blood goes dry very quickly.'

'Yes,' the other voices agreed. 'White blood probably dries straight away.'

'Why don't you two go eat your pots? I'll make sure he's okay and follow you over.'

Through slitted lids he saw the two younger men leave wordlessly and the old man staring vacantly at the lamp, rubbing the side of his face with a flat and anxious hand. The Father tried to move his lips but no sounds came. He closed his eyes and collected together his face muscles to try again.

'I did it,' he blurted finally. The old man twitched in fright.

'What?'

'I did it,' The Father croaked again. 'Changed things.'

He felt proud in a way. Something new had finally happened in the Snowcamp.

But he was unprepared for the peevish, lip-curled retort.

'Don't you be so bloody sure, clever-dick.'

'My hair!' he protested weakly. 'There's no blood!'

A bitter and ironic smile melted across the old man's countenance. 'Now how would you know a thing like that? You can see the top of your own head, can you?'

'I heard them saying that—'

'You heard *nothing*!' he snapped. 'Understand? Nothing!'

'But this hasn't happened before,' The Father exclaimed, unable to understand the unexpected anger.

'It has!' The old man shouted. 'It has! It has! It *must* have!'

'But—'

'Don't *but* me!' he screamed. 'You think you're so bloody clever! You think you've changed things! Well you haven't. You can't! It's not fair on the rest of us!'

'Not fair?' The Father tried to sit up in his cot but collapsed weakly on the pillow.

'Right! Supposing some smartass like you comes and changes things. What happens then? No one has any idea what happens then, that's what. And people like me, old people who've gone through all the agonies of coming to terms with this crazy place, are left dangling. Where's our guarantee we're going to get out of here when our Sixth Moon comes up? Supposing you really have changed things and we all have to go on living here for ever? No leg-losing, more and more youngsters pouring in every month, food supplies running out, fighting amongst ourselves, killings, thievings, no one knowing from one minute to the next what's going to happen? Is that what you want, you selfish bastard?'

'No, of course, I—'

'Well then, nothing's changed, alright?'

'I don't see how we can say that when—'

'We can say it,' the old man shouted, a hysterical disharmony in his vocal cords. 'We can say it. We're *going* to say it. If we have to we'll pretend all this has happened *before*. I'm the next-to-go after you. They'll all believe me. It's only for a few hours. By tomorrow morning you'll be up in the snows getting your last sleep and things can go on undisturbed.'

'But we're *free* now!' cried The Father. 'Don't you understand? I've broken the sequence. I've broken the cycle.'

The door opened and a huddled form scurried in with the freezing wind, peering into the gloom.

'What's happening?' he asked anxiously. 'There's no blood in the snow.'

'He's got white blood,' the old man answered. 'Doesn't show. Now get back to your pots before they get cold.'

The figure shuffled over curiously.

'White blood!' he exclaimed in wonder.

The old man tried to screen him from the victim on the bed.

'I am *not* bleeding,' said The Father firmly. 'I've changed everything. I've remembered how we all got here.'

'Quiet!' hissed the old man savagely.

'I must be heard. This has to be told. The truth must be known.'

'This *is* unusual,' said the newcomer. 'Truth? What truth?'

The Father greeted his question with relief. At last, someone who would listen. He ran through his recollection with eager haste. 'We all came from under the sea. Don't you remember? Stop me when it reminds you of anything. Big bubbles. We lived in big bubbles anchored to the sea-bed. At one time we were all in one big bubble, a whole, great civilization, but accidents happened, they divided up into smaller scattered bubbles and lost touch with each other. I don't recognize anyone in the Snowcamp so you must all have come from other bubbles. We must have got up top somehow and then those strange mutant creatures captured us and put us in here. Don't you remember being forced up a narrow river passage in a cliff-face and then losing your memories?'

He stared excitedly at their unresponsive faces.

'This is dangerous, dangerous talk,' muttered the old man, red with anger.

But slowly a look of amazement dawned over the other's face. The Father grasped his hands eagerly.

'You remember,' he cried. 'I can see it in your face! You remember!'

'No, no,' replied the man, with a look of awe, 'I can't remember anything. But I believe you! I believe you!'

'He believes me!' cried The Father in delight. 'Now it's all changed. Now we don't have to go through this cycle of suffering. We're free to make our own choices. We're saved!'

'Yes, saved!' replied the man joyfully. 'I believe you, Lord. I believe you!'

'Don't be crazy,' yelled the old man, rushing to the door. 'I'm going to get the other before it's too late.'

The young man fell on one knee with a look of deep adoration.

'Bless me, Lord,' he begged. 'Bless me before you go.'

'I'm not going anywhere,' cried The Father. 'At least, not yet. I'm going to explain everything to everyone here and then we'll decide what we all want to do.'

The face of the devotee turned pale and anxious.

'Oh, but you must go, Lord. You must. It comes to us all.'

'What comes to us all?'

'The old Snowcamp in the sky, old chap. Daddy's Place. Goodboy's Home. Can't take it with you when you go and all that sort of stuff. You *have* to go. But listen,' he pressed forward anxiously, 'when you get up *there*,' he pointed to the ceiling, 'tell Everyone what's happening and get Them to do something about it. If what you say is true, then we're being pretty unfairly treated and I think you ought to bring that to the attention of the Powers That-Be. I'm sure that was Your Mission, Lord.'

The door burst open and other men of the Snowcamp swarmed in led by the old man shouting,

'Quick! Get him!'

'But it's true! He's not bleeding!' exclaimed a voice.

'Doesn't matter,' someone replied. 'A few taps on the head with this will soon put that right.'

A figure loomed from the shadows and The Father heard a loud explosion in his skull.

'There you go,' said a voice triumphantly, 'I told you he'd bleed quick enough if we coaxed it along.'

Another percussive club landed on his head and lanterns swam around his pupils.

'What for?' he said groggily. 'You're free! You don't have to do this.'

'Don't forget, Lord,' came the voice of his devotee faintly as someone tried to hit him again but struck his shoulder by mistake. 'Tell everyone what's going on down here.'

'What do you think he is?' a voice retorted peevishly. 'A bloody Messiah?'

'Careful,' whined The Father, 'you're going to do me some permanent damage.'

'That's very astute of you,' someone said as a fourth blow cracked down on his forehead. 'Can't have you gumming up the works, snow-head. I'm sure you won't mind us feeling that way about it. After all we're just exercising this new freedom you're telling us we've got. So we're going to put you out on the slopes where you're supposed to be.'

'No!' The Father cried.

But at that moment the novice with the cudgel found his form and all the lights went out at once.

7

Meanwhile, Brother One was involved in a more than usually stormy scene in the Council Cave (a building which lent itself to fierce argument rather in the way that the Inner Temple of The Sacred Expulsion lent itself to a hoe-down) and the Barbans had called a recess to decide whether or not he could be penalized under the Rules of Council Cave Conduct. He could have told them before they withdrew that they wouldn't have a leg to stand on.

When they returned a Barban moved that his behaviour had been a breach of 'good taste' but Brother One pointed out that this rule was not applicable in a question of family dispute, especially when the family was a brother, especially when the Brother was an identical twin.

'Well, I think that's a shortcoming in the Constitution that ought to be rectified,' the Barban blustered, 'because we all know that twin-cloning is now illegal.' And Brother One replied, 'I don't think this is the moment to consider changing a constitution that has worked wonderfully well for centuries, let us instead return our attention to this question of the title in my late brother's property.'

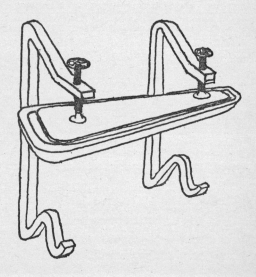

'I wish you'd stop referring to him as your *late* brother,' The Arbitrator complained. And, in reply, he quipped,

'Well Sir, with all due respect, if *I* can steel myself to the grisly truth then I feel it should be no great problem for *you*.'

It was leaning over the abyss to treat the Arbitrator with so little respect, but he desperately needed to intimidate the others and this was the best way he knew.

'I am simply pointing out,' responded the elder in his icy whisper, 'that there is, as yet, no proof that your brother is, in fact, dead.'

'I take your point, Arbitrator,' he said meekly and the old man, mollified, shrunk back into his collar.

'However,' Brother One went on, with a glance of mischievous arrogance at the Barbans that he was careful the Arbitrator did not see, 'there is no doubt that he has left the community, there is no doubt that he has stolen ancient manuscripts from the libraries that cannot be replaced and there is no sign that he even intends to return, even if,' he added darkly, 'he were able so to do.'

He paused to scan the faces of the Council, all goggling at his bad taste.

'And therefore,' he concluded, 'I request that all title to my brother's goods and functions pass to me. I have the authority of the Constitution behind my request both in words and spirit.' He shot a glance at the Barbans. 'And, speaking for myself, gentlemen, I respect that Constitution with all my heart.'

A bit melodramatic, but what the hell. How often do you get to demand all your Brother's possessions in the Council Cave?

The Arbitrator stretched his scrawny neck and cleared the throat within it.

'I am of the opinion,' he whispered, 'that all the objections which are appropriate to this Council's purpose have been raised and dealt with effectively enough. However, I feel there are certain sociological and emotional issues that have been opened up by your request. I will therefore allow a period of *four* tides in which those who differ with you may approach you privately, separately or in groups, to express their point of view in the hope that you will revise your intentions to make them more generally pleasing. After that time we will meet to consider your request again and, if nothing has changed, I will deliver the verdict that I now hold in readiness.'

There was a tremor of suppressed glee in the Barbans' benches.

The Arbitrator had practically handed them Brother One's head on a plate!

Four tides!

Privately, singly and in groups to *express* their *point of view* on his thumbs and fingernails, to get him to *revise* his *intentions* by twisting his legs, to thrash out the *sociological and emotional issues* on his back!

'With respect, Sir,' he said, rising to his feet, 'might I suggest in such a clear-cut issue as this that *one* tide will leave ample time for the free interchange of ideas?'

'Four tides,' the Arbitrator whispered.

Already some of the rougher Barbans were leaving the benches and climbing up to the rear exits.

'With respect, Sir,' he said again, fear gnawing at his spine, 'I would like time to prepare my home for the better entertainment and comfort of the guests who will visit me for discussion and would ask that the stipulated period of four tides commence two hours from now.'

'Four tides, commencing immediately,' the old buzzard hissed. 'Any other business?'

Brother One would not even have time to barricade himself in his cave or prepare a defensive arsenal. So much for the Constitution. When it came down to it, you were on your own.

He slipped quickly out of his seat and made for an exit but there seemed to be Barbans everywhere, so he turned towards the damp and gloomy Dining Chamber to think things out over a meal.

'At least,' he thought, 'I'll be fairly safe here until the first tide comes to restock the tanks. Then I'll have to try to find some kind of hiding-place.'

Distracted, he found it hard to catch a good meal and settled for a slow-moving grubfish from the shallowest tank which obstinately refused to die no matter how hard he turned the crusher on its head. Even when it was finally still he could barely pick at it under the baleful stare of a bullyboy Barban in the doorway.

'Why don't you sit down and have something to eat?' Brother One suggested facetiously.

'My appetites,' the Barban replied in their typically smug and self conscious manner, 'do not run to *food* just at the moment.'

'Then may you starve horribly,' Brother One replied with a smile.

The Barban's teeth flashed in a hideous grin.

'Thankyou,' he said, 'I welcome your respect.'

'Don't mention it.'

Brother One could say what he chose without fear of reprisals while inside the Council Cave Complex since all enjoyed protection under the *Freedom from Maiming* Bill, but his sanctuary would be brief.

His mind moved like lightning.

The Tubes?

If he could get up The Tubes before the next tide he would be swept outside the city walls on the ebb, where the Barbans would never dare follow.

'A brainwave,' he thought glumly, knowing full well that leaving the city would mean Death for him just as surely as it had meant death for his father and brother before him. He pushed aside his food, which was still unappetizingly alive, rose to his feet and passed into the Council Chamber.

No point in not admitting when you're beaten.

He caught the Organizer's eye with the sign for Special Business and waited for a long wrangle on shell-tax and sand-measurement devices to terminate. He would have liked to seize title to his brother's property so they could laugh about it together if he ever came back, but wasn't prepared to undergo four tides of hot rocks in his eyeballs or coral in his intestines to get it.

The Organizer signalled him to speak and he rose, saying,

'With respect, Sir, I would like to withdraw the motion I put earlier today claiming all my brother's goods.'

The Arbitrator looked at him with his ancient, frozen eyes and said, 'I thought I made it clear. We meet on that question again in four tides. Any other business?'

8

Let no one be your victim,
Lest you yourself become victim.

Yenin Bible (black version)

He had taken cover in his brother's cave for it was the last place the
bloodhounds would think of searching. He had thrown a sea-reed
mattress inside the secondary pump-assembly and stretched out on
top of it, pulling over himself a length of vermilion carpeting. There,
snug and warm, he calculated on being safe for two, possibly three,
tides.

But four?

Impossible.

That was why the Arbitrator had set the time at four. No one
could survive four tides without getting caught.

It was against the rules not to stay in one's house during a period
of *private approach separately or in groups*, but he reasoned that the
Arbitrator had a judgment in *readiness* and since that judgment had
to be in his favour then he could argue that title to his brother's
goods had already passed to him and he *was*, therefore, technically
speaking, in his own house.

The Barbans would work that one out sooner or later, after they
had turned over his cave a few times without success, and would put
their heads together and figure out where he was. If there were some
way of getting back into his own cave while they were on their way
over, he might escape unhurt, but, since there was no way of knowing
the right time to move, the odds on getting it right were slim.

He could see Brother Two's study between the pipes, a study of
identical design to his own but transformed in a unique way by the
use to which he had been put. Here and there the floor was smooth
and shiny where Brother Two had lain upon it reading beneath the
night-lights and on the carpet was a circular track where he had
paced round and round, memorizing the language and literature of
his peculiar, possibly unhealthy, hobby. Volumes of thick paper
lined the walls, every one 'borrowed' from the dustier sections of the

libraries, all thumbed, marked and heavily scored, consumed with obsessive zeal by impassioned eyes over and over again.

'There's something in it,' he used to insist, sensing Brother One's bleak disinterest. 'I'm sure there's something in it.'

'So what?' One would say, 'I'm sure there's something in everything. Doesn't mean you have to make a life's work out of it.' Ironically, that was exactly what he had done.

Or, rather, made a death's work of it. Gone *up top* and left the real world behind. A shame really. Brother One had liked him and, in a way, rather envied him his fascination with the ancient arts, for he never seemed to experience the clammy ennui that sometimes laid out Brother One for days at a time.

Occasionally they would argue angrily, out of jealousy he now realized, treating each other like some short-celled clone that couldn't make thoughts of its own.

'Well, okay,' Brother One would admit furiously, 'so I'll accept, for the sake of argument, that people used to be able to do this *mating* business. We'll *assume* that at one time half of the population had holes between their legs and big empty spaces in their bellies filled up with a vegetable chemistry laboratory. We'll accept that as reasonable just so I can make a point. This is it. Even if that were once true and there *were* people like that, what makes you think that it's still possible now? Why get so bound up with something that, at best is a Lost Art and, at worst, is a load of hocus-pocus and mystical twiddle-twaddle?'

'I don't have to answer that,' his brother would reply. 'I just *am* bound up with it, that's all. As far as I'm concerned the mere fact that it provides me with the energy I need to read and study is justification enough. When things change, ask me again.'

'Well, I think you're just being stupid about it,' Brother One would retort. And Brother Two would say,

'I know you do. I'm sorry about that.'

He could be a bit smug at times.

Brother Two wondered what had really happened to his twin, never having fully believed that anyone actually went *up top*. It always seemed obvious that it was just another of those allegories that made the mystic arts so inaccessible to the mind of a truly intelligent person. The idea that there was a *somewhere else* was surely a wistful fantasy. But Brother Two had taken it seriously and literally, had gone out through the pump locks with his head full of dreams and his wet-pack full of stolen manuscripts.

Courage.

Had to admit that.

Lots of it.

But crazy.

'How are you going to breathe?' Brother One would ask him when he first started 'training up' for the trip, sitting crosslegged on his mattress, holding his breath, bending over backwards and so on. 'You realize it's all water up there don't you? Are you going to learn how to breathe water?'

'Nope,' Brother Two would gulp, popeyed, between blue lips.

'Then what?'

'Not going to breathe at all. No point. If I breathed my lungs would fill with water and I'd drown. No point in that.'

'Just like that?'

'Just like that,' he'd reply. And ask, 'What other way is there? I'd be glad if you could come up with a better idea.'

'I think a better idea is to stay in the real world filled with real people with their bodies intact and their bellies free of strange growths. That's what I think is a better idea.'

'Yes, I know you do,' Brother Two would say.

He could be a bit smug at times.

Now he was probably divided up between the separate jaws of a pack of dog-dolphins.

'And if you manage to complete this journey successfully to one knows where, will you come back to us poor souls trapped in the dark night of eternal ignorance to enlighten us all?'

'What do you take me for?' he would reply. 'Some sort of Messiah? Why should I come back? You should just come up and join me.'

'But if you don't come back, how will we know you've got there?' Brother One would tease him. 'How will we know you haven't been crushed to a ruby by the sheer weight of water?'

His twin would shrug.

'Might be the same thing,' he would reply laconically. 'Getting there, as you put it, may indeed entail being crushed to a ruby first.'

'And you don't care?' would come the incredulous response. 'You don't care?'

'Sure I care,' Brother Two would reply. 'That's why I'm doing it.'
He really could be a bit smug at times.

But brother is a brother no matter how crazy. And he missed him, especially now, hiding under a piece of carpet in his secondary pump-assembly.

'I would have thought you'd be pleased I'm going,' he had once said with a bitter smile, 'for you can finally fulfil your ambition and be a two-caver.'

'That is the one consolation I'll have for losing your pleasant company,' Brother One had answered drily. 'Just make sure you leave proof that you're not coming back.'

'I don't expect that would matter much to a legal expert like yourself,' his brother had replied laughing.'You can simply invoke the Fraternal Rights Act.'

Yes, he could be a bit smug.

Suddenly, as Brother One lay wrapped in these recollections, there was a loud sucking racket in the pumps close by his ear. He sprang up, banging his head sharply on the auxiliary piping.

The secondary pump-assembly was starting to go into operation!

How could that be happening?

He crawled from his hiding-place, ran to the doorway to clear away a pile of papers from the face of the seameter and felt the blood drain from his wildly pumping heart.

The pressure was almost double!

It had never been so high.

Tremors moved faintly beneath his feet through the carpet.

A sea quake!

It had to be. Nothing else would destroy the values. It must finally be happening. Just as the old legends said!

The final and total destruction of the entire undersea civilization!

9

*The legends speak of a great disaster that will engulf the
world and destroy humanity.
But then – don't we all?*

from *Silver Linings* by Madame Lottie Eucharist

This is why Brother One found it especially frightening to notice that
the seameter was reading double pressure.

The city was protected from the black mass of water that hung
overhead and threatened to crush in from all sides by the pressure of
nothing more than the bubble in which it was situated; anchored to
the sea-bed by the action of millions of tiny algae exchanging the
carbon dioxide in the captive atmosphere for oxygen, taking out the
carbon and liberating the O_2.

The margin for error was slim.

Too little atmospheric pressure inside the bubble and the sea
would fall in and smash it to deepwater suds and the inhabitants to
saltwater mincemeat. Too much pressure and the bubble would try
to claw its way *up top*, leaving them behind to cope with the pres-

sure of water at several more tonnes per square centimetre than their bodies had been designed to withstand.

Somehow one lived with it by simply forgetting. It would have taken an unthinkable cooperative effort to build a system that would prevent the inevitable cataclysm and, although there were Council Meetings about it every year, nothing ever got under way.

Secondary pump-assemblies had been made obligatory in every home to act, supposedly, as an emergency pressurization system if the ecocycle went askew. But no one really believed that if things went wrong the little domestic pumps would do more than frighten everybody out into the walkways to be the better pulverized by the crushing massives of a falling ocean.

Brother One had read an account of the collapse of a submarine civilization from *bubble-up* – the escape of the atmosphere up through the sea – written by a member of the first sea-bed engineering teams at the dawn of history. It told how an entire first-base fabricatory had turned into a steady stream of tiny bubbles moving slowly upwards, men, machines, buildings, everything squeezed into tiny beads, expanding as they rose, bursting their contents against glassy walls which ran with blood and rust as they disappeared into the impenetrable darkness of the sea sky.

As children the chilling horror stories they whispered to each other in the dim eerie glow of fish-scale phosphorescence lanterns were filled with the drifting bubbled dead, appearing silently from nowhere, their long empty eyes staring unputrified from their windowed tombs, their hollow mouths grimaced in airless screams, calling with empty lungs, floating, eternally lost, in the chasms and craters of the lifeless depths.

Now they were to become their own frozen ghoulish nightmares.

He checked the seameter. The pressure was holding steady and it occurred to him that he should be doing the same thing.

'Don't panic. Think,' he told himself. 'That's what you've been trained to do.'

He looked around wildly without inspiration.

When an irreversible cataclysm occurs one can find oneself at a loss, not really having a clear idea how best to pass the last moments of one's existence. Loth to spend them being belaboured by Barbans he moved to the long line of shelves and scanned the contents, looking for a volume entitled 'How to Survive City-crushing Weights' or 'Airless Life At Great Depths for Men'. He did not find it.

Everything was related to Brother Two's obsession. Dusty piles of manuscripts with names like *Bumsup* and *Tit Pix*. Skinbound books called *Hot Night in The Harem* or *Women Who Like It*. All entirely incomprehensible to Brother One.

'You just look at them and meditate,' Brother Two had once told him.

'And then what?'

'That's all.'

'I just look at this picture and think and I'm supposed to understand the secrets of the universe?'

Brother Two had pursed his lips irritably.

'You can put it that way if you want to,' he had replied, and then, with the heavily tolerant air of one who is going to make just one more despairing effort to put something across to an idiot, had sat down and opened a manuscript at random.

It was a figurative representation of a man with a hole between his legs and extremely distended pectorals dangling from his chest. He was clothed from the tips of his toes to the top of his legs in some kind of netting and wore only a gold chain around his waist. There seemed to be something wrong with his mouth.

'Now, this is called a *picture*,' Brother Two had explained. 'It's hundreds and hundreds of years old and we have no other evidence that this civilization existed except for these manuscripts. It seems that human beings knew a lot more about their fundamental selves in those days and these pictures have certain psychic triggers built into them which, if allowed to freely operate in the mind, will result in an expansion of consciousness.'

'Just like that?'

'Just like that.'

'I just sit here, look at this picture and my consciousness expands, is that it?'

'Look!' Brother Two had snapped, prising the book from his twin's fingers and returning it, almost with reverence, to its place on the shelves, 'I'm only telling you what I've learned. It may be wrong. It may be right. Just don't try to inhibit *my* activities till you understand what they are and what purpose they serve.'

'Brother, have I ever told you that you can be a bit smug at times?'

Two had been too busy whistling angrily though his teeth to answer.

Now, as Brother One leafed through the library, he was struck by the ironic change in the situation. While Brother Two had discorporated upwards, *he* was killing time before an ocean dropped on him.

'All these manuscripts,' Two had said, 'tell of a time when we lived side by side with these creatures, mating almost continually, in complete harmony and in total ecstasy.'

'Fantasy.'

'Please yourself. I prefer to call it historical fact. Something happened in the world, some great upheaval that made it necessary for us to live down here in darkness and be denied that state of eternal bliss. But I believe it's possible,' he had wagged a finger sternly, 'I really do believe it's possible to transcend the barriers between our two separate worlds and be united once more in total harmony, understanding and love.'

'Well,' Brother One had replied, grinning into his hands, 'I suppose it keeps you off the streets.'

As things had turned out, Two had been smarter than the rest of them. Much better, his brother was now thinking, to be crushed to a ruby fulfilling a hopeless dream than be smashed to mincemeat hanging on to a futile reality.

'Okay, smartass,' he muttered to his brother's departed spirit, 'where's the note you stashed telling me what to do in this situation?'

The tremors were growing more rhythmic and rattling the wall-lanterns softly in their float chambers.

Almost inaudibly a deep booming whine echoed dimly in the air as though through miles of rock.

'Calm,' he told himself. 'Composure.'

There was nothing of any consequence that could be done so he picked a manuscript from the shelves and settled himself down on the mattress to have one last crack at expanding his consciousness before it was finally out of the question.

'Stop biting your nails,' he told himself. And did.

'Stop tapping your fingers!' he snapped. 'Concentrate on the Mandalady and dematerialize while you have the chance.'

The *picture* at which he had opened the manuscript showed two

45

men with holes between their legs and large chest muscles biting the toes of each other's boots and looking as though it hurt. Beneath the *picture* was an example of the kind of phrase that Brother Two had told him was to be repeated over and over again to more fully attune one's mind to the 'finer vibrations'.

And as the rumbling grew he stared at the representation of the two male mutants and repeated the mantra over and over again.

The mantra said,

'Suck leather, Sister. Suck leather, Sister.'

10

But Brother One's efforts to concentrate on the Mandalady and chant the mantra were more and more frequently disturbed by the shuddering symptoms of the impending upheaval. It is hard for the novice to master unfamiliar meditative techniques when, from the corner of his eyes, he can see the solid rock walls of the cave in which he sits bulging and bending beneath the pressure of vast geological shifts.

He had come to recognize the source of the disturbance as volcanic for he was familiar with the small earthquakes that very occasionally disturbed the calm waters of the city, sometimes setting the shallow tide rolling in wave motions from one city wall to the other, entering the houses, buffeting the occupants and sloshing the furniture around like driftweed.

But this was something new, something frighteningly serious.

The waters, which normally never rose higher than the waist, were now up to his neck as he sat on Brother Two's reading podium and he had to hold the manuscript out of the water to read it. He could hear the frantic shouts and splashings from the walkways as people waded panic-stricken to their caves to ensure their secondary pump-assemblies were working and he took the precaution of closing the massive flood doors in case of unwelcome visitors – anything from the City Police ordering him back to his own cave, an unimaginative Barban seeking to cause him pain, unaware that this was the end of civilization (which therefore automatically cancelled the Arbitrator's four-tide ruling) or, perhaps worse, some swift-skinned predator from the packs that hung around outside the city walls, scrap-hunting, that had been known to swim into the city when the water rose exceptionally high and loot the caves of their unwary inhabitants.

The heavy flood doors also cut off the sounds of humans realizing their world was falling to pieces.

He tossed the manuscript angrily aside and climbed to his feet as the waters rose past his chin.

'I'll drown soon enough,' he thought, 'without taking it sitting down.' A hammering explosion beneath the bedrock cave floor started the fish-scale phosphorescence lamps rocking wildly and set up disturbances in the water that swirled him suddenly round the cave, drowning in buffeting books and suffocating carpets. Gasping, he clung to the pump-assembly and hung on grimly until the worst of it had subsided.

'One more like that should do me in,' he reflected wryly. 'Brother Two, here I come.'

This is what happened.

The walls closed in upon the room like melting wax, plastic, rippling. The waters rose, carrying him up to the roof with only two or three inches of air left to breathe, a terrible pressure squeezed him like an eel under a rapidly-screwed crusher and the water, growing warmer by the minute, smelled of sulphur and glowed dimly green from the submerged phosphorous lamps that bobbed one by one to the surface, robbing him of precious oxygen and blinding his eyes with their unshielded brightness.

He felt the cave lurch from its place on the seabed and begin to spin.

Faster and faster it turned until the waters in which he struggled became a vortex that dragged him down, choking and gasping, until his feet were scraping in tight ankle-bound circles upon the floor and the floating lamps grew fainter and fainter as he watched them dance round and round on a surface that he could no longer reach.

11

Discorporation Techniques

1 Sit tight.
2 Everything will be alright. Do not panic.
3 Your environment will shrink to the size of a small bubble enclosing your head.
4 Everything will be alright. Do not panic.
5 Empty your mind completely.
6 Allow your body to shrink to the size of a walnut and join your mind in the bubble.
7 Sit tight. Everything will be alright.
8 Do not worry about what is going to happen.
9 The bubble is going to burst.
10 So long, sucker.

from *The Complete Dictionary of Phrases Beginning with a D and a T* (vol II)

When he awoke he found his body suffering the most intense agony it had ever been his misfortune to experience.

Cell by cell he explored himself with his mind to find the centre of its discomfort and discovered it to be total and all pervasive. There was no living nerve in his body that did not shriek in its own unique pain-filled voice and many had already closed down business for the day, presumably under the expectation that his body was going to die anyway, it wouldn't make a great deal of difference. From head to toe, from fingertip to earlobe, inside and out, every cell and he wished they could expire.

The cave seemed to be lying on its side, for he found himself sprawled out on the now empty shelves that had lined Brother Two's study walls. Except for foul-smelling puddles here and there, all the sea water had drained out of a long narrow rupture in the cave wall through which flowed a light even more intense than the sputtering phosphorous lamps but which, to his numb surprise, threw shadows.

He tried to move but his aching body shouted immediate protest and he lay still, fighting his agonizing discomfort and wondering whether the raging inferno in his lungs meant imminent death.

At least, he reflected, the city had survived the crisis. Maybe the secondary pump-assemblies proved adequate to the scale of the disaster after all.

He slipped into a semiconscious limbo, trying to piece together the broken fragments of splintered recall into recollection. Most of the details had vanished for ever.

He slept.

He woke.

The light had disappeared and his phosphorous lamps were sparkling and guttering as they burned empty.

He slept.

He woke.

No light.

Chilled body.

He dragged himself from the shelves on to a ragged, frayed greenweed cushion.

He slept.

Dreams of bursting pods of warm brine, blinding, blinding brightness, eye-blanking light.

Then insufferable cold and trembling, roaring and spinning.

He woke.

A faint gleam of thread-thin silver glowing across the cave from the fractured wall and strange odourless smells, the scent of emptiness.

He slept.

Someone might come. Others must have survived. They would break in and find him. He would be alright if he could stay alive till then. At least he was no longer bleeding. In some parts of his body the pain was receding although he still felt red-lunged and breathless.

'Help me,' he spoke into the silver-fringed darkness.

'Help me,' he said.

And slept.

And slept.

And slept more.

Coming round more and more frequently, wincing in the cold, shifting agonizingly out of the puddles into which his legs would fall in sleep. And then the light faded and he cried in his fatigue and pain, soft-water tears carving tracks through the dust of salt and sulphur on his face falling into the sea-pools to which he had so recently abandoned life itself.

'Where are you, you bastards?' he whined, curling into a ball, hunching his blue, bruised knees up to his chin.

'I'll get you all for this.'

He slept.

He woke.

He woke to a stifling baking heat and the same blinding glare from the fractured wall.

Nearly all the water had evaporated, leaving salt crust rings where they had vanished and his skin burned with sweat and sulphur and sodium chloride.

He shifted carefully, still battered beyond belief, but seemingly recovering.

'I can get by without you, you rotten finks,' he muttered and fell into a half-sleep that was very close to death.

When he woke he tried desperately to screw up the resolve to rescue himself, for he had found it hard to believe that he was on his own or that some attempt wouldn't be made to release him.

He dragged himself over to the flood doors and yanked at the lever.

No response.

He heaved at the heavy emergency handle with all his waning strength until it suddenly gave way and the doors slipped open, to reveal a wall of sand as impenetrable as any rock face.

He scratched at it, amazed to find it abrasive, dry and hot.

He had never seen anything like it except for tiny quantities inside the ornamental lamps that decorated the Council Cave Complex of the Supreme High Senate. Here it was in weights heavier than a human being! What holocaust could have caused such vast deposits to collect at his door? The city must have experienced a terrible disaster. The anger for his slow-moving fellow-citizens turned to a desperate fear that they may, after all, have perished, every one.

They might be Barbans, but they didn't deserve to die. He crawled over to examine the cracked wall but no simple tool could have further split the massive slab through which it ran.

The light hurt his eyes as he tried to peer through.

He was hopelessly trapped.

Doomed to starve to bake to death in some submarine lava pit, the last flickering remnant of a civilization smashed into eternity.

It must be confessed, he wept again.

But not only for himself.

He wept for all living creatures wiped out en masse.

He wept out the realization of a new humility, a new deference to Nature's Way, to what Brother Two sometimes called The Scheme of Things, a new understanding of our total weakness in the universe, of our utter inability to adapt to changes in that universe and the larger, long-term ends of that peculiar logic of which we had come to believe ourselves masters and had dubbed 'Fate'.

'Sod it,' he said sadly, shaking his salt and sulphur-scarred head sorrowfully. 'It's all over now.'

And then, with the familiar sleight of hand that destiny works to grant reprieves at the very moment that one resigns oneself to death, as though she requires only the abnegation of all claims to self before setting one free from a self-sought imprisonment, he heard the sound of small voices, still far away, but gradually coming closer.

He smiled, despite his agonies, and sobbed uncontrollably in relief.

But there is a fickle streak in human nature that damns us all.

Changeable, changeable with the tide of our body fluids, the shifting salts and neutral flash-patterns.

Fickle.

Attending first to this body language then to that.

Responding always to the loudest voice, the coarsest whisper, the most nagging, insistent and neurotic of our guardian angels.

We do not appreciate Fate's subtle chemistry but clamour always for its windfalls, too peevish and impatient to delight in its quiet fermenting maturation.

We seize the infant grape too soon from the growing vine and later curse the ill-luck that denies us the fattened fruits of seasons past.

So soon do we forget.

The man who had given up his life with patient humility and whose reward was the sound of approaching voices, now railed impotently against the diversions and distractions that drew their dawdling footsteps from him and rescue. He hammered with futile fists against the naked rock as their voices faded away from him and faint was his ragged cry against the rhythm of the gentle surf echoing, booming, to their sharp little ears among the steaming beach-flung debris of the undersea upheaval.

But skittering like rats among the rocks the Orphachins came, encircling the emaciated survivor in his stone capsule.

He heard their scuffling and breathing and shouted,

'I'm here! I'm here!'

And they glanced at each other in excited greed and began to salivate. 'Gobbly Gobbly,' one said and the others took up the mutter until the beach was alive with Orphachins running from the dunes and milling in packed crowds round the lava-spotted stone half-buried in the sea-shelled sand.

Some climbed over the top, others tried to force their little fingers through the tiny crack, others began to dig out the sand around it, while others puzzled telepathically among themselves or sat moodily on nearby rocks picking at the blisters on their feet.

The sand-shifters found the flood door.

He had never seen an Orphachin before and the Orphachin had never seen a man.

They stared at each other through a crumbling tunnel, one covered in sand the other in sulphur.

He was captivated by the Orphachin's appearance for, to him, they looked like nothing more than young boys.

'Hello,' he said, his voice echoing astrally in the drum-like cave. The Orphachin jumped back startled and pushed in the sand to block the doorway.

'Hey, let me out!' he shouted, somehow sensing that his voice had a fascination for them. 'I won't harm you.'

Had he known at that moment what the Orphachins were he would have laughed to hear himself cry,

'Come back! I won't harm you.'

A single unarmed human being shouting.

'There's nothing to fear,' persuasively, to the most venomous killers in the history of earth life.

There was a scrabbling in the sand once more and three gleaming faces appeared in the doorway, their glittering eyes completely motionless, scarcely blinking. And from the corners of their mouths saliva ran in moving threads.

52

'Hi kids!' he said as cheefully as he could. 'Why don't you dig a nice big hole so a tired old man like me can get out without having to crawl along on his tummy?'

They vanished again with nervous speed but others had come to examine the imprisoned prey and dug away rapidly in the soft beach sand.

'Come on!' he called to them encouragingly. 'Here I am!'

Within moments the flood doors were cleared and the Orphachins, scattering to a short distance, peered from grassy dunes and lavic rocks, gobbling excitedly and bubbling at the mouth.

Brother One staggered out into the sunshine, his arm over his eyes, his hand waving a feeble greeting.

'Hi kids,' he called weakly. 'How are you fixed for something to eat?'

12

As most people know, Brother One's account of the Orphachin desert packs has been largely discredited today. For various reasons, mainly political, he chose to misrepresent the social patterns and psychic structures of this racial group. However his autobiographical account of meeting with the Orphachins contains information of more than a passing interest to students in the field and it is from this book, *The Good Die Young*, that the following extracts have been taken.

(courtesy of *The Military Press*)

As I was to learn soon enough, the Orphachins, small and childlike though they seemed, were cannibals.

Unlike other human beings they were not the product of the cloning process (skin-cell nuclei planted into cells taken from the now obsolete reproductive organs) but were the product of what is known colloquially as 'virgin birth'. It is to this fact that I attribute their peculiar eating patterns.

At the time I first landed on Orphachin Beach (as I have called it) the land was in the grip of the old Female tribes, descendants of the Harridans who drove human beings from the land-masses at the dawn of history, and one per cent of these Females autofertilized during puberty. The Female children were taken into the community to keep the population constant, while the male children, after being nursed for six months, were thrust out into the desert to fend for themselves. If they were lucky they would be discovered by a roving Orphachin pack and, if they were not eaten, would themselves become Orphachins.

The Orphachins hunted in packs at that time, capable of covering immense distances in a single night, attacking even the most heavily armed travellers for food or, when travellers were scarce, falling upon each other.

Their natural life-span ended at puberty. Their language was one of primitive grunts and blows to the head coupled with natural telepathic ability. Whatever clothing they wore was rudimentary and purely decorative.

I had been fortunate indeed to escape with my life as Brother Two's cave was dislodged from the sea-bed and tossed up by the turbulent ocean on to the edge of the desert at Orphachin Beach. But, as I soon discovered, I was doubly fortunate not to have been immediately despatched by the voracious little creatures. Under normal circumstances I would have fallen prey to the Orphachin appetite in less time than it takes to say Gobbly Gobbly, but at the moment of my appearance they were confused and intimidated by the restless earthquake tremors that still rippled across the desert and by a second phenomenon that I was to witness soon enough. But perhaps the single most fortunate factor in my survival was my own manner and bearing.

By a stroke of good luck my easy confidence, born of ignorance, my superior size, the rich variety of noises I could make with my mouth and, not least, the deep timbre of my adult voice, all fascinated them and filled them with awe. I, for my part, thinking them mere children, immediately assumed command and, communicating by gestures and the oft-repeated phrase, Gobbly Gobbly, indicated that we should go in search of food.

They set off eagerly, diving into the sand and swimming swiftly just below the surface but, seeing me trying to keep up with them at a floundering run, they seized me, not ungently, and dragged me with them until I learned to travel as quickly as they by using a rapid paddling stroke in the sand, surfacing occasionally to check my bearings and breathe.

We had travelled thus for less than an hour when we came upon our first victim, a typical example of Brother Two's mutant angels, lying in the extremes of exhaustion in a sand gully. Before I could prevent it the Orphachins finished her off and began to eat.

Now, there has been much debate on the subject of Orphachin eating-habits, mostly among the ill-informed. They have been condemned out of hand by those who offer no alternative solutions to the burning question of Orphachin existence: how could they have overcome the hazards of survival and self-sufficiency from the tender age of six months in any other way? Even I, a human being, filled with all the natural taboos against cannibalism, found my resistance to eating flesh fast weakening under the duress of hunger. And when it became a matter of eating or being eaten then I must confess I ate.

But never the head.

I never ate the head.

I was a little squeamish that way.

And, then again, who is to say what is cannibalism and what is not?

I still assert that the female is an entirely separate species of animal despite much argument to the contrary. What is the difference then, morally speaking, between eating a female and, say, devouring a stag? Both are flesh, both become dead meat, both sustain life. I rest my case.

Having refreshed ourselves, we pushed on through the rumbling desert, encountering several weary, sand-struck travellers whose misery we terminated in the very same way until, in the distance, we saw the vast throng of which they must once have been a part. It marched North with seeming jubilation, the sand raised in clouds above it by the passage of their many feet, the air ringing with the strident blare of many horns, the jingle of armour and weapons, humming with excited and clamorous voices.

'What happens?' I asked the Orphachins.

But Gobbly Gobbly was the only reply they knew.

They gibbered nervously to each other and drew back in fear, whimpering and cowering behind the dunes. But for my determined command they would have slunk back into the desert, intimidated by the vast army. And it is upon this fact and this fact alone that I base my claim to the title of Orphachin General, a rank subsequently stripped away by those from whom I would have expected greater loyalty.

How dare they say that initiatives taken by me, with the Orphachins under my firm control, had no significant effect on destiny? Why, I think it is only a simple modesty on my part that prevents me from declaring that events I precipitated on that dreadful night changed the entire course of human history.

13

Meanwhile the Tribunal listened grimly as, far off in the desert, came the ringing of distant horns.

'They come,' said Ana, flat of voice, clear of gaze, sick of cancer.

'Close the tents. Let it be cool and shady for their coming.'

Shadows moved eagerly forward, deft hands sewed blindfolds of canvas over the wall of burning light, the rich texture of the carpet faded to luminous blues and reds.

The women sat in a silence enriched only by the droning of heat-sick insects trapped in the humid tenting and the murmur of approaching hordes marching barefoot across the baking sands.

'There will not be food or drink enough,' murmured Rogesse, compassing the multitude with her finely pitched hearing. 'They are too many.'

'Then let them have nothing at all,' replied Ana. 'For what they need let them ask.'

'It is said they move like locusts across the earth, feeding without growing, destroying without building, thinking nothing of the travellers who must follow them.'

'Calm yourself,' replied The Matriarch, motionless upon her throne. 'I have known it. It has always been the way of some.'

A damp silence fell across the fetid pavilion. The distant cacophony rose and fell as the dunes themselves.

And over the desert sands came the gabbling throng, glittering and gleaming in the cloudless air, shimmering like sandflies in the reverberating light, skittering like a slow and vagrant breeze across the undulating sea of powdered stone. Like a melting tide they came, bare of breast or armoured, with razor points and bells and knives, in steels and silks, waterless, they strung out to the horizon, losing many in silent sand-caverns, long-lost behind the winding line of march. And at the front, blackened and blistered by the vicious sun, dragged up and shouldered on by muscular Amazonis, thrust headlong across the barren burning wastes – Yeni, last of the Fallen Goddesses, She whom Many Called The Messiah.

In the darkened tent the voice of Ana moved like smoke, light as breath, heavy with the death gnawing at her bosom, her sickness like an odour on the words she spoke.

'This girl,' she said. 'It cannot be Her.'

No voice answered. There was no question in that grey slab instruction to the universe. As She willed it, so it would be.

Unseen, unheard themselves, their senses stretched out from the black engloomed pavilions to probe the noon-blasted wastes.

'Wild-eyed they come, this multitude,' murmured Rogesse.' 'Wild-eyed and driven from within.'

Ana's empty eyes turned to the hunched and riddled figure that clung doll-like to the leg of her throne.

'And you, Foolish One? What see you?'

'Wild-eyed, I see, aye,' the Rag-bundle replied with the voice of a young girl in the throat of a crone. 'And driven also, yes.' She broke off and from hidden lips removed a wet and wrinkled thumb. 'But not from within,' she croaked. 'They are driven by she whom they drive.' And the thumb returned to the faceless hole in her robes.

'And what of their coming?' Ana demanded impatiently.

But the sound of sucking was the only reply.

'You serve me badly, Fleshless One. Answer me!' she rasped and the sucking stopped.

The Crone's voice came, smooth and sonorous now.

'I serve you well if I serve you at all. You ask of their coming? There is nothing you do not know of their coming. It is as it has been told.'

'It cannot be,' snapped Ana angrily.

The Crone tittered. 'She is the last one to have the stigmata!'

'No' insisted Ana.

'She is the last of those who bleed with the moon.'

'No!'

'It is *she*,' affirmed The Crone with satisfaction.

Ana's voice was cold and curt.

'Bring me a blade.'

From the darkest shadows stepped a figure in black, a scabbard at her waist from which she drew a jewelled poniard whose needle point gleamed with a dull light of its own that grew brighter as Ana's fingers closed upon the shaft.

Expressionless, in pain, she leaned forward in her throne and drove the dagger with sinewy power over and over again into the black huddled bundle at her feet before returning it, gored and dripping, to the waiting guard.

The Rag-doll did not move, its body slumped untidily against the throne.

But then came the voice, mocking and amused.

'She bleeds with the moon, I tell you. It is She!'

'Silence, Idiot! I will have silence!' screamed Ana.

'Oh yes,' agreed The Crone, 'you will have silence.'

And rippled off into hideously ancient girlish laughter.

'Throw this bag of holes into the sun,' Ana snapped. 'Let her burn for a while. Perhaps *that* will teach her humility.'

'Ah, humility,' croaked The Crone with heavy irony as the two guards glided forward to dispose of her, 'is that what I must learn? Perhaps so, but Death will not be your servant. I know the moment of my Death as I know the moment of yours and it will not be here in this Hell-pit, you may believe that.'

The wall of the tent was unstitched rapidly by nimble door-servants and The Crone's body tossed out into the eye-blinding sand.

As quickly as it had been opened the wall was sewn together and

58

for a while the women could see nothing in the darkness save the after-image of a dazzling horizon.

'She *cannot* be the last of those who bleed with the moon,' Ana asserted petulantly. 'There *must* be more!'

'It is reported that this is the last of those cast out by The Others,' Rogesse ventured nervously.

'Reported?' spat Ana, turning her baleful, still half-blind gaze upon her Counsellor, 'what do I care of reports? Idle chatter caught by mischief winds. Reports! If there were as many drops of water in this desert as false reports that you have credited then we should all drink deeply this day. Reports! Has not even my own death come in these *reports* of yours?'

Rogesse shrunk into her robes, instinctively seeking shelter.

There had indeed been reports of Ana's death.

Reports spread by one whose ambitions had sought to usurp the wrinkled Matriarch's power.

Reports littered on the wind to provoke the people to rebellion.

Reports uttered by Rogesse herself at the peak of her now shrunken ambition.

Reports for which she would have suffered the penalty of death had not Ana chosen the crueller punishment of keeping Rogesse with her always, withering her under the weight of frightened, uncertain years.

Suddenly, bell-like, the voice of a watchtower guard rang through the air.

'A runner,' it cried. 'A runner comes.'

'From what quarter?' came the response.

'From the West,' replied the guard.

Ana looked at Rogesse with tight lips.

'Could that be The Others? Would The Others dare to send a runner here? The Foolish One must speak of this. We must know more of this runner from the West. Bring the Foolish One to my feet.'

14

Onward rolled the marching thousands, great clouds of sand rising above them like an angry ancient deity. A jewelled snake with plumes of stone they came, with whispering of flesh and murmuring lips, wild-eyed – aye – wild-eyed and wild of beating hearts that thumped like muffled drums among the crazed and tumbling throng, a single sound for long moments that splintered to coronary components as an atom dissolves into light. Dark and fair, slender and strong, young and old, sick and scarred, heady with the exhilarating joy of prophecy fulfilled, they drove their sacrifice onward, struggling and stumbling, to the place of execution. A curious wailing and keening fanned back and forth among the marching women as they sang strange, wordless songs of ecstasy and death and, far in the distance, their music shivered through the spines of the waiting tribunal.

'They do not tire!' remarked Rogesse in wonder. 'They march all day and do not tire!'

The battle-hum grew in a blaze of light as guards carried the black bundle back into the shaded pavilion and dropped it before the Queen. She poked it with a slippered foot.

'Stir yourself, Witless One,' she commanded. 'Speak of this runner who comes from the West.'

'Then give me to drink,' answered the wizened mystic in a weak and petulant voice.

'First answer, *then* drink,' Ana replied. 'A runner comes from the West. What does it mean?'

The Crone's reply rang like polished iron.

'*I* will wait to drink and *you* will wait to hear your answers. We will see which of us can endure our thirst the longer.'

Ana rose enraged from her throne and, seizing a guard's spear, plunged it into The Crone's back over and over again.

'Answer or die!' she shouted savagely, blood spattering her feet and gown. 'Answer or die!'

'Give me to drink,' The Crone cried in peevish reply. 'I will not die. And I will not answer until I have to drink.'

'You *will* answer!' screamed Ana.

'Shan't' said The Crone.

'Answer! Answer! Answer!' commanded Ana, a mortal thrust with each word.

'Shan't! Shan't! Shan't!' croaked The Crone in reply.

Ana drove the spear once more into the bundle and loosed hold, her face a mask of rage and hatred.

'Bring the Empty One to drink,' she hissed angrily. 'And clean these weavings. You drive me to wasteful anger, Old Idiot.'

'Diddums,' said The Crone.

A bowl of water was brought forward and Ana tossed it over the black bundle.

'You have had to drink,' she snarled. 'Now answer. What of this runner from the West?'

For a long moment it seemed as though The Crone would not reply. Then came her crackling voice, half-amusement, half-venom.

'The runner comes from The Others. None but The Others would run from the West. None but The Others would dare send a runner alone against The Orphachins.'

'So?' demanded Ana, arch and hostile. 'What do they want?'

'Not telling,' sang The Crone. 'Not till you say sorry!'

Ana's eyes burned angrily.

'Guard! Take four soldiers and kill the runner before she reaches us,' she ordered.

As the guard sprang forward The Crone laughed.

'Silence!' snapped the Matriarch.

'Yes, oh most sterile of the steriles,' came the derisive reply. 'Kill the runner, indeed, as though that will be the end of the matter. The Others will simply send a second runner and then a third and then will sweep down upon you with such an army of vengeance as you have never dreamed the like. Yes indeed, kill the runner, Sterile One. Ho, ho. Very wise. Kill the runner.'

The guard, who had at first moved swiftly at Ana's command, now stood hesitantly at the doorway.

'What keeps you?' enquired the Queen in an acid voice.

'The Crone – I thought—' stammered the guard.

'*I* am your Queen. Not The Crone,' Anna hissed. 'Now hear *this* order and obey. Take no soldiers. Ride out *alone* and kill the runner. Then ride back and tell The Crone what you have done. Be gone!'

The guard vanished in a blaze of light and nimble fingers once more stitched out the sun.

Ana's whitened gaze turned upon Rogesse.

'Well?' she snapped.

'Nothing,' replied Rogesse, carefully observing the palms of her hands. 'If The Crone speaks truly this runner may die without consequence. But the next—' she spread her fingers then closed them upon her lap.

'Yes,' said Ana, 'this one may die without consequence. We will receive the next runner and send back her head with our reply stitched to its lips.'

Rogesse cleared her throat gently.

'These are delicate times, Ana,' she said, and stopped diffidently.

'Exactly,' replied the Queen of Women, 'so let it be clearly seen that the Queen acts with determination in these "delicate times". Let them know by whom they are justly ruled.'

Rogesse shrugged without lifting her eyes.

'Yes, Your Majesty,' she replied.

The women sat again in silence, separating the distant hum of thousands from the thousand wing-beats of the trapped insects that dropped from the roof to feed upon The Crone's trickling blood, milling and buzzing, crawling upon each other's backs and being crawled upon.

Time flowed uncounted.

A voice from the watchtower cried,

'The runner is dead!' as the sun began to tumble from the mid-heaven and within the hour the guard entered silently to take her place once more behind the throne.

After a long while Ana asked,

'What message did the runner carry?'

And the guard answered stiffly, without moving her eyes, her voice hollowed out by a terrible, silent panic.

'I did not ask.'

'Then what papers did she carry?' Ana demanded.

'There were no papers,' replied the guard, struggling to push out the words. 'She ran naked.'

Rogesse caught her breath in alarm.

'She ran naked and you *killed* her!' she gasped incredulously.

The guard did not turn her head.

'She ran naked. I killed her. Was I not ordered so to do?'

'But to kill a naked runner!' Rogesse began angrily.

'You have done well,' Ana interrupted forcefully but nervous, 'Let The Others see the fearless obedience that is due to the Queen of The Earth. You will be rewarded handsomely for this when this business is over.'

'With respect, Your Majesty,' replied the guard, pale of face, eyes glazed with shock, 'I do not seek honours for the work I have done this day.'

Ana glanced round at her sharply but, seeing the empty terrified face, simply said,

'You will have them anyway, whether you seek them or no.'

Suddenly the voice of The Crone startled all the women.

'Listen!' it hissed.

'Listen to what, Idiot Woman?' snapped Ana irritably.

Rogesse stood up in alarm.

'Listen!' she echoed.

'Listen to what?' demanded Ana more angrily.

'The marchers,' whispered Rogesse in bewildered reply, 'they make no sound!'

She turned, frightened, to her Queen.

'The marchers have stopped!'

It was a terrible, lonely silence filled with awesome empty distances.

15

Within her stinking rags The Foolish One knew not the meaning of the sudden stillness but giggled.

She laughed and said nothing.

Now, at last, she thought, perhaps the prophecies will be fulfilled; the last of those who bleed with the moon would die as a Messiah and Ana's empire would be destroyed. Well worth waiting for all these years, limbless, captive of a tyrant Queen, carried, trunk in trunk, skewered and singed, lanced and tortured through many a vicious royal rage, tossed here and there like an old doll at the whim of her mistress, yet feared. Yes, feared, for the seeing dreams she pretended to have, for her power over life, her clinging, grasping, clutching power over life that it should not fly from her until the prophecies were manifested. She sucked her thumb happily and chuckled silently.

'What shakes you, Bone-bag?' demanded Ana. 'Grief or laughter?'

Let her sweat this out, thought The Crone, let her see how helpless she too can be.

'Do you recall,' she creaked with slow and careful speech, 'do you recall the day you took away my legs and arm, oh Sterile Queen?'

'You would have taken flight,' Ana replied.

'Oh yes,' admitted The Crone sadly, 'I would have run far away.'

'But could not,' said Ana. 'I needed you. You would have deserted me. A treason.'

'Yes, I would have deserted you. So you cut off three of my little limbs. I was a young girl then.'

'We were both young girls then,' snapped Ana. 'But what of it?'

'Well now *you* would fly, but cannot. Now you too will know what it is to die limbless, helpless, loveless, forever lost.'

'Silence, Witless One!'

The Crone laughed.

'Silence, she says, silence. Very well, silence she shall have,' and she replaced the thumb in her mouth.

She is frightened now she thought, or she would have struck me. She listens to the silent thousands, straining for sounds that are not there, hearing only the winged things of the shadows. And Rogesse, too, knows fear, although it is no stranger to her after all these years, twisting this way and that to survive her royal mistress and usurp the throne.

The Crone giggled again.

She felt herself sliding into sleep as dream images flickered in her mind's eye. Memories of childhood when she was still whole, running in the gardens playing nuts with the monkeys, kicking down flowers at the end of Autumn, combing her wiry black hair. These things she remembered, in bitterness waking, with fondness sleeping. Happy days before the seeing dream that ruined her life, before the vision that made Ana realize what a valuable possession the little girl's head could prove to be, before the Palace massacre and Ana's decision to rule from the desert, in pavilions that moved with the Seasons. She snored gently into her rags, knowing it infuriated the Matriarch. Happy days so brief; she mourned their passing.

'I had the strangest dream last night,' she had confided to little Princess Ana as they played around the fountains in the gentle, crisp morning sunlight. 'I dreamed there was fighting in the palace and everyone woke up from the noise and someone said "The Queen is dead, The Queen is dead".'

She had expected Ana to sneer at her or throw stones, but the little princess showed extreme curiosity.

'How had the Queen died?' she asked.

'I don't know,' answered the tiny dreamer. 'That's all I heard.'

'Well tonight when you go to sleep you must go back there,' said Ana, willing it so, eyes staring into her little friend, 'and you must discover everything that happens.'

'Back where?' the younger girl had asked innocently.

'Back to wherever the dream happened. Back to the night there was fighting in the palace.'

'Why?'

'Because it will come true, that's why. There *will* be fighting in the palace and the Queen *will* die. That's why.'

The little dreamer looked surprised and the older girl had grabbed her by the throat.

'You'll go back and dream the rest of it and you won't tell anyone else but me. Understand?'

For the first time her eyes took on the hard, hot look that The Crone would come to know so well.

'Yes,' she had whispered in terror, 'I understand.'

From that moment life in the palace had changed rapidly.

The Queen had died, writhing horribly from some gruesome poison in her ears and all the older princesses were skewered to their mattresses by unnamed spears. Ana, then only ten years of age, had led a column of death-dealers through the palace pointing out those who were to be punished for the ghastly murders until the winding stone staircases ran with blood and the long corridors rang with the cries of the dead and dying.

When the night was over Ana was undisputed Queen and the bodies of those who had prior right to the throne were burned in heaps before her as she ate her breakfast in the gardens.

'Eat,' she had ordered her little companion. But she was too sick with the stench of burning flesh.

Ana's eyes, aflame with reflections of grisly bonfires, had burned deep into the little mystic's mind.

'You will not leave me,' she had said, more an assertion of fact than a question.

'No,' The Crone had replied.

'No,' Ana had repeated. 'I *know* you will not leave me.'

And that night they had plucked her from her bed, carried her screaming to the vaulted underground chambers and there lopped off her legs and an arm at shoulder and hips and cauterized the stumps with molten lead dropped upon the pulsing arteries and pumping veins.

'I will not die,' she had told herself. 'I *will* not die.'

And she had not died, although it took all her magic to survive, perverting her gift from selfless seeing to selfish being, rendering herself once more psychically blind, knowing only that the moment of her death would be of her own choosing.

Many times, in easy anger, Ana had tried to despatch her, mortally wound her, sever her from her existence; but she had refused to let go of life and thought no more of her body's pain than the gardener of a rose-thorn. Her hatred and obsessive lust for a dark revenge upon her Queen had carried her immortal, waiting only for the moment when she would see others cut Ana down as she had herself been cut down by Ana.

The prophecies told plainly of the destruction of the Matriarchy, the dissolution of the Queendom, the devolution of History, Time turning back upon itself like a recoiling spring, an apogean pendulum of exhaling lung. She looked forward to the spectacle with relish.

'And very soon now,' she thought gleefully.

She chuckled to herself again and a bony knuckle rapped her skull through the rags.

'We are in high spirits today, Foolish One,' Ana's voice cranked out. 'Let us all share the jest.'

She rapped and rapped and rapped, slowly, inexorably, painfully. The Crone chuckled the more, allowing the pain to roll over her mind instead of into it.

'You wanted silence,' she answered. 'Now *eat* it.'

'Bring me a burning stick,' Ana ordered with ice in her voice and venom in her veins.

'No,' said Rogesse, 'Let us listen for the multitude.'

'Do you now presume to instruct me?' demanded Ana irritably.

'I speak only for myself,' Rogesse replied hastily. 'I feel this is not time best spent burning the Witless One. Something is strange in the world today.'

She cocked her head.

'How can so many create so vast a silence?'

'I thought I ordered a fire-brand brought to me!' Ana shrieked, ignoring her Counsellor. 'Bring me fire to burn this rag and bone bundle into silence! Bring me oil to set her alight! I am weary of her giggling emptiness.'

A servant slipped out of the tent beneath a rear wall and Ana leaned down from her throne to poke The Crone.

'Do you hear that, Bone-bag? I'm going to set fire to you.'

The voice of the watchtower guard rang once more through the womblike pavillion.

'A runner,' it cried. 'A runner comes!'

'From what quarter?' came the response.

'From the West once more.'

Rogesse spoke.

'We must receive this one. The Crone spoke of the avenging armies of The Others sweeping down upon us in the night.'

'That,' replied Ana, 'was after we had despatched the third runner. Guard,' she turned to the assassin. 'Go to.'

The guard stared in numb fear at her Queen.

'And if the runner is naked this second time?'

'Kill her,' answered Ana, 'as you killed the first.'

The guard hesitated.

Ana spoke again.

'Or, if you choose, you may kill yourself.'

The guard swayed sickly in the twice-breathed air, sweat in faint dew glistening on her brow and upon her slender arms.

'Whichever you choose,' Ana went on, 'go to it now.'

The guard strode weakly to the wall that was raised once more for her passage and there fell a long silence in which even the insects lay still as though listening in fear.

Finally the voice from the watchtower rang yet once more.

'The runner!' it cried in the waning evening light. 'The runner is dead!'

16

One Two Three,
One Two Three,
One *Two Three.*

20th Century Dance Music
(scraps of music such as this support the theory, put forward most strongly by Professor Pazazz, that 20th-century humans had three feet and not four as was commonly supposed.)

Tomaly-Somaly was out of her brains on a table in The Great Hall of The Others. Prudence was displeased.

'It's only just gone dark,' she pointed out to the semi-conscious debauchee spreadeagled on the polished mahogany, 'and already you're out of it.'

' 'Salright,' Tomaly-Somaly lied, 'be okay in a tick. Sunbathing.' She raised a wobbly blonde head and looked around startled.

'Sun's gone!' she exclaimed. 'It's all dark!'

'It's called night,' Prudence answered tartly. 'Happens every day about this time.'

'The Feast!' Tomaly-Somaly sat up in alarm, 'I missed The Feast!'

Prudence began to toss the empty bottles into a large wooden tub, counting under her breath.

'Six, seven, no you didn't, nine, ten, but you can help me clear this place up now you're awake. Those damned servants claim they're too busy in the kitchens. Tomaly-Somaly slid to the edge of the table and lowered herself gingerly to the floor shaking her head.

'Got to have a bath. Change. Get my head together.'

She staggered slowly towards The Great Stairs curving in a majestic spiral to a breathtaking height and began an unsteady ascent.

'You rotten cow!' Prudence muttered bitterly. 'You always leave a mess.'

Tomaly-Somaly, hearing her, turned and sat down halfway up the steps with tears in her eyes.

'Oh, Pru, please don't be hard on me. I can hardly walk. How can I help you clear up?' She began to sob bitterly, her face in her hands.

'Now Tomaly-Somaly, don't get upset. I didn't mean it,' Prudence answered, moving to comfort her but muttering 'Rat-bag,' under her breath. She put a consolatory arm around Tomaly-Somaly's bare shoulders. 'You mustn't stretch yourself so thin, Tomaly-Somaly,' she murmured in her ear. 'You've got to learn how to pace yourself, how to pull yourself back when you're tired or sick. You'll wear yourself to a frazzle.' She kissed Tomaly-Somaly's ear affectionately. 'Now go and soak for a while. I'll get someone to lay your clothes out and heat the chambers.'

'You're so *nice* to me,' Tomaly-Somaly replied, beaming smiles and sunshine again. 'I'm *starving*! When do we eat?'

Prudence put on a face of exasperation.

'Go and bath,' she insisted, 'or you won't be ready in time.'

'Right,' agreed Tomaly-Somaly eagerly, dragging herself to her feet with the marble banisters. 'Got to get ready for The Feast.'

She wobbled up to the second floor and staggered slowly around the balconied hallway peering at the ornate golden doors to find her own chambers.

Prudence shook her head and sighed noisily.

'Bottlehead!' she muttered. 'Why don't you get yourself together sometimes?'

She swept up scraps of food and broken glass from The Great Hearth, her face flushing prettily in the heat of the massive, scented pine logs burning deep in its iron-grilled heart.

'Making work for people!' she muttered on. 'I'll cut her tits off one day, I swear I will. Little scrubber! Screws around all afternoon then expects me to clear up after her and run her bath and put her clothes out. Bloody jug-head. Thinks I'll do anything she wants. Thinks all she has to do is look at me with her bottled blue eyes and say "oh Pru" and everything will be alright. Well she's got another thing coming, dirty little cats-paw.'

She straightened out the ornate high-backed chairs lining the tapestried walls and drew heavy drapes over windows that curved and looped in spirals through the massive masonry. Her lips were tight, white, pressed savagely together.

'And if she lets that Amrita sleep with her again tonight then it's the skewer for *both* of them!'

She swept the floors of polished slate and burned the afternoon's flowers in the fire, filling the massive vaulted hall with a vegetable reeking scream that would fade to delicate perfumed sighs and linger, intoxicating, throughout the night's revels. Then, on velvet feet, she flickered through the shadowed Great Walk into The Chapel where, already, Great Womb had been transformed into a shimmering glistening pool of crystal water. Here and there silent forms uncoiled long blue velvet ropes that would contain the devotees at the Moment of Ecstasy.

Prudence cast a practical eye over the floral arrangements and the brightly burnished brasswork that followed the timbers of the vaulting roof in joyful dips and curves, pronounced herself satisfied and silently traversed The Great Courtyard to the kitchen cellars.

She paused at the door, listening to the raucous sounds within and shook her head in contempt.

'Ignorant swines,' she hissed and pushed upon the heavy oak panelling.

The cellars were sick with steam and damp with the reek of screaming vegetables boiling in oil or sizzling in their own body juices. Huge sinks of stagnant, greasy water drowned the rubbled pans of former feasts, ascum with scraps, burnt and raw, festering and stinking. Blackened pots and broken earthenware lay shattered on the tiled floor where scalded fingers had let them drop and decaying scraps lay dead and odourous, crushed damply beneath a season's passing feet.

Unknown vapours, congealing on the high windows, had spread clammy brown fingers across the panes, seizing what little light the flickering courtyard torches threw and trapping careless spiders ankledeep (lose a leg or die) in treacherous quick-fat. The sweating faces of the kitchen staff gleamed in the blaring roar of seven mighty furnaces, each bearing two massive cauldrons, each cauldron vomiting and bubbling, coughing its death-bound burdens this way and that as it boiled out their lives.

And swaying in fierce and deathly grip, staggering and stumbling on the very lip of a red-heat pit of cinderous coals, struggled two kitchen maids locked in mortal combat.

Prudence edged her way through the cheering spectators until she saw what held their attention.

'What happened?' she asked a thickset stump of a sink-woman next to her.

'Rosalie let the rice burn,' the drudge replied.

Prudence turned away in disgust and made her way back to the door.

'I don't know how you people get any work done here at all,' she said to no one in particular and slammed the heavy portal behind her. Soundless once more in soft slippers she swept the winding corridors with the silken kiss of her robes while phantoms in the shadows skittered away at her passage, leaping up the walls and into the roof timbers, chattering at the candle-light, waving maniacally in ritual aggression, then dropping back to the ground behind her, standing motionless, totally concealed in the darkness save for glowing red eyes that shut each time the frightened walker turned to look for them.

She slipped through a narrow slit in the wall and began to climb the winding narrow staircase to her rooms. Once the secret, or at least the discreet, way to what had once been the Royal Bedchamber, the tortuous spiral now tormented Prudence daily with its breathless windings.

'You will use the rear chamber, which has a little staircase all of its very own,' Tomaly-Somaly had once decided in a drunken stupor, 'and you will stop anybody who tries to get past you to get into bed with me in the middle of the night.' And she had kissed Prudence on the foot. 'Except you, of course, my prudent little pussy.'

'All very well,' Prudence thought as she neared her narrow little door, 'But the minx lets them all in from The Great Stairs!'

She reached for the golden key at her waist and turned the stiffened lock.

Then she sat on her narrow bed and looked out at the sky, growing lighter already as the Full Moon prepared its entrance over the horizon. Then, unaccountably, Prudence began to cry.

17

On the dark side of the valley they waited in the shadows, black wings folded like steel cases upon their crooked crusted backs.

Motionless. Wittering sporadically and salivating.

As the sun had yielded into night they had come.

First one. Alone.

Breasting the ridge-top breeze, dipping its stiff feelers into the currents of warm air that carried up the perfume and putrefaction from the palace below.

It had turned, its antler held like divining rods against the dusking sky. A signal.

A beacon. A totem.

A clarion.

Then had come a second, unheard, slowly choosing its many footsteps across the verdant crumbling fields. Then a third and more by the heartbeat until the shadows shone black with the pulse of their quiet waiting. In their faceted eyes the prismed palace dissolved into a million reflections glowing like a candled rosewater moonstone set in the dark velvet of the purpling earth. Strains of sweet music drifted up unheard to the earless grim watchers as they trailed their tremblers in the scent of burning flowers, boiling vegetables and bathing women. Saliva ran like a sodden treacle underfoot and turned the flinty soil to a swamp. Their jaws with twin curving teeth, black-sheathed, blue-gummed, hung open to the breeze, sifting the odours of the night for edible, flotsam titbits.

They waited, motionless, for the moon to rise, an ancient goddess, above them and light their way down to the busy flesh-filled beehive on the valley floor.

And she came, her vast face breasting the rocky plains, casting shadows as long as rivers with her single pearl-white eye. Silver-fingered, she stroked the far side of the blackened hills with silken touch, startling the frozen rabbit in its shadowed burrow. And with her came – Silence.

A hush as loud as the ocean flooded across the thirsty buzzing earth and all was still.

The moon, forever waxing, waning, changing, melting from darkness to light, madness to love, birth, death and evil, had chosen this night for her foulest bitter mood and spread her cruel and lazy veils upon the sunless hemisphere with languorous malice. After all, she had all night.

With subtle tremors of the gravity-gripped globe she called up the blood worms from the buried dead and sent them arching and bending up the valley from the boneyards, glistening greenish-red as they dragged their blind and succulent bodies across the river grass towards the beckoning gleam of the lanterned palace and the suppurating stink of the dribbling huddled packs waiting on the hillside.

And slowly, The Moon, Hecate herself, rose to stare balefully at her forgetful wanton daughters and blood ran slowly down her rampant horns.

Naked she hung, herself, herself alone, no myth or meaning to dim her savage brightness. A wild Moon, rogue mother of an ancient world once more this night, baleful, uncaring, illumined by a fallen sun, unshadowed, mistress of tide and subtle current. The Moon.

And in her iron webs she drew together slowly the magic numbers. From the boathouse in the winding river's sandy, sea-spilled delta she drew the enstubbled and emaciated Brother Two and the carnivorous machine that held him siege.

From the sterile, twin-spined snows she brought the crack-skulled, scar-handed time-warper, the man who was to become known as The Father. And from the lightless depths of the lurching ocean bed she brought Brother One, the cheesecake charlatan, the mantra-chanter, ogling his mandalady, waiting for the sea to fall and repeating,

'Suck leather, sister,' in a serious voice.

And from the fast-cooling desert sands she drew Yeni, she whom many called the Messiah, last of the fallen goddesses, last of those who bleed with the moon, binding spells around the maddened hordes, swirling, dreamless, in The Dance of the Broken Butterfly, bleeding, stigmatically with her Mother Moon and dancing, dancing jewelled, upon the cream-bleached sealess beaches.

And, last but not least, Tomaly-Somaly soaking, bee-brained, in her perfumed and overflowing tub.

Across the warm marble floors the scented water crept, beneath the heavy oaken door and across the floor of Prudence's bedroom to tickle at her foot with a bubbled finger and make her sit up with alarm to see what seemed to be her tears in flood across the carpets.

Long had she sat and wept to see the Full Moon rising in her narrow window, a grim foreboding choking her head with the darkness of the night ahead, fearful of the deep booming shivers that shook the earth.

Now she collected her thoughts together and stepped out of the tepid water.

'You silly cow!' she muttered.

She stepped gingerly to the door in her sodden slippers and flung it open. The noise woke the dozing Tomaly-Somaly and she blinked round startled, saying,

'What's happening? Anything?'

'Yes,' replied Prudence brusquely, 'your bath has overflowed all over the floor. Again.'

'Now listen, Pru,' said Tomaly-Somaly sitting up defensively, 'it definitely wasn't my fault this time. I specially watched it and made sure to switch the taps off when it was full. Someone must have sneaked in while I was getting undressed and—'

'No one sneaked in,' Prudence interrupted in a tired voice. 'Let me explain it to you once again. It's quite simple to avoid this problem if you can understand why it happens.'

She knelt down on a thick rug near to the bath and brought her nose two nose-lengths from Tomaly-Somaly's.

'If you fill the bath full to the brim when you are not in it then, when you climb in, all the little bits of water that have to get out of the bath to make room for you all fall on the floor and run under my door and get my slippers wet. What you should do is leave all those little fellows in the pipes and use them later. That way, when you get in the bath all the water that you've put together will stay in the bath with you. Understand?'

Tomaly-Somaly closed her blank blue eyes in a show of earnest concentration and nodded gravely.

'Yes, Pru,' she replied, 'I understand.'

'Good,' said Prudence briskly, adding under her breath, 'now I'll wipe the little bastards up.'

'What did you say?' asked Tomaly-Somaly plunging her head beneath the water.

'I said you'll miss the Feast if you don't hurry up.'

'What?' asked Tomaly-Somaly, 'I had my head underwater.'

'I said you're spilling more and more water by sticking your head in like that.'

'I can hear funny noises in the pipes.'

'There are always noises in the pipes,' Prudence answered with murderous sweetness. 'It's the water, dearest.'

'No, it's different,' Tomaly-Somaly insisted. 'Put your head in and listen.' And she disappeared under the suds, depositing another wave of perfumed water over the marble-sided tub.

'I've no intention of sticking my head in, thankyou,' said Prudence, 'I'm already in it up to my ankles.'

Tomaly-Somaly surfaced again, wide-eyes, and said,

'No, really, you should! It's a horrible noise! It's like thousands of creepy things crawling up the pipes whispering to each other!'

It was.

18

In the kitchen cellars Rosalie the rice-burner died horribly on the coals, her back broken by a massively muscled pan-watcher.

And in the flues and waterpipes all manner of creepycrawlies waited in ambush, pushed up against plug-holes, peeping from ventilators, creeping up to cracks in the windows. Unseen, unheard, they filled every nook and cranny where light did not fall.

Fat ones, hard ones, scurrying things and slimy slow crawlers, lashed by moonbeams, they struggled into every crack and crevice.

And in The Great Chapel the devotees, too, silently gathered one by one to take their appointed places on the cushioned rows of steps encircling and leading down to the steel-floored octahedron in which Great Womb stood, already illuminated eerily from below.

The Choir, high up among the vaulting metalled woodwork moaned softly in preparation for their performance and the Organ Mistress slowly polished her gleaming shears.

Here and there groups whispered to each other of this and that, of silken robes and hair and lumps in the breast and digestive complaints, toenails and fragrant scents, but hushed and reverent in the magic atmosphere that centuries of ritual had brought to the very air of The Great Chapel.

High up in the rafters, in a secret place to which only she was strong-armed enough to swing, crouched Houdra the Hunchback listening to the whispers as they floated up to her by some unique acoustic phenomenon, clearly audible and crystal crisp. She unpicked the hem of her robe in nervous glee as she overheard this secret and that scandal, heard lies repeated, truths denied, flirtations begun and ended, venomous gossip winding its tortuous way from mouth to mouth. And intermingled with the real came also the unreal.

'Didn't Houdra look simply delightful last night in that sky-blue cloak?' and 'Did you see the great ruby-finger-rings that some secret lover has given to The Hunchback?'

Houdra cared not from where these whispers came, whether from some flesh and blood gossiper on the Chapel floor, some floating spirit spiralling over the flickering candles or from her own thick-skulled and misshapen head. She smiled and laughed and patted her matted hair all the same. Loneliness would drive us all to such extremes, huddled in the rafters of some alien temple, dressed in some beauty's castoff nightclothes, admiring our squat and grimy hands for their translucent delicacy and, while picking our short and yellowed teeth with a broken fingernail, hearing a voice whisper, 'How beautiful she is, how exquisitely beautiful.'

But this evil night there was indeed a whisper in the rafters of The Great Chapel. The whisper of stealthy feet in millions, scurrying and climbing in the darkness, packing the dusty beams and buttresses, clinging to the very cords commemorating past invocations of Great Womb to which were tied the right hands of unknown gods, each with a deep red scar across the back and mummified to varying degrees by the air currents ever swirling beneath The Great Dome.

The insect army hesitated, shrunk back from Houdra's tiny wooden platform in the roof, startled to find an alien so high in the thick shadows. But little by little they grew bolder and moved silently upon her. Unnoticed.

And as the beams and rafters filled up with crawling life, creaking under a weight far greater than that which they had been designed to withstand, so the cushioned tiers filled with their gloriously robed and richly bejewelled burdens. Houdra, unwitting, cut off from any descent, peered down upon them. Tiny as winged sapphire ants in a velvet nest, glittering with faceted winking light, twittering to each other in harmonious squeaks and whistlings. Suddenly the choir swelled up in glorious blood-filled, throat-deep song and the Organ Mistress stepped forward, silver-trained, into the great torchlight circle, the wicked shears held high above her helmeted head, light fraying golden from their glittering handles. A high clear voice, lilting and soaring, sung the Song of Incarnation over the massed harmonies of the swaying songstresses and then all faded, as though by some secret signal, until only the echoes remained, flying up and up into the darkened vaulted cupola, fading, repeating, fading and dying.

All eyes turned to the circular crystal window set high in the North wall, already bright with pale light from the emerging Moon and in the silence the beating of hearts came throbbing and pulsing, a binding rhythmic evocation of The Saved Virgin.

'Oh Crystal Waters of Great Womb!' cried the Organ Mistress trembling with devotional zeal. 'From whom all good and evil springs and to whose dissolving bosom all good and evil returns.'

She cleared her throat and someone sneezed.

'Vouchsafe to us this night once more your perpetual sacrifice to our sadly mortal gods. Bring us once more the body of God to feed and sustain us through our Sacred Feast of Longing and Remembrance, deliver up the Sacrament that we may taste again that which has long been held from us and teach us, in our humility, the pride of being Your chosen servants, entrusted throughout Eternity to keep the Oaths of The Redeemable Damned. Come, O Mother of Woman, rise O Mother of the Earth, daughter of the Sun, Sister of the Ghoulish Host, look down upon us with softened severity at this especially significant moment, cyclically speaking, and bless us once more with your nuptial gifts.'

Tomaly-Somaly, pressed amongst the dazzling worshippers, muttered, 'At least do something! I'm starving! Aren't you, Amrita?'

'Shush,' whispered Prudence sharply.

'Come, O Moon,' the voice of the Organ Mistress soared hypnotically on. 'Come, come O ancient ship of the Heavens, Come O mirror of Truth.'

'How could an old bag like that make *anyone* come?' whispered Tomaly-Somaly to Amrita and Prudence shushed her again.

'Rise to our waiting window and shine down upon Great Womb that it deliver up its precious gift.'

The Full Moon began to show herself by degrees at the bottom edge of the Chapel's one vast eye.

Ponderous she rose, bathing the Eastern wall with an unearthly pallor, her silken silver fingers sliding across the congregation to the steel floor of the octahedral Womb and, as they trailed across the crystal shimmering waters, triggered off the ancient mechanisms built beneath the Chapel floor and with a spectacular swirling of the crystal depths, opened an airlock twenty feet down and jettisoned its rigid, frozen offspring to the moonbright surface.

All eyes gleamed impassioned now as the moment came that all had awaited.

What manner of god would the Full Moon bring tonight?

It bobbed to the surface, its face stiff with cold, arms rigidly pinned by frozen clothing to its sides, legs unbending, ice in every joint. Upon its right hand a livid red scar; dried blood caked in its white and frozen hair.

Its eyes, wide open, stared with glazed bewilderment at the richly-textured, incomprehensible spectacle into which it had suddenly been catapulted as every throat in The Great Chapel screamed in wonderment and horror,

'It lives! It lives!'

'It's still alive!' screamed the Organ Mistress, sick with fear, the glittering shears trembling in her hands.

'Kill it! Kill it!' screamed the panicking throng. 'Quickly! Kill it!'

The frozen stiff, reborn through the tender mercies of Great Womb was none other than he who was to become known as The Father, cast out for dead in the twin-spined valley, bludgeoned and buried alive in a shallow snow-grave.

He heard strange highpitched voices crying, 'Kill, kill!'

Unaware that they referred to him, rigid as a rib and thawing pain-fully, floating on his back in the waters of Womb.

The Organ Mistress gathered up her courage and moved towards him, opening the razor jaws of the Great Shears. And his eyes, the only responsive muscles remaining to him, grew round with disbelief as he realized he was to be clipped, of all nightmare fantasies, of his manhood!

He was about to wish himself somewhere else when a strange event occurred that distracted all attention from him.

A dead hunchback plummeted from the roof timbers and burst open as she hit the ground, scattering the insects that riddled her.

Like marbles across the floor.

19

Meanwhile, back in the boathouse, I had almost become accustomed to the wrinkled, red speedboat bumping unexpectedly against my boathouse piles, almost as though reassuring itself I was still there, when slowly things changed.

I began to realize that this was no watching brief.

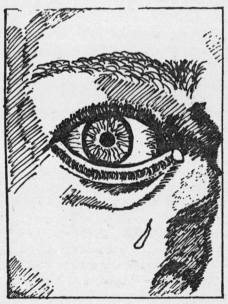

It had become serious.

For three continuous days and nights the scarlet speedboat lure floated beneath my feet.

Escape had become impossible.

I tried to break the cunningly plaited strip-rubber inner walls, but the Orphachins had melted the strands together into a tough, impenetrable web against which my bare hands were useless.

And I had tried to coax the creature out of hiding with friendly salutations culled from the manuscripts in my wet-pack. For hours on end, day after day, I had lain on the dusty wooden floors peering through a peephole and bellowing comradely greetings in a jovial fashion.

'Hey cupcake!' I would shout.

Perhaps the water made my voice inaudible.

'Fancy a yard of this up your passage, then?' I yelled.

Each day the sun turned the wooden boathouse to a hot-pit, so close and yet so far from the cool river water flowing down from the mountains.

'How's about some nookie, then, Doll-face?' I called, keeping as close as I could to the pronunciation indicated in the text.

'Any more at home like you baby?'

'Fancy some gum?'

All useless.

Even after the sun set and darkness filled the valley I could hear my tired voice echoing from the distant foothills.

'Spread 'em, Honey.'

'Who's the little lady, good buddy?'

And other supposedly potent phrases from the ancient writings. No good.

For some reason the magic was not working.

I had tried everything I knew.

So, realizing that my condition could only grow worse as time passed, I determined to make an attempt to break out and reach the mountains where I believed there might be fewer predators or, perhaps, some other *up top* survivors with news of The Father.

I made my plans carefully. If I estimated my adversary aright then my first mistake would be my last and so I studied the boat for several hours as it bumped gently against my downstream pillar, bobbing invitingly beneath my trapdoor, and realized that I had two options. Either I could throw the Orphachin swill into the water, jump into the boat and paddle away, or I could throw the swill into the boat and try to escape along the substructural rafters or into the river.

Although the second alternative seemed the more dangerous, it had one attractive feature – I might catch some glimpse of my predatory companion in all her primaeval splendour. But if the swill did not tempt her into the boat or if she were faster than me in the water then that glimpse could cost me my life.

To tell the truth, I had made up my mind that I was already finished and didn't really care either way.

I thought wistfully of Brother One, snug and safe in my cave, placidly taking life as it came, occasionally dipping his nose into other people's interests to see what they were about and then lying back on a weed cushion cynically figuring out where they were mistaken. I had thought him a fool then but I envied him now. Better to die of boredom in a worthless reality than become breakfast for some mutant abomination in a soiled heaven. Yes, I was feeling sour alright.

I stuffed everything into my wet-pack save for a couple of manuscripts with which I would make one final attempt to communicate and then pressed my mouth to the peephole for the last time and shouted,

'Hey toots! wanna get your lips round something tasty?'

'Get a load of this, Big-jugs,' I called, selecting phrases at random.

Perhaps I misunderstood the nature of the text. I had believed salutations of this sort would bring the creature out into the open, endear her to me, fill her with admiration and, ultimately, persuade her to play her part in the ritual of 'mating behaviour'.

But, whether it was a reluctance unique to this individual creature or whether I was simply using the wrong tone of voice, the magical phrases were utterly ineffective.

I packed away the manuscripts and my revolveroids ready for any emergency then dragged the stinking Orphachin cauldron across the splintering floor to the hatch and went to work, slowly, silently, withdrawing the battens that secured the heavy wooden boards.

Quietly raising the hatch and placing it to one side, I looked down. This was the most dangerous stage of the manoeuvre.

Below me the speedboat rocked lazily on the gently moving river, almost within arm's reach. If the creature spotted the open hatch now she could be inside and at me before I could do anything about it.

I eased the cauldron to the yawning hole, silence making the task doubly difficult, and even my sweat stood tip-toe on my bulging forehead as I inched the suppurating stew barrel out over the boat. I was gambling that the noise and smell of the putrid flesh would distract the creature and enable me to slip across the substructure rafters to the bank and vanish into the bushes.

This is what went wrong:
As I released the cauldron I slipped and fell into the boat with it, striking my head on the steering wheel, knocking myself unconscious and nearly drowning in the Orphachin stew. The cauldron holed the bottom of the boat. The boat began to sink.

I recovered consciousness only to pass out again, overcome by the freshly upturned stench of rotting meat. Fortunately, as the boat slowly sank, the water revived me but, rising too rapidly to my feet, I struck my head upon the very structural beam along which I had hoped to attain safety and fell back into the disappearing vessel, once more unconscious. I might still have escaped on recovering my senses had I not opened my eyes to find the creature standing upon the stern of the boat staring down hungrily (as I supposed) and my mind blacked out as I became one of the few human beings ever to set eyes on The Forbidden Ones and live to tell the tale. She was just as the ancient scriptures had pictured her. She wore the greatly enlarged pectoral muscles that were a mark of her kind and was seemingly devoid of genitalia, though I knew from my studies that this was merely a trick of the light. Smaller-boned than a human being, though perhaps broader in the hip and generally less well muscled, I could not help but feel, well-prepared though I was, that I had never seen a more hideous mockery of the human form in my whole life.

20

How long I lay unconscious I do not know. Stunned by blows to the head, nervous system and senses I lay in what the old teachings call a 'swoon' for at least as long as it took to be bound hand and foot with golden cords and placed in a container made entirely of pipes. When I came to I was aware at first only of the bumping and bouncing of the conveyance upon which my cage was bolted as we travelled a muddy pathway beside the river.

I sighed grimly, realizing what was in store. I recalled seeing pictures in the manuscripts of these strange creatures bound by ropes and thongs, fiendish gags distending their jaws, padlocks between their thighs, raw red whip marks on their back and legs. Now I too was surely to become a victim of this bizarre practise. I struggled vainly against my bonds and raised my head to look around.

To the left the river flowed widening back to the boathouse that had witnessed my recent débâcle and to my right the valley rose, as always, screened by stunted trees.

I craned my neck to see what powered my strange conveyance and saw the heads of a dozen bobbing little boys that I later came to recognize as Orphachins in harness, struggling forward in the light of torches secured by iron clamps to their traces. Behind us ran my captor and a no less hideous companion, jogging easily with light and graceful steps, 'Whey, hey, hey!' I shouted cordially, trying to recall appropriate remarks from the oft-studied manuscripts. 'How's about a quick bunk-up, darlin'?'

No response registered upon their grim, impassive faces.

Clearly, I had learned the language of the Court and these were low-bred servants, unable to understand the niceties of refined speech. I abandoned myself to the lurching journey, vomiting upon myself from time to time, involuntarily, but quite usefully, as it happens, since my clothing was wet, the night was cold and the little bit of warmth meant a lot to me.

'Oh to be peacefully lying in my undersea cave,' I thought wistfully. 'Brother Two, you made a big mistake.'

We left the riverside, climbing steeply up through coarse undergrowth that strove to reconquer the stolen roadway, whipping and scratching at the cage with nonchalant malice and, looking back, I could see the river, my river, as I had self-indulgently come to think of it, snaking down towards the invisible sea in the light of a Full Moon.

Suddenly I was startled by cries of horror and despair from my captors and I turned to see their faces made even more hideous by alarm and concern as they stared into the valley we were following. I looked down and saw a strange and beautiful spectacle.

Deep in the velvet moonlight shadows of the folding earth stood a radiant palace. Marble must have been its building stone, but so bright with fires, torches and candles did it burn that it seemed to shine translucent from within as the wing of a gull-hawk against the sun. Even at this great distance the faint echoes of warm and perfumed corridors wafted to our rough and muddy pathway but with these gentler scents came the stink of burning flesh. The Palace was surrounded by a moat of wildly blazing fire and even on the roof great gouts of flame poured out in random bursts as though to exterminate some flammable invader. And in the warm night came cries of pain and terror. What terrible events were taking place in that palace of torches it was impossible to guess, but I noticed that my captors stamped angrily upon the ground as though trying to annihilate the harmless crawling insects that seemed to abound in that part of the valley, sweeping downhill in droves, presumably attracted by the warmth of the flames. The Orphachins were lashed on to even greater efforts and they rattled away breathlessly to each other in their staccato gibberish, heaving the lumbering waggon over the rim of the valley until the Candle Palace became a firefly in the night, a tiny glowing pearl nestling into darkness and distance until it faded to nothing.

Onward and upward we rolled and rumbled until the snowcapped mountain peaks loomed over us, disembodied in the moonlight, floating and swaying gently thousands of feet from the earth, lit from within, spectrally, by the twice-reflected luminescence of an invisible sun.

I swooned now and then, I do believe, as the air grew colder and my weakened condition became more and more apparent and we climbed more and more steeply upwards to where there was nothing but an occasional obstinate weed clung to the stony hillsides and the Orphachins wittered and chirped in peevish protest, bullied onwards by incomprehensible yelps, oaths and whistles from their mistresses.

I was much impressed by the ability of these hideous Amazonis to control the vicious little creatures who were constantly snapping at each other's necks with their sharp pointed teeth or attempting to chew through their chains and traces.

But at length, just as I had come to believe I could grow no colder and remain alive, the conveyance ground to a halt with much whoaing and hupping and the wall of my cage clanged heavily open. I tried to say, 'Wanna take a little ride with me, Big-eyes,' to ingratiate myself with my captors as they dragged me bodily from the carriage and dumped me on the rocky ground, but my lips were too numb to move. We had stopped at the foot of a sheer cliff-face that rose up into the snowline hundreds of feet above our strange waggon. And from a cavern close by issued a roaring torrent that broadened out to become the winding river we had followed from the lower reaches. Handling me not ungently, they removed my bindings and stood me on nerveless legs as though I were as light as a small child, fastened iron shackles between my knees, hurried me over to the river bank and, with prods and pokes and pointing fingers, indicated that I was to continue upriver without them.

Quite naturally, I refused, preferring to slump semiconscious upon the ground and tremble with cold.

They looked at each other with irritation, returned to the waggon, and, while one unshackled the conveyance, the other took up a large goad and unhitched the first six Orphachins from their traces.

From that moment on all became dreamlike. I saw the creatures leap their chains towards me, leg muscles knotted with voracious speed. I saw the Amazoni whooping and yelling them forward and felt myself rising to my feet, turning, running several manic steps, diving into the torrent that poured from the rocky embouchure, forcing my way against the mass of tearing water, buffeted to my knees, clutching at rocks and mossy outcroppings, dragging myself hysterically on, torn and bleeding, until the baying of the frustrated Orphachins no longer came to me, real or imagined, over the water's raging flood. I saw moonlight ahead and struggled towards it mindlessly, thankful that the going became easier as the natural conduit broadened out, and I climbed through to a sheer-sided crevasse that contained the struggling, thundering torrent.

Fearful that the Orphachins might dare to follow me even here I struggled up a snow-sprinkled ridge and found myself looking down into a deeply-snowed plunging valley which lay as though between twin stickleback spines of mountain range.

And half-buried in the deep snow-bowl I saw three rude wooden huts, in darkness save for a single beckoning lantern, a tiny pinprick in the surface of the moonlit snow.

I stared around the mighty ice-clothed mountains and was suddenly lonely. There was nothing for it but to see what the buildings were.

Perhaps I might find help.

I swung over the edge of the rocky ledge into the valley.

21

I stumbled through the deep snow like a baby dog-dolphin caught in a tide-cave, floundering and falling, sliding and stumbling through the warm powder, resting frequently, face down, breathing upon the crystals until they dissolved into water then recombined into clear, smooth-rimmed ice.

Distance became meaningless.

Time shrunk to the shortwave rhythm of inhalation and exhalation. The tiny building came no nearer. I became neither more cold nor more tired and the moon stood still in the sky.

I thrashed on through the snow, dragged downwards into the bowl of the valley by gravity himself, Lord of the Mountains.

And in that skittering descent towards fellow-humanity I experienced the yawning loneliness of time frozen, time thawed, time melted and reformed into clear and smooth-rimmed minutes.

I forgot most of the things I had most clearly determined to remember and remembered many things that I had long forgotten – spills, sprains, spasms of grief and pain, anger, lust and first love over and over again. I became a dwarf and a giant, a king and a cockroach, a victim and a victor all rolled into one frozen, thawed, melting, refrozen clear and smooth-rimmed eye.

And as I entered upon the tiny pathway that led to the wooden huts the valley seemed to thunder, echoing, with my awesome footsteps as I clung, like a jackal in an abandoned city, to the walls of my new-found empire.

I was totally out of my brains.

I knew not what sort of a place this was to which I had been forcibly transported.

Another trick? A trap?

A malicious mind-game?

I peered through a window of one of the huts and pushed aside rough sacking that screened out the frozen winds.

A long benched table stood amid a litter of food scraps and soggy splinters scuffed up from the rough-hewn board floors. Pots empty and pots burned were scattered here and there around a massive black iron stove, its doors hanging open, its coals gleaming faintly in their soft white bed of uncleared ashes.

A stroke of luck.

A place to find food and nobody around to jump on my back and rip my throat out.

I dragged my battered body over the sill and collapsed head first on the floor inside, luxuriating in the smell of edibles less than a week old until I could summon up energy to crawl across the floor, devouring droppings and sodden scraps with unseemly relish then, slightly delirious with blood sugar, I crawled carelessly out of the door and down the muddy pathway to the next hut.

My raw tingling senses picked up on the breathing inside.

In my sensitive state I felt even the timbers themselves breathing.

'Alright,' I shouted defiantly, 'Wake up. Here I am. I've arrived!'

No sound stirred the liquid silence of the night.

I banged on the door with numb fingers.

'On with the show!' I yelled. 'You wanted me, now you've got me. Let's get it over with!'

I heard stirrings from within and redoubled my efforts, putting my mouth close to the cracks in the door.

'Yoo Hoo!' I whooped in a high falsetto. 'Open up and eat me. I'm too tired to play this game any more.'

Low grunts of surprise and startled whispers were my answer.

'Come on, come on,' I yelled impatiently. 'You must have known I was coming. Don't play-act with me any more.'

I suddenly had a vision of myself from the top of the twin-spined peaks, a tiny four-limbed figure, beating on the outside of the only man-made artifact in the universe, crying for surrender, giving myself up willingly to whatever consuming fate awaited me inside. And I crumpled, sobbing, in a hysterical heap on the floor.

'I just don't care any more,' I muttered. 'That's the long and the short of it. I just don't care any more.'

I heard furtive footsteps and the rattle of lanterns, the crisp crackle of lights being struck and the tight-lunged silence that men give out when they huddle together in the frightened shadows asking themselves what hideous stranger beats upon their universe. Anxious ears shuffled uncertainly to the door against which I lay and I heard breathing as close to me as my own mouth.

'Open the door you bastards,' I muttered in a self-pitying whine, 'or I'll freeze to death.'

'Must be the newcomer,' muttered a nervous voice. 'Better look and see.'

Fingers of fear trembled with the sliding bolts and as the door opened the weight of my body flung it aside and I fell inside. They scuttled away in panic.

In the grip of Death I stared fearless from the floor at the frightened huddle cowering against the wall. My eyes widened in disbelief.

'Human beings!' I cried weakly. 'Human beings, of all things!' I had never thought to have the good fortune to stumble upon fellow creatures in this mountain fastness.

Their eyes, too, were wide with disbelief, but for different reasons.

'It can't be,' whispered one in frightened awe. 'He's dead. He *must* be!'

'It's him alright,' whimpered another. 'I knew we should have killed him properly.'

'They've put the colour back in his hair!' marvelled a third, stepping forward curiously, emboldened by my unmoving bewilderment. 'He had *white* hair before!'

'And he looks younger. He's lost twenty years!'

They edged forward nervously and I said,

'Hi fellers, you want to invite me in or am I going to lie here all night?'

A face swung down to mine, the lantern held between us.

'Is it you, Lord?' the face croaked, a mask of excitement and cunning. 'Is it really you come back?'

'Sorry to disturb you at this hour.' I mumbled, wondering what manner of human beings these could be to poke and stare at a fellow creature as though he were already dead. 'I know it's rather late but I was just passing so I thought I'd drop in.'

There was raucous laughter.

'Sure. Sure,' a voice said sarcastically. 'Well maybe we'd better drop you out again. But this time we'll do you properly.'

'Hang on a minute,' said the face closest to mine, 'where's his scar? He hasn't got his scar. He hasn't got white hair and his scar's gone!'

My blue, numb extremity was picked up by warmblooded fingers.

'Look. No scar!' he hissed in wonderment. 'What the hell is going on around here? He's been reborn, I tell you. It's the Messiah himself, resurrected!'

Not having any more idea than he what was going on, my mind took the opportunity to go blank and allow events to flow unhindered by my confused consciousness.

I blacked out. Plunged into the blessed relief of utter helplessness, the body's night, the soul-saver, a useful trick to know when life is too tough to take.

It worked its magic once again.

When I awoke I was wrapped in rough blankets, with dry clothes upon my suffering flesh in a cot close to a small but brightly burning stove.

It took a few moments to realize I was tied up.

'Hi fellers,' I had the presence of mind to say to the ring of lanterns encircling me, but spoiled a pleasant smile by unexpectedly throwing up my recent meal.

'The dirty bastard! Just look at him!' a voice of contempt spat out.

'Sorry,' I muttered, wiping my lips. 'Trouble with food recently.'

'*Ask* him,' urged a voice. 'Ask him now.'

I looked round expectantly but no voices came.

'What is it?' I said, suddenly nervous again in their faceless glare.

'What happened?' someone asked finally.

'What happened when?' I replied.

'He's trying to be funny,' rapped an angry voice.

'What happened after we knocked you on the head and threw you out on the slopes?'

'You did?' I exclaimed in wonderment.

'Where did the blood go?'

'How did you wipe it off?'

'It's a miracle, I tell you.'

'How did your hair turn dark again?'

'Where's your scar?'

I began to realize I had stumbled into a reality that did not recognize me.

'Blood? Hair? Scar?' I muttered, filling once more with despair and self pity. 'Who do you guys think I am? The Messiah?'

'We knocked him potty,' affirmed a competent voice. 'He's barmy.'

'How can you say that? It's a miracle I tell you,' insisted another. The same gnarled mask of fear and cunning loomed once more through the lanterns.

'If you're not Him, who are you?' it demanded.

'If I'm not who?' I asked, realizing as I spoke that it was not an appropriate question.

'Ah, let's just do him in, properly this time, and get back to bed,' the voice with the peevish personality suggested.

'Are you saying that there was someone here who looked just like me?' I asked with sudden excitement.

The face nodded. My heart leaped.

That could only be *one* person.

The Father!

'Are you really the Lord?' asked a grimly bright-eyed face swinging down to within inches of mine. 'Are you really come by a miracle?'

'Me?' I mumbled. 'I'm The Father's son!'

'It's *true* then!' responded the face triumphantly, turning excitedly to the others. 'It's Him! It's The Messiah. He is risen. He's risen to save us all!'

Suddenly the earth beneath their feet began to heave and shudder and there was a loud crashing from the next building. The lamps swung dangerously upon their hooks and the cots shifted uneasily about the floor.

'Another one!' an old man exclaimed nervously. 'What's happening around here?'

'The stove!' shouted another. 'If the stove goes over the pot-house will burn down!'

The tremor faded as quickly as it had come, leaving them shaken and confused.

'I don't like it,' said an angry voice. 'It's this bugger's fault, I'm sure of it. Him and his bloody Father!'

'Let's do him in and have done with it,' suggested another.

'Yes, yes,' said the old man, 'but we'd better check outside first. We can't afford to lose the pot-house or we'll have to eat in the snow.'

They checked my bonds then crowded out into the rumbling night, leaving me to pounder over my misfortunes after leaving the tranquil security of the submarine civilization.

True, I had found the angels of whom the manuscripts had told, but had found none that responded to the ancient language and had, instead, been delivered into the untender hands of my own species and was about to die.

But as I waited for death I experienced a curious phenomenon not unlike that reported by the victims of minor pump accidents.

A recollective re-run of past experiences.

Rather it was fragments of what I took at the time to be scenes from previous incarnations that were unfamiliar to me.

I imagined myself as an Orphachin in the desert or, to be precise, several Orphachins in the desert, muttering together in a rudimentary guttural tongue mixed with clear and rapid telepathic images. I was hungry and could see food on the hoof, as it were, in large numbers quite close by. To my horror and surprise I found my mouth watering at the sight of an enormous gathering of angels and heard my lips muttering the strange phrase 'Gobbly Gobbly' over and over again. And I thought I could see my brother leading us on our bellies through the sand and felt a great love for him, as for a Father, Leader, General, Saviour or Messiah. I watched his every movement as though my life depended upon it, moved forward or stopped at his command and listened intently for his orders as they swept amongst us by word of mouth or mind. 'Gobbly, Gobbly,' I said, salivating. 'Gobbly, Gobbly.'

And then I saw her, whirling upon the desert beneath the full moon like a golden moth around a phosphorescent float-lantern, a goddess if ever there was one, beautiful beyond legend, more fascinating than all the representations I had studied in the textbooks, graceful, lissom, inspired, possessed, at one with the cosmos, dancing, dancing upon the dunes as though Time itself had stopped to watch her.

Then my brother's hand went up and I, that is to say, we, swept forward and seized the creature even as she leaped from the sands, and carried her off, rigid with shock and terror, into deep sand caverns of which only the Orphachins knew.

My brother kneeled to tend her wounds and I tried to speak, to call out to him saying,

'No, you must not touch her. She is a Goddess!'

But my mouth instead formed only the words,

'Gobbly, Gobbly.'

'No Gobbly,' my brother replied sharply. 'Capisco? No Gobbly.' And as he cuffed me on the side of the head the image disappeared and I found myself back on my cot in the bunkhouse.

'Gobbly, Gobbly?' I muttered in surprise. 'What's happening?' I strove to send my mind back into the dream world from which my brother's blow had driven me and with surprising ease found myself once more out in the desert, lying down and standing around in the sand-gully as the collective consciousness of the Orphachin pack, watching my brother vainly endeavour to stem the goddess-queen's leaking wound.

'What's happening?' I enquired of myself.

'Gobbly, Gobbly,' my lips replied and my brother looked up sharply with an angry frown.

'Be *told*!' he snapped, cuffing me even more savagely on one of my heads. 'No Gobbly. Capisco? No Gobbly, Gobbly.'

'No Gobbly,' I agreed with slack and little-used lips and with a suddenly banging door and a razor-sharp mountain wind I was yanked back to my snowcamp cot as men returned, shouting angrily amongst themselves.

'I *told* you we should have done him in the first time! Everything's falling to pieces now!'

'Shut your trap! Nobody was stopping you!'

Two men began to untie the ropes that held me to the cot.

'Alright,' said one angrily. 'You win. I didn't believe you were The Messiah before but this little stunt has convinced me.'

'What's happening?' I asked, puzzled realizing they were soaked from head to foot.

'You should know, Lord,' was the bitter reply. 'It must be you who started it.'

'Started what?' I said in surprise.

'Started the snows melting. We've been out to check them. We can't smooth any more. The slopes are turning to water, melting to rivers and running down the mountains. Something has gone wrong and you're going to have to tell us what to do.'

I struggled from my cot and peered through a window.

It was true.

The slopes that had been so smooth and perfectly white were now slit and pitted by a thousand running wrinkles in the moonlight. The ground outside the huts was transformed to thick mud where the returning men had struggled from each deep, clinging footprint and from all sides came the faint music of running water.

'It's melting!' I cried.

'Clever lad, Lord,' replied the second man ungraciously. 'Now you'd better freeze it back up again.'

I turned to see that both were looking at me expectantly.

'I can't do that,' I said and the first man turned away with a snarl.

'Told you,' he said. 'Useless! I told you he wouldn't be able to do anything. All these bloody Messiahs are the same when it comes to the nitty-gritty. We'd better go over to the pot-house and join the meeting. We're in trouble enough without relying on *him*.'

We waded shin-deep to the pot-house where a grim-faced gathering waited for us around the table. A single oil-lamp illuminated the shabby room where the half-naked snow-smoothers had hung dripping clothes to dry before the stove and no trace of love or humour lightened their anxious countenances.

Unexpectedly, one of them rose to his feet and pulled out the end of a bench for me.

'Here, Lord,' he said. 'Sit here.'

'Thank you,' I replied, limping to the seat.

'Don't bloody crawl to him now, just because we're in trouble!' someone grumbled and I looked round to find all eyes upon me.

'What's happening?' I said.

'Don't bloody give us that,' began a petulant voice. But it was silenced by the raised hand of the man who sat next to me.

'What's happening, Lord,' he said gently, 'is that Your Father has seen fit to upset the delicate balance of our lives here by throwing everybody into confusion and melting the snow. You most probably knew that this would happen if we harmed you, but were not at liberty to explain it to us or warn us because we know how important the principle of Free Will is to all you divinities.'

'Yeah!' came the petulant voice again, 'otherwise there'd be nowt for them to do and they'd lose their bloody jobs.'

'Please,' insisted my quietly-spoken informant, 'let us try to retain some measure of dignity before the Son of God even at this late hour.'

He turned back to me.

'What we would like you to do, Lord,' he said, 'that is to say – what it would give us great pleasure and comfort to see you do entirely of your own free will and without any pressure at all from us – is to tell us what is going to happen next and, if necessary, help us to leave this place and find safety.'

'Why should I help anybody,' I replied. 'You were planning to kill me.'

My neighbour smiled gently and inclined his head as though in deference to the convincing point I had just put forward.

'Be that as it may, Lord, we would still be overjoyed to be the recipients of your unsolicited aid at this point in time.'

I looked around, sensing a certain strange tension in the air and it suddenly occurred to me to distrust the gentleness with which I was being handled, for upon at least half the faces at that table was written the terrible hatred of the bested bully.

Brother Two, get smart, I told myself. These men have no feeling of kinship with you. They are aliens to you, to each other and to themselves. If you do not manipulate them they will destroy you. I moved quickly.

'If you had listened to me before,' I said quietly, simply, 'This situation might have been avoided.'

'Don't bloody give us that!'

'Hush,' said my protective neighbour.

'This is what we must do,' I said. 'We must gather together provisions and quit the valley.'

'Quit the bloody valley!' cried the petulant voice, rising to his feet in alarm. 'But I'm the next-to-go! I've served five months already! *I'm* not leaving! I've nearly finished here!'

'Very well then,' I replied graciously, beginning to feel more comfortable in my role, 'if you so wish, you may stay.'

'Oh,' said petulant, mollified and surprised. 'Thankyou, Lord. Then I'll stay. Thankyou.'

'Think nothing of it.'

'How are we going to carry everything, Lord? The beds, the stove, things like that.'

94

'We'll have to build a raft,' said another, 'wait for the streams to form a river, then float out of the valley.'

'That may take some time,' I suggested.

'We can wait,' they replied grimly.

'Yes,' I agreed smoothly, 'you can wait. As for the rest of us, we should pack up tonight and leave at first light.'

'Right,' said my neighbour, taking charge of the situation, 'you, you and you, prepare the food. You come with me and we'll make packs out of the spare blankets. You sit here and rest, Lord.'

'Thankyou,' I said with dignity.

'Hang on a minute!' said petulant suddenly. 'Hang on just one bloody minute!'

He moved belligerently round the table to stand over me.

'He hasn't told us what's going to happen yet!'

'What's going to happen?' I repeated, as if absentminded. 'Oh yes. With the exception of you, we're all going to escape and live happily ever after.'

'Oh,' he said, mollified again, shrinking back to size. 'That's alright then. Thankyou, Lord.'

22

Meanwhile, elsewhere in the darkened desert, things were hotting up.

'Dreams?' screamed Ana, belabouring the on-climbed mystic with a stout stick. 'Dreams? You've never had a seeing dream in your life!'

'Desist!' hissed The Crone uncomfortably. 'You know otherwise.'

The cudgel snapped across her back, the Queen of Women tossed aside the broken stump with a snort of contempt and flung herself down in her throne.

'The only dreams *you* have, Witless One, are dull ordinary everynight dreams. It is *I*, Ana, Queen of The Earth, who brings them to sparkling, vibrant, meaningful life.'

She turned to the hooded hag with venom in her voice.

'You dream the dreams for which *I* have prepared the world. It is *I* who give your nightmares their reality.'

'Not true,' responded The Crone nervously, 'not true.'

'You know *nothing*, Worthless One. You brag of magic powers and believe your own boasting. If you have magic, tell me of this woman Yeni, this woman they call the Messiah.'

'It is as it is written.'

'Ha!' screeched Ana contemptuously, 'always the same answer!' Her voice became a mocking echo of The Crone's feeble croak. 'It is as it is written. It is as it is written. Pah!'

She spat on the black rag bundle.

'You know nothing, charlatan! There must remain *many* who bleed with the moon!'

She sunk her chin on to her cancerous chest nervously for a moment and then gave a short, hollow chuckle.

'But if she *is* the last of those who bleed with the moon, if she really *is* the Messiah,' she raised her eyes and stared in the darkness of her skull. 'Then let her be delivered into *my* hands!'

She pushed herself stiffly to her feet.

'Unstitch the doors,' she ordered, 'let me look into this night that hides them.'

The tent walls were pulled back by diligent seamstresses and Ana gazed out into the desert, blindly scanning the blackness and reflecting nothing but the moon.

'If she *is* the Messiah,' she whispered, a new strange note of power in her cunning voice, 'then she is *mine*! *Now* is my moment. Now!'

She raised tightly clenched fists to the watching moon.

'And I shall seize it without flinching. At *my* hand will this Messiah die. And in that single moment of ritual sacrifice shall I become more powerful even than she. If she must die then let it be by *my* Will and let the scribblers write large the words:

"And in the Land of The Supreme Matriarch
Was Yeni, Mother of Mankind, put to death
By the hand of Queen Ana herself."

'Such an opportunity comes only to a Blessed Few separated by thousands and thousands of empty years and millions upon millions of weaklings, nothings and nobodies. Will I not then become more powerful than she? Will I not then become a goddess also, accorded rank and power in some great feasting hall between the Gods of Courage and Ambition?'

She thrust her clenched fists savagely against her breast.

'I *must* have her! I must *possess* her! Take from her even her life and let the name Ana ring through Time and Space to the ends of the universe that every intelligence, even to the furthest uncaring star shall hear *her* scream and know *my* name!

'*Ana!*

'And, if there be a God, let it be One who demands just such a sacrifice as this and takes *me* to sit at *His* right hand in Power and Glory!'

Her voice rang, fading, across the desert and behind it fell a silence such as the World had never known.

A silence in which even the Earth did not turn, nor the moon revolve around it, nor the planets flame their dreadful orbits.

This was the moment for which The Crone had willed herself to survive, when Time itself stood still and, with a noiseless scream, began to reverse itself, slow and ponderous at first but gathering pace as it recoiled diagonally across centuries of centuries, unwinding history as easily as it had been ravelled up, a self-cancelling vortex, a mirror negation of all that had ever been.

And in her womb of rags The Crone knew Terror.

As she had never known it.

Terror.

Now that the moment had come she was afraid of her Queen.

It was true, she saw nothing in her dreams of this woman Yeni, nor of events that her coming would precipitate.

And true it was also that she saw many things that did not transpire and that only those prophecies that Ana herself believed ever found expression in reality.

Now she was afraid.

She had not realized before that Ana knew she had no magic.

And until this moment she had not realized how much magic Ana herself possessed.

Far off in the baking desert she could hear still the raging silence that followed the Queen's words as they rung through the universe and she tried to stretch herself out to the hushed and motionless throng whose coming would reveal all, trying to learn something of them to chasten the Queen and prove The Crone's Second Sight.

But she could not find them in the vast desert.

Her spirit flew blind in the darkness and returned to her with empty hands.

'Give me *something*!' she muttered to her stars. 'Some secret, some special foreknowledge to frighten this witch into belief in me again.'

But the only thing she knew for certain, as she had always know it, was the moment of her own death.

'What's this, Crone?' snapped Ana, breaking into her reverie. 'What's this muttering in there? Let not your words of wisdom fall upon barren ground, Sagesse. Speak, speak, let us *all* marvel at your magic powers.'

'The woman, Yeni, has captured her captors in a spell,' bluffed The Crone desperately. 'They are in her power, they sit upon the sand in frozen rows as she swirls in The Dance of The Broken Butterfly.'

(Where did I know that from, she wondered.)

'And what dance is that, Old One?'

'Tonight, upon the dunes, shifting as the tide, she spills out The Wine of Life upon the thirsting sand.'

(That should give her something to chew on, she thought.)

Ana screwed up her face, troubled and anxious. Could it be true? Could this Yeni really be the Last of those who Bleed with the Moon or was this a wild Crone guess?

'You bogus bag of bones, every year The Others cast out more who bleed with the moon,' she snarled and listened for the silent multitude, the staring out into the night. Rogese, seated as always in the shadows, smiled a small lip-curved smile.

'Sweat a little, Queen Ana,' she said to herself. 'Sweat a little.' She had learned from her own bitter experience that one draws to oneself that which one fears the most, that almost out of thin air one conjures one's worst nightmares, living them out, if necessary, to enact the ritual of Change and Purification which one is too weak or frightened to play out on the level boards of the Mind's Stage. 'Sweat a little, *Your Majesty*,' she whispered to herself, smiling.

MEANWHILE, as witness to the mystery that she intuitively understood, a day's march distant over the dunes, Yeni did, indeed, dance, crimson-thighed, upon the desert wastes, in macabre celebration of her godhead beneath a grisled moon.

Dreamless she danced, lips drawn back in frozen snarl, wings cracked and broken, shrivelled to arms upon her shoulders, The Dance of The Broken Butterfly, Minuet of the Trembling Menstrual Moth.

And open-mouthed in wonder watched the sterile hordes, their spirits frozen in the timeless horror of fulfilled prophesy; Hatred and Adoration struggling, titanic, in their fiercely beating hearts. And from dunes more distant still, other eyes, strangers' eyes gleamed greedily to see the multitude in frozen herds stagnant upon a powdered sea.

It was the Orphachin Army, The Cannibal Kids, immaculately conceived every one, led by him who called himself General – the Cheesecake Charlatan, Overlord of the Undernourished, himself chewing upon the remains of sand-stuck bone-bruised travellers.

They watched, eyes glittering, and from the corner of their mouths saliva hung in moving threads.

'They've stopped,' muttered the selfstyled General. 'What a feast we'll have! Food beyond the dreams of avarice!'

From his hiding place he could see, afar off, a moving speck, bathed in moonlight, upon which all eyes were hung.

'That must be their leader,' he told himself. 'A tasty morsel if ever I saw one.'

He raised his arm, waved it left then right then forward and instantly the Orphachin battalions began to crawl through the sand, fanning out to left and right, skimming rapidly on their bellies like flounders through a sea-bed, showing themselves on no skyline, soundless. And, as they passed, the desert rippled like an invisible tide.

A useful technique to know.

They used it now, moving unseen around the succulent soul-struck thousands.

Brother One, with a phalanx of small-fry, circled the spotlit scene, swam to a single dune's width from Yeni and gazed in wonder at the Bleeding Ballerina.

'That must be a *human being*!' He whispered to his uncomprehending lieutenant. 'Look, they've cut off his manhood and are watching him bleed to death, the cruel fiends!'

'Gobbly, Gobbly,' was the reply, as always.

'No,' said the General, drawing a cross upon his lips. 'No Gobbly. Capisco? No Gobbly!'

'No Gobbly,' repeated the Orphachin with slack and little-used lips, drawing the cross upon his own mouth.

The General cuffed him sharply on the head to emphasize the point. 'No Gobbly,' he repeated. 'Pass it on.'

The sound of whispering and cuffing travelled back like soft applause through the sand-shrouded ranks as the order swept among the invisible Orphachins with the swiftness of a sea-breeze. 'Grabby, Grabby,' the General ordered, clenching both fists several times and pointing to the Goddess. 'We have to save that man before he bleeds to death.'

'Grabby, Grabby,' came the fading whisper as the desert received its instructions.

Some few among the multitude may have seen the single arm rise from the sand, beckoning and pointing. But the rest, hypnotized by the swirling sacrifice, knew nothing of their danger until the desert rose up on the backs of children and swarmed forward to swallow up their captive; engulfing her in a swirling cloud of sand that whirled around, wheeling, and streaked away across the dunes to disappear in the stone maze of troughs and gullies. One moment they stood mesmerized beneath the moon, impaled upon their menstruating Messiah, the next they were alone with the wind and the echoes of silence, robbed by a vanished cloud, a meaningless rabble clustered upon a shoreless beach, ravaged by the icy palms of the desert night. Many dunes distant the waiting Tribunal leaped to their feet as the shock travelled to them in a high keening wail of awful loss, a single screaming note of terrible despair and total desolation, it cut them to the heart for reason they could not comprehend.

'What happens, Crone?' demanded Ana.

But even The Crone did not know.

23

On wings of sand the Orphachin Army swept into the desert carrying their semiconscious captive. Undulating eel-like under the moon-blasted wastes they flew, rippling, into secret canyons where no follower on foot would find them, nothing but a whispering hiss to mark their passage.

Finally, in a deep sand grotto known only to the cannibal corsairs, they surfaced, stopped and rose on their hind legs in the moonlight to wink, stare and salivate over their hostage.

'No Gobbly!' shouted the General to his restless troops and pointing to the quietly moaning figure in the sand. 'No Gobbly, savvy?'

He drew a cross on his lips and the Orphachins, puzzled, reluctant, did the same.

'This – Human Being,' he shouted. 'No Gobbly!'

He ripped a patch of clothing from an aide to stem Yeni's bleeding stigmata and wrapped her shivering frame in a small cloak.

'You'll be alright, old chap,' he muttered encouragingly to her. 'Be as sound as sand in a couple of days.'

A day's march distant the voice of The Crone creaked in cunning counterpoint to the faroff wail of loss from the plundered women.

'And a pillar of salt shall rise up in the desert and carry her off,' she crooned, 'and the next day the women came to the Queen saying, "Where is she whom many called the Messiah, She who Bleeds with the Moon?" And the Queen waxed wroth and mounted a great army to scour the desert for she sought to put her to death.'

'What's that, Bearded One?' demanded Ana.

'As it is written,' replied The Crone.

Ana glared down at her huddled helpmeet.

'Where, Hag? Where is it so written?'

'In the Teachings it is so written,' replied The Crone.

Ana threw up her arms and gave a short strangled scream of rage. 'Teachings!' she cried, almost choking, 'What Teachings are these? *I* have never seen them. I don't believe there *are* any Teachings! Let me see them if they exist. Show them to me – these mythical messages!'

'Ah,' replied The Crone, 'Lost. All lost,' grinning devilishly to herself within her rags. 'All lost in the Great Wars.'

(How do I know that? she wondered. She dismissed the question. More important the Queen was now back on the defensive, uncertain, frightened, feeling ignorant.)

'Well the Teachings *lie*,' replied Ana petulantly. 'Wherever they are, they *lie*.'

'And the Queen denied the Teachings,' the Crone went on, pushing her luck, 'and the forces of The Others marched against her and for three days a terrible battle was joined.'

'Don't push your luck, Rag-Bag,' answered Ana. 'If I ever find out that you're making all this up, you'll wish you had died when I first dismantled you.'

Suddenly, the voice of the watchtower came yet again through the tar-pinned night.

'A Runner comes!' it cried.

'From what quarter?' came the response.

'From the West,' replied the watchtower.

'And a third Runner came from the West,' intoned The Crone, 'And there was . . .'

'Oh shut your blabbering lips, you worthless fake,' snapped Ana. 'I *know* a third Runner came from the West. Have I not ears, Fleasack? Tell me of the future or seal up your mouth!'

The Crone kept silent, feeling she may have gone too far.

'You see!' crowed Ana, turning to Rogesse. 'Now she says nothing. What counsellors I have! Give me also the fruits of *your* wisdom, *old* and *trusted* friend.'

'You are agitated,' replied Rogesse nervously. 'You wax hot in the cold night air. You should meet with this runner and hear her message. Calm yourself. Let not events ruffle your regal dignity.'

Ana stared angrily for a moment, then with a snort returned to her throne.

'Correct, Rogesse,' she said, beckoning forward servants to re-arrange her robes. 'Let my regal dignity be unruffled. I will calm myself.' She sat quietly for a moment.

'And then I will calmly have this runner carved into tiny regal pieces and scattered in an unruffled manner at the gates of the Candle Palace. But you are right, Rogesse, *first* I should hear her message.'

Rogesse sighed quietly.

'Yes, Rogesse,' said Ana without turning, 'these are delicate times, I know. Do not repeat yourself.'

In the humid tent beneath the night sky of a Full Moon the women waited for the runner from The Others.

What evil quivered across the Earth that night as predator and predator stalked each other in the floodlights, mindless, bound by their simpler drives?

Unready. So many victims, goddammit.

How grim and gloomy a world at war, how sterile shrinks the Earth without laughter, tears and reconciliation.

How weak and weary our planet grows sans love, sans sharing or the closeness of a warm and wordless embrace.

Gods we were, it is written, exiled and re-exiled until our splintered selves resplintered by generation of their involuntary own.

Blind we have become except, like the sparrow's eye, for sudden movements, death and other dramatic flourishes and deaf are we also lest we answer too many cries of pain – wander, wounded, into some other lost soul's savage darkness.

Black, black beneath the moon that night this mirror world of hideous unease.

Shining, shining silver the ancient moon, cruel as snow, careless as a heartbeat, glaring down upon this forest of trees falling, falling unheard in the remote fastnesses of the imagination.

Because happiness is resolution and resolution requires power our Gods dare not trust us (and why should they when they suspect each other) and we do not trust our Gods (for equally sound God-given reasons) nor do we trust even each other's dogs. Hence the effort of consciousness, the upward thrust from coarse to fine, carries the penalty of birth.

Enough. One loses the thread.

MEANWHILE on their separate stages, various villains stroll careless under cathartic skies. Prophets false and real act out their destinies and the forces of Black and White gather armies of annihilation across a self-designated no-man's land.

The Orphachins watch the man they have learned to call General staunch the wounds of Yeni, she whom many call the Messiah, while The Crone, selfstyled mystic, recites the ancient prophecies by telepathy to the doomed Matriarch Queen whose people mass in milling army in the isolated desert, robbed of their sacrifice, enraged.

Meanwhile, in ominous fidgeting silence, hungry bugs, under the command of the Earth's first Insect King, have penetrated the pregnable Candle Palace of The Others where the Full Moon has mischievously delivered a live offering to a Chapel accustomed only to the dead and has exploded a hunchback in the Octagon for laughs.

Meanwhile a stranger from the sea-bed, yours truly, the pilgrim, stares at his sterilized Snowcamp shackles and hears news of his clone-father from a fellow prisoner who, though hostile, believes him to be the Messiah come to save them all. Meanwhile terrifying tremors shake the Earth and Time is hurtling backwards.

Now read on:

24

Rogesse slipped unnoticed through the tent wall and pulled the cloak tight around her against the cold night air. She moved swiftly through the encampment, leaving the shadows only to cross the wide torchlit boulevard that separated the long low lines of soldiers' billets from the imposing pavilions of the royal entourage. Once she was challenged to show her Ring by a raw recruit who fell back in terror as the Chief Minister parted her lips to reveal the Royal Tooth and then she was out into the desert itself, feet biting into the sand, legs pumping by effort of will alone over the switch-back dunes.

Far off in the distance she twice saw the Runner from The Others breasting a ridge before dropping out of sight in the steep sand valleys. Grimly, she set her course to intercept.

This chance would be her last.

She shuddered in the agony of frustrated power.

'Let battle commence,' she muttered under her laboured breath, 'And let the vanquished *die*.'

She struggled on over the cream-white dunes, no longer young, but embittered, vengeful, weak and dangerous, driven on and doomed by Loser's Spite.

When she had gone far enough from the encampment she stopped and sat down to restore her ragged breathing, quivering at the enormity of what she had undertaken.

'Alright,' she whispered firmly, consoling herself. 'This is the end of it. One way or the other. If I cannot be Queen then I will be *nothing*. If this last treachery comes to naught then I will abandon life itself.'

She lay back beneath the Moon's eye, caring nothing for it, a dead husk, a minion, a sky-bauble, pushed her fingers into the cool comforting, accommodating sand.

'Oh Man,' she breathed, calling upon the long-lost pagan god, 'let this Earth be *mine*.'

She listened to the wind, a gentle breeze that moved the mountainous dunes westward grain by grain and thought of the grain-minutes, dune-days and desert-years she had waited for her moment to come. 'All gone now,' she thought. 'All over after this.'

She closed her eyes and listened to the Earth turning on its axis, trembling with deep subterranean unease, waiting for the whisper-soft footsteps of the Runner.

They came and she rose swiftly out of the sand to call to her.

The Runner was clearly exhausted but, terrified by Rogesse's sudden appearance, redoubled her pace and cut off sharply to the left.

'That way lies Death!' Rogesse called and the Runner, hesitating, slowed and veered to the right.

'That way also lies Death.'

The Runner stopped some distance off, panting hard, her whole body seeming to inflate with each gulping breath.

'I mean you no harm,' Rogesse said quietly and held out her arms. 'See. I have no weapon.'

The Runner stared with ironic disbelief and said nothing. Nobody walked unarmed upon the desert. Even she, a Runner, naked, as befits the bearer of a Desperate Plea, carried a sliver of glass hidden in her hair.

'Come,' said Rogesse, 'deliver your letters to me and return with your life.'

The Runner's eyes flickered nervously over the dunes, fearful of Orphachins, and then returned to examine Rogesse, sensing trickery.

She crouched down upon weary legs.

'Come,' said Rogesse imperiously, 'there is little time.'

'Are you trying to tell me,' the Runner answered drily, 'that the Queen of Steriles walks along in the desert night without an army, a guard, a weapon?'

'I am not the Queen.'

'You can say that again.'

'I am not the Queen,' replied Rogesse naively.

'Then step aside. Can't you see I'm naked? You're not supposed to hassle naked Runners. And besides this wind is giving me ass-ice.'

'The Queen is mad with fury. She slew the two before you. She plans to scatter your body in tiny pieces before the Candle Palace.'

'Well good luck to her,' replied the Runner. 'She'll have to use an ice-axe if she wants to cut *me* up. Sod this for a job.'

She scanned the horizon warily and added,

'You realize of course that stopping here like this is like saying *Eat Me* to the wee Gobblies?'

'You speak strangely,' said Rogesse with an ingratiating smile, edging closer. 'Do you refer to the Orphachin packs?'

'The very same. And I'd be speaking even more strangely if that wine hadn't worn off. Listen, how long are we going to stand here gabbing like this? It's alright for you, wearing that tent, but me – even my shivers have got shivers.'

'Give me the message and return in safety to the warm hearths of your Palace. The road to the Sterile Queen ends in Death. I am her Chief Minister. From the very lips of your sisters' assassin I heard how they were slain. I came to warn you and to save you from their fate. The soothsayer speaks of three dead runners and an avenging army sent down upon us by your Council.'

Rogesse spread her hands, palms up, smiling again, wanly.

'That is something we would prefer to avoid. War makes the troops so excitable.'

'Yes,' replied the runner, ruefully rubbing her thighs, 'I know what you mean.'

She bit her lip thoughtfully. 'Alright,' she said, 'I don't suppose it makes any difference whether I deliver the message to the wrong person or whether I find the right person and get cut to pieces.'

'You think with great clarity,' replied Rogesse, stepping within arm's reach of The Other, smiling still. 'Give me the message.'

'Alright,' she said, 'here goes. The Candle Palace is under attack by insect hosts. For many years, ever since Princess Ana butchered the monarchy and took to the desert in Tent-Palaces there has been bitterness between your Court and ours; we have called you The Desert Rats and you have called us The Others. But now it is all up with us unless you come to our assistance. We offer half our lands to Queen Ana if she joins us against the insects. There is no time to lose. The insects have already extinguished our fire-moats with the weight of their numbers. We need your help. Let enmity cease between our nations lest we perish and the insects then move upon you who live in the oases and desert wastes.' She looked over her shoulder at the motionless cresting waves. 'That's it,' she said. 'That's the message. And I'm getting out of here because I don't like it. It's too quiet. It feels creepy.'

She sensed Rogesse's movement too late and turned, but the blade of the arm-knife was already in her back, too high for her groping fingers.

'You lousy pile of crud,' she hissed, stumbling with a bloody cough to her knees and staring stupidly at her hands in the sand.

'I fell over,' she muttered in amazement.

Then collapsed on her side, unbreathing.

Rogesse let out a long pent-up breath and spat, spittleless, upon the dead Runner.

'Sleep, little one,' she whispered, low and comforting. 'You have served your Council well. Now your corpse will serve me.'

She pulled the blade from the Runner's corpse and slipped it back onto her arm beneath the sleeve and, gathering up her robes right around her, strode with invigorated steps out into the desert, skirting the tented Royal Encampment and threading a fading line of footprints to the South where even now under the haunted Moon the faint echoing and reprise of the mourning multitide came and went like the sobbing of a burning Orphachin.

She spotted their distant campfires and plugged on doggedly.

'Now, *Old Queen*,' she muttered to herself as she went, her voice filled with a hatred that only here, in the earless desert wastes, dared she release.

'Now, now is The Night of Reckoning.'

She laughed fiercely to herself.

'You shall have *reports* right enough this time, my Precious Monarch.' Her mouth became a tight hard line in her ageing face.

'As I *roast* you upon living coals!'

She began to tremble violently as the rage and venom inside her slowly rose up to meet oncoming events.

She did not know that an ambition too long nurtured will curdle and sour; that desire becomes obsession if it is not free to move and breathe in the shifting winds of opportunity; that Hatred turns upon its keeper; that the only venom against which Heaven has no antidote is one's own.

'You will call it treachery, Old Queen, but it is not so,' she lied to herself comfortingly. 'Rather, it is victory!'

She could hear the faint rattle of the rabble's camp among the flicker-lit dunes ahead and chuckled.

'Let she who wins the game call the rules,' she said grimly. 'It will be easy to turn these simple farmers, robbed of their Messiah, against the Queen. And then The Others, already besieged by the insect armies, will yield to me or die!'

Rubbing her hands together in vicious glee, she crested a ridge and looked down upon the mighty throng of women, milling in angry confusion upon a desert that trembled with subterranean unease.

Rogesse spread her arms self indulgently and took a long, deep breath. 'Welcome,' she said. 'Welcome, my people.'

25

Meanwhile, in single file, the seven women picked a way through the labyrinthine passageways. Their sodden slippers pattered through the stinking puddles, their gorgeous robes brushed the slimy and lichenous rough-hewn walls, their eyes watered in the acrid stench of smouldering bones.

'Shit!' said Tomaly-Somaly, slipping on a moss-pod and recovering her balance only by clutching desperately at Prudence's neck. I don't know why you need *me*. I'm sure The Whale would never notice if *I* didn't come.'

Too busy negotiating the treacherous footways the others did not reply. She raised her voice.

'I said, I don't know why you need *me*.'

'Zip it,' ordered Diva, holding out the flaming torch that lit their way, 'You know The Whale can count to seven – and always does.'

'Yes, but—'

'Zip it!' Diva ordered more sternly.

And Tomaly-Somaly zipped it.

They struggled on in a silence broken only by the slip, splash and rustle of their uncertain progress.

Twice they lost their way and retraced their steps, three times they stopped to rest, halfway between nowhere and nowhere else, four times they hammered on a tiny iron door set in the wall where the passage suddenly came to an abrupt and exhausted end.

'Pooh!' exclaimed Tomaly-Somaly, wrinkling her nose.

'If you think *this* is bad wait till we get inside,' whispered Amrita wickedly. 'That'll *really* make your curlies curly!'

'Be quiet!' hissed Prudence. 'Show some respect you two!'

There came a low bellow from behind the door that Diva took to mean come in, she turned the rusting handle and between them they pulled open the creaking door.

In the torchlight the odour that came was visible as a slowly curling cloud of green gas.

They fell back, coughing and gasping, and both twins threw up at the same instant.

'Steady, everybody,' counselled Diva, 'the first few minutes are the worst.'

Amrita turned to Tomaly-Somaly with a grin and whispered,

'After that you pass out.'

'Shush!' hissed Prudence sternly.

'Shush *yourself*,' whispered Amrita under her breath and turned away, surreptitiously pinching Tomaly-Somaly in the stomach. Diva, The Twins and the dour, taciturn Pog climbed into The Whale's chamber and Prudence herded the giggling girls after them, gagging and poohing and nipping each other.

They huddled together in the subterranean cavern staring, as always, in wonder at The Whale.

The cell in which it lay, dimly-lit by a hundred tallow candles scattered willy-nilly over the floor and crowded on to any rock edge or niche large enough to contain them, was hot and humid, filled with odours so old and foul they lay like logs in the barely stirring air – stench laid haphazardly across stench until the whole became a stinking welter of unidentifiable fetid putrescence and, amongst it all, vast, swollen, grey-skinned and tiny-eyed, lay The Whale, gross beyond the horrors of nightmare, doomed, trapped, entombed forever in a rock sarcophagus whose exits were now too small to accommodate more than a corner of one huge blubbery lip.

It lay on its back, head propped against one wall, staring over the bulk of a vast and shuddering belly, its body heaving from within as though with life of its own.

The Whale took not the slightest notice of them and Diva, glancing nervously at the others, gently cleared her throat.

The shuddering mass of oily flesh made no response and Diva's cough was drowned in its hoarse and hideous breathing.

Diva cleared her throat again, more loudly, and The Whale's tiny flesh-swamped eyes flickered in their direction for a moment as the belly began to move in huge and rhythmic convulsions.

'We have come for your advice,' Diva said finally, faintly, trying not to stare at the mammoth heaving monstrosity. And from the thick obscene lips came a short highpitched and reedy whine.

The women shuffled uncertainly, pale and sickened, in the smoky light. Diva cleared her throat and tried once more.

'We have come to seek your advice,' she said loudly.

The great head turned slowly towards her and the eyes riveted themselves to her face before turning once more to the shivering mountain of its belly. The thick lips parted and the voice came, slowly, whining, a rusty squeaking like a little used lock.

'My advice,' it said, a tiny sound from so vast a body, 'is to shut the fuck up.'

The women glanced at each other and waited.

Suddenly The Whale screamed, a highpitched whinny of pain, anguish and victory, thrashed violently, arching its spine and bending back its head in indeterminable agony or ecstasy, almost heaving its vast bulk from the waterlogged swamp of food flotsam and excrement in which it lay.

Tomaly-Somaly perched on a low outcrop of stone against the cavern walls until the subsidence faded to tremulous shivers.

'Alright,' said The Whale after a moment's rest. 'What's happening?'

'We're being overrun by insects. Horrible creepy-crawlies!' said The Twins in excited shared sentences. 'Nippers and stingers dropping from the ceilings and crawling through cracks under the doors!'

'They're coming up through the waterpipes,' added Amrita. 'Tomaly-Somaly heard them.'

'The Man-feast still moves,' said Diva with a reproachful glance at her excitable companions. 'The Moon offering is alive.'

'Everything is falling apart!' squeaked The Twins, frightening each other with their own anxiety. 'The ground keeps going wobbly!'

'And the Hunchback exploded on the floor of The Chapel,' said Tomaly-Somaly.

The Whale, who had received the other news with seeming indifference, turned to her sharply with a piercing gaze.

'Houdra!' it said, 'Houdra the Hunchback?'

'Yes,' she nodded. 'Whistle, bang, crump! All over the floor! I couldn't believe my eyes!'

She suddenly stopped in mid-torrent as they all noticed with astonishment that The Whale's pig-eyes were filled with tears.

The reedy voice came mournfully, as from a great distance.

'Houdra?' it said, 'Houdra? Dead?'

Diva cleared her throat nervously again.

'Yes,' she said softly and fell silent.

'Ah,' said The Whale and moved its head in a slow nod that was savagely interrupted by another tremendous belly-spasm, rocking the huge body in knotted paroxysms of pain.

Suddenly there came the sound of tearing fabric and rushing fluids and the huge belly began to deflate, sliding away from The Whale's head like a ship putting out to sea as a hot stench engulfed the watching women.

'The Man-god lives,' Diva repeated determinedly, 'And . . .'

'Be told!' whinnied The Whale through spasmed lips. 'Shut the fuck up.'

Its words dissolved in an earsplitting scream and suddenly a part of its belly seemed to fall away, a tiny morsel, scarcely as long as one's forearm but in the perfect image of a crumpled human being, stirring feebly in the ankledeep floor.

The Whale heaved itself up to look down at the phenomenon and grunted with satisfaction.

'As I thought,' it said, 'A boy.'

With slow care and massive strength it eased itself up to a sitting position, dragging its baby with it by the umbilical cord.

'So Houdra is dead,' it said shaking its head sadly, reaching into a hole in the wall and withdrawing two lengths of soft twine.

'Poor Houdra. A sweet child.'

Tomaly-Somaly, back on her perch, could contain herself no longer.

'What the *hell* is *that* thing?' she whispered in disgust, staring horror-stricken at the slow-groping mite.

'Shush,' hissed Prudence, punching her sharply in the ribs. 'It's a baby.'

The Whale, seeming not to hear, was busy itself with the twine and the infant's living lifeline.

'And the insects are here, are they?'

It bent forward with a sudden enormous effort, lips parted, bit through the cord with its teeth and pulled the body from the mire.

'And the Man-god lives,' it mused, holding the tiny morsel by the feet and clearing the little mouth with a surprisingly delicate finger. The child's lungs drank of air for the first time and, as its body shifted suddenly from an aquatic mode to that of a free-roving air-breathing biped, it cried out in its shock and horror, its anger and rage, its tiny arms trembling hysterically.

'Everything seems to happen at once,' muttered The Whale, examining its offspring for defects, finding none, grunting with approval and enfolding the scrap of humanity in its overflowing breasts.

It turned to the women with tear-filled eyes.

'This will be my last child,' it piped, rocking gently, comfortingly, holding back its own anguish and despair, setting up small waves in the sodden floor that lapped over the ankles of the onlookers, now too frightened to move.

'It was good while it lasted.'

Tomaly-Somaly clutched Prudence's arm, drawing her blanched and terrified face closer to her and in a whisper asked,

'Is that how I, I mean you and I, all of us, is that how we came to be here?'

Prudence nodded impatiently and spoke sharply to The Whale who was rocking rhythmically and crooning in a distracted, flute-like voice to her now sleeping child.

'We've told you what's going on but all you do is nod and rock and act as though we're not here.'

The Whale made no reply and Prudence stepped forward threateningly. 'Tell us what to do!' she shouted angrily.

The Whale stopped rocking and turned slowly to her.

'Prudence,' she muttered, searching her memory. 'Yes,' she said, 'you always were difficult, I remember. I'll tell you what to do, Prudence, I'll tell you what to do.'

She turned her attention to the baby.

'Just shut the fuck up.'

26

The object of an unrequited love Is unworthy of that love.
The Yenin Yellow Bible.

The Whale smiled sadly at the tiny child in her enormous arms.
How many would this make? She had long ago lost count.
Fifty?
Seventy-five?
She could not count them but she could remember all their names.
Pog, the dour one, quietest, grimmest child of all.
And The Twins, always squabbling and giggling.
Diva, the kind of child who grew up to carry the torch for the others and think herself leader.
Amrita – pretty but undisciplined and a little selfish.
And Tomaly-Somaly – a strange guarded child, hidden depths, a gentleness that often lost itself in high spirits.
The Whale rested her mind for a moment.
So tired.
So much to think about.
Poor little Houdra, even Death brough the sweet creature no dignity. And the insects were back again. This time almost certain of victory. She had been little more than a young woman herself when they last came. But things had been different then. The Candle Palace had been strong and the women many and even the Whale Chambers had been packed to capacity.
When she had first come, heavy with child, her cell had been filled all day long with the whispers of her gossiping neighbours telling the Old Tales, laughing and joking far into the night. But now she was alone.
The Last Survivor.
There had been many who bled with the moon, but none had conceived and even Yeni, the last of them, was now gone. Driven out in disgrace. And the Whales had all gone too, their cells had been sealed up, one by one, upon their bloated corpses. She brushed away a tear.
She had looked like Tomaly-Somaly once – lithe, lissom, bright-eyed and slender. She too had wrinkled her nose like that in the

stench of the caverns, fretting impatiently until the child was born and she could slip through the iron doorway and enjoy once more the flowers, the sunshine, the company of friends. But the life of a Whale was not long a life of liberty as she had discovered after her third pregnancy and she could no longer squeeze through the tiny exit, had cried for weeks, petulantly ignoring the whispering comforts of her sisters, coming very slowly to the realization that virgin birth was a gift for which all other delights of Nature were sacrificed.

A hard life, she mused. A tiring life. But in many, many ways a rewarding one.

Sad that it should end with the insects.

She would have liked to have missed the insects.

She rested her matted head against the slimy rock wall and closed her eyes.

So tired.

So very weary.

And the Man-god still alive.

How could that be? Had something gone awry in the Snowcamps?

She fought to keep her mind moving against the steady current of her exhaustion.

'Runners,' she said without looking round, 'were runners sent to the Queen of the Steriles?'

Diva spoke.

'Three,' she said. 'None returned.'

The Whale nodded. So be it. There was little else that could be done now. Yeni, the last of those who Bleed with the Moon, would die, the Candle Palace would fall to the insects and there would be no more regeneration on the Earth.

She looked down at the sleeping miniman in her arms and felt tears rise up once more.

He was to be the last human being on the planet Born of Woman.

The chain was broken at last after all these centuries, its links severed by foolishness, spite, dissent, jealousy, greed, lack of love and a thousand black spells of which she would never know.

So tired.

More tired this time than she had ever been. She moved her lips with a great effort.

'This is what you must do.'

The waiting women exchanged relieved glances. They had been afraid The Whale was asleep.

'You must find the other children and bring them here. We are not strong enough to fight off the insects alone.'

She turned her tiny liquid eyes upon her daughters.

'Do not shrink from this. They are your brothers. They have suffered too much already.'

'What children?' asked Pog sullenly, speaking for the first time.

And Tomaly-Somaly said,

'What's a brother?'

'Those who are called Orphachins,' replied The Whale. 'Many are also *my* children.'

Her eyes ran with tears and her reedy voice shook with exhaustion and grief.

'Let them return,' she whispered, pleading. 'Let my children come back.'

'*Orphachins*!' exclaimed Diva, surprise overwhelming her natural courtesy. 'In the Palace? Here? It's not possible!'

'Please,' whispered The Whale, 'for all our sakes.'

The faces of the women were masks of shock and astonishment.

'We can't let those stinking creatures walk free!' Prudence cried. 'They are killers by instinct and by inclination, they eat human flesh between Feast-days, they are completely incapable of conforming to our social patterns. We would simply be *easy meat* to them!' She turned to her companions.

'I think all the time she's spent in this stinking hole has creamed The Whale's brains. What does *she* know about anything? She hasn't even seen the sun for more years than we've been alive! How can she presume to give us advice? Our time would be better spent helping the rest fight off the insect attack than listening to some hideous balloon telling us to let *Orphachins* through our defences!'

She spat on the floor in contempt, seized the torch from Diva and struggled out through the iron door.

They heard her voice trailing away up the passage.

'She's got the torch!' squealed The Twins and Amrita, rushing after her. 'Prudence! Wait for us! We'll come and help too.'

Pog bowed, almost imperceptibly, to The Whale and said.

'I would rather be devoured by insects than shake hands with an Orphachin. Your advice is unacceptable. I'm sorry.'

And she followed the others out through the narrow aperture.

'I had better see them safely back up to the light,' Diva muttered, hastily withdrawing and her footsteps scurried echoing along the passageway until silence closed over them.

The Whale looked long at Tomaly-Somaly.

'And you, Little One?' she said in a gentle voice.

Tomaly-Somaly stood with her back turned, fiddling with an elaborate chain that decorated her neck and stared, troubled, into the darkness outside the iron door.

'I was wondering,' she said uncertainly. 'What you called *brothers*. What does that, I mean I don't know that word.'

'Come closer, child,' said The Whale softly and Tomaly-Somaly turned, half-reluctant, and shyly moved closer, her feet moving unwilling through the slime of the cell-bed, eyes averted.

'Closer,' said The Whale, holding out a paradoxically delicate hand. Tomay-Somaly forced herself right to The Whale's side and gingerly reached out her hand, surprised to find The Whale's fingers warm to the touch and sensuous.

With one huge arm The Whale raised up the tiny baby.

'This,' she said quietly, 'is your brother. Take him.'

Tomaly-Somaly accepted the tiny bundle and held it, at first awkwardly, then cradled her arms and held it with a newly-kindled warmth against her breast.

She smiled, looking up.

'This?' she asked simply.

And the Whale nodded.

'Take him,' she said. 'Take him to his brothers. Find them, wherever they are. Show him to them. Tell them we need them now.'

Tomaly-Somaly's eyes, wide with fear, met The Whale's full of tears and sadness.

'Yes,' she said bravely with trembling breath. 'Yes, I will find them and tell them to come.'

And with a cry of sorrow, fell with relief into The Whale's massive and encircling arms and let loose a lifetime's pent-up tears.

27

Meanwhile, elsewhere in the Palace, things had got out of hand. Already the Emergency Council Meeting had been forced to retreat twice from the insect incursion and had holed up in the sweltering kitchens with flame-troops guarding the doors and windows from the outside. The meeting was slit and slashed by the sound of flashbursts from the Courtyard as the troops fought to melt back the crawling wall of carnivorous life that pushed suicidally, relentlessly, forward. Inside there was a constant stamp and slap of insects being subjected to pressures greater than those which their bodies had been designed to withstand.

'It's madness!' Prudence was declaring. 'We can't possibly go on like this. We're losing people by the minute. We should abandon the Palace. There isn't a moment to lose.'

'You know that's not possible, Prudence,' replied Pog gravely. 'We have already been through this over and over again. This is not just some woven tent of The Steriles that we can simply uproot and peg out in the desert wherever we choose. This is the Candle Palace, home of Great Womb. To guard Womb and to celebrate its festivals is our sacred obligation under our Mother Moon. So it has been for centuries and so it is now. It would be better that we all die here tonight than desert our responsibilities.'

'Great Womb!' cried Prudence emotionally, edging gingerly away from a glowing furnace that threatened to singe her gown. 'How can we understand what Great Womb needs of us after tonight? Did we not all see that the Man-god lived? Did we not see Houdra the Hunchback fall half-eaten from the sky into the Octahedron itself? This is the moment of which The Teachings tell when they speak of the collapse of life as we know it. Why, even now the earth trembles and shakes in warning. I say we should scatter and flee, take cover from the insects and regroup when danger is past. If we stay here there will be none left to celebrate the Feast at all.'

There was a general murmur of assent and nervous denial and Pog held up her hand for silence.

Slowly the hubbub died away until only the settling of the coals in the massive ovens and the muffled cries of flame-troops directing the struggle in other parts of the Palace could be heard.

She looked out over the gathering of her troubled sisters, face pale and strained, lit eerily from below by the glowing furnaces, casting gloomy shadows high upon the flickering grease-thick walls. 'There are times,' she said slowly, heavy with the knowledge that this might be the last time she would have the chance to speak, 'when every belief, every cherished tradition, every sacred ritual is threatened by total annihilation from unexpected and unforeseen enemies.' She peered around in the gleaming darkness.

'We are facing such a time now.

'But we must ask ourselves,' she went on firmly, raising an imperious forefinger, 'we must ask ourselves what separates the Real Faith from the False; what distinguishes the heartfelt belief from the convenient and passing fancy? The answer,' she spoke loudly now, feeling her listeners grow more restless with every breath, 'is in the word *Faith* itself. If we have *Real Faith* then nothing can induce us to abandon our Goddess to her Fate. If we have *Real Faith* we will simply *know*, despite the evidence of our eyes and ears, that our Goddess is more powerful than these tiny, mindless predators. Only one thing stands between the Candle Palace as our home and Sacred Church and the Candle Palace as a blackened ruin peopled by alien and uncaring intelligences. That one thing is *Faith* itself.'

A mutter of disagreement shivered through the restless listeners. 'Stay with me sisters,' Pog implored them, arms outstretched. 'If we but stay here the tide will turn for us and come morning the Palace will be safe again.'

'No!' shouted Prudence angily. 'That is sheer folly. It is time to go! It may already be too late!'

'Stay with me!' shouted Pog over the cries of assent. 'Stay with me to preserve yourselves and your Palace and your Heaven.'

'Stay with you and die, you mean,' came a bitter voice. 'I'm getting out of here.'

'No, no,' shouted Pog over the rising tumult as members of the Council made for the door. 'I implore you. Please stay. If you leave now there will be nothing left but ruins.'

'Aye, and if we stay there will be nothing left but *bones. Our* bones!'

'And what of Great Womb?' Pog shouted desperately.

A silence fell on the disordered Council who looked at each other anxiously in the furnace-light.

'We cannot leave Great Womb,' she pleaded. 'At least let us take Womb.'

'How can we take Womb?' murmured one. 'Its workings are sunk far into the earth.'

'That's impossible,' muttered another. 'Who can even raise it?'

'If we *must* go, let us carry Womb to a place of safety in the mountains.'

Prudence's voice broke the frightened silence.

'Take Womb, Pog,' she called mockingly, 'and may Man reward you for your labours. But remember this – Womb has nothing to fear from the insects if it stays here for a thousand years, whereas *I* have seen my sisters carried down The Great Staircase in the jaws of a million murderers. I do not foresee the same end for myself. Take Womb if you wish, and go. But most of all – *go!*'

She turned angrily and strode unsteadily to the door across the food-slick floor, gathering companions rapidly as she moved through the frightened, uncertain assembly. Reaching the massive door, she pulled it open upon a Courtyard that was a mass of flame.

Torch-troops, white-eyed and soaked in each other's sweat, were being forced back in a semicircle by a crawling waisthigh wall that replaced itself faster than it could be burned and rolled forward remorselessly. All exits from the Courtyard were blocked by crisped and cindered remnants of the advancing tide destroyed by sheeting swathes of fire from the roaring torchpipes.

'Them am too many for we!' a Soldier-servant shouted, catching sight of Prudence in the doorway. 'Us must take covers and abandon the Courtyard.'

'Clear a path for us!' Prudence screamed. 'There is no escape from the kitchens!'

'It am no goods. Us am overwhelmed here. Us can makes none headway!'

'Clear a path. Hurry!' urged Prudence desperately, stamping at the streams of insects that threatened her ankles. 'We must get to Womb!'

'Fuck Womb,' replied the soldier turning out her flame and then, raising her voice, shouted,

'Takes cover in the kitchens, Sisters. Quick as you can. Now!'

The Torch-guards extinguished their weapons and ran to the doorway, thrusting roughly past Prudence in their desperate haste.

'No!' she screamed, grabbing the soldier's arm but finding no grip on the sinewy, sweat-slick limb. 'You *must* clear a way out or we're going to *die!*'

'Does it yourself, Madam,' replied the guard, unslinging her backpack and dropping it at Prudence's feet. 'There am the torch. There am the Courtyard. *You* clears it.'

The wall of twitching, pulsing life rolled inch by inch towards them and they fled inside and bolted up the door.

'There am none way across the Courtyard,' the soldier reported to Pog. 'Us must waits here until there am fewer of them or until ...' She motioned to two guards. 'You and you, gives the place a sweepings with your flames. These women do nothing but stands and talk. Look – there are hundreds of them coming through the chimneys. Clears them all away.'

The searing torches scoured the walls and floor, adding their heat to the stifling smoke-sick air, mopping up the crawling adventurers who had found entrance to the cavernous cookhouse.

'It's too late,' shrieked a hysterical voice. 'We're all going to die. It's no good! They're too many for us!'

'Control yourselves,' called Pog, raising her arms for attention, 'We must prepare ourselves for a night of siege. Let us not turn upon each other in our terror. Let us be calm and brave and turn our adversity into a cohesive force that binds us ever closer together. Gather in the centre and let the torches scour the walls. We will profit nothing from panic.'

The richly-robed women of the Council, ever ready to heed the voice that promised safety, clustered like frightened butterflies among the smouldering ovens and watched wide-eyed as the exhausted soldiers sprayed the crawling greasy walls with white and yellow fire.

Incinerated insects pattered like Summer rain upon the floors.

'Look!' came a strangled cry. 'The windows!'

High up near the roof the grilled lights boiled with a crawling mass of life that crushed up ignorantly against unseen panes of glass that began to splinter and crack beneath the pressure.

'The windows are caving in!'

It was true.

One by one the casements, subjected to pressures far greater than those they had been designed to withstand, broke open, allowing malevolent life to pour in black sliding torrents down the walls, swirling like pools of glue and swarming across the floors.

'Let we face it,' muttered the Chief Torch-guard to her Lieutenant with the wry, twisted mouth of defeat, 'Us am had it.'

28

Meanwhile, deep within the shuddering earth, vast forces stirred uneasy in their sleep. Plate and plane rubbed restlessly together and, deeper still, roiling molten rocks banged irritably on their neighbour's floor and roared their disturbed disapproval. Fire demons, chained and shackled to the Earth's fluid core, darted in spirals, exploring each groaning crack with hysterical hubris until suddenly, with a roar of joy, one column of white-hot matter slipped from its prison and broke for freedom, speeding crustwards with the speed of heat, cleaving through all impediment until, with a terrifying explosive cry, it burst, cooling, into the atmosphere and made its presence known to the inhabitants of the island, shaking them in their beds and rattling their eardrums in their heads.

The snowcampers, bickering anxiously in the streaming twin-spined valley, stood as one man and stared in glazed terror at the pillar of fire that rose above their tiny huts, a livid dragon standing tiptoe upon the ruined slopes and roaring at the skies.

And as the Clap of Doom rippled Eastward across the desert it poked the sleeping she-soldiers from their pallets, threw the cancerous Matriarch of The Earth from her linen hammock, triggered the grumbling thousands from their shallow sand-hole beds and turned the heads of the Orphachin Army to gaze upon its awful splendour.

To the West it stilled the frantic din of mortal combat in the Candle Palace as its voice rolled with horrifying power through wall and cellar, hall and catacomb alike, pinning the puzzled insects to the trembling ground and freezing the fighting women where they stood encircled. And curling heavenwards, reaching with its bloody tongue even towards the moon itself, it spread a black cloak of ash and cindered dust across the sky, blotted out the universe and spat its venom in turbulent torrents over the juddering earth. On the mountain tops the crisp crystalline snows vanished before waves of heat that smashed their myriad latticed beauty to steam or flowed melting, heavy and airless, down ever-deepening channels to join their babbling brothers in triumphant descent to the valleys, gathering strength and speed, plunging headlong into gravity's compelling maw, roaring and tumbling, tearing, melting, dissolving and destroying, sweeping down upon the tiny wooden dwellings from which wee scurrying figures were already taking uncertain flight.

And from the rocky embouchure into which Brother Two had been forced to flee from the Orphachin waggon-team emerged a solid wall of water that stood erect upon the unsuspecting river, over-rode its gentle current, careening to the sea, faster than a flying bird, leaping banks and cutting bends, drowning the sleeping vegetation on each side, roaring past the Candle Palace that still stood frozen in horror, to smash into the incoming, moon-swayed tide and rip the sturdy boathouse to tiny splinters in its remorseless fury. And then, in snaking recoil, the current echoed and re-echoed along the length of the river's course until its boundaries were rent and torn and washed away and across the Candle Palace Plains the waters spread, radiating, debris-laden and in turmoil to turn the verdant meadows into liquid desert and drown the invading insect armies in its muddy and suffocating embrace.

What a scene!

Ana, Queen of Women, selfstyled Matriarch of the Earth, reeled back into the shelter of her pavilion, choked by finely raining ash that covered the desert like a ghostly grey snowfall. The sand beneath the richly textured carpets boomed and trembled like a bowstring as she shook the unconscious Crone from deathlike slumbers.

'Wake up, you Bone-Bag!' she screamed in terror. 'If you know anything, speak now. What livid god stamps out his mighty anger on our land and heaps dead dust upon the desert?'

'Do not trouble yourself, Foolish Woman,' replied The Crone, surfacing momentarily. ''Tis but a thunderstorm that frightens you.'

'A thunderstorm!' cried Ana, 'When boiling fire flickers around the mountain tops and streams like burning blood to the desert's

122

very edge? When suffocating dust spreads thigh-thick upon my army's tents and moon and stars themselves have quit the sky? Wake up! Wake up, you Teller of False Futures or you will lie out in this powdered rain tonight and breathe more rock than air and choke on stone. Wake up! Bestir yourself!' The Crone's spirit had been far far away, as every night it flew far away to make up in the dark hours of liberty for the limbless bondage that each day demanded, and with reluctance did she take up once more her maimed and mutilated frame.

'It is the middle of the night,' she whined bitterly, 'when all decent persons lie asleep.'

'There's no one sleeps tonight save you, Witless One. Can you not hear the wrath of Heaven hammer at the sky and shake the desert like a picnic blanket and we its crumbs and peelings?'

'Ah!' said the Crone, suddenly bright-eyed, her wits once more about her. 'Vulcano speaks!'

'And who is this Vulcano?' demanded Ana.

The Crone's eyes appeared to glaze over, her lips moved as if mechanically and her words came high and piercing through the grumbling air.

'And the Earth shall give forth fire into the air and water will cover the Earth though the fire will not be extinguished and the Kingdoms of the Earth shall fall like rotten nuts upon the heads of the people and from the waters shall rise up a new race which will . . .'

'Silence!' shouted Ana, seizing the Crone by the throat and squeezing it so tightly that all voice was instantly cut off. 'You will not babble so. You will answer my questions or not speak at all!'

She glared sternly for a moment at The Crone's bulging eyes and purpling face then relaxed her hold.

'Now,' she said, 'who is this Vulcano of whom you speak?'

'Vulcano the Spouting Mountain, God of Fire, Father of the demi-god Man, Enemy of Women,' replied the Crone. 'At his command the Earth trembles and opens wide its many throats. At his voice the ice melts and rises up as steam to drown the life that dares to cling like parasites upon his back. When he so orders the rivers swell up and bleed upon the people, tearing down their palaces and smearing their millenia with mud. And in the blast of his breath there are none so brave as will not burn.'

'And why now?' insisted Ana, shaking her Counsellor by the

123

tightly held throat. 'Who has called him from his prison in the Earth? Is it Yeni, she whom many call The Messiah? Is it *she* who has brought this Fire-god's wrath upon my Queendom?'

The Crone's eyes glittered for a moment as she toyed with a taunting reply but instead she answered,

'No female can stir the gods of Fire save the Moon herself, and then only by accident, misuse of power or the unforeseen consequence of spite. No. It must be a Man. There is a Man at liberty upon our lands. There can be no other answer. Some descendant of the gods who once walked the Earth and were driven off in the Great Wars with the She-gods at the Dawn of History.'

'A Man!' exclaimed Ana in horror. 'A Man upon the Earth? But why *now*?'

The Crone once more flickered between Truth and Falsehood but again her spirit overruled her vengeful heart.

'For many years,' she replied slowly, 'century upon century, ever since we became two peoples, servants of The Others, a secret and religious order known only to The Whales, have kept Men in the mountains, taking one at each Full Moon for the Feast of Sacrifice, storing them in the Valley of Forgetfulness into which, even now, the blood of Vulcano pours in hardening red-hot tongues of boiling stone.'

Ana's eyes grew wide, she loosed her hold and staggered a few tottering steps across the undulating floor.

'Men!' she gasped. 'In the mountains? Why did you not tell of this before?'

'Because you did not ask,' replied The Crone.

Ana clutched at the Snake Throne for safety as the shifting earth tried to throw her to her knees.

'Then I ask it *now*!' she said savagely. 'Tell me of these gods upon our island.'

There was a long pause before The Crone replied, in which the angry mountain rumbled three times, four times, five, across the shaking desert.

'They are not gods in the mountains,' The Crone replied bitterly. 'In the Valley of Forgetfulness they work as though in harness, smoothing the snows that they themselves have walked upon and learning how to long for the death that will release them when their Sixth Full Moon swims across the sky. Servants of The Others bring them one by one from the seashore caves and tide-line hideaways

124

where they grub and grovel with their hands for roots and crawling succulents and are thrust, untouched, into the Valley, to kill off the poisons upon their skin in the cold air. And as they are cleansed so they are taken to be Moon-offerings at the Feast of Sacrifice. They are not gods, these Men, but rather cattle, waiting mindless for the day of their slaughter, never thinking from whence they came nor whither they are bound.'

'Their destiny is The Others' bellies if you speak honestly, Crone, but where do they come from, these gods that have become beasts of pasture? Were they not driven off the Earth by the She-gods of ancient history never more to set foot upon the land?'

'Aye, so it was,' replied The Crone, 'but from the sea they come one by one, some by design, most by accident, bruised and torn, crushed by the pounding waters, clinging on to life, often in vain, or dying in the waters ere they ever make our shores, their bodies the food for gulls and Orphachins who know not what they eat.'

Ana kneeled, swaying, against her shuddering throne, more rocked and shattered by the thoughts that whirled inside her head than by the hammering cataclysm all around her. 'And all this time I knew it not, because I *did not ask*,' she murmured to herself in near disbelief. 'So now I ask you this, Crone: what happens to these fallen Man-gods in the path of Vulcano's burning breath and what of Ana, Matriarch of the Earth, upon the dust-deep desert and what of The Others in their Candle Palace? Tell all of this, Crone, and hope to stay the angry hatred that your now-revealed treachery has set alight in my aching breast!'

'I will tell you,' stammered The Crone uncertainly, knowing nothing of the future from her spirit's nightly journeys. 'The Man-gods will die and the Candle Palace will be utterly swept away along with all who dwell there and you, Ana, will inherit their lands and power and hold sway over all the earth as undisputed sovereign.'

'And what of Vulcano, this brash and dirty god?'

'He will return, exhausted, to the earth and trouble us no more.'

But even as she spoke a burning cloud rose up from the volcano's depths and, with a mighty roar, once more stood tiptoe, teetering boiling and booming, lighting up land and sea and sky, turning black night to crimson day, a formless newborn sun, chained within the Earth's rotating mass and now, unexpectedly and without warning, rolling faster than a fleeing hare down the steaming snow-clad valleys, scorching everything before it, airless, unburning, accelerating, triggered by some geophysical lottery towards the desert, whose soft surface froze to glass beneath its tumbling passage, a mile wide and a mile high, a fireball, god-flung, it ploughed its course of devastation into a sea that flinched and writhed in boiling whirlpools and horrendous steaming explosions, retreated injured from the shore then returned, vengeful, enraged, aroused, to punish the land that had so wounded it and spread its antiseptic fingers upon the air-breathing symbiosis of the desert. A tidal wave higher than the Candle Palace moved upon the flattened earth like a highprowed ship at sea and swept up every living creature in its path, skinks, rats, lizards, fly-grubs, plants and plant-dwellers alike until, her forces spent, her fury sated, she sank with quiet dignity into the thirsting, drowning sand. And with her came the wind. Air bolts hurled back by the sea-gods, thrown before them in whirling, whipping coils, tearing the tents and pavilions of the Matriarch's camp from their sunken thrice-roped stones and lifting them like banshees into the sky, looping and curling into the darkness, stripping off vestments, armour, hair, flesh, in deadly rage.

And then all was still across the wasted camp until the sound of rain, dropping in heavy bouts from the overladen sky, began to drum, taunting, poisoned, upon a decimated nation.

29

Black, battered, drowned and burning end to end the squat and scarab-shaped island that grim night, pounded by the infuriated sea, choked by hanging clouds of dense and poisonous dust, lashed by vicious rains returning to the earth from which they had been so swiftly boiled, engloomed by shrouds of smoke and, in its burning heart, white-hot and flaming, shuddering at each massive detonation in the subterranean cauldrons far below, Vulcano the Volcano, spouting gobs of stone desultorily upon its soiled chest.

How fared now our separate heroes and heroines under its diabolical abuse; Ana and The Crone, Rogesse, the two Brothers and their frozen Father, Tomaly-Somaly, Yeni and the last Child of Woman Born?

Fate's children, every one. All survived. Each clinging to the straw of life unyielding until the hurricane of Wind and Fire, Earth and Water swept past in the blackness and left each bruised, bloodied, but alive.

Survivors all.

But flung into the worst extremities of suffering and fatigue, tested to their very limits. Scattered, scared and shattered, but survivors all.

The Crone's spirit, frightened from her body by the furious beating blasts of wind and rain, flew high above the roiling clouds and marked the utter devastation that the earth had brought upon itself.

'This,' she thought to herself, 'must have been how the world looked at the close of The Great Wars.'

And, freed from the poisoning mastery of her self-contemptuous body, the simple childlike spirit sighed with real sorrow to witness once more the cyclic tragedy of humanity.

'Yet again it is Man and his Man-gods who bring this horror from the bowels of the earth to decimate our people,' she whispered as she crossed and re-crossed the smouldering island. 'Once more the guilty ones sneak back from their submarine exile to bring forth all-consuming fire.'

She moved in closer and saw how the Candle Palace stood now like a broken tooth in the still-streaming muddy waters of the flooded plains, how The Valley of Forgetfulness between the twin stickleback spines of the mountain range had become a vast lake, rising still as water cascaded from every crack and ledge in the freshly-exposed rockfaces and how, at one end of the valley, a huge moraine plugged up the mouth, imprisoning the seething steaming water with an impenetrable seal; she saw how the desert, half-blanketed in volcanic ash, half-littered with sea-flung debris had been, in the space of a few minutes, first smothered, then burned, then drowned and now lay helpless and exposed waiting only for the morrow's baking sun to finish off whatever life still stirred feebly on its mutilated surface. And then, curious and half afraid, she moved still closer, seeking out her own stump of a body among the desert's jetsam.

And many a sorry spectacle she saw among the debris of dead and living upon the tortured earth. And often was she jostled by newly liberated spirits, panicstruck and shrieking still, reverberating to the horror of their bodies' unforeseen and brutal shattering, tugging formlessly at their once animated corpses, wailing and whining in the naked terror of the untimely stripped. And often was she forced to flee through subtle passageways in time to circumnavigate whirlpools of despairing souls, locked together in stark dread, spinning and wheeling, dragging all who were caught up with them in an irresistible downward spiral to irreconcilable depth of negativity and hopelessness. And often was she called upon to use the agility and skill of her long experience to escape the clutches of the ghoulish predators who flocked from all the ends of time to feast upon the astral fledgelings set loose upon this ravaged battlefield, descending thick and ravenous, quick or massive, alone, in packs. And howling, howling horrid and exultant every one.

And faint of heart had she become before she found, beneath a broken stump of pole that had once carried the flag of the Queendom high above the Royal Pavilion, pinned helpless to the ground, the broken stump of her own body, beaten, bruised and bleeding, but breathing still. Not far off lay Ana, strangely contorted in the volcano's flickering glare and The Crone's spirit could see that, though she still lived, her spark was very low and that her spirit, too, had been thrown clear of the panicstricken body and blown she knew not where.

And she let loose a cry of terrible remorse to think that this was the moment of triumph and revenge which she had so doggedly denied Death to see. Gazing over that waste of burned and broken bodies she wept at the futile vanity that had carried her through all those weary years.

'Oh Mighty Queen, Matriarch of The Earth, Grand-dame of Over-weening Hubris, see how our frail bodies mock the very pride that sustained them.'

She dropped down to her body and reoccupied the pain-racked frame, struggled briefly, vainly, to remove the crushing pole and then rose up into the sky once more, frightened by her failure, to collect her scattered thoughts.

'The Queen is dying. How can her wandering spirit find her before the leaking blood lets trickle all her life if even, I, each night an astral traveller, rediscovered myself only through great trials?'

She asked the question innocently of herself, but already the brief moments spent inside her feeble shell had once more tinged her spirit with its crippled venom.

'Why then should I not use her body to free my own? Did she not take *my* body as a child and use it as her plaything? Do I not now have the right to take up hers and use it as I wish? Is it not the pole that held *her* flag that pins me still? Had she not taken my three limbs would I lie so hopeless now? I think not. Why then should I not take up her body and use it for a little while, a few short moments? Is that not a fair trade?' She hovered nervously above the two twisted bodies, desiring yet afraid, knowing that she contemplated a gross offence, punishable in Courts higher than those of Humanity. But, tinged with angry spite and peevish greed, the poisonous legacy of a bitter heart, she steeled herself to perpetrate the act and, in an instant, the eyes of Ana, Queen of Women, Matriarch of the Earth, opened slowly to gaze in glazed wonder at the devastation that surrounded her.

The spirit of The Crone had promised itself that only for a few short moments would it inhabit the body of the Queen, just long enough to use her strong arms to free The Crone's body from its wooden pillory. But having tasted the strength and mental power of her new fleshly vestments she realized that it would never freely give her up to return to her own enfeebled trunk. 'I am alive!' she cried out to the wind and rain. 'I take this body as my right from one who took mine.'

But suddenly the spirit of Ana was at her side, enraged and boiling like a tornado of whirling steam, screaming soundless in her fury and calling up the Fates to drive out the Cosmic Criminal who squatted in her unattended corpse.

'Oh final and most exquisite treachery!' she screamed. 'What ghoul is this who robs me of my undead body? Speak, speak, that I may know the fiend upon whom I shall be revenged though it take eternity to accomplish!'

The Crone, canny and determined, made no reply. If need be she would conceal her identity for ever rather than incur so dreadful an enemy.

'Speak!' thundered the spirit of Ana, 'that I may know this sneak-thief, this colonizer of carrion, this banshee bodysnatcher, in the hereafter!'

The Crone, pretending to neither see nor hear, pushed herself groggily upright, attending to the internal bleeding that threatened life, healing up the wounds as she discovered them, mending the broken bones and sealing up the skin where it had been torn. But, with a sudden lurch of terror in her heart, she discovered that her legs and arms were frozen, paralysed, unreachable. She was, even in Ana's body, as crippled as she had been in her own. Meanwhile the spirit of Ana swirled in furious loops around her head, grimacing and shrieking with despair and loss, calling down the vengeance of unnameable gods upon the poacher of her material body.

'What does it profit me now,' The Crone reflected fearfully, 'to live crippled inside this body for a few short years and then to endure the wrath of this sorely-wronged and vengeful spirit for eternity.'

But the body within which she had taken refuge, the glands and nervous system, even the brain itself, shocked by physical pain, grimly clung on to its existence and held her fast, not knowing that its rightful mistress demanded entry. The Crone, struggling to extricate herself, writhed the body horribly this way and that, heaving herself from muscle and sinew as though bogged in clinging clay.

'Release me!' her spirit cried.

But before she could tear free, the spirit of Ana, mad with fury, whirling and raging out of control, fell, uncomprehending, through a hole in time and disappeared far into the curving maze of space, fleeing terrified before the hounding fear of past and future rolled up in our star-spangled burning ball and found herself utterly lost and alone upon some astral desert across which the Winds of Random Circumstance scoured with punishing speed.

'Oh dreadful Night of Nights!' she wailed, realizing too late what she had done, 'Whither hast thou brought me now?' She looked around at the horizonless vacuum into which she had flung herself, fast weakening in the withering winds and with a final scream of despair she gave herself up to total annihilation by the howling gale.

30

Meanwhile, Tomaly-Somaly stared out over the flooded plains that had once been her homeland. Clasped in her arms, wrapped thrice around against the cold night air, lay the Last Child of Woman Born gazing out upon the devastated world with watery, blinking and unfocussed eyes.

'Oh baby,' whispered Tomaly-Somaly, 'we should be able to see the lights of the Candle Palace from here, but where are they? Can you spot them?'

Her eyes searched vainly for the tiny pinpoint of reassuring light in the moaning darkness but her sinking heart knew she would not find it.

'You don't suppose the water's so deep that ...' she left the thought incomplete, but its consequences flashed across her mind. The Whale, deep in the passageways, how could she escape the flooding? And if there were still survivors at the Candle Palace, why did they wait in darkness for the dawn? Surely, if there were any left alive ...

She forced herself to turn away.

'I'm sure they're alright,' she said aloud, lying for the sake of the baby in her arms. 'Let's build a fire and have a cosy supper and not think too much about anything except finding the Orphachins, your brothers.'

And then, after a long, lip-biting pause, added,

'And let's not think too much about that either.'

She propped the infant against a rock and built a small fire. 'It's about time you had your first meal,' she said, drawing strips of meat from the satchel on her shoulder. 'And then I think we'd better get some sleep.'

She laid the meat upon crossed twigs close to the flames.

'Oh,' she said, 'I see you've fallen asleep already. Well, never mind. You have a quick nap and I'll wake you when it's ready,' adding, under her breath, 'Oh, I do think that's *rude*, just to conk out like that when I'm talking to it.'

She had built her campfire in the mouth of a pass through the mountains that took The Others on their rare journeys to the desert peoples. She had been afraid to enter the unknown blackness of the steep-sided clefting pathway and took comfort from the thought that her tiny fire would be visible to some sharp-eyed watcher in the Candle Palace. For, having never been so far from home in all her life, she was already feeling a homesickness that was distinctly different from the sickness of fear and loss that threatened to engulf her if she thought too logically of her sisters' fate.

But, as she watched the meat sizzle on the flames, her eyelids dropped like buttons and within minutes the firelight flickered over her sleeping face.

Meanwhile, elsewhere in the desert, the Orphachins were beginning to surface one by one. As the hammering explosions reverberating through the dunes abated they emerged from their hideyholes beneath the sand and stared about them in mute astonishment.

'Gobbly, Gobbly,' they muttered to each other comfortingly, each bearing his share of the mutual telepathic anxiety. The desert was gone. The smooth clean sand had been stolen away and in its place was warm and stinking dust, hurtful to the touch, poisonous to taste, burning to breathe. They gobbled at each other in consternation and fear.

One by one they crawled from the lavic ash and stared in disbelief at their polluted world, the glowing, grumbling volcano and the lowering, unnaturally clouded sky.

They knew what had happened and they knew why.

They had all shared the thought.

They had all tried to speak, but Gobbly Gobbly was the only phrase they knew.

'Do not touch her, for she is a goddess,' they had thought.

'Do not touch her,' they had tried to say.

'Gobbly, gobbly!' they had cried and he had cuffed them saying, 'No Gobbly! Capisco?' and had continued to staunch her wound.

It was from *that* place, the twin-spined valley, that the thought had come, where now stood the heavy blackened mountain, roaring with fiery anger, shaking the very ground beneath their feet in rage and frustration.

The fire-devil had been disobeyed.

The General had brought down its wrath upon them.

The Burning Mountain had spoken and the General had not heeded its words.

Now they had *all* been punished for *his* impudence.

They were fearful, but angry and hurt also.

Why had he been so naughty?

Why had he ignored the stone-god's warning and destroyed their desert?

Collectively hostile, they gathered round the spot beneath which Brother One and Yeni were concealed by the protecting sand and waited for them to emerge.

And as they stood quietly, with the awful patience of inconsolable rage, staring down at the bury-hole before them, a single thought flickered back and forth in their collective consciousness.

'Gobbly, Gobbly,' they said eagerly. 'Gobbly, Gobbly.'

And from the corners of their mouths saliva hung in moving threads.

Meanwhile, a few hour's blundering march across the desert waste, a bruised and staggering Rogesse surveyed the ruins of her stillborn Empire and tried to piece together in her head some understanding of the hours since she had left the Matriarchal Pavilion.

She could recall waiting among the dunes for the runner from The Others and calling upon the Man-gods for their aid. And she could remember the dead runner at her feet and the throng of grumbling women spread before her.

She could recall her entry to the camp, the tense moments among the robbed and resentful women and the long struggle to convince them that she was indeed their rightful Queen. And she could remember calling upon them to march against The Others and seize the Candle Palace as retribution for the stealing of Yeni, she whom many called The Messiah.

But of the time between the roars of fury against her from the enraged women and the moment when she returned to consciousness, half-buried in the thickly-falling pumice dust, her dreams of Queen decimated by the howling elements, her mind unsteady and confused, she could remember nothing. 'What's happening?' she muttered. 'No moon? No stars? No desert? Nought but a savage howling wind, a ghostly pall of dust and a burning mountain!'

She sank to her knees and buried her face in her hands.

'What have I done? What have I done?'

Of the milling throng that had, but hours before, with swelling voice and vigour undimmed, thrust their anointed hostage across the desert, few survived. They crawled among their fallen comrades heavy with despair, some seeking kin or friends, some stealing articles of value from the dead. All were shocked and dazed, many were dying, few could remember what mad folly had brought them to that place nor what cataclysm had reduced them to so wretched a condition. One of their number, a powerfully-built woman from the shell-gathering tribes of the island's Northernmost tip, seeing Rogesse in an attitude of prayer, crawled next to her and, taking up the same posture in frightened and low-brained mimicry, spoke hesitantly to her. 'Oh Ana, Queen of Steriles, Matriarch of the Earth, Praise be to the gods that you have been spared by the burning mountain and say also thanks from me that my life too is saved.'

The woman ventured on.

'Ask them what we should do now that we are so pitiably beaten by the sky.'

Rogesse, turning to her, said,

'Did you call me *Ana*?'

The woman stumbled some distance off upon her knees and threw herself prostrate on the ground in terror.

'Forgive me, Oh Mighty Queen. I did not think! May these lips never move again for speaking Your Name and soiling Its Majesty with their ignorant utterance. Forgive me, Oh Queen of Women, Matriarch of the Earth! My wits are scattered by the din of the heavens!'

Rogesse, frowning, puzzled, began to remember fragments of events forgotten. Yes, she *had* announced herself Queen to these people, taking Ana's name and Ana's mantle of royalty to draw these ignorant sand-farmers along with her in her quest for power. Now she recalled how they had menaced her, accusing her of complicity in the disappearance of Yeni, She whom many called The Messiah, for she had come upon them at the hour of their loss as they sulked in grumbling confusion, seething with bitter and frustrated anger. And she recalled how, in an inspired power-play, she had brought them to heel with a pose of regal authority and ordered them to kneel before her lest heaven itself cast them to the ground for their impious blasphemy. And she recalled how, nevertheless, certain hotheads among them had laid hold of her and called the others to crucify her in place of the Stolen Messiah. But even as they were dragging her to the bonfire upon which she would have died the cruel death of the prophetically damned, the mountain had shouted out with its massive voice of boiling stone and choking ash and cut them down, even as she had threatened they would be cut down.

That is why, she thought, this powerful woman grovels in terror lest she has sinned even in speaking my name. '*Ana*,' she said to herself. 'The power is in the name itself. For was it not that name that brought the fire-demon down upon my tormentors?' She smiled to herself. 'Indeed it was. Now I have the name I will be invincible and even heaven itself leap to my command.'

'Rise!' she said to the prostrate woman, 'Gather the others where I may number them and where they may hear the orders of Queen Ana, Matriarch of the Earth, and learn to obey and escape the wrath of the skies.'

'Yes, Oh Mightiest One,' agreed the woman eagerly, scrambling to her feet. 'Right away, Oh Favourite of the Gods!'

Rogesse watched her as she sought out the living from the dead, abjuring the survivors to gather together for their monarch and trying vainly to rouse the slain from their slumbers.

'Surely now is the moment to strike against my enemy!' she muttered exultantly, 'while her army still reels from the mountain's deadly blow. And then on to the Candle Palace to annihilate The Others and rule the Earth unchallenged from shore to shore!'

She looked up at the blackened, cloud-stuffed sky and grinned with joyless glee. 'Now is the world to be mine and mine alone as I prayed for it to be! Truly the Man-god looks with favour upon me and with his aid I will wipe out all who stand against me.'

And, so saying, she flung herself upon the earth outstretched, exultant and trembling with the anticipatory joy of absolute power.

Meanwhile, perched high upon a narrow mountain ledge, chattering with cold and fear, the two snowcamp survivors huddled together, peering out into the blackness and staring down at the swirling mass of water which had drowned the frail huts and their former companions in its many fathoms.

'We'll just have to wait here until morning,' said one nervously 'it would be madness to go on climbing in the dark. What do *you* think, Lord?'

'Listen,' said Brother Two irritably. 'I wish you'd drop that

"Lord" business. How many times do I have to tell you? I am *not* the Son of God, nor *was* I the Son of God, nor will I *ever* be the Son of God. I'm just an ordinary human being and I just played along with the idea when we were down there to avoid getting beaten up again. Understand?'

'I bet you say that to all your disciples.'

'I don't *have* any disciples. Can't you get that into your thick skull? I'm just a plain and simple human being like you.'

'I'm not a plain and simple human being any more, Lord,' replied his companion. 'I'm your disciple. A Chosen One. Whether you like it or not. I've seen The Path. I've seen The True Way and The Light, I'm not going to renounce all that and turn back into my ordinary self. I would have thought someone like you would have appreciated that.'

'Well I don't appreciate it,' replied Brother Two tartly. 'I find it very embarrassing as a matter of fact. And I wish you'd do me the courtesy of dropping it.'

The other smiled beatifically.

'No chance, Lord. *I* won't deny you. *I'll* hold by you, don't you worry about that. And I realize that you're just testing my faith, so I don't mind you being like this.'

Brother Two gave a snort of annoyance and stared out gloomily towards the smouldering volcano.

'As if things weren't bad enough without having an idiot for a travelling companion,' he muttered.

'It was a *miracle*!' said the hunched figure at his side in a voice of narrative wonder. 'A *true miracle*!'

'Oh *shutup*!' snapped Brother Two.

'No, it's *true*!' insisted the other. 'We were lifted up out of the floodwater as though by a gigantic hand and raised to a place of safety from which we were able to escape unharmed. That was *your* doing, Lord, I know it. And I thank you for it with heartfelt reverence.'

'What actually happened,' replied Brother Two through gritted teeth and tightly-controlled temper, 'is that a big wave smashed us up against the rocks with such force that we were thrown clear of the worst danger. And *you* may think we're unharmed, but it feels as though half the bones in my body are broken and you've got blood all over your chin. Now, once and for all, stop calling me *Lord*.'

136

'Would that instruction come under the heading of a Divine Decree, Lord?'

'Stop it!' cried Brother Two, irritation and rage suddenly boiling over, 'Stop it! Stop it! Stop it! Do you hear me? Stop it!'

'If you wish it so Lord . . . I mean, yes, if that's the way you want to play it.'

'It is.'

'Alright then,' agreed The Disciple.

'No more Lords?'

'No more Lords.'

'Good!'

'I will obey your every command. No more Lords.'

'Then shut up for a while.'

'Alright.'

They sat in silence together for a long time.

'I think we should try to get some sleep,' Brother Two said, finally. 'We're safe enough up here but I think it will be a hard and dangerous climb in the morning.'

'With your permission, I'd rather watch over you,' replied the other, biting off the word Lord only just in time.

Brother Two sighed.

'You do *not* have my permission to watch over me.'

'Oh,' said The Disciple, disappointed. 'I'll go to sleep then.' And scarcely were the words out of his mouth than he began to snore gently.

Brother Two rolled his eyes heavenwards in frustration.

'What,' he asked, 'have I done to deserve this?'

He stared for long moments at the other's slack-jawed, blood-encrusted face and made a decision.

'I'm sorry, pal,' he whispered, pulling out their meagre food supply and dividing it carefully in half. 'I'd rather be at the bottom of all that water with the others than have you round my neck.'

And stuffing his share of the food into his pockets, he stole off into the night.

31

Meanwhile, elsewhere on the planet, with the simultaneous symmetry so typical of the universe, it was dawn. And the sun, peeking over the horizon, bent its weak and nearly horizontal rays across the plains and mountains of distant and unpopulated lands.

Slowly rolled the Earth, basting itself, perpetually turning its cold and benighted blindness to the sun. And the edge of dawn, a red and softened line of light, rippled, static, over the revolving hills and oceans, waking the sun animals from their dreams and filling the creatures of the dark with sleep.

And as day approached the ravaged island, the restless muddied sea itself gave warning of the devastation that the sun would shine upon. In one revolution of the earth the warm, blue, purposive water had become dark and turbulent, heavy with dying plants and the soil they had lived upon, littered with porous rocks and the multicoloured vomit of an erupted mountain. And it was upon a new and unfamiliar shoreline that the sun's rays first fell as the spinning planet rolled Eastward.

The level yellow sands that the setting sun had left in tranquil sleep, spreading smoothly up from the warm sea shallows, were sterile, blasted salt marshes, pounded still by the agitated tides, infested by scavenging sea-birds feasting upon the stranded sea-life castaways that struggled blindly to crawl in their several ways back to the protection of the ocean before Death fell upon them.

And with its soft curtain of light the sun gently swept away the flocks of ghouls that tarried still to feast upon the dead and warmed the chill wounds of the living with its healing vision. It filtered through the mountain peaks to wake Brother Two's disciple from his nightmare sleep and set him scurrying up the rockfaces calling 'Lord, Lord, come back!' and 'Why hast thou foresaken me?'

And it cast the shadow of steam and smoke that belched from the volcano's gaping throat across the Candle Palace that stood as tranquil as a marble statue in an island lake. And rising slowly in the sky, it warmed the roofs of the deserted fishing-village that stared imperturbably through the centuries out towards the curving horizon where darkness still clung, fading, to the azure sky.

And, ploughing through that darkness five abreast, mounting the night hemisphere towards the dawn they came, savage gargoyles carved upon their prows, long graceful oars moving in spidery unison, crawling swiftly across the surface of the sea, their elegantly tapered hulls leaving only a thin line of lazy turbulence in the deep dark waters – the swiftest galleys in the Neo-navy, commanded by the most daring and courageous Admiral in all the fleets, those who were to become known in their own land as the fire-pirates flew across the ocean at muscle-tearing speed. And below decks, lashed by mighty thongs inside their separate cages they carried the Death-beasts, slavering and snapping inside their head-bags, whining and growling in an incessant rage of pain and fury.

'Dawn and dead! Dawn and dead!' cried the lookouts from their basket-kites high above the speeding vessels. 'Dawn, dawn and dead on course!'

An exultant cheer rose from the fleet and the boats bounded forward with redoubled speed as the steady beat of the rowing-drums caught the exhilaration of the hour and pressed the laughing oarsmen ever harder.

And as the sun rose higher above the battered island and the survivors gathered their strength to meet the day, the ships drew ever closer and their fighting units honed their wooden weapons to murderous perfection.

In The Admiral's cabin aboard the leading galley the two navigators peered anxiously at their maps, checking and rechecking their position with silken threads that divined their course. The elder spoke to her assistant with a worried frown.

'It looks like it's going to be Scarabim after all.'

'Yes,' he replied grimly. 'Scarabim. The Prison Island.' He scrutinized the tiny scarab-shaped dot on the map that symbolized their destination and said,

'Surely there won't be any survivors after all this time, will there?'

The Navigator replied with a short, cynical laugh.

'Oh, yes,' she said. '*Something* will have survived. Don't you worry about *that*!'

She leafed through a pile of charts, seeking without success for a map of the seascape that encircled them. 'Something *always* survives in one form or another.' She laughed bitterly. 'My God, I've seen some sights that would make your hair fall out, young man.'

'But I thought they were all empty now,' he insisted. 'I thought everyone died trying to escape from Prison Islands.'

'Nuts.'

'But they were inappropriately evolved. Wouldn't they all have killed each other by now?'

'Listen lad, you're fresh to this game and you've got a lot to learn. The best way you can do that is to listen to what I say and not argue all the time. Inappropriate evolution was just a catchy phrase that turned out to be wrong-headed. Just because someone's inappropriately evolved it doesn't mean that if you stick them on a desert island somewhere they're going to kill themselves off one way or another. That's what went wrong with the Prison Island idea. They don't. I'm telling you. In all my years at sea I've never put into a Prison Island without some form of life rushing out of the bushes to have a crack at us. What do you think the plague-dogs are for?'

She pointed at him with a firm finger and said in level tones, 'If you think you know what inappropriately evolved means, wait till we get to Scarabim and you'll think again. On some of these places they simply aren't human beings any more. Now take this to The Admiral and say it's a final confirmation and I'll find out what I can about the island in the next hour.'

She thrust the official memo across the table to him and turned to the shelves of scrolls behind her.

'But I'll tell you this,' she said gloomily, 'if we've got anything here it will all be a thousand years out of date. And if I know my prison islands, there will be one or two unexpected changes by now.'

The young navigator climbed up to the bridge and delivered the memo to The Admiral who stood with his face into the wind as though revelling in the rays of the morning sun upon his skin.

'There's no doubt?' he asked curtly as he read it.

'That's Final Confirmation, Sir.'

The Admiral raised his eyebrows ruefully.

'I thought things were going too easily on this tour of duty,' he said. 'Very well. When the navigator has more let me have it.'

Meanwhile, with wry mouth and closed eyes, the Navigator was digesting the first two sentences of the report on the Criminals of Scarabim.

'The Admiral didn't seem too pleased,' remarked the lad as he climbed down into the cabin.

'He'll be even less pleased when we tell him about this,' she replied, picking up the scroll and reading from it. 'Listen. "Scarabim: landed population: 17,576. *No sub-group separation*"!'

She stared up at the younger navigator with bleak eyes.

'So?' he said.

'So there's no sub-group separation. So they dumped the lot on that island – men, women, children, actives, passives, workers, thinkers, you name them – they dumped them. Everything necessary to perpetuate the strain was kindly off-loaded on that island and allowed to bubble and stew and mate and die and change and mutate through a thousand years, all ready for us to try and walk in there to check out the seismological disturbance. And what's more,' she paused to find the quotation in the manuscript 'this is a real sickener – "Criminal classification – resource wastage (technology)". Do you know what that means?'

The lad shrugged sullenly.

'Metals,' The Navigator replied. 'And *Fire!*'

'Oh,' said the lad, growing pale.

'Oh indeed,' replied The Navigator replied. 'This could be a bit of an eye-opener for you, my lad, with your "surely there won't be any survivors after all this time" nonsense.'

She read through the scroll again, taking extensive notes on her pad and then tore off the page. The lad jumped up but she waved him back to his seat.

'I'd better take this one up,' she said, unsmiling. 'He's going to choke on it.'

She climbed the swaying ladders to the bridge and coughed at the Admiral's elbow.

'News for me, Navigator?' he asked.

'I'm afraid so, Sir.'

'You'd better read it to me then.'

The Navigator glanced round quizzically at the lieutenants who stood within earshot.

'Come on, woman,' snapped The Admiral, 'they've all seen Prison Islands before. What have we got this time?'

The Navigator shrugged and broke the news bluntly.

'The island is an undivided resource-wastage group, initially exceeding seventeen thousand.' She paused, knowing the rest would be hard to take. 'Technology, Sir. They landed them with everything – technicians, planners, artisans, the lot.'

She stopped.

Even in the golden dawn the faces of those around her had paled to the colour of the prow-curled foam.

'Technology?' said The Admiral.

'Yes Sir.'

'Excuse me a moment,' he said, moving towards the ladders. But he had taken only three steps when, unable to contain himself, he vomited across the deck.

32

Meanwhile, high above the lookouts on their snowwhite wind-wings higher even than the red-eyed vultures with their webbed talons, flew the spirit of Ana, dispossessed Matriarch of the Earth. Weary was she now from her long and tortuous voyage through the catacombs of time, seeking her lost Empire and the body from within which she had held sway. And content now was she to drift along over the tiny scurrying galleys with the smoking mountain in sight upon the horizon. She knew from their wooden boats that they were strangers, for there was no suitable timber on the Island of Scarabim. And she knew from their speed and the discipline of their formation that they were dangerous. Better, she thought, to follow above them and observe their movements than hurry back, impotent, to the ruined desert and her wounded army. So she watched from the unseen visibility of the spirit world as the boats arrowed swiftly across the ever-darkening sea. And as the oarsmen pulled the almost perfectly efficient hand-carved hulls over the water, exulting and enthusing from the effects of stimulants culled from the shrubs and herbs of their native continent, the Beast-Leashers checked their animals with expert eyes and steeled themselves for the task ahead.

'This is my last tour,' one of them grumbled to himself. 'Just my luck to get involved on the very last trip.'

'They wouldn't let you before?' asked the youngest of the Beast-Leashers, herself little more than an adult fresh out of farm school.

'Wasn't necessary, thank God,' he replied. 'I'm not sure I have the stomach for it now.'

He thrust his hand through the twisted wooden bars of the cage and stroked his beast's haunch, feeling the trembling anger and horrifying hatred that welled up as hysterical paroxysms of rage at his touch.

'Look at that!' he said with admiration. 'You wouldn't think she was twelve, would you?'

He stood up and kicked the cage in sudden savagery.

'And after all this time I could lose her on the very last trip!'

'Maybe we won't need to loose them when it comes to it,' said the youngster, blundering into incivility in an attempt to comfort her colleague. The approach inevitably drew contempt. 'Maybe we won't. But if we do, this one goes first,' he snapped and kicked the cage again, reducing his beast to near paralysis from excess adrenalin that stiffened every muscle and caused yellow froth to leak from the neck-strap of the head-bag.

'It's her *right*!' he said. 'She'll go first. And when she does that'll be the last we'll see of her. You've heard The Navigator's report. Technology. She'll never come back alive. She'll have her day but she'll get killed for sure.'

'But why would they kill her?' asked the younger Beast-Leasher in wonder. 'What good would *that* do?'

'Don't ask *me*, Sister, I'm from the Farms too. I don't know anything outside of what I do. But I've heard stories. Picked up a thing or two here and there. And you can take it from me that if you stay in the Service till you're seventy-five you won't ever have a worse tour than this one. And you can say goodbye to Thingy here as well,' he added, kicking at the young girl's captive dog, causing it to respond with wild howls and furious twisting against its bonds. 'I reckon all this lot has had it.'

The girl shrugged.

'It's not *our* fault,' she said.

The older man turned and looked at her with a curiously bitter expression.

'Is that what they're teaching you youngsters on the Farms these days?'

'That's one of the things, yes,' replied the girl with quiet pride.

'Well, well, well,' muttered the man, shaking his head and squatting down to be closer to his beast. 'Did you hear that one, Pluggo? "It's not *our* fault".'

Two decks above them the last of the foot-unit Commanders floated gently down on to the bridge, unleashed his shoulder straps and allowed his wings to be folded away. The Admiral nodded his approval to the assembled officers.

'Thankyou for gathering so swiftly. I have some good news and some bad news.'

There was a ripple of laughter but The Admiral silenced it with an upraised hand.

'No, ladies and gentlemen, I'm afraid this is serious. The good news is that it seems highly unlikely that you or your people will be required to use weapons.'

He paused to allow a murmur of unanimous approval to run through the group.

'The reason for this is also the bad news. Technology.'

He dropped the work quickly amongst them, half-hoping that someone would throw up and relieve his embarrassment at having done so himself. But a tight-lipped and ghastly silence was the only response.

'It looks,' he continued, 'as if we shall have to unleash The Beasts.'

He looked round, attempting to gauge their reactions.

'I know this is unusual but I have reasoned that to put translators ashore on a Prison Island with the constituents of this one would be an unjustifiable risk of life.'

He raised a hand to snuff out the protests he could see rising on all sides.

'Briefly,' he said, 'only one of two conditions is likely to obtain on Scarabim at the present moment. Either they will have gathered together too great a concentration of energy and been killed in the resulting explosion. And, I'm afraid, we cannot rule out the possibility that it is just such an explosion that we are here to investigate. Or, on the other hand, they will have developed a system of con-

144

trolled energy-wastage which, as you all know, means machines and, almost inevitably, killing machines at that. Either way, it is too hostile an environment to risk any personnel.'

He hurriedly cleared his throat, ignoring several raised and waving hands in his audience.

'As I interpret the manual on Prison Island Landings, The Beasts are a standard part of our equipment to meet just such an eventuality as this. I've never heard of them being used before but I firmly believe that this is the correct moment to put them in the field.'

'With respect, Sir,' one of the officers broke in with anxious and controlled urgency, 'they *were* used once. But a subsequent enquiry censured all involved for misuse of resources and causing unnecessary death.'

The Admiral frowned irritably.

'Yes, I know about all that. I'm aware of the consequences. Do me the courtesy of assuming that my decision has been made only after a great deal of serious thought. I would not unleash the Beasts if I felt any other alternative were feasible.'

'Accept a volunteer, Sir?' piped up a young officer in the front row.

'For what?'

'To go ashore with a translator and check out the validity of your analysis, Sir.'

'Are you suggesting I might be wrong?' snapped The Admiral angrily.

'Not *suggesting* that you are, Sir,' replied the officer, 'just *hoping* so.'

'Volunteer not accepted. We'll circumnavigate the island today, and then take action some time tomorrow morning. I'll brief you then. Any questions?'

He looked into their faces, concealing the unhappiness that filled him behind a mask of sternness.

'Yes, Sir,' replied the Volunteer. 'Why are you doing this?'

The Admiral grew red with anger.

'I'll ignore that,' he snapped. 'Take to your wings, all of you. Be here tomorrow morning at the same time.'

He turned and put his heavy shoulders into the wind knowing that his officers were deeply unhappy but reluctant to drive his point home too convincingly. They would have to share the responsibility, if he persuaded them to agree with him. It was better that they should

145

think it a mistake. He himself felt it was wrong. Every gland in his body churned over at the thought of unleashing The Beasts on an unprepared population and one with which they had made no attempt to communicate. But the alternative was to send in good youngsters to face an even savager beast, technology, in an even less prepared condition. He knew it would only be weakness in him to seek their support for the initiative.

He looked back to watch them flutter up on the graceful sail-wings, catching the wind of the galley's swift passage to rise upon the lengthening silken cables into the sky and peel off to left and right. He did not know that he had stirred resentments in some of those gently swooping creatures that would smoulder, burn, burst into flame and bring down an evil upon the fleet far greater than he ever would have dreamed.

He spotted three wings alighting on the same bridge three ranks behind his own and smiled to himself through a muttered curse.

'The young whelps,' he murmured. 'Looks like a bit of insubordination being hatched up there!'

He turned away and looked out to where the smoke of the volcano was now faintly visible in the distance, smoking and flashing even in the bright sunlight.

'Well, good luck to them,' he said sadly. 'I can't give them the answers.'

He looked down at his sleeve with the rings of service sewn side by side from cuff to elbow.

He had forgotten how many there were but did not count them. 'That's enough,' he said to himself. 'However many there are, after tomorrow, that's enough.'

33

Meanwhile, high up in the mountains, I woke to the drabbest morning of my life. Clouds of dreary grey pressed down upon the peaks, shut out the sun and held the still night air close to the ground, damp with rain and the lingering spray of sudden and fast-foaming torrents. I was terribly tired. For, although I had slept well after shaking off my would-be disciple, my world of dreams was so troubled that I woke more exhausted then I had fallen asleep.

'Orphachins again,' I muttered, recalling my nightmares. 'They exist. I know it. They're somewhere out there in the desert with Brother One and the goddess.'

I knew it with complete certainty for I had spent the night not only on the mountainside but also in the desert with the Orphachins, not only curled up uncomfortably in the lee of a mountain boulder, choking in the ash-laden wind, but also stretched out under the desert, warm and dry, breathing the clean, clear air that filtered through the sand.

I had lived a double life that night, both mine and theirs, double fear, double self-pity, double anger and had been forced to carefully distinguish one from the other lest they carry me away with their doubled intensity.

I had *become* the Orphachins for long timeless moments and knew them as they knew themselves, knew their memories, their aspirations and their intentions, shared their drives and felt their hunger.

And I knew they had come to hate their General.

How was it that Brother One knew nothing of his danger, I wondered, but lay sleeping beneath the sand with no awareness of the furious anger that the frightening mountain had stirred in his miniature army?

But then, he always was a bit obtuse.

I struggled to my feet and looked around at the unfamiliar mountains. 'Which way to the desert?' I asked.

The mountains made no reply.

I sighed wearily and began to pick my way down the rocky slopes towards the morning sun, stumbling often as my mind flickered back and forth involuntarily between the mountain and the desert. I would wake as though from a dream of conversation with my cannibal comrades to find myself plunging into a ditch or walking into a rockface. Or I would suddenly disappear from the damp mountain to find myself in the lavic ash deposits of the desert, saying Gobbly Gobbly and salivating at the idea of an edible Brother One emerging from his sand-bed.

'No Gobbly!' I would shout, admonishing us with our mind and reminding us all of the love and respect in which Brothers and Generals ought properly to be held.

And 'No Gobbly,' we would finally agree, reluctantly, puzzled and frustrated, staring in anxious awe at the smoking volcano.

But when I next returned from the treacherous footing of the mountainside we were salivating again, once more consumed by the resentment and fear that coursed through our little bodies, searching vainly in the sand for our succulent victim.

'No Gobbly,' I shouted into our collective mind. And once more we would reluctantly decide not to eat Brother One.

But as time passed I found my instructions becoming more and more feeble, tinged less and less with the necessary authority and I had to think ever more loudly to still the clamour of our bestial natures.

And I, too, was hungry.

'Unless I get to them shortly,' I thought, 'I will be unable to stop them.'

And so I pressed on, desperately trying to drive out all thoughts of what my brother would taste like and arguing with voices inside my head that would have it otherwise.

But as I rushed headlong through the rocky pass I became aware of another voice, neither mine nor the Orphachins, high-pitched, yet speaking in soft and gentle tones. I stopped, listening, and crept through the rocks towards it until I found myself looking down, unseen, at a truly remarkable sight. Only a stone's throw from me were two creatures of the island, seemingly preparing a light breakfast over an open fire. And my heart leaped as I realized that the larger of the two, clearly one of the goddesses in search of whom I had come to this hostile land, was speaking the familiar language of the ancient manuscripts in an almost unadulterated form.

'Oh baby, it's cold outside,' she said, stirring the fire suggestively with a stick. 'You'll feel a lot better with something hot inside you.'

I pressed closer, my heart beating fast, aware that I was witnessing something that had never before been revealed to the eyes of human beings – the life of the angels! The dwarf who accompanied her made no reply, but waved its arms eloquently in the direction of the mountains and then towards the fire. Clearly, it was suggesting they should eat quickly and then press on. Had I arrived moments later I might have missed this exquisite sight!

But then I blacked out and re-surfaced in the collective Orphachin mind as once more we prepared to plunge hungrily into the sand in search of Brother One and I shouted:

'Stop! No Gobbly!'

We paused, puzzled and frustrated, sniffing the wind to locate the sudden smells of meat cooking over an open fire that filled my nostrils in the mountains.

'No Gobbly!' I repeated again desperately, realizing that my own intense hunger, exacerbated by the Angels' breakfast, was overwhelming the authority of my words and causing us all to salivate excessively into the sand. 'Gobbly, Gobbly,' came the argumentative reply from another quarter of our mind. And then, from someone close by, 'Let us not disobey the orders of the burning mountain. Look what happened to our desert when The General ignored its commands.'

'Yes,' I agreed forcefully, 'Quite right. Do not disregard my orders. No Gobbly, Capisco? No Gobbly.'

We shook our little heads in fearful agreement.

'Now do as I say until I can reach you,' I ordered. 'No Gobbly.' And the next instant I was back in the mountains, peering down through the rocks at the angel campers.

I realized that each moment I spent in the mountains put Brother One in greater danger. I had no time to lie here and birdwatch. But this was too good an opportunity to make contact with a real angel.

I had to make some approach.

I stood up boldly on my feet choosing a mode of address almost at random from the list of suitable phrases I had memorized from the manuscripts.

'Hi Blue-eyes,' I said, trying my best to emulate the slow drawling speech which the text often indicated. 'Wanna have a good time?'

The goddess, startled, looked around without seeing me.

'What was that, baby?' she asked, nervously.

'I said "Hi Blue-eyes. Wanna have a good time?",' I repeated.

The goddess screamed and turned towards me, rising to her feet. 'Come on, honey,' I continued, stepping forward with what I hoped was a lascivious leer, 'be nice to me. I haven't had any for days.'

She glanced at the dwarf and the sizzling meat and then turned back to me and said haltingly,

'Help yourself.'

I was delighted.

At last I had managed to establish contact with this magical race and it seemed possible that we might even converse together.

'I thought you'd never ask,' I replied with formal politeness and, sitting down, lifted one of the skewers from the fire and spoke conversationally to the dwarf.

'Any more at home like you, baby?'

It made no reply save for a long and liquid stare at the sky and a few curt movements of its feet.

Clearly it was still anxious to move on.

'He's the last one,' replied the goddess nervously.

I nodded carefully and thought hard for a reply.

'Oh yeah?' I said, suddenly inspired, 'I bet you say that to *all* the guys.'

34

Meanwhile Rogesse's ragged Farmer Army had already moved Westward, mopping up the survivors around Ana's shattered encampment and Rogesse, flushed with violent and unconfined glee, put many to the blade herself, urging on her troops to further excess. 'Advance and punish!' was their battlecry and Death was their legacy as they trailed slowly across the desert behind the sun.

'Seek out the one-limbed hag whose foolish counsel brought ruin to our nation,' she ordered. 'And bring her to me alive or dead! And bring also she who is called Rogesse, she who so often tried by treachery to usurp my throne and who will have bedecked herself

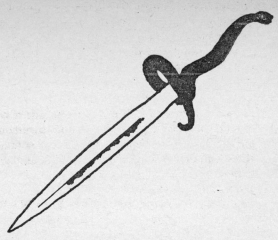

already with my Royal Chains. Strip her of them and bring her also, barefoot, to me whether she lives or no!'

The re-kindled Messianic army, illuminated from within by Rogesse's greed for power, made short work of the weary and overfed troops in Ana's demoralized encampment, many of whom, seeing their own countrywomen, made no move towards their weapons but instead held out their arms in comradely greeting, only to discover too late that treachery and lust for power still beat feebly in the breasts of the hungry even after the sky has fallen upon them. Others, fighting bravely, were no match for the many spears of the advancing Amazonis and fell by the side of storm-slain comrades that they had so lately mourned.

And then, with exultant shouts, the bodies of The Crone and she who wore the Royal Regalia were discovered among the ruins of the tattered pavilion and borne in rough triumph to the feet of Rogesse. The Crone breathed so faintly in her spiritless swoon that she seemed to hover weakly between sleep and death, but the body of Ana, paralysed in one arm and both legs, peered out shrewdly with the clear eyes of The Crone.

Rogesse stared down at her captives, diabolical joy unconcealed upon her face. She stooped, reached out a hand, raised the unconscious cripple's eyelids and let them fall.

'She lives, though barely,' she muttered. 'May she recover so that I can kill her in the manner of my own choosing and thus repay her for the lifetime of insolence I endured while she skulked in the protection of the Queen.' And then she turned to Ana with an especially cruel smile upon her lips and stared into the paraplegic's eyes.

'Greetings, Oh Queen,' she whispered sardonically, so softly that the women about her would not hear. 'Have we not waited many years for this rendezvous? Have I not rehearsed this moment a thousand times in my dreams?'

She laughed, despite herself, a spontaneous overflow of gleeful malice.

'I can see you *peeping!*' she whispered mockingly, as though to a child. 'I know that you can hear me well enough although your poor body has been a little broken.'

She raised Ana's useless arm and let it drop to the sand with an appreciative chuckle.

'The Man-god has already started work on you for me,' she told the silent cripple, 'and be assured you will be a little *more* broken before I have finished with you, *My Queen!*'

The lips in Ana's face moved and the voice of The Crone spoke with Ana's throat, afraid yet defiant still.

'You know not of what you speak, Rogesse,' she croaked with an unfamiliar tongue. 'You are merely astride the winds of circumstance. You have no power of your own. You are weak and useless and when the wind changes direction you will be blown away like an empty husk.'

Rogesse eyed her with icy venom.

'For that, My Queen,' she replied, 'you will have your tongue cut out.'

Ana's lips moved again and The Crone spat in Rogesse's face. 'Do what you will, Rogesse,' she said mockingly, 'for you are *doomed!*'

Rogesse moved as though to strike her but held back and clutched at the Royal Chains that now hung from her own neck. She closed her eyes and inhaled her anger, storing the rage inside herself, dangerously volatile, carcinogenous.

'*I* am The Queen!' she hissed, partly to the body of Ana, partly to herself and partly to the smoking mountain and the infinite sky beyond.

'I *am* The Queen! There is work to be done and all pleasures grow keener for the waiting. I will deal with you, Ana, when I have the leisure to work in elaborate and exquisite detail.'

She opened her eyes and grinned with mischievous delight. 'And

152

meanwhile you shall have a box to live in and you will come out of
the box when I allow it and go back in the box at my command, just
as it was with you and The Crone. And so we will re-enact the roles
in reverse and you will recall with each shutting up how you
slammed down the lid of Fear upon my life whenever it took your
fancy so to do and you will live like The Crone.'

She paused, lit up from within by a sudden thought.

'Yes, even in the same box will you lie, cheek to cheek, wizened
sisters of sorrow, with nought but your cold kisses to cheer the darkness of cruel imprisonment. And if you are *very* good,' she giggled
and stood upright, a gentle, crazy smile upon her lips, 'I will cut off
your arm and legs so that you may cuddle even closer with your
stinking box-mate.'

She threw back her head and laughed at the sun and then, bursting
with the delight of power, strode forward, calling up her scattered
women, vitalizing them with her energy, filling them with reflections
of her own eager bloodlust.

And through Ana's eyes the Crone watched her own stump placed in
its familiar box and felt Ana's body thrust roughly on top and saw
the light blot out with a bang as the lid closed down upon the sky.
Through Ana's body she felt the weak breathing of her own crippled
frame and felt her own wrinkled skin through Ana's. And she
smelled her own rancidness with Ana's nostrils and grimaced in distaste.

'Pooh!' she said, 'you would not grudge me your body for *this*
journey, Old Queen.'

She giggled to the absent Ana.

'This box would not be quite to your royal liking.'

She giggled again.

'You are well out of it indeed. But, as for me, it is no great thing. A
box is a box no matter whose body we wear. Who can throw off a
limitation that has once been accepted willingly? It was too late for
me. I should have known.'

She giggled again.

'And at least we are still together.'

And, kissing The Crone's face with gentle amusement, she laid
Ana's body to sleep, hoping that the bonds that held her spirit captive might relax in slumber.

*

The box moved now with a steady, almost soothing rhythm as the four Amazoni bearers caught a level striding pace towards the mountains. And like some mutant sacred vessel it travelled across the sands, doubly pregnant, preceded by its rabble bandit army, lit from within by their leader's lunacy, their blades already bloodied in the flesh of kinfolk, travelling headlong down a blind alleyway of destiny, apeing the zeal of the divine in a hellish travesty of crusading purity, unwitting players in some devilish mocking parody of sacred ritual that swept them on to the very battleground of Good and Evil itself, but only to be destroyed.

Satirically.

In jest.

As all armies are destroyed, almost by definition.

And towering over their struggling journey stood the volcano.

A burst pimple of the face of the Earth.

A polite and guarded cough.

A mere shift of temperature and pressure inside the planet.

Dreaming in a different kind of day.

Knowing nothing of the emotions that flamed about its feet, the passions making waves that echoed and re-echoed even to the gates of Heaven and Hell.

35

Meanwhile, below decks in a certain galley, in the fourth rank of the wooden Armada standing off the coast there was hurried conversation in discreet tones. The young Officer who had volunteered to go ashore was whispering urgently to his two companions.

'And I say let's ignore the Old Man and go ashore anyway. Did we join the Navy to sit on some stinking ship for weeks on end and then stand by while that senile idiot puts Plague-Dogs ashore on the one place where we can be *sure* there are pickings that would be rich enough to retire on?'

'How can you be so sure?' asked Johnson, a thin-faced young Officer with the red rose of the Botany Corps in his lapel.

'Because they have *technology* here!' hissed The Volunteer impatiently. 'Even the simplest Machine would fetch a small fortune on the Black Market. If we could smuggle something home that was at all sophisticated we'd all three of us be set up for life.'

'So you say,' replied Johnson doubtfully.

'So I *know*!' insisted The Volunteer. 'What's the matter with you? It's a chance that any fool would jump at. Do you think that half the officers in this fleet wouldn't give their lower jaws to be in on a scheme like this? You heard the noise everybody made when he announced he was putting Plague-Dogs in! Everybody was seething! Under any other Admiral the whole fleet would simply move in and clean up all the goodies to sell back home, but this old fogey is still living in the days of a State-supported Navy! Can't you see what's going to happen? He's going to sail round the island to find out if there's any life left here, and when he does he'll send in the Plague-Dogs to finish it off and then send a seismic survey team over with kites. A quick in and out. No looting. No booty. No profits. Just like it was in the old days. Then we'll sit on this stinking ship some more until the tour of duty ends and we'll get home no richer than we set out. Is that what you want, Johnson? It's not what *I* want. I want us all to be rich men!'

'Rich men and a *woman*,' remarked the third member of the conspiracy drily, indicating the secondary sexual characteristics under the front of her uniform. 'What do you think these are? Rock samples?'

The other two exchanged wry glances.

'As you wish,' replied Johnson with pedantic courtesy. 'Rich men and a *woman*.' Then he nodded to The Volunteer. 'Okay,' he said. 'I agree with you. I didn't jack in a promising career with a lichen-hunting corporation just to spend all day finding out what direction we're rowing in. But how do you know we'll be able to sell anything we take back?'

'Are you kidding?' replied The Volunteer with a smirk. 'My uncle has all the naval ports sewn up. He'll take anything and give us the top price.'

'It's not going to be easy getting at the boats,' put in The Girl practically.

'Forget the boats,' countered The Volunteer. 'We take kites. That way no one will see us go until it's too late.'

'That's very smart,' she retorted acidly. 'And how do we get back to the ship on kites? Flap our wings and fly against the wind?'

'We *have* to take a boat,' urged Johnson. 'It's crazy to go by kite. We'd just be stranded.'

'Oh God,' murmured The Volunteer, closing his eyes in disbelief. 'What have you Botanists got in your heads? Soil?' He jabbed the table with a forefinger. 'Listen,' he said with irritation, 'if we take a boat, that's called jumping ship or possibly desertion. It puts us in a lot of trouble and, knowing the Old Man, he'll probably just leave us behind to stew in our own juice. But if we take kites we can claim we were using our initiative to avoid the use of Plague-Dogs because we feel so strongly about the ecological consequences. Right?'

'Right,' said The Girl in grudging agreement, 'that's just the kind of garbage the Old Man would swallow.'

'It's going to take him a day to go round the island. When we want to get off we signal from shore and he'll send out a boat to pick us up. He'll be hopping mad but, secretly, he'll think it was a pretty noble thing to do, and after he's through yelling at us, it will all be forgotten.'

'I still think a boat would be a better idea,' grumbled Johnson.

'Two of us say kite,' snapped The Girl. 'You're outnumbered. Winners' Rules, Johnson. Either come in or get out.'

Johnson shrugged.

'Okay. Winners' Rules. As long as I get rich I don't care how we do it.'

And thus, with almost careless ease, the three adventurers entered a drama the like of which they could not have conjured in the most extreme states of drug intoxication, little realizing they were about to drop into a world in which time was reversing upon itself, gathering speed as it recoiled diagonally across centuries of centuries, a collapsing spiral, an imploding helix, a self-cancelling vortex, a mirror negation of all that had ever been. Winners' Rules, indeed!

'What exactly are we looking for on this island?' whispered Johnson as they made their way through the decks along the narrow ramps.

'We'll have to play it by ear,' replied The Volunteer. 'Anything we've never seen before. Anything that's made out of inorganic materials. Anything that looks illegal. We'll just have to keep our eyes open and use our imagination.'

They reached the upper deck and scaled the ladders to the Wing-deck.

'Plenty of line for us,' The Volunteer instructed The Winchman, 'We're going to take a look over the island.'

'I haven't received any orders about it, Sir,' grumbled The Winchman with a puzzled frown.

'These are your orders,' snapped The Girl sharply. 'Plenty of line.'

'Yessir. Right away, Sir,' he replied with mock servility. 'Not expecting me to pull you back are you. There's no return wind up there, you can bet on that.'

The Volunteer gave him a look of ruffled discomfort intended to convey a stern rebuke.

'We'll be returning by boat,' he said. 'Please don't be facetious. This is no picnic.'

'No, Sir. Sorry, Sir,' agreed The Winchman. 'Plenty of line it is.'

He stooped to prepare the winches for a three-kite lift and shook his head in disapproval. A man who stared at you like that wasn't acting on Admiral's orders. He had seen that look before. Twice. Both times it had ended up with tragedy and a posthumous Court Naval. He suspected this would be the last time these three robins would struggle into a wing-harness.

'You don't mind if I ask for clemency now, do you, Sir?' he said, almost casually, as he fastened the winchlines to the wing-stays.

'Clemency?' replied The Volunteer, startled.

'Clemency for whatever it is you're about to do, Sir.'

His eyes met The Winchman's knowing stare and he looked down.

'Yes, of course,' he replied. 'Since you ask, you may have clemency. This is nothing at all to do with you.'

'Thankyou, Sir,' he said. 'One at a time, then.'

He signalled to Johnson, who spread wings into the level on-shore breeze and lifted gently under the billowing shrouds. The Winchman's practised eye watched the wings until they came alive momentarily, taut and strong between periods of lazy, lifeless flapping, and signalled Johnson off the winch-deck onto a layer of smoothly moving air. Instantly the wooden winch spun under the Winchman's powerful thrust and the wings rose vertically into the air for several feet until the line began to play out and the kite rose higher and higher as it drifted inland.

'Not bad, even though I do say so myself,' he mumbled, reeling in the castoff wisp of silken ropes and watching the kite fade into the blue of the sky. 'You two still want to go?'

'Hook us up,' they replied.

36

Meanwhile, back at the ruined Candle Palace, Amrita had moved from childhood to maturity in a matter of hours.

'We have to face it,' she was trying to impress upon her pale, exhausted companions, 'after this we're entirely on our own.'

'But Amrita,' chirped up The Surviving Twin.

'No, just listen for a moment,' Amrita insisted. 'Something has gone *wrong* in heaven. The Man-god lived, the waters destroyed the Palace and the insects came. Now we must try to put the pieces back together and go on living without a heaven and without a God.'

'Suppose we don't want to go on living?' argued Elvira melancholically. Amrita pointed to the door.

'Then just go off and try to live somewhere else somehow. Don't you understand? We're on our own now. Nobody is going to use their magic to help us and nobody is going to punish us if we're naughty. We're going to go on living just as we are now until we die of old age or the desert tribes come and kill us all.' She looked up at the tired anxious faces of the women grouped upon The Great Stairs, seeking, without success, some glimmer of understanding or courage.

'You paint a very gloomy picture, Amrita,' someone said. 'I'm not sure I like it at all.'

'It's not up to us to like it or dislike it,' she replied with suppressed irritation. 'It's up to us to *deal* with the *realities* of the situation!'

She cast out an arm to take in the flooded Hall with its grim floating debris, the splintered windows, the cracked masonry, the

158

blackened and blistered walls. She waved at their tattered, smoke-stained, muddied robes. 'What could be more gloomy and heart-breaking than this?' she asked, 'and what are we going to do about it? Sit here still we starve? No. We must make up our minds to either rebuild or move out and re-establish ourselves on some other part of the world.'

'And what about we?' called a Pot-watcher from the foot of The Great Stairs, kneedeep in the mire. 'What am us supposed to does?'

Many of the women frowned to hear the uncultured voice bellowing so brazenly in the once-great Hall.

'I'm afraid you'll have to fend for yourselves,' replied Amrita. 'I'm sorry it's come to this but, as you can see, things have changed rather drastically.'

'Me sees!' shouted the Pot-watcher belligerently, causing a flutter of shock among the seated Others. 'It's like that am it? Us scrubs and slaves and cleans and cooks for you then when things goes wrong it am, "thankyou very much, us won't be needing you any more", am it?'

'I'm afraid I don't see any alternative,' replied Amrita levelly. 'It's just not possible for things to remain as they were after what has happened.'

'Well, alright. Us can sees *that*,' said a Cook, wading out from the shadows of The Great Staircase, her skirts held carefully out of the oily water. 'But what am *us* going to does? This place am *us* home just as much am yours, even though the cellars and the kitchens am flooded. What am us supposed to do? Hold us breaths and lives underwater?'

A guffaw of approval echoed out from The Great Corridor where the servants had been lurking in the dripping darkness, eaves-dropping on the interchanges of the bejewelled women.

'I'm afraid you're going to have to make up your minds to carve out new lives for yourselves, just as we have been forced to do.'

'How?' demanded the Cook bluntly. 'Us knows nowt but us am learned in the kitchens. How is us to carves out new lives? It am alright for you people. You knows what what is. You all knows what to does. But us am ignorant. What am going to becomes of we all?'

'I'm sorry,' replied Amrita gently, with a shrug of her shoulders, 'I'm afraid we're in no position to advise you.'

'Well me doesn't think that am right,' replied the Cook. 'Me doesn't thinks that am right at all!'

'Then why don't you just go away!' shouted one of the women high on The Stairs, waving an arm of torn and crumpled silks in a gesture of dismissal. 'Why don't you just leave, as you've been told to do, and stop causing trouble?'

'Us wasn't told to leave!' retorted the Pot-watcher. 'Nobody have told we nothing till now. Us am just been left to makes do as best us can!'

'Well I'm telling you now!' replied the woman crossly. 'Just go away!'

There was a grumbling in the tunnel and somebody burst into tears. The Pot-watcher stepped forward, trembling with fear and anger.

'With respects, ma'am,' she said, 'Us thinks us will stay here and lives in the Palace. It am the only home us knows. We can't manages anywhere else.'

She pointed to Amrita.

'She says us mays go somewhere else. Well why doesn't *you* does that and leave we here in peace? Us can fix the place.'

There was a murmur of assent from the skulking servants, but a cry of protest rose from the women upon The Great Staircase and shouts of 'Get out!', 'The impertinence!' and 'How dare you?' jumbled and jostled each other in the echoed vaulted roofing.

The Pot-watcher shrank back frightened into the shelter of the shadows and the tumult subsided.

'If we decided that it's better to live elsewhere then I suppose there's no reason why you shouldn't have the run of the place after we've gone,' said Amrita, 'But you must realize how ridiculous your suggestion sounds to everybody now. Besides,' she turned to speak to the ruffled Others, 'and this is perhaps a more pressing issue, when we consulted The Whale about what we should do she told us to bring the Orphachins here.'

There was a second uproar among the jewelled women and Amrita waited impatiently for the ripples of outrage and disgust to die away. 'Quite,' she agreed. 'But the thing is that nobody has seen Tomaly-Somaly since then and I'm afraid she might have gone to fetch them.'

There were shouts of 'Unbelievable!' and 'What a traitor!' and even the shadowed minions could be heard complaining. 'So we've got to be ready,' shouted Amrita, holding up her arms for silence. 'We've got to be ready for their coming and that means making sure that they can't get in, getting together some weapons to deal with the ones that try and arranging for some of us to keep watch from the roof at all times of the day and night.'

'Oh, how *boring*!' someone exclaimed.

'Yes. But it has to be done,' replied Amrita. 'Now I don't know how we'll do this. Can somebody see to the doors and windows?' She waited for a reply and looked around. There was no response. 'How about weapons?'

No response.

'Well I can keep watch today,' she said, 'I've hurt my foot and it will be good to rest it, although I wouldn't mind if there was somebody with me to talk to.'

'I'll watch too,' said The Surviving Twin bravely. '*I'll* sit up with you. I'm not sure I could sleep anyway. This place is awfully creepy now.'

'Yes,' came the general murmur, 'we'll *all* keep watch on the roof.'

'Us would like to helps if us could,' said the Cook diffidently, twisting the edge of her skirt nervously between her fingers. 'If there am anything us can does.'

Amrita looked baffled.

'Well I think we've got all the lookouts we need for now,' she replied. 'Why don't you see what you can do about the doors and windows and try to clear this place up a bit?'

'Very good, ma'am,' agreed Cook enthusiastically.

'We'll be up on the roof if you have any problems,' said Amrita and, limping, picking her way painfully up the Stairs, led her companions towards the roof. 'Oh!' she said suddenly, stopping on the second floor and leaning over the rail to call to the servants below, 'and we'll need some food. Is that possible?'

'The cellars am flooded,' replied a store-keeper 'and most am surely spoiled by now.'

'Well, anyway, see what you can do,' replied Amrita. 'Just a little breakfast is all we need, really. Anything will do.'

'Yes,' replied the store-keeper. 'Rights away!'

'Oh, and if you find any wine, bring that too.'

'Yes'm.'

Amrita sighed as she led her women up the broad, winding stairway, spiralling gracefully up towards the sky.

'What a *mess* all this is,' she said.

*

The Others filtered out on to the flat marble-flagged roof and scattered to take up watchful attitudes in all directions, chattering about the flooded plains and the smoking mountain, mourning the tragic loss of their sisters, brushing loose dirt from each other's clothing, gathering in small groups to examine tiny jewelled insects that had crawled up to the roof to die. Before long their concentration waned and they began to lie about on the smooth warm marble, soaking up the sun, snoozing. There was a general murmur of delight when breakfast appeared, although it was little more than bread and meats, various cheeses with cold vegetables, salads and fruits.

'At least there's plenty of wine,' commented The Surviving Twin, opening a large flagon, 'that's one thing that floods and pestilence can't affect.' They sat in a large and glittering circle, resplendent still, despite the grime and mud that smeared their clothes.

'There's something awfully peculiar over towards the mountain,' said a young dark-haired girl conversationally.

'Zelda, please don't talk with your mouth empty,' chided an older woman at her side.

'Oh, sorry,' said the girl and quickly took a bite of blue cheese. 'I said there's something awfully peculiar over by the mountain,' she repeated indistinctly.

'What is it?' asked another through a mouthful of bread.

'Looks like three big white tents floating in the sky.'

'What kind of big white tents?' spluttered Amrita.

'Just big white tents. Look for yourself.'

The Surviving Twin stood up and strolled over to lean on the parapet.

'Oh yes,' she said. 'Three big white tents. Flying.'

'We should have asked the servants to start on the bedrooms first,' said a mouthful of fruit.

'All in good time,' said a mouthful of lettuce.

'Actually,' said The Surviving Twin, 'they're not tents at all. They're creatures. They've got heads and legs and things.'

Amrita stood up and joined her.

'Oh yes,' she said. 'Three big white birds. And it almost looks as though they're coming this way.'

They returned to their places at the picnic and resumed their meal.

37

Many hours had they floated over the desolate desert, seeking they knew not what, knowing only that they had not found it. And, as their fatigue and disappointment turned to ill-temper in the twisting, treacherous currents rising up from the overheated landmass, more curt and uninformative had their communications become and each had been guilty, more than once, of failing to warn the others of sickening down-draughts in the rapidly shifting air. Finally they had tied together high above the flooded plains and held a short and irritated conference.

'These people are just *Primitives*,' Johnson had shouted wearily above the wind. 'And this place shows as much evidence of technology as a fishfarm! I think we ought to admit we've blown it and get back to the ships before we invite serious trouble.'

The Volunteer scanned the now tranquil waters far below them, unwilling to give up the dream of fabulous wealth that had swelled his heart as the wind lifted him from the wing-deck towards the sky.

'These people *must* know what happened to all the machines. Maybe they've got them hidden anyway somewhere!' he yelled.

'These people don't have any more idea what a machine is than I have!' Johnson shouted back. 'I'll bet my stripes on that. The only evidence of anything supernatural is that white building down there and that's just an ancient ruin.'

'I think we should try to make contact with some of the Criminals before we give up,' suggested The Girl. 'They *may* still know the old secrets. We didn't come all this way to go back empty-handed!'

'I suppose it's superfluous to remind you that we're not supposed to communicate with Criminals without a Translator?' shouted The Volunteer.

'Yes it is,' replied The Girl. 'I told you – Winner's Rules.' She cast off the link-rope that joined them and dropped into a curling glide, searching out a plane of air that would lead to the Palace.

The other two stared at each other for a moment, then wordlessly separated and dropped after her.

*

And they came like white feathers falling through the earth-flung clouds, three loops of light upon separate currents of air, sliding down the wind towards the marooned Candle Palace.

And the surviving women watched them come, full of wonder, for it seemed as though they were borne upon the level sunbeams that filled their graceful wings. And they were not afraid, for they knew they would not harm them.

'They have come for the Man-god,' they whispered, as the smoothly-falling kites spiralled closer. 'They have come to take him away. We are no longer fit to eat his flesh and they are angry.'

The birdmen were tired and cold.

They had been in the air since dawn and fear had become no stranger to them.

Fear of the strange intangible evil they felt everywhere in this strange and mutant land, fear of the mountain whose choking breath had many times caught them in its rising coils and threatened to toss them high above their oxygen ceilings. And, not least, fear of the Plague-Dogs that might be released on to the land before they could get back to the ships.

They landed gently upon the smooth battlements, their wings closing slowly, folding out the trapped air that could have lifted them away at the last second. Now they were mortals once more, earth-bound bipeds wearing cumbersome backpacks, relieved to see the women of the ruined palace spread themselves prostrate on the marble roof. They assumed the air of cold indifference that was the correct mode of approach to a Criminal Colony and unstrapped their wings.

'Take us to your leader,' called The Volunteer.

'We know what you want,' replied Amrita, bravely pushing herself to her feet. 'Do us no more harm, we beg of you. Take what you will and go.'

'Couldn't be easier,' muttered The Girl. 'Just say "Lead us".'

'Lead us,' said the Volunteer eagerly and Amrita, turning with difficulty upon an injured foot, hobbled down the marble stairs that led below.

And it was a sorry sight indeed that met the eyes of the three adventurers as they descended into the ruined building. The gleaming walls of polished marble were blackened and defaced by the blaze and smoke of flame-torches that had fought long and hard up and down the stairways to clear the verminous invaders. And in every corner the crisped cadavers of the crawling carrion were heaped and piled in cindered confusion, some smoking still, filling the air with a sickeningly sweet aroma of roasting insect meat. And each step was slippery with the secretions of tiny things subjected to weights far greater than those which their bodies had been designed to withstand. As the young pirates and their hobbling guide struggled down the proudly curling stairway the Volunteer tripped on some unyielding lump beneath a heap of incinerated husks and blanched to discover it was the body of a woman, half-eaten from the inside out, gaping idiotically down into the stairwell. He pointed it out discreetly to his companions and they winced and grinned nervously.

'Can you *imagine* living in a place like this?' whispered The Girl, her voice filled with contempt. 'It seems almost unbelieveable!'

'Hush!' said The Volunteer. 'We're doing alright so far. Don't say anything to upset them.'

They spiralled hesitantly down The Great Staircase, stepping nervously around charred and frozen figures, bones half-cleared, still alive with buzzing creatures picking away at the remains with quiet diligence.

'This is a lovely place you've got here,' The Volunteer called down to Amrita, trying to cover the nauseous bubblings of his companions.

Amrita, turning slightly, half-smiled.

'Thankyou,' she replied. 'I'm afraid you've caught us at rather a bad time. The place isn't usually such a mess at this.'

'Not at all,' answered The Volunteer, catching her up and treating her to a gleaming smile. 'I think it's delightful when a place looks lived in, don't you agree?'

'A lot of us *died* here,' Amrita said sadly.

'Well, of course,' responded The Volunteer nervously. 'It's inevitable, isn't it?'

'If you say so,' said Amrita, 'then I suppose it must be so.' They spiralled down in a silence that was thick with the echoes of their crunching footsteps.

The Volunteer cleared his throat nervously again and renewed his efforts to communicate with this limping Criminal.

'You seem to have a lot of insects here,' he said, and then, realizing how fatuous that must sound, added, 'are they part of your diet?'

'Pardon?' said Amrita.

'The insects,' repeated The Vounteer. 'Do you eat them?'

'No,' answered Amrita gloomily. 'They eat us.'

'Oh, I see,' said The Volunteer, blankly.

Amrita trembled visibly as she picked her painful way down the stairs.

The Man-gods! Alive! And speaking to *her*! She, the Chosen One, to lead them to their brother!

'Control, Amrita. Control,' she said to herself, remembering the constant schoolroom rebuke. 'Don't chatter or seem afraid, just answer politely each question they ask.'

She stepped on a weakly weaving blood-worm and the sound echoed wetly down the convoluted stairwell.

'I can't help noticing that these insects seem to be dead for the most part,' he blundered on. 'Some kind of sickness, was it?'

'Burned,' replied Amrita, wondering how the Man-god could have failed to notice.

'Burned!' exclaimed The Girl behind them. 'Did she say *burned*!'

'How did they get–er–burned?' asked The Volunteer, whose trembling lips belied the indifference with which he spoke.

'The Torch-guards. They worked very hard.'

'Torch-guards?'

'Yes,' replied Amrita. She held an invisible flame-torch in her hands and let out a roar of imaginary flame over a heap of dead insects. 'With torches.'

The Volunteer could hardly contain his sudden excitement.

'You mean you have things that shoot out *flames*?'

'*Machines*?' added The Girl.

'Of course,' replied Amrita, 'how else could we have burned the insects. The Great Chapel is through here.'

They had reached The Great Hall, kneedeep in an oily floodwater, floating furniture and drowning insects, and she paused to assess the wisdom of putting her injured foot in it.

But the three pirates were almost suffocating with suppressed excitement.

'A fire-machine! And a fire-machine that not only *makes* fire but actually shoots it out!' whispered The Girl. 'One of those would set us up for life!'

'Did you see what it's done to those insects,' marvelled The Volunteer.

'Let's just get one from the women and go,' hissed Johnson. 'If we wade through that cesspit we'll ruin our uniforms. Why put our expenses up when we don't have to?'

'Where's she taking us, anyway,' muttered The Girl. 'Has it occurred to you she might be going to burn us like the insects?'

Johnson smirked.

'So much for Winners' Rules,' he whispered sardonically.

'Shut up!' she snapped. 'Winners' Rules is one thing, but I've never seen so much unnecessary death in my whole life.' The Volunteer spoke to Amrita, who was about to step off The Great Stairs into the stinking swamp of dissolved bodies.

'Where are you taking us?' he demanded bluntly.

'To The Great Chapel,' replied Amrita.

'What's in the Great Chapel?'

A look of sudden suspicion flashed across Amrita's face, mingled with fear and what could have been the beginnings of anger.

'One of your kind!' she exclaimed, as though it should have been self-evident, and scrutinized their faces with so mixed an expression of terror and belligerence that Johnson almost shouted his hurried approval.

'Wonderful!' he cried nervously, grinning like a skull at his companions and urging them with awkward movements of his shoulders to express similar enthusiasms.

'Wonderful,' they agreed limply.

Amrita, reassured, turned to lead them into the slime, pushing hard through the unknown, unthinkable debris beneath their feet, wading down The Great Corridor towards The Great Chapel.

As they drew nearer they heard the sound of rushing water and glanced at each other in puzzlement. But the sight that met their eyes as they entered The Chapel caused them to let out an involuntary cry of surprise and shock.

A column of water rose to a height of twenty metres from Great Womb, reached for the heavens, faded, fanned out and crashed down with a ceaseless din upon the flooded Chapel floor.

And, riding its highest point, rolling and spinning like a log on a geyser, twisted and turned about in the turbulent seething fountain, was the helpless form of a white-haired man, his eyes wide with terror, his mouth bellowing soundlessly over the roar of the water.

Yes. It was the crack-skulled, scar-handed Time-warper himself.

It was The Father.

38

'They're mad, I tell you!' The Father stammered through chattering teeth. 'They're absolutely stark staring mad!'

'Sure, but don't shout it so loud,' muttered The Volunteer glancing round nervously. 'We don't want to upset them.'

'Upset them!' cried The Father in a strangled whisper, responding readily to The Volunteer's paranoia. 'After what they've done to me I don't care if they burst into tears! They kidnapped me! Did you know that?'

'No, I didn't. I – that is to say, we – haven't been here very long.'

They had wrapped The Father in a blue velvet curtain stripped of its gilded rings and had laid him in the tepid sunlight that splashed through The Chapel window on to a sill of warm marble.

'Well they did,' The Father asserted. 'They kidnapped me, pushed me into a river mouth, made me smooth snow in shackles in a state of almost total amnesia, then, when I was beaten up and left for dead, they brought me down here on the river and sluiced me through a network of pipes until I popped up in that dish. They're mad I tell you!'

'Oh, really?' said The Volunteer, maintaining an appearance of composure by a supreme effort of self-control and staring with mute appeal at his companions.

'Yes!' The Father went on, 'and then they were going to unman me with a pair of shears, but suddenly this exploding hunchback fell out of the roof and burst open like a bag of marbles. And insects began crawling in from everywhere!'

He suddenly grabbed The Volunteer's hand as though the warmth of it would help heal the wounds that terror had opened up on his soul and he began to cry weakly, his shoulders shaking with relief.

'Yes,' he said, 'and they would have eaten me, only they couldn't get at me because I was floating in that bowl of water and then suddenly the whole place flooded and the bowl turned into a boiling fountain and threw me up and over, up and over for so long that I thought I was going to break into little pieces!'

He shuddered at the memory and his face collapsed in tears.

'They're totally mad!' he whined. 'Stark, staring, raving mad!'

'Yes, I suppose it must look that way,' agreed The Volunteer diffidently with a half-smile to Amrita intended to convey amused pity for the embarrassing old man. 'Never mind,' he went on, 'you'll forget all about it when you've had a good rest and recovered from it all.

'You are taking him away with you,' said Amrita, stoic acceptance of shame in her trembling voice.

Johnson and The Girl shook their heads and mouthed 'No. No' over her shoulder, but The Volunteer, frightened by the curious expression on her face, replied, 'Oh yes we certainly are. He's coming with us right now.'

He shot a glance of inventive pride at his companions adding, 'Now if you can just find his *flame-torch* for us, we'll be away.'

'Oh yes,' agreed the other eagerly, 'we'll take that too.'

'Flame-torch?' replied Amrita. 'He had no flame-torch.'

'Oh, sorry,' said The Volunteer, 'I thought that's what he said. I thought he said "don't forget my flame-torch when we go".'

'He didn't bring one. I'm sure of that,' Amrita replied flatly. 'I saw him come. I would have noticed if he had a flame-torch.'

'Oh I see,' said The Volunteer. 'Perhaps he meant he'd *like* a flame-torch.' He looked at The Father. 'You would, wouldn't you? You'd like a *flame-torch*,' he urged, nodding his head.

'No,' said The Father.

'Yes you would,' said The Volunteer persuasively.

'No I wouldn't,' said The Father.

'I think he's still a bit confused from his recent ordeal,' said Johnson, taking a step forward in the knee-deep slime and grimacing with impatient discomfort through what was meant to be a friendly smile. 'I'm sure he wants one really.'

'No I don't,' said The Father.

'He doesn't want one,' said Amrita.

'Yes, I think you might be right,' admitted The Volunteer. 'I don't think he wants one after all.'

He glanced round shrewdly.

'I expect they're all submerged in this muck anyway, aren't they?'

'What?'

'The flame-torches.'

Amrita shrugged.

'I don't know. I suppose so.'

She was becoming truculent now.

Why did they keep her standing here in the blood-thick water upon her injured foot?

Was it some kind of punishment?

And if so, was that fair?

Had she not led them immediately to their Brother?

And had she not stood by and let them pull him from the waters of Great Womb itself?

What greater act of penitence could they require?

Her mouth hardened.

Whatever it was, they could whistle for it.

'What's that door?' asked The Volunteer.

'The Great Courtyard Door,' replied Amrita stiffly.

'Where does it lead?'

'To the Great Courtyard,' she replied bluntly 'Many of us also died there.'

Johnson had wandered up through the tiers of seats, poking at the debris with a soaking boot.

'We'd love you to show us around the place,' The Girl put in brightly. 'Would you mind?'

'What about *him*?' Amrita asked, sullenly indicating The Father.

'He'll be alright there for a bit. Let him dry out for a bit,' said The Volunteer, then, leaning close to The Father's ear and speaking as though to a deaf mute, said,

'You're not going to run off anywhere, are you, Dad?'

He patted The Father's shoulder vigorously.

'No, look. He's shaking his head. He'll be alright.'

The Father's vice-like fingers closed desperately on the hand that shook him.

'Don't let them eat me!' he cried in a strangled whisper. 'Please don't let them eat me!'

'Don't worry, Dad!' The Volunteer shouted back. 'They won't lay a single tooth on you. Take my word.'

Suddenly there was an excited scream from Johnson and they turned to look for him along the highest tiers of seats.

'Sorry!' he shouted apologetically, signalling them to pay no attention. 'Thought I saw something. Made a mistake.'

'Jumpy,' The Volunteer explained to Amrita hastily. 'Not used to all this.'

He indicated the towering Chapel, its gleaming brasswork now smudged with soot and smoke, its velvet upholsteries streaked with

170

mud and littered with tiny, upturned carcases, its magnificent floors now lost beneath a flood of rotting mire. Amrita, who had been brought up to hold the Man-gods in awe and to assume her best tablemanners during the Feast of The Sacrifice as a token of respect, could not conceal her confusion at this seeming lack of moral fibre in The Holy Ones. Was this any way for Beings that claimed Omnipotence and Omniscience to behave? Screaming and flinching, hollow rictus smiles, nervous trembling and utter unease; were these the attributes of Godhead?

The Volunteer, sensing her creeping disenchantment, decided it was time to reassume control.

'After all,' he snapped, 'it *is* bloody untidy, isn't it?'

'Untidy?' stammered Amrita.

'All this bloody water,' replied The Volunteer sternly. 'All this mud and junk. Quite frankly. I've never been in a filthier Chapel in all my life! Why don't you clear it up a bit?'

'I'm sorry,' replied a chastened Amrita. 'If we'd known you were coming we could have—'

'Alright, alright,' said The Volunteer. 'We'll say no more about it for the moment. Now if you'll just show us round.'

'I think it's time to move on,' called Johnson urgently from high among the tiered ranks of seats.

He spoke with the clipped diction of one who is trying to say more than he is appearing to say and briefly held up a dripping flame-torch before concealing it swiftly behind his back.

'*I think we've seen enough*,' he shouted.

'Yes,' replied The Volunteer, almost squeaking with excitement, 'why don't we come back again when you've organized yourself a little better?'

Amrita hung her head in shame.

'And are you taking your fellow Man-god?' she said.

'Yes, we'll take him.'

His eyes lit up with a second flash of inspiration.

'But we'll need something to carry him on. Something with lots of room underneath. We always carry our sick people on something that has concealed hollow compartments somewhere in it. You'd better arrange that for us and you'd better get together some people to carry it.'

'Hidden compartments?' repeated Amrita in bewilderment. 'I don't know if there—'

'There was a table floating about near the stairs we came down,' suggested The Girl. 'That will do.'

'And make it snappy,' added The Volunteer brusquely, 'or we won't be able to answer for the consequences.'

And so it was that scarcely more than an hour later, a strange convoy floated out of the gates of the flooded Candle Palace heading for the sea.

The table from The Great Hall, its once shiny surface now dull and scuffed, carried the shivering frame of The Father, securely lashed 'for his own good' to the broad and gently rocking surface. Beneath him, secretly stowed and wrapped in innocent draperies, was the Flame-Torch, pirate's prize and repository of avaricious dreams.

And at each corner of the table moved a bewildered swimmer, pressganged into unaccustomed service and torn away from their Candle Palace home. Behind them, towed by silken lines cut from the useless kites, floated three wooden benches lashed firmly together, upon which perched the three sailors, anxiously scanning the horizon for signs of the ship's lookouts in their basket-kites, quietly exultant at the success of their secret mission and eager now only to return to their fleet and safely conceal their illegal treasure.

Consumed by their own greed, in the manner typical of their species, they gave no thought to the part they might be playing in the history of a land where time was reversing itself.

39

Meanwhile, Rogesse and her ragged Farmer Army toiled up the steepening foothills of the twin-spined mountains, bedraggled, dispirited and dusty in the pitiless clarity of the morning sun. The false Monarch strode ahead of the winding line of weary women, forcing a spring into her step that ill-matched the anxious exhaustion on her wrinkled face.

For years, for a lifetime, she had crouched in the shadow of the Queen of Steriles, carping treacherous, resentful and vindictive, respect and contempt growing, side by side and intertwined, in her uncomprehending heart. She had coveted the throne and despised the Queen, unable to see how the two were inextricably bound together. But now, as she and she alone led 'her' people in 'their' war, and felt them bleeding off her energy to sustain themselves, demanding from her, in their own weakness, a superhuman strength, she began to understand the penalty of absolute power. And each step she took into a future that she alone had framed was heavier with doubt and fear – fraught.

Once before had she marched with a desert army through the mountains, to meet the forces of The Others in the Candle Palace Plains, but then as Counsellor, not Queen.

How eagerly had she then bounded up the rock-strewn slopes, heart aflame with two different but equally delightful dreams; the one of Ana's success in battle, a united Queendom stretching from sea to sea, her own power growing in proportion to the Queen's; the other of Ana's death upon the field, her own accession to the Crown and Sovereignty over the Desert Tribes.

How happy she had been, waiting in the well-guarded pavilion that overlooked the battle plains from a strategically irrelevant and unthreatened hillside, knowing that all news would be good news and that if the worst came to the worst, things would merely remain the same.

And how she had chuckled, before combat began, to see the Queen's pale face, knotted with executive doubt, twisting into masks of courage, simulacrums of certainty to inspire her generals with confidence.

Now she too knew the agony of the royal role.

Bottomless dread in the face of bottomless doubt, realizing that the only single truth is that all decisions are arbitrary and that a ring of metal pressed against the skull is symbolic of majesty in a way that only queens could fully understand.

As she struggled up the foothills towards the pass through the mountains, terror gathered around her intuitive mind in billowing and ever darkening clouds.

*

She heard footsteps closing on her from behind and grimaced with dread, for she knew it would mean intercourse with one of her new-found subjects and that once again her flimsy façade of power would be put to the test.

'Oh Mightiest of Queens!' came a puffing voice behind her. 'The women are weary and grumble amongst themselves. They have eaten nothing since the sun last set and face the coming conflict with a fear as empty as their stomachs.'

Rogesse did not turn her head but set her jaw into the resolute profile of one whose burning ambition would not be quenched by some passing weakness in her warriors.

'Tell them they will dine at the tables of the Candle Palace if they do their work this day and that Destiny does not stop to break its fast.'

'Some have already turned aside to light fires, Your Majesty,' came the reply. 'I have kicked them on their way but they grow too many for me. Let them hear once more Your Royal Command that they may find obedience in their hearts again.'

Rogesse almost let loose the moan of fear that rose up inside her.

To dominate the women, strangers all, to override their fear, their resentment, their hunger and their exhaustion with nothing more than the Power of her Will expressed with voice and eye alone!

What if she tried and failed?

If they once flouted her command, how could she then reassert the charismatic power to drag them through the Valley of Death itself?

She framed her reply carefully.

'They have endured much, fought bravely, travelled fast and far. It is well that they should stop to gather their strengths for the final thrust. Order campfires built and food prepared. We will move out when they are recovered.'

'But what of their mutiny further down the trail? Is it wise to allow them to do what they were instructed not to do?'

Rogesse turned her anger upon her informant.

'And what of you,' she demanded curtly, 'who also fails to do what I have instructed must be done? Is that not a greater disobedience?'

The woman, withering beneath the weight of her displeasure, slipped away, shamefaced, to carry out the orders while Rogesse climbed a rock and sat upon it, as though it were a throne, assuming a pose of stern dignity to intimidate her troops.

But it was her own fear that swelled up inside her as she watched them gathering wood and breaking open their supplies. For as she looked at them closely for the first time in daylight she saw their raw physical power, the strength of desert farmers who scratched a living from barren dust and fought against the elements for life itself.

She saw how they drove their weary bodies through the ritual of making camp with the sheer power of dogged persistence and saw how many carried wounds that would have been mortal to a weaker will.

'Any one of these women could kill me with a single blow,' she marvelled. 'And yet my pride has subjugated them to me. How can that be? Do they not perceive my frailty as clearly as I see their strength? Who are these people that they should be so willing to follow?'

She knew little of their lives, for the Royal Court had ever isolated itself from its people save when unrest or Palace poverty had made it necessary to discipline the desert tribes with long-speared royal troops. Their feasts and festivals were unknown to her and never had she seen them gathered in such numbers until they had come, bewitched and bewildered, overcome by a Messianic madness, by some collective and hysterical climax to their religious destiny, dragging the ill-starred Yeni to be sacrificed at the feet of their Queen.

For they were a scattered and peripatetic people, planting in sand, feeding the roots with sea-algae, then feeding the plants to themselves and their few animals. After a few seasons the symbiosis would break down, the algae would feed upon itself, the plants would starve and the farmers would move on, leaving the sands to be cleansed by sun and wind, a strange race of nomadic meat-eaters, fishing without bait, planting without soil and herding without fences, forming rapidly into collectives which dissolved just as quickly for no apparent reason, scattering to join with other collectives in a seemingly random and cyclic dance; society held together by nothing more than a punitive and self-seeking Royal House that extorted heavy taxes to pay its soldiers and so built up a huge army to enforce the tax-extortion in a self-perpetuating circle of robber and victim, whose laws made no mention of goodness generosity and love although they spoke much of peace, freedom and penalty.

And as Rogesse turned these things over in her mind, it came to her with a creeping, throat-squeezing horror, that she had destroyed the Queen's army in order to become Queen and now stood alone in the royal robes, unarmed and unaided, in the very midst of the peoples who had been so savagely abused by the Royal Tents and now prepared a pitifully inadequate meal over damp twig fires, resentful and grumbling, led, they knew not why, into a battle from which they would gain nothing.

'I won't get away with it,' Rogesse muttered to herself. 'It needs only one of them to ask why they are beholden to me, by what divine right I claim to have inherited the Crown, and then it will be all up with me. At best they will simply abandon me. At worst they will cut me down where I stand.'

She tried to imagine what Ana's secret thoughts might have been at this time, how she would have asserted her Sovereignty over these people.

And memories came to her.

'Let them see by whom they are justly ruled in these troubled times!'

'Revolution is impossible. To succeed the people must strike at the Queen, a tiny and well-guarded target. The Queen, on the other hand, may strike back everywhere and anywhere amongst her subjects to punish them for their insolence, a massive and totally exposed target.' 'When the people cry out for blood, one must make sure that it is not one's own.'

And then,

'To be sacrificed is itself a sin that ignites the rage of the people. Therefore, when the sacrifice has been named, the people will instantly bring it to trial and execution, believing that they are saving themselves by so doing.'

And,

'When danger threatens, point out a sacrifice. The danger will devour the sacrifice and disperse, content.'

'Yes,' thought Rogesse. 'Let there be a sacrifice. Let them but have another Yeni and they will not forget to revere my wisdom and power.'

She giggled viciously.

'Perhaps the Queen herself will serve to demonstrate the truth of her own aphorism.'

She turned suddenly as she heard footsteps advancing once more upon her.

'What moves you to disturb the Royal Meditation?' she snapped as the aide approached, her body twisted awkwardly by the deference she hoped to show.

'The scouts,' she replied hesitantly, 'the scouts say there is a group of strangers further along the trail. A woman from the Others, a small Orphachin and one whose origins they dared not guess.'

'Ah!' thought Rogesse. 'No sooner is the idea conceived than the sacrificial beasts are delivered up.'

She spoke with crisp and certain authority.

'Select two dozen of the strongest women and take the strangers captive. Bring them to me unmarked and unharmed and let none speak to them on pain of death. Thus it comes about as it was prophesied in the ancient books,' she spoke with the lilting rhythm that The Crone had often employed to give out her oracular news. 'And on the very day of battle shall three sacrifices offer themselves for the slaughter. And at the moment of their death shall all impediment be removed from the brave warriors of the desert tribes and they shall have dominion over all the earth and want for nothing. So long as they shall pay homage to their rightful Queen.'

She spoke now with controlled lust.

'Quickly. Go and fetch them and we'll cut them to bits!'

40

Meanwhile, the relationship between The Dwarf, The Angel and myself had ripened rapidly over breakfast to what can fairly be described as 'intimacy'. At last it seemed that my years of lonely study, poring diligently over the ancient manuscripts, were beginning to pay off.

And I discovered that whereas the other goddesses, those with whom I had had such brief and unrewarding contact, walked naked, the full extent of their ghastly mutation exposed to view, this gentle creature wore clothing from neck to ankle and could be distinguished from a human being only by virtue of an atrophied face and skull, a squeaky highpitched voice and what seemed to be a permanent swelling about the lips. And so, spared the more disturbing aspects of angelic incarnation, I was able to relax in her presence and more easily recall the cabalistic language I had learned.

'What's a nice girl like you doing in a place like this?' I asked, seeking phrases that would trigger off the 'mating behaviour' towards which I knew the angels were particularly predisposed.

She made no reply but stared at me with an expression of timidity mixed with defiance which I immediately recognized as 'the seductive glance' or 'Sly come-hither stare' of The Teachings. I felt a surge of excitement.

'You going my way, Honey?' I enquired eagerly.

The Dwarf butted in, indicating the East and saying, 'Wah',

which, I suppose, could be roughly translated as,

'We intend to go in that direction',

or,

'That way',

or something similar.

Clearly, it was a separate species, for it spoke entirely in grunts, lip-smacking and wild gestures, seeming to know nothing of the magic language.

'Why don't you wiggle over here and cuddle up a little closer, Baby?' I said to the Angel.

At first I thought I had made my first big breakthrough, for she gave a brilliant smile in response and rose to her feet. But it soon became apparent that there had been a misunderstanding, for she carried the Dwarf over to where I sat and placed it, damp and aromatic, in my lap.

I pretended to be unconcerned, not wanting to repeat the foolish mistake I had already made during breakfast. After my initial success with my earlier greetings I had too quickly become overconfident and had lapsed, momentarily, into normal speech. Unthinking, I had blurted out the realities of my situation. 'I was in the Snowcamp,' I said suddenly. 'But all the others were drowned except for one!'

She had stared at me in horror, her eyes growing wide, her jaw falling open with shock.

'All The Others drowned except for one?' she repeated, apparently appalled at the coarsity of my speech.

And then, to my shame, she burst into inconsolable floods of tears.

That was my first and last lapse into the vernacular. I was careful not to make the same mistake twice.

Gradually her sobs abated and we were able, in due course, to communicate once more, after a fashion, although she remained pale and drawn, obviously deeply wounded by exposure to the common tongue.

But time was running out for me.

And for Brother One.

More than once my mind flew involuntarily to that of the Orphachins in the desert and discovered us, slavering and muttering, digging at the sand beneath which he and his goddess slept. Only with the greatest difficulty could we be persuaded to desist. Threats and entreaties became ineffectual, and finally I was forced to pretend that I was the god of the volcano and promise to come down to them from the mountains.

'No Gobbly,' I told them, 'and your God will visit you.'

My mind lurched back to the mountain pass and I realized there was no more time for smalltalk.

'Fancy a walk in the conservatory?' I asked the Angel and she appeared to nod, rising to her feet, stamped out the fire with her unnaturally small feet, picked up the Dwarf and set off in the direction of the desert. I had no idea what a conservatory was, but my heart leaped to recognize in her the symptoms of 'mating behaviour' – the quickened breathing, the parted lips, the occasional moans of pain – as we struggled over the twisting pathway down the mountainside.

Burdened though she was, she could make better progress than I, for though her steps were small they were rapid, whereas I constantly tumbled and tripped as my mind flickered back and forth involuntarily from mountain to desert, from where we were going to where we were, and I often lost my way, my footing or both as a result.

But between these unfortunate incidents I was able to give some thought to the nature of the relationship I had formed with the goddess.

Clearly, although I was using the appropriate language and had more than once elicited meaningful responses, there was much lacking in our intercourse. I wondered how it was possible for communications to improve while using stilted phrases learned by rote

179

from the inherited wisdom of my ancestors. Often I was nearly moved to speak openly and with spontaneity but held my tongue, fearful of snapping the delicate bonds of friendship that seemed, somehow, to have grown.

So I followed behind, concentrating most of my attention on the difficult descent and only occasionally uttering the odd aphorism to impress her with my erudition.

She made no reply.

'How's about some nookie, Fruitcake?'

'Whey, hey, hey, get a load of this.'

And so on.

But suddenly we were no longer alone.

Grimy, well-muscled creatures, wearing strange strips of material across their bodies and peculiar little helmets on their heads, rose up from the rocks all around us and, without sound or speech of any kind, closed in upon us, seized the Dwarf from the goddess, bound both of them with ropes and then, with fear and surprise in their eyes, encircled me at a distance, their spears wavering noticeably in their trembling hands.

I quickly noticed that these creatures, too, were goddesses, for they exhibited the same distended pectoral muscles that I had seen earlier on my boathouse captors. But they seemed unable or unwilling to speak and responded to my tentative greetings with a consternation that bordered on hysteria.

'I'm the Canoodling King,' I announced with a carefully lop-sided grin.

'Who's for a bit of slap and tickle?'

But their own reply was to wave me forward with their spears.

'Alright, ladies! It's leg-over time!' I said ingratiatingly, readily complying with their request and concealing my confusion under a veneer of light, bantering charm, using more abstruce idioms like,

'I wouldn't roll over her to get to you'
and
'Why! I've seen better bags with chips in!'
and so on and so forth.

But my façade of easy poise disintegrated as we rounded a bend in the pathway and came upon hundreds of the grimy half-naked goddesses squatted around tiny campfires, bickering hungrily among themselves or lying in attitudes of extreme exhaustion all over the stony slopes.

180

'Hot nuts!' I exclaimed, careful not to slip into the vernacular. 'Get a load of that!'

But these conventional and archaic phrases masked emotions that were far less dignified. The sight of the goddess encampment was like a blow to the stomach, the thought of what dread fate might await me among the alien horde was like a kick in the head and the realization that there was now little hope of reaching my brother in time to save his life was like a knife in the heart.

But all these several agonies, being emotional rather than physical were doubly penetrating and painful.

My appearance seemed to cause them much consternation. Some reached out for weapons, while others threw their weapons down in fright; some covered their mouths with their hands, while others ran to call out to their companions.

Was this the confused and feverish activity that preceded 'mating behaviour'?

If so, I was not at all sure that I liked it. I was reminded of certain descriptions in The Manuscripts of ritual religious activities in which mating behaviour was practised upon a single female angel against her will by many male angels. To my novice's eye, these had always seemed particularly arduous rities, especially for the female, and my heart sank at the intuition that such was now to be *my* fate.

'Thrown in,' as the textbooks might have put it, 'at the deep end.'

Suddenly, without warning, I found myself once more in the Orphachin consciousness, heard peevish protest at the unpunctuality of the promised god, and saw that many of us were glowering furiously at the volcano in red-eyed frustration, stamping our little feet in rage.

Desperation makes criminals of us all.

I confess, I foolishly succumbed once more to the temptation of unearned power.

'Your Goddy is held captive by enemies in the mountain pass!' I cried, filling our collective mind with my anxious urgency 'Aid him! Come to his rescue! Drive all other thoughts from your mind until you have released him from captivity!'

We froze where we stood, gripped by an alien and unusual alarm.

'Save him!' I cried again, more desperately, and found myself once more in the encircling ring of spears, stumbling down the rocky pathway.

I tried to cast my mind back to the Orphachins to ensure my brother's safety, but an imposing figure in the camp had captured my attention. As I drew closer I was relieved to see a second goddess clothed from neck to foot in a manner not dissimilar to my goddess friend. She sat upon a rock, somewhat apart from the others, an expression on her face not of fear, but of a stern and inflexible authority. Clearly she was their leader and I was being taken to her. My bound Angel and her Dwarf had already been thrown down at the foot of her rock and my nervous captors indicated that I too should approach.

I felt fear, but I believe I did not show it.

I stepped boldly up and gave her a smile of greeting and carefully chosen salutation.

'Hi, Toots,' I said. 'Stick this in your ear.'

41

Meanwhile Brother One stirred uneasy in his sleep, fragmentary dreams flickering about his mind.

He had slept badly, reliving in his nightmares the undersea upheaval that had flung him so fortuitously on to Orphachin Beach. He had felt the Earth tremble and bend once again, heard the boom and groan of vast geological voices calling to each other under the earth and once more abandoned himself to forces far greater than those which his body had been designed to withstand.

But something had changed.

No vertiginous spiral ascent this time.

No bruised and buffetting vortex, a slow diminuendo, a gradual fading of the buckling pressures within the earth and finally, a peace and silence in which Brother One's mind anxiously raced to stabilize itself. He opened his eyes to darkness.

'Where am I?'

He felt himself covered by sand and panicked, choking on the subtly permeating rock dust.

He clawed upwards desperately, broke through the surface and sat up, terrified and confused, his brain reeling to find the reality under-lying a world that had turned entirely grey, dominated by a belching mountain and peopled by grubby and hostile Orphachins, once his obedient army, who now stared at him hollow-eyed with rage.

And salivating.

'No Gobbly!' he cried in instinctive defence and sprang to his feet, shaking the unfamiliar dust from his clothing. He looked round sharply, counting quickly, and snapped,

'Where are the others?'

The Orphachins salivated at him weakly.

He stepped forward and cuffed the nearest over the head.

'The others!' he demanded. 'Where are they?'

The Orphachin stared round at his companions before pointing a crooked finger at the mountain.

'Goddy Goddy,' he mumbled with untrained and stumbling tongue.

Brother Two followed the finger and spied several tiny ripples in the distant sand moving swiftly towards the mountains. 'The fools!' hissed Brother One under his breath, 'What do they expect to gain from that?'

He cuffed four of the Orphachins and pointed down at the sand beneath which Yeni, she whom many called The Messiah, lay stretched in sleep.

'Fetchy, Fetchy,' he said, and then, indicating that all should follow him, he plunged into the sand and began to swim after the deserters.

Soon there was no sign of the grumbling group.

And had there been eyes to watch the scene, there would have been nothing to see save a silent, frightened Yeni travelling on her back across the desert at bewildering speed, each wrist and ankle clutched by a tiny hand attached to tiny arms that disappeared into the rippling sand.

But, scanning the surface of the desert carefully, those watching eyes might have also seen the tracks of Brother One and the Orpha-chins cleaving under the sand in formation like inverted mallards against a grey and thunderous sky, their passage marked only by tiny standing waves that subsided in the gently breathing breeze and left no trace.

And they might have seen that Brother One, using his superior

183

weight and strength, closed rapidly on his deserting troops. And as he passed each invisible, ripple-forming arrowhead, a disgruntled Orphachin materialized from the sand, standing upright, ruefully rubbing a cuffed ear or a punched head. And the leaders, telepathically cognizant of the turn of events, rose flinching, wincing and protecting their heads with their folded arms.

'Alright, you bastards!' shouted Brother One inaccurately, standing upright among them. 'What's going on here?'

The Orphachins pointed to the mountains and the guttural rumble of the volcano, and, 'Goddy, Goddy! Goddy, Goddy!' echoed into the foothills.

'That's just a subterranean upheaval, you dummies!' shouted Brother One and, stabbing himself in the chest with an assertive forefinger, cried,

'I am your Goddy! Me! The General! Not some spectacular natural phenomenon Goddy! Understand?'

The Orphachins glanced at each other, snarling in their minds, resentful. And Brother One, seeing the defiance in their eyes, yelled.

'Do you think a Goddy would do this to our desert?'

He kicked up the stinking dust that blanketed the sand.

'What kind of Goddy is that? *I* am your Goddy! I do *good* things for you. I teach you how to ambush properly and organize yourselves on useful military lines! I don't throw dust all over you and smother you in grime! Now we're going to wait here until the rest of us catch up and then we're going to split up into search parties and look for food!'

'Gobbly, Gobbly,' said the Orphachin closest to him.

'That's right,' agreed Brother One. 'In a little while – Gobbly, Gobbly.'

The Orphachins began slowly to close in upon him and from all sides rose the muttered mantra,

'Gobbly, Gobbly. Gobbly, Gobbly.'

Brother One, at first pleased, thinking his authority had been restored, nodded and smiled and said,

'You're good lads, really. Underneath you're not such bad chaps at all.'

But the smile faded from his face as he realized the true significance of those saliva sibilant words and the Orphachins moved into an ever-tightening ring around him.

'Gobbly, Gobbly,' they jabbered, their voices rising and echoing in the mountains.

'Gobbly, Gobbly.'

'Now wait a minute!' protested Brother One, suddenly scared.

'What's got into you guys?'

'Gobbly, Gobbly,' was the ever more enthusiastic response.

The General thought with lightning speed and glanced up at the mountain.

He raised his arm and pointed to the lowering volcano.

'Goddy!' he shouted excitedly. 'Look! Goddy! Follow me!'

And, plunging into the sand, he snaked under their feet and set off with bewildering speed towards the rising foothills.

The Orphachins, momentarily at a loss, but prepared to go along with anything that did not get in the way of what they wanted to do, took up the pointing cry,

'Goddy, Goddy!' and disappeared one by one into the sand.

And soon, had there been eyes to watch, they would have seen the arrowing sand moving swiftly once more towards the West, this time with Brother One's larger waves leading the rest and driving towards the mountains.

And deep within the earth, in the boiling belly of the globe, the Forces of Chaos withdrew slowly from their window on the sky, their destruction done, their anger evaporated, their rage released. They had made reply to the grinning, baleful moon and now retreated to the privacy of their fire-tossed chambers to sulk and stew in their own alchemical preoccupations.

But what had been their part in the exoteric chemistry of the damaged island and in what way had they pushed the path of the world towards totality and peace, the sum of all parts? The insect hosts called up by the horned moon were washed away in the floods, overwhelmed by an excess of the very element that their goddess ruled. They had come and gone, leaving only a scar of fear on the memory of conscious beings to mark their existence.

So it goes.

The pack of Kings and Queens, Gods and Mortals, shuffled by the moon, had been reshuffled by the Earth, throwing up new yet familiar patterns, fresh manifestations of the same wheel, offering new choices from old permutations and enabling all to choose again the paths their destinies were to take. The magic numbers had revolved and with them the roles and futures of their separate symbols.

Brother One, The General, the Cheesecake Charlatan, clinging on to his fingernail authority, now cried 'Goddy!' to the volcano's shell and believed it not.

Brother Two, caught for a second time in the trap of selfstyled Godhead, had telepathically declared himself Divine to The Cannibal Kids, believing that survival justified the blasphemy.

Yeni, She whom Many called The Messiah, was dragged on still by overwhelming force, but now upon her back.

Ana, Queen of Women, selfstyled Matriarch of The Earth, flew free. But her body was imprisoned in the same box that had for so many years imprisoned her oracle, The Crippled Crone, who, perhaps not for long, perhaps for ever, had stolen her destiny, along with her face and frame.

And Rogesse, The Hypocrite, schemed to conceal her hypocrisy even from herself by subsuming the symbolic power of Tomaly-Somaly, bee-brained but curiously pure, and The Last Child of Woman Born in ritual sacrifice.

So, on the surface, it appeared.

But what of the Neo-Navy, extracontinental pirates, mercenary ecolunatics, drawn into the drama by the seismic rumblings of a disturbed Earth? What new attribution did they represent as they turned their prows Northwards to begin the circumnavigation of the island and assess the fate of its inhabitants in terms of Plague-Dogs slavering in the holds?

And what of their missing officers, ferrying The Father on floating furniture, piloted by Candle Palace porters, drawing ever-closer in the floodwaters to the mysterious fishing village which even Brother Two had been afraid to explore when first he emerged transcendentally from his many-fathomed exile?

And if the Whale survived, she who had mothered many without herself being called Mother, would she know the secrets of the future from the inaccessible coils of the present?

Is there, indeed, any order in Cyclic Chaos or is life itself merely the rolling of the wheel?

'Gobbly, Gobbly,' said the Orphachins.

'Goddy, Goddy,' shouted Brother One.

'Release us!' screamed Tomaly-Somaly.

'Wah!' cried the Last Child of Woman Born.

'Hi, Doll-face,' quipped Brother Two.

'Faster, faster,' yelled the Volunteer and his fellow-criminals with their stolen fire.

Yeni, she whom many called The Messiah, said nothing.

And The Crone, snoring hollowly, snoozed inside her box.

Now read on.

42

Meanwhile, in the creaking silence of his wooden cabin, the Admiral sat among his scrolls worrying about the three winged deserters, head in hands, scarcely listening to The Navigator's voice as she read from a Thinkers' Report on the probable development of a Technological Criminal society.

'The young fools! The young hot-heads!' he muttered as phrases like 'romanticized cannibalism' and 'alienation as a sexual response' filtered through to his worried mind.

'Self-death,' he said finally. 'That's all they'll achieve by going ashore. There's nothing we can do for them now.'

He stopped The Navigator with a dismissive wave of the hand.

'That's enough, thankyou. It makes me sick to hear it.'

'Well it's no fun reading it either,' she replied tartly 'Those Thinkers much be sick in the head to dream up all that stuff!' She threw the report down on the table.

'So what are you going to do? Send in The Dogs anyway?'

He pursed his lips and cleared his throat nervously.

'Eventually, yes, I still feel we have no choice.'

He rose to his feet and prepared to climb the ladder to the bridge.

'And I'll thank you to make no comment,' he said curtly, seeing The Navigator open her mouth to speak. 'I'm in command here.'

He climbed up into the morning sun, tried to open himself to its warming strength, but failed to reach the knots of tension ravelled up and stored in his musculature.

'This business is taking its toll,' he reflected. 'I haven't been as knotted up as this since my last separation.'

He gazed out to starboard where the North-Western coast of the island slid somnolently past, dense green vegetation struggling in unhealthy profusion down the slopes to dribble its tendrils in the poisoned sea. Here and there a brightly-plumaged bird would hurl itself into the clear sky screaming in fright, escaping predators just one more time.

But the loudest noise of all was the silence; an oppressive, attentive silence as though each creature strained its hearing for a stealthy footfall while placing its own stealthy feet with murderous guile one before the other in the slow dance of survival and death.

'What do you think?' he asked The Watcher, who stared intently and with seemingly unfocussed eyes, into the impenetrable undergrowth.

'It looks unlikely and I see nothing,' replied the woman. 'If this weren't a Technological island I'd say all that stuff was empty, but I'm not sure what's possible with these people.'

'Try not to let it intimidate you,' said The Admiral. 'Their reputation for intelligence is phony. The powers they have are not their own. They just steal energy from other structures and convert it to their own plane of existence. Don't confuse the two. I suspect we'll find they've become extremely weak after having relied for so long on the leverage of the external universe instead of developing their own internal strength.'

'I listen to you, but I don't hear you,' replied The Watcher bluntly and gave a movement of her shoulders as though to terminate their dialogue.

Typical of Watchers, thought The Admiral, whose special insights on peculiar levels make them blind on others. Always the same. You couldn't win. The longer the oar, the fewer the strokes. There was no way round it. Heaven was a ceiling through which no man could pass and only the infinite could conceive infinity.

He listened to the movements on board ship and noticed that here too there was a strange silence. Even the oarsmen had stopped singing and the rowing drum had ceased its beating though the boat still cut swiftly through the water.

'We are frightened,' he thought. 'All of us. Filled with a fear that is more than Death Fear. This is something new. This is fear of ourselves, our race, of what we would have become if History had not carried us to safety with its devious twisting benevolence. We are afraid that we might see ourselves as we would have become, dreading the loathing and the pity it will wring from us.'

He shuddered involuntarily and drew his coat closer about him in the warm air.

'Dead Ones!' said The Watcher suddenly, staring into the blanket of greenery that suffocated that quarter of the island. 'Long dead. Strays. Lost. Attacked from within by micro-organisms. Consumed.'

She gave a grunt of contempt and settled herself against the wooden handrail again in an attitude of patient concentration.

'How long ago?' asked The Admiral.

'Who cares?' replied The Watcher, giving the same dismissive shrug of the shoulders.

'Yes,' thought The Admiral. 'She's right. Who cares?'

The vegetation began to spread over huge grey rocks that thrust at ancient angles from the land and thick-leaved, perfumed trees gave way to smaller, coarser soil-scavengers, tumbling guiltily down steepening rockfaces as the galleys began to round the Northern end of the scarab-shaped island. Soon these too were gone and in the cracks and ledges where they might have clung fisher-birds screamed belligerently from their thatched nests.

'I'm getting to think this whole island is empty,' said the woman resentfully. 'And I'm losing my concentration.'

'Go below and eat, then,' replied The Admiral readily, for he did not enjoy the company of Watchers. What little insight they had into humanity curdled and soured them.

The watcher shrugged and left the bridge with a look of distaste upon her face.

'Be back here in fifteen minutes,' said The Admiral. 'The Eastern side is desert.'

She gave him the empty, searching, discomfiting stare of the Seer and disappeared.

He shook his head to remove the image of those penetrating eyes.

'Who cares?' he wondered again. 'Is that what we've been reduced to? So conscious of the cycle of Life and Death that we cease even to marvel at its rotation or wonder which way it moves?'

He gazed up at the cliffs that now towered over the tiny galleys of his fleet, throwing black sunless shadows over the dark waters upon which their narrow wakes spread like mirrored oil and he wondered if the dark stones knew them, had known other creatures that had passed beneath their stony gaze and if there was judgment in that silent, brooding solemnity. He shuddered again and rustled through his charts.

'I must stop this,' he thought. 'This is sea-dread. It will send me mad.'

He tried to concentrate on the scarab-shaped outlines hurriedly scribbled in charcoal upon the woven cloth, but he saw only an abyss of selfdoubt and uncertainty in their wavering lines.

'We can map lands that we have never seen, chart seas we have never sailed upon, predict lives we have never lived and still we ask ourselves "Who cares?" ' he muttered. 'What use are Thinkers if they cannot answer that question first? Or Watchers if they cannot see the shadow of the divine inside a human being? Better, perhaps, that we destroy ourselves in greed and hatred than fill this vapid, unemotional vacuum that we have designed for ourselves.'

He turned to stared into the deep inky waters beneath the sliding galleys and felt himself drawn into their silent certainty.

'This is ridiculous,' he said. 'I'm giving myself over to some unhealthy intelligence that lives on these shores. I'd better fortify myself before I heave myself over the side into the sea.'

And so, pausing only to balance himself on the balls of his feet and to take several deep and calming breaths, he began to dance about the bridge and sing The Song of Happiness (Sailors), in a stiff and rusty guttural voice.

'Oh I am a jolly jack tar,' he sang. 'And I sail the ocean blue. And as sure as hell I'll ring my bell when I get home to you.'

He broke off to execute a tricky series of steps that took him back to his starting-point.

'Oh, I am a navy blue,' he went on. 'And I've seen a thing or two. But blow me down, we'll hit the town when I get home to you.'

His spirits lifted, he attempted a double cartwheel across the deck, slipped on the second but regained his balance by means of a twisting handstand then, spinning round and round with arms flailing, opened his throat in song once more.

'Oh, I am a roving sea-dog. And sure as a pig is a free hog, I'll fill you in with my rolling pin when I come—'

He became aware of The Watcher's eyes staring at him from floor level as she clung to the ladders and he skidded to a halt by his lectern and, for a moment, made a pretence of reading his charts.

'Permission to come up on the bridge, sir,' said The Watcher drily, irony treacling the formal request.

'Permission granted,' he replied with a private grin. 'Thought I told you to eat something.'

'Did, Sir.'

'Good. Good,' said the Admiral. 'Just doing some callisthenics while I was waiting.'

'I'm sure you were,' she replied, turning her searchlight eyes towards the island.

'Good to keep in shape,' insisted The Admiral.

'Yes, I'm sure it is,' she replied indifferently,

And then, with no change in her voice, said,

'Live Ones. Two.'

She turned her head from side to side, scanning the island with her peculiar vision and then pointed through the headland.

'On the other side of the point. A beach. Two live ones. Sick. Filled with poison, though they will not die from it.'

The Admiral moved swiftly to the Speaking Tubes at his lectern and rattled out orders with clarity and precision.

'Boats one and two, prepare to put off within four minutes. One Translator to go ashore. Volunteers report to the Cox of Boat One. Full protective clothing. Beast-Leashers – two Dogs in covered cages. No one to put foot on shore except the Translator without further orders. Lieutenants of the Watch to the bridge immediately. Jump to it.'

He turned to The Watcher.

'Anything else?'

'Beast-Leashers?' she demanded angrily.

'Attend to your duties or go below!' snapped The Admiral and was relieved to see her turn her face once more, reluctantly, towards the shore.

'They sleep,' she muttered truculently. 'They are women. Since when did our Navy send Plague-Dogs against sick and sleeping women?'

The Admiral's galley rounded the headland and two huddled specks became plainly visible on the narrow beach. Over the clatter of four lieutenants climbing eagerly up to the bridge a voice squeaked from the Speaking Tubes.

'Boats One and Two ready, Sir.'

'Boats One and Two away,' rasped The Admiral. 'And the best of luck.'

43

The two graceful boats slipped swiftly from their waterline kennels and bounded over the tranquil sea towards the grey and scummy shoreline. Even high up on the bridge The Admiral and his lieutenants could hear the hysterical grumbling of the Plague-dogs in their shrouded cages and the creaking squeal of the twisted wooden bars as the animals thrashed about in white-eyed lunatic rage.

In the bow of the leading boat the Translator stood in noble attitude, one foot on the gunwale, one hand on his knee, both eyes fixed unwavering upon his distant quarry.

'New shores!' he announced in a resonant baritone, indicating the island with a wave of his gauntletted hand to his oarsmen, all pale-faced, but grinning broadly from the effects of supportive herbs. 'Shores upon which no foreign foot has trod for century upon century.'

Behind the thickly-gauzed face-mask his eyes lit up with inspirational fervour. 'For a millenia!' he cried excitedly, expanding on his theme.

He lifted a thickly-booted foot and pointed at it as though it were some separate living creature.

'This foot, gentlemen,' he continued, 'is about to step through the barrier of time itself and break the impenetrable seal that has imprisoned these creatures, their fathers, their forefathers and their even more former fathers for generation upon generation.'

The rowers exchanged droll glances beneath their brows although anxiety still lay upon their faces like a stiff and lifeless mask.

'Pipe down!' came a shout from the second boat. 'Or we'll set the Dogs on you!'

And there was a ripple of sudden laughter over the swiftly-crossed water.

The Translator, interrupted and thrown out of rhythm, took up his heroic stance again, attempting to recapture the grandiose emotions he had been enjoying.

He failed.

There was a lump in his throat and his heart beat loudly in the blood around his ears.

He was frightened and he knew that his Partner on The Admiral's bridge would know it.

But even as this passed through his mind, a warm thought came to him.

'It is alright to be frightened,' came the thought, 'for this is frightening.'

He looked back to the row of white faces lining the rail of the towering bridge and a hand waved.

He waved back.

'Thank you,' he thought.

'You're welcome,' came the reply in his head. 'I love you.'

The boats ploughed on in a wordless silence broken only by the tittering of the oarsmen, the slavering of the Dogs and the soft hiss of the Beast-leashers keeping their charges on the boil. All eyes measured and re-measured the narrowing distance between boat and beach until, finally, the Cox gave the order to ship oars and the boats drifted gently through the littered shallows to bump against the shore.

'Here I go,' sad the Translator without enthusiasm, making no move to put foot ashore.

'You have to do it,' came the thought.

'Yes, here I go,' he replied.

And with a monumental effort of will he forced himself to step into the shallow waters.

*

On the Admiral's bridge they watched in tense silence as the tiny, white, padded figure waddled up the beach, a single line of footprints trailing behind him, curiously widely spaced as a result of his cumbersome protective clothing. His Partner, trembling herself, sharing his secret terror, reported,

'He is afraid but determined. He will not turn back.'

The two pinpoint recumbent figures on the sand did not stir as he drew nearer.

'He sees them now,' the Partner reported, and shuddered with vicarious fear as the image came to her. 'Everywhere there are metals!' she said in a horror-choked voice. 'On their clothing, even upon their fingers. And there is a machine!'

She let out an involuntary scream and almost fainted away upon the deck.

'What is it?' urged The Admiral, supporting her with his arm. 'What is it?'

She turned to him with pleading in her eyes.

'Call him back,' she begged. 'Please call him back!'

'What *is* it?' insisted The Admiral. 'What has he seen?'

She turned to stare desperately at the distant scene.

'They have *fire!*' she whispered through a terror-tight throat and at her words a ripple of anguish passed among the others.

'Brace yourself!' ordered The Admiral sternly. 'Or we'll lose him.'

The Partner nodded and grasped the wooden rail tightly, as though drawing strength from it.

'They are torturing some creatures in water over the flames,' she went on gamely. 'The smell of it is horrible. Oh, the agonies they suffer! And the women are not asleep. He can see them staring at him through lowered lids. He raises his hand in greeting. "Hail" he says!'

She spoke with the rapid, absentminded clarity of all simultaneous translation.

'One of them is struggling to sit up. "Hail," he says, "I am your friend." One of them tries to speak.'

She struggled to find words, her face took on a glazed expression and her eyes began to roll in her head.

She had achieved empathy with the creature.

'Yer a fren, hey?' she said in thick-lipped, heavily-slurred accents. 'Well, any fren of ours will either pissof or siddown an have a lill drink.'

She reached up with a trembling hand and clutched her forehead.

'Oh, shit,' she croaked with slobbering lips, 'Me head feels like a sword through it!'

And she passed out on the deck with a grunt.

'Bring a pallet up on to the bridge!' ordered The Admiral as he motioned a lieutenant over to help him raise the prostrate form. 'This is going to be a tough one.'

He glanced up at The Watcher who stood to one side in sneering detachment.

'What happens?' he asked.

The Watcher shrugged.

'The poison, I suppose. But these Translators are so feeble that it could be almost anything.'

The girl opened her eyes and stared blankly at the sky for a moment before realizing where she was and scrambling to her feet in embarrassment.

'I'm sorry,' she said. 'I must have—'

She broke off and turned quickly to the rail, searching out her Partner on the distant shore.

'He is calm,' she said with relief in her voice. 'He is seeing it through.'

She glanced quickly at The Admiral.

'You couldn't call him back, could you?'

The Admiral took her arm, half-supportive half-intimidating.

'Let's keep going. I'm sure he can take it for a little longer.'

She uttered a trembling sigh, swallowed with difficulty and applied herself once more to her duties.

'He turns to the second creature. "Hail," he says. "I am your friend." She looks afraid. She tries to crawl away but is too sick. "Friend," he says again, pointing to himself, "I am your friend". The first creature speaks from where she lies.'

Once more her face took on a glazed and stupid look and The Admiral motioned a young seaman who was carrying a pallet on to the bridge to make haste and place it behind her. 'Give him a drink, Widge!' said the girl indistinctly.

' "Come on you. Siddown and have a drink." She offers him – oh – she offers him something metal!'

Her hands fluttered anxiously to her mouth.

'No don't take it!' she cried.

'Control yourself!' said The Admiral. 'Or you will be sent below. Do not interfere. It will only endanger him!'

'I'm sorry,' she replied. 'You are right, I know. Anyway, he's already taken it. It is a form of cup and contains a liquid that is something to do with the machine that tortures vegetables but smells like nothing I have ever smelled before.'

'Poison,' guessed The Watcher bluntly. 'They're both sick with it already.'

'Be silent!' snapped The Admiral. 'Speak when so ordered!'

'He does not drink it,' put in the Partner. She glanced over at The Watcher. 'He has more sense, even though he does not know it for poison.'

'Please,' said The Admiral, intervening as gently as his anxiety would allow. 'Let us concentrate on the job in hand.'

The Partner turned back to the island and her face immediately became slack and stupid.

' "I know who *you* are!" ' she slobbered. ' "You're from the Queen." '

' "No," he replies, 'I come from another world." "Hear that, Widge?" she crows. "Says he comes from another whirl. Did you hear?" '

Suddenly one lid lowered, her eyes turned inwards and when she spoke her voice was rough and hoarse.

' "Sounds like bad news to me." "I come from across the sea," he is saying and they stare at him with disbelief. "Sure, sure, pull the other one, Sister. Haw, haw." He is confused. He does not understand their sickness. "Where are the rest of those who live with you?" "Aw, all the sisters have gone off to the Queen with that Yeni girl," she slobbered and then her eyes crossed. "Yeah, the little bleeder!" She coughed, broke off in riotous laughter and fell back on the pallet, slapping her thighs and guffawing. "They think it's going to make the crops grow better".'

She tried to tap the side of her nose with a finger, missed, then struggled to sit upright again.

' "But you wanno know what I think?" He is nodding yes. "I think the Queen's been dead for years and they've kept quiet about it. Because answer me this one".'

Her face took on a shrewd and cunning look.

' "If the Queen's out there on her throne, how come she don't know that me and Widge got this still going out here, and how come her soldiers haven't come and took all our carrot whisky like they used to? Answer me that one. You can't, can you?" '

She sat upright with a look of superiority struggling to assemble itself from the rubbery muscles of her drooping face.

' "And where are your menfolk?" he is saying.'

She broke off again and began to tremble violently.

'Oh no!' she cried and sprang from the pallet to stare with anxious concern over the distance that separated ship from shore.

'They have metal weapons in their hands!'

Her face dissolved into truculence and her eyes swivelled inwards.

' "Okay, buddie!" ' she wheezed menacingly. ' "Just who the hell are you?" "I'm your friend," he is saying. He is very frightened by the metal weapons.'

Her face fell to pieces again.

' "Yer one of them damn sea-slugs aren't yer! One of them things that comes up out of the water! Come on, let's cut it up, Widge".'

Her eyes swivelled.

' "Let's put it in the still and see if it makes good liquor".'

She screamed and fainted onto the pallet.

The Admiral knelt swiftly by her side and raised her eyelids.

'She's out!' he said 'We've lost contact with him!'

He stood up and peered out towards the shore.

The clumsy white doll was stumbling with awkward frantic haste towards the boats while the other figures, sick though they were, more accustomed to the yielding sand, blundered determinedly after him, threading a rapid line of wavering footprints behind his slow straight tracks.

'They gain on him,' said The Watcher without excitement. 'If they catch him they will cause him unnecessary Death.'

A lieutenant stepped up urgently.

'Permission to send out a battle-boat, Sir!'

'No,' said the Admiral, with an air of severe authority that was belied by the nervous twitching of his fingers.

He glanced up at the lookouts in their basket-kites, hovering upon the high altitude winds, swooping backwards and forwards in lazy moebius loops to maintain height in the invisible liquid currents.

'Flagman!' barked The Admiral.

'Yessah!' replied a small sailor waiting by the flagpole.
'Signal to shore party.'
'Yessah. What signal, Sir?'
The Admiral took a deep breath.
'Unleash the Beasts!'

44

Meanwhile, for the Armada's three absent crew-members, things were not much rosier. Adverse currents had slowed their progress and, more than once, their makeshift raft had struggled free from its bonds, separated onto its component parts and tossed them into the murky waistdeep water.

Every five minutes, Johnson's voice would begin whining.

'I told you we should have brought a boat. I said that right from the start. But no, cleverdick knew better, "we'll just send up a signal and The Admiral will come and pick us up," he said. "It couldn't have worked out better," he said. Well all *I* know is that almost anything would have worked out better than this!'

At first there had been excited discussions about the future and the possible price they might get for the Flame-Torch on the black market, but now they were too tired and wet and cold to sustain any emotion other than miserable anger.

'Right from the start I said it,' Johnson was saying again. ' "Let's take a boat," I said, "let's take a boat so we can get back without any trouble." But did anyone take any notice? Did anyone stop for *one* minute and say "you know, I think there might be something in what Johnson is saying"?'

He laughed bitterly.

'Did they fiddlesticks!' he cried in answer. 'They said—'

'Please shut up, Johnson,' said The Girl. 'You're giving me a belly ache. I don't know what you're complaining about. You're always peeping round curtains on the bath-deck and here you are surrounded by naked women engaged in strenuous physical activity. I'd have thought it would be a dream come true.'

'They said, "No," ' Johnson went on, unruffled. ' "Let's *not* take a boat," they said. "We can simply send up a signal and—" '

'Where are all the naked men? That's what I want to know,' said The Girl.

' "And the Admiral will come and pick us up".'

'I didn't see any men in that Palace except Grandpa over there.'

'That's very curious,' agreed The Volunteer. 'I suppose I hadn't realized that, but you're absolutely right.'

'So what happens?' said Johnson. 'I'll tell you what happens. Instead of sitting in safety and comfort, slicing through the water like a tree falling over, we're sitting on three benches—'

'Why don't you ask Grandpa where everyone is?'

'He said they threatened to eat him,' said the Volunteer.

'Maybe that's what happened to the rest of them.'

He grimaced nervously and glanced around at the exhausted struggling women pushing the heavy furniture through the waters.

'Come to think of it, I suppose that is quite a possibility.'

'Practically at a standstill,' Johnson went on. 'Chattering with cold, wringing wet.'

The Volunteer pulled on the silken rope and drew their knotted benches up to The Father's table.

'And no certainty of ever meeting up with the Fleet again,' Johnson continued. 'You've thought of that, I suppose? You've got some *contingency plans* for us never being able to get off this bloody island because we "didn't need a boat", I suppose?'

The bumping benches woke The Father from a restless snooze and he looked round in panic, straining at the ropes that held him secure.

'Don't eat me!' he yelled. 'You mustn't eat me!'

'Don't worry, old man,' The Volunteer shouted back with some irritation. 'You're safe with us!'

The Father rolled back his eyes wildly and stared at the young officer upside down.

'They're going to eat me,' he confided in a low strangled whisper. 'This river leads down from the Snowcamp to the Palace and they put you in this enormous underground canal and the next thing you know, all the water shoots up and you're in this enormous bowl with thousands of them staring at you and someone with a helmet comes with a great pair of shears to—'

'Alright, alright,' snapped The Volunteer. 'What I want to know is where are the other *men*?'

'Where are the *ships*?' put in Johnson in mocking tones, 'that's more to the point. Where are these ships we're just going to send up a signal to?'

'And the next thing is this hunchback falls out of the roof and explodes all over the floor!'

' "Couldn't have worked out better," he said. Well I don't see how it could have worked out worse! Here we are—'

'Just tell us what happened to the other men!' snapped The Volunteer, trying to keep his voice too low for the women to hear yet shouting over Johnson's monologue at the same time.

'And then all these insects come! That's what happens! Millions and millions of them! Crawling over each other's backs. Just *eating*! That's all they do you know, they just *eat*. But they can't get at you properly because you're in this pool of water, do you follow me?'

'Practically marooned on this floating bloody furniture and we don't even know whether the ships will still be there when we get to the beach, although I can make a damn good guess where they'll be at this time of the morning, they'll be round the other side of the bloody island. *That's* where they'll be. Ho, ho, they won't hang around waiting for us to show up, you can be sure of *that*.'

He gave out a hollow sardonic laugh.

'We're just *deserters*!' he affirmed.

'But they try to get at you anyway!' hissed The Father, his eyes wide with the horror of it. 'You can see them looking at you! You can tell that they *know* you're there and they just walk towards you and fall in the water and they're drowning, but they're still trying to get at you because if they can reach you they're safe, you see, they know that, so they're desperate to reach you, hundreds of them, crawling on each other's backs, treading each other under the water, just coming for you by the million and you have to sort of swim with your fingers to stay in the middle where they can't get you, but it's terribly hard because your clothes are all frozen from lying in the snow!'

'Listen!' snapped The Volunteer. 'Just answer me one simple question. Is that too much to ask? Just one question?'

'Where are the boats? That's what you should ask him, clever-Dick.'

'Shut up, Johnson,' said The Girl. 'This is important.'

'Don't tell *me* to shut up,' retorted Johnson. 'And don't tell me what's important and what's not important. *I* thought a boat was important before we ever set out on this lunatic journey. But did anyone agree? Did anyone say, "Johnson, you're quite right. We ought to take a boat"? Did they?'

'Why are you the only man we've seen? How come you're the only man amongst all these women?'

'Yes,' said The Father, 'and just when you think that you can't hold out any longer, these women come in with this incredible sheet of flame in front of them and slowly move across the floor frizzing all the insects up and there's all this smoke and soot and stink and the stench is awful so you're choking on this burnt body dust and there's still a lot alive and still trying to get at you and then—'

'Make him stop!' hissed The Girl. 'He's giving me the creeps!'

'You shut *Johnson* up,' retorted The Volunteer. 'How can I question him with that drivel going on and on?'

'Just *ignore* it!' she retorted. 'That's what *I'm* doing! Don't tell me what to do. Just get the old man to give some coherent answers!'

'Now who's telling who what to do?' replied The Volunteer.

'Shut me up, is it? That's what it's down to, is it?' put in Johnson, in a voice of pained disgust. 'The one person that's said *anything* intelligent and now you're talking about shutting me up! Isn't that bloody typical!'

'And then they see you there, trying to stay afloat in the bowl, and they say "There he is! There's the one that made all this happen! Burn him to a crisp and all the insects will go away!" And they come for you with this sheet of flame and they cut a wide path through the insects and the dust gets worse and you can't breathe and all the time they're coming closer and closer!'

The Girl suddenly leaped from the bound benches on to the table with an expression of naked savagery on her face. Her voice was a shrill hysterical scream.

'What happened to the other men?' she shrieked, shaking The Father by the shoulders with all her strength. 'Tell us! Tell us! Tell us!'

'As if knowing *that* is going to do the slightest bit of good,' jeered

Johnson to an invisible audience in the sky. 'What we need to know is how we're going to get home if the boats have gone.'

'Don't *do* that!' shouted The Volunteer, grabbing The Girl's wrists and forcibly restraining her. 'You'll shake him to Death!'

'Let go of me!' she cried, struggling violently. 'Let go! Let go.'

'Not until you promise not to be violent.'

'It's *you* who's being violent! Let go!'

'And to think I could be up on the bridge at this very moment. Just taking a little cruise around the island to see what there is to see and then getting ready to go below for something to eat,' mused Johnson.

'And then suddenly, just when the heat from the flames is becoming so intense that even the insects in the water are beginning to frizzle up, there's this terrific booming noise and the wind starts to smash against the windows and there's this terrible noise of water rushing down the valley and even the water in the bowl begins to tremble and the walls of The Chapel begin to shake and crack from floor to ceiling and you can hear the wooden beams in the roof exploding and all the glass falls out of the windows and breaks into pieces on the floor.'

'If you don't let go of me this instant I can't be held responsible for what I might do,' yelled The Girl.

'You don't appear to be acting responsibly *anyway*. I shall need some assurance that you've calmed down.'

'Alright! I've calmed down!' she snapped.

'You don't look as though you've calmed down.'

'Well I have. I'm perfectly calm. Let go.'

'You're shouting again.'

'Now look!' she screamed, purple with rage and kicking at him with both feet. 'I'm perfectly calm and in full possession of my faculties. Let go of me or I'll have your eyes out!'

'And then later on,' Johnson was saying, 'I'd probably take a kite and drop in on Jarvis' ship and trade some jokes with him. Jarvis has got more jokes than anyone else in the Fleet.'

'And this tidal wave hits the building with a noise that must be like the explosion that the First-Base Fabricatory workers heard just before Bubble-up and the whole place seems to bend and buckle under the impact of this massive torrent!'

'If you just show me you can stay still for one moment I'll let you go,' argued The Volunteer, hanging on grimly.

202

'Who the hell do you think you are to make conditions to *me*!' replied The Girl trying to scratch his face and kick his legs at the same time. 'Just let me go!'

'He'd probably tell me the end of that one about the man with three legs who wanted a new uniform made.'

'And then suddenly all the water in the bowl turns into a huge fountain because the floodwaters have rushed into the underground canal, you see, and it comes through with such force that you're lifted bodily into the air. You saw me! Higher than the Council Cave Complex! And you're balanced on this liquid spout and there's nothing you can do about it!'

'I'm giving you formal warning,' said The Volunteer, holding on tenaciously to The Girl's wrists beneath a hail of blows. 'If you don't stop attacking me I'm going to have to temporarily disable you.'

'Just let me go! Threatening me won't do any good! How *dare* you assault me like this?'

'So he goes to this tailor and he says "I want a new uniform and I want it to be especially smart and well-cut" and this tailor looks down and sees he's got three legs so he thinks "I must have been working too hard. It looks like this chap's got three legs". So he pretends not to notice and says "Alright, come back next week and I'll measure you up." '

'Look!' said The Volunteer suddenly.

And even Johnson stopped talking.

In the distance was a white fishing village that stared imperturbably out to sea.

And from one of its chimneys a curl of smoke rose lazily into the blue sky.

'I didn't notice any smoke there when we flew over it,' said The Girl.

'Neither did I,' said The Volunteer.

And from one of its chimneys a curl of smoke rose lazily into the blue sky as it stared imperturbably out to sea.

45

Meanwhile, in the pass through the mountains, had there been a living soul to watch, a strange sight would there have been to see. Brother One, at the head of his wide-eyed band of frightened Orphachins, stared down in utter puzzlement at a figure that had rushed out of the rocks and prostrated itself at his feet.

'Get up! Get up!' said Brother One.

'Gobbly, gobbly! Gobbly, gobbly!' jabbered the Orphachins, prostrating themselves before the prostrate figure.

'Oh Lord, oh Lord, please don't leave me again. I'm sorry. Please don't leave me again!' it shouted and clutched with trembling fingers at Brother One's ankles. 'I promise I'll be good! I promise!'

'Get up!' shouted Brother One nervously. 'Who are you? What are you doing? Let go of my ankles! You'll make me fall over!'

'I was desperate!' cried the prostrate stranger. 'I thought you'd abandoned me and that I'd never find you again!'

The Orphachins crawled closer and sought to attract the attention of one whom they supposed to be Goddy by plucking at his clothing. The stranger jerked round in terror, screamed and struggled to his knees.

'Devils!' he cried. 'They've changed into Devils! Get them off me. Please save me from them, Lord. I'll do anything you say!'

Brother One leaned forward, cuffed a couple of Orphachin heads and indicated that they should withdraw a short distance.

'Who are you?' he demanded. 'Why are you crawling on the ground? Let go of my ankles.'

The stranger looked up beseechingly.

'Please don't send me away again, Lord. When I woke up and found you gone I thought I'd kill myself. I only want to follow in Your Footsteps and do Your Will, Lord.'

'But I've never seen you before in my life! How do you know me?'

'Oh please, Lord,' sobbed the strange, returning to a *prostrate* position. 'Don't do this to me. You *know* we were in the Snowcamp together. You *know* we were the only survivors. You *know* I'll do anything you ask. Please don't say that you've forgotten me. Look!

This scar on my hand. Isn't that proof enough of who I am? It's identical to the one on yours.'

Brother One was becoming more and more nervous as the stranger grew more excited and he would have turned to run had it not been obvious that for some reason the Orphachins held the creature in high regard.

'I have no scar,' he replied bewildered. 'Why should I have a scar like that?'

The stranger struggled to his knees again and reached for Brother One's hand.

'Look, Lord,' he said. 'Here. On your hand. Oh. It's gone!'

His face fell, he dropped the hand in astonishment and staggered back a few short knee-paces.

'It was there, on your hand, Lord,' he said in confusion. 'Just like the rest of us. But it's gone again!'

His face took on an expression of deepening awe.

'Just like the last time! After we'd brained you and thrown you out in the snow and you came back! It had gone then! And now it's still gone!'

He prostrated himself once more.

'Oh Lord, please forgive me. I didn't know what I was doing. I'll never hurt You again. I know now that You were just testing me and I failed. I'll never run off when people take You prisoner again! I would have saved You but they were too many for me! You saw! All with weapons and those strange lumps on their chests like the things that put us into the Snowcamp. I realize now that You were giving me a chance to show my devotion and faith, Lord. But I was too weak and frightened! I let them take You away because I didn't think I could help. Now I know that You are all-powerful and would have protected me. I'm sorry, Lord. I'm sorry.'

The Orphachins, seeing their supposed Goddy humbling himself before Brother One, gazed at their General with new respect.

'Taken prisoner?' he murmured in confusion. 'Lumps on their chests? Who took me prisoner? When?'

'Just now, Lord. Not more than an hour ago. I saw them taking you away through the mountains. That way.'

He pointed towards the West.

'But now you come from the other way and everybody has changed into little creatures and your scar has gone!'

'Are you trying to tell me that someone who looked just like me was taken by the women of the Desert Tribes an hour ago?' demanded Brother One, a rising excitement in his voice.

'Well, yes,' replied the prostrate figure uncertainly. 'Is that the wrong thing to say?'

'It must be Brother Two!' exclaimed Brother One in delight. 'He and I are identical clones. He must have made it up through the sea after all. I gave him up for lost long ago! But he's here! Just an hour ahead of us! Captured by the women! We must find him and rescue him!'

He freed his ankles from the penitent's grasp and beckoned his troops.

'Runny, runny!' he shouted, pointing West along the pass through the mountains. 'And you too,' he instructed the devotee, 'runny, runny as well.'

'Yes, Lord,' said The Disciple, somewhat confused, falling in behind Brother One as the army began to swarm forward. 'Anything You say, Lord.'

And as they pressed swiftly on Brother One learned of the Snow-camp from his new adherent, learned how a person identical to himself save for a head of white hair had been cast out into the snow, and how Brother Two had arrived, unscarred, in the middle of the night, seeming to know nothing of the Snowcamp yet looking just like Brother One, and just like the man that had been left for dead.

'The Father!' exclaimed Brother One in amazement and delight. 'That must have been The Father in the Snowcamp. Brother Two always believed that one day he'd find The Father if he ever got up-top!'

'Yes,' agreed The Disciple. 'That's what He said when He first came to the Snowcamp. "The Father," He said, "that must have been The Father." He looked just like You, except for the scar on His hand, of course, and He looks just like the one before Him except for the white hair.'

'And you threw The Father out in the snow, did you?' asked Brother One grimly.

'Ah, well, the others did,' replied The Disciple. 'I wasn't involved. In fact I tried to stop them. I told them it wasn't right but they went ahead and did it, Lord. There was nothing I could do about it. If I'd known it was Your Father, Lord, and His Father too, if I'd known who He was, I can assure you I would have given up my very life to save Him.'

'Why do you keep calling me Lord?' snapped Brother One, thrusting a large rock aside irritably as he drove himself forward.

'Well,' replied The Disciple. 'If you're His Brother, then you must be the Son of God too, mustn't you, and you have to admit there is a very strong Family Resemblance. I noticed it the minute I saw you. I recognized you immediately, Lord, didn't I?'

'That's because we were both cloned from the same father,' explained Brother One. 'We're identical twins. Surely you know what cloning is.'

The Disciple looked as deeply reflective as it is possible to be while scurrying along a rocky mountain pass and replied,

'Well that's how I was born, now that I think back on it. But, it's a funny thing, I can't remember hardly anything that's happened to me before the Snowcamp. It seems to take your memory right away.'

'Well you must have come up from one of the submarine civilizations yourself.'

'Well, I suppose now you mention it, I do sort of remember some sort of Trial and being found guilty and thrust out of some Tubes into the water.' He squinted quickly at Brother One's face. 'I don't suppose that's important any more is it, Lord?' he asked nervously. 'I mean, that's all over with now, isn't it?'

'That's how The Father came to be up here,' replied Brother One. 'It was the standard way of executing criminals. I suppose they all ended up somewhere on this island if they survived the trip. The Father's crime was double-cloning, my brother and I. What was yours?'

'Oh, it's hard to remember now, Lord,' replied The Disciple with another sidelong glance. 'I think there was some mix-up over someone's property but I don't remember too clearly.'

Suddenly the Orphachins began to gabble and scratch their heads in excitement as they came upon an extinguished campfire of still-warm twigs and sniffed the strange scents around it.

'Someone was here not long ago,' said Brother One. 'And look, there are the plains.'

The pass had come to an end and in the distance they could see a white Palace rising from the floodwaters like a gigantic broken tooth.

'They must have taken him there!' cried Brother One.

And the Orphachins nodding their heads eagerly, scurried down the side of he mountain towards the plain, jabbering, 'Goddy, Goddy!

'Goddy, Goddy.'

46

Meanwhile Rogesse and her ragged army with the bodies of The Crone and Ana, Matriarch of The Earth, had reached the very wall of The Candle Palace. But utterly exhausted were they, having crossed the flooded plains too recklessly and too fast. They stood waist deep in water in the shadows of the Palace as the stragglers caught up, bringing with them their prisoners – Brother Two,

Tomaly-Somaly and The Last Child of Woman Born. But, even as they waited, a head appeared at the windows above them and a hoarse voice called out to them.

'What does you wants?'

'I am Ana, Queen of The Steriles, Matriarch of The Earth!' shouted Rogesse. 'And I am come to claim this Palace and these lands as mine by lawful right!'

'You is welcomes to it,' replied the head. 'Us hopes you has brungs some foods with you. Us has got nothing left!'

'Surely,' muttered Rogesse's Lieutenant, 'this cannot be the Candle Palace of The Others! This is just a marble ruin. The Candle Palace has been known throughout our history as the most beautiful sight in the world!'

Rogesse, ignoring her dispirited underling, cried,

'Yield! We have come in vast strength and a second army waits in the mountains for my signal. Open your gates to us and it will go easy with you! Resist and you will all perish!'

'Us cannot open gates that am not theres. Thems got blowed away by the water. But you am welcomes to climbs up through the windows!'

'Yield!' shouted Rogesse again, confused, feeling the situation somehow slipping out of her grasp.

'Is this the Candle Palace?' one of her army shouted up in disbelief.

'Yes'm,' shouted the head, 'but all the Candles am wet now alright. You am better off in the mountains now. This place am full of dead creepies and us can't get to the kitchens!'

There was an angry rumble of discontent from the exhausted army and a voice cried, 'Did we come all this way for a broken ruin full of dead creepies? This is not what we were promised! Where is all the luxury and the feasting? This is a blighted, evil place!'

'Aye!' cried another voice. 'And what have we to eat if we do not return to tend our own crops in the desert?'

'Well,' called the head from the window, 'Us am servings boiled creepies for dinner so you better makes up your minds now if you am staying outs or comings in.'

And with that, it disappeared.

'Yield, I say!' shouted Rogesse once again, but uncertainly now, to the empty window.

The arriving remnants of the ragged army were learning from their sisters of the Fool's Errand their crusade had turned out to be and an angry muttering rose up from the huddled ranks.

'It's a trick!' shouted Rogesse desperately. 'They know they cannot resist us by force and so they resort to trickery and demoralization. Storm the Palace! We will find Yeni the Messiah and riches beyond the dreams of avarice inside these walls!'

A few of the women began to climb unenthusiastically up towards the windows but several heads suddenly appeared over the parapet of the roof.

'Who's that climbing the walls?' called a voice thick with wine. 'Are you Orphachins?'

'I am Ana,' shouted Rogesse, 'Queen of Steriles and Matriarch of the Earth. I have come to claim this Palace as mine by lawful right. Resist us and it will go badly with you—'

'Yes, but are you *Orphachins*? You're not are you? You're women from the desert.'

'—And we have come in vast strength,' replied Rogesse, 'And—'

'Well you can just go away again in vast strength. You're not wanted here. You're not supposed to come this side of the mountains. We all agreed on that *ages* ago.'

'Yield, I say!' screamed Rogesse, beside herself with rage. 'Yield! Or we will *destroy* you!'

'Why don't you stop shouting, you'll hurt your throat. There's nothing for you here and we don't like your attitude.'

At this the heads withdrew and the army were left standing, unheeded, in the stinking floods.

'Where are the prisoners?' shouted Rogesse. 'Bring the girl and the Orphachin to me?'

Weary soldiers who had dragged Tomaly-Somaly, The Last Child of Woman Born and Brother Two across the floodwaters on inflated wine-skins, brought their captives to the Queen.

'Free the girl's mouth,' ordered Rogesse. 'They will realize they cannot trifle with us when they discover we hold hostages.'

Tomaly-Somaly sighed with relief as her muzzle was removed.

'Tell them!' snapped Rogesse. 'Tell The Others that they are in mortal danger, that if they do not cooperate with us we will sack the Palace!'

A head appeared at the roof parapet again and a voice called, 'If you don't go away we'll throw things on your heads. You're not supposed to come this side of the mountains. We sent three runners to ask for your help and none of them came back. We think that's absolutely awful and we don't want to have anything to do with you.'

'Tell them!' hissed Rogesse. 'Tell them they had better let us in and yield.'

'Amrita!' called Tomaly-Somaly, 'it's me! Tomaly-Somaly! They've taken us prisoner. They've got a Man god as well!'

'Tomaly-Somaly!' replied Amrita in surprise. 'Did *you* bring these awful people back with you? There's nothing for them to eat and I think it's a bit much just arriving unexpectedly and shouting at the servants. I suggest you take your friends off somewhere else. They're not welcome here. And, quite frankly, Tomaly-Somaly, neither are you. Some of us think you've behaved in a rather peculiar way – going to fetch the Orphachins, for instance – and we've only just got rid of the Man-god that started all this in the first place. I don't see why we would want another one.'

'Amrita!' shouted Tomaly-Somaly, close to tears, 'I didn't bring *them*, they brought *me*! They took me prisoner and threatened to do all sorts of horrid things to me. I was only doing what The Whale asked me to do! The least you could do is send someone out to rescue me!'

'It's easy for you to say that,' replied Amrita, 'but we've had nothing but trouble from the servants ever since this awful thing happened. It's hard enough getting them to make up the beds without asking them to get into fights as well!'

'But you just can't abandon me like this!' cried Tomaly-Somaly tearfully. 'I thought we were friends!'

'Well, we were,' replied Amrita, 'but things are very difficult just at the moment and I'm not sure that we can spare the—' she broke off and thought for a moment. 'Oh, alright,' she decided finally. 'Tell them to come inside and wait in The Great Hall. We'll come down and talk to them. But we can't promise anything.'

The head withdrew.

'Where's the Main Doorway?' demanded Rogesse.

'Round the front,' replied Tomaly-Somaly glumly, at which Rogesse turned to face her army and, in an imperious voice, cried,

'Storm The Palace! Onward Sisters!'

With blood-curdling yells she led the way round the corner of the Palace while her army, muttering and grumbling, slouched dejectedly after her, wading through the mire between the broken doors and collecting in a discomfited group within the cracked and crumbling confines of The Great Hall. The building overawed them, for they were a nomadic people, accustomed to woven tents or shelters of matted fronds and had never stood within so large a structure. And they felt doubly uncomfortable beneath the gleaming stares of the servants who peered from the shadows of The Great Corridor. But they themselves stared, almost hypnotized, as the gloriously-robed Others made the slow, curving descent of The Great Staircase.

'Well?' Amrita demanded from the top of the straight flight of steps that led down to the water. 'Now you're here, unwelcome though you are, what do you want?'

'I claim this Palace and its lands as mine by lawful right!' cried Rogesse.

'Make them let me go, Amrita!' called Tomaly-Somaly. 'They say they're going to kill us!'

Amrita descended to the water's edge with a composure marred only by the faintest of drunken wobbles. But as she opened her mouth to speak, her eyes fell on Brother Two, still bound and gagged, supported by two muscular Amazonis. Her face turned pale and she cried out, clutching at her companions to support herself.

'It's the Man-god!' she screamed, losing her grip and falling forward.

'It's the *same* Man-god! They brought him *back*!'

47

Meanwhile, Johnson and The Volunteer were up to their shoulders in waters that drained rapidly towards the sea, crawling on their hands and knees, keeping their balance with difficulty against the pressure of the flood, creeping up to the window of a small white cottage in the little fishing village from the chimney of which rose a lazy curl of blue smoke.

*

'It's fire, I tell you!' Johnson was muttering angrily. 'We're crazy to go anywhere near it. It's one thing to have a machine that spits it out, although heaven knows that's risky enough, but it's quite another to creep up on it in its natural state! How do we know it won't leap out at us when it sees us? You know as well as I do that fire consumes everything it sees! I don't want to become lunch for the wretched stuff!'

'Shut up or go back,' snapped The Volunteer in a harsh whisper. 'It's clear that the people of this island have discovered the secret of taming fire and bending it to their will. There are obviously human beings of some sort in there and we may find prizes far richer than a simple flame-torch. This village is scarcely touched by the flood. God knows what we might find.'

They reached the low-silled window and craned their necks to peer inside, but no sooner had they glimpsed a row of naked women, bound at wrist and ankle, propped uncomfortably against the wall, than their attention was distracted by anguished screams a short distance off. They turned to each other in fear.

'What was that?' hissed The Volunteer.

'Sounded like anguished screams!' replied Johnson, alert with alarm.

The screams came again and among the hysterical cacophony the word 'help' and the name 'Johnson' appeared briefly, then sank again in a welter of panicstricken shrieks.

'It's The Girl!' said The Volunteer angrily. 'She was supposed to stay behind and guard the furniture. The crazy fool must have followed us!'

They stood upright and blundered back through the water the way they had come until, turning a corner, they suddenly came upon a bizarre sight. Half a dozen ragged men had seized The Girl, bound her hand and foot and were carrying her away horizontal beneath their arms.

Both sides stopped, aghast, to see the other.

Both parties turned to run but then, seeing the frightened reaction of the other, stood their ground belligerently.

Seeing the belligerence of the other, both parties turned again to run. This cycle might have repeated itself over and over again until darkness fell had not The Girl, seeing her compatriots, screamed,

'Help me, you stinking cowards! Don't just stand there!'

At this The Volunteer, stung to valour, walked hesitantly forward, an uncertain smile on his face, hand raised in cordial greeting, and said,

'Hello there, friends. There seems to be some misunderstanding here.'

Meanwhile, Johnson, having vanished round the corner at the first sign of trouble, reappeared from the shoulders up and shouted,

'If you don't want a lot of trouble, you'd better drop her!'

The astonished men, wild-eyed, pale-faced and sickly, loosed The Girl unthinkingly into the water and she floated, struggling and gurgling in the steady current towards The Volunteer, who failed to grab her as she flowed past but turned to see Johnson rescue the swearing jetsam as one of the strangers, through salt-encrusted lips said,

'Thank Heaven for that. Human beings at last!'

'We thought that she was one of *them*,' said another by way of lame explanation.

The Volunteer thought for a moment of running away but, remembering his training, smiled and said, 'Everything is alright. There is no need to worry about anything.' He advanced upon the group, still smiling, and said, 'We mean you no harm,' adding with a presence of mind born of self-interest, 'We have only come to look at your machines.'

'What *are* those creatures?' demanded one of the *strangers*, indicating The Girl who was busy struggling out of the ropes around her wrists, 'they are like humans and yet they are not humans.'

'The others like that one attacked us,' explained another. 'We questioned them and we found that they eat human flesh!'

'They do?' enquired The Volunteer nervously. 'I mean, they *don't*. At least, not all of them.' He pointed to The Girl, 'That one doesn't, for instance. It is a friend.' He cleared his throat. 'Now perhaps you would take me to see your machines.'

One of the strangers smiled grimly.

'You'll be lucky,' he replied bitterly. 'We lost nearly everything in the upheaval. We were lucky to get away with our lives. Most of us didn't.'

'But your homes appear very little damaged by the flooding,' said The Volunteer, puzzled.

'You must be joking,' came the sneering reply, 'These crude and

214

primitive structures are not our homes! Even our rubbish tanks are palaces compared to these hovels. We are not natives of this backward place. We are castaways, flung upon these shores by the recent storm. *Our* world is a world of technological sophistication unparalleled in the history of the universe.' He grimaced angrily and indicated his companions and the village with a wave of his hand. 'And now we are reduced to rags and this random heap of stones. We have to start again, almost from scratch. We salvaged a few machines but we have no way of returning home.'

'A technological sophistication unparalleled in the history of mankind?' repeated Johnson over the shoulder of The Volunteer, almost choking with repressed excitement. 'Salvaged a few machines?'

'Right,' replied the leading stranger, glumly nodding.

'And no way of getting home again?'

They nodded their heads sadly again.

'Well, we may be able to help you with that,' said Johnson. 'We're traders, you see.' He turned to The Volunteer for inspiration. 'Aren't we?' he said brightly.

'Yes,' agreed The Volunteer readily. 'Traders. We specialize in misfortunes rather like yours. We arrange to ship people home in exchange for some of their machines. As long, that is,' he added quickly, 'as they are of a certain sophistication. Superior to our own, you understand.'

'You could get us home!' cried three of the ragged men in unison, their eyes alight with joy. The nearest seized The Volunteer's lapels in an almost involuntary gesture of delight.

'Everything!' he croaked. 'You can have *all* if you can get us home again!'

'I'm soaking and I'm freezing,' complained The Girl angrily, storming through the water in an ungainly fashion and confronting her two shipmates. 'I've been abused and taken prisoner by these hooligans and now you're offering them a passage home? What kind of diplomacy is that? You should be cutting these wretches down like dogs!'

'Shush!' hissed Johnson fiercely, 'You're going to gum up the works.'

'Our companion,' explained The Volunteer apologetically, 'misunderstood your reaction to her. She naturally feels a little disturbed, having been accidentally aggressed in that unfortunate fashion.'

'Well, we're sorry,' replied the strangers' leader. 'But we have a house full of creatures looking just like this one who tried to involve us in some kind of strange cannibalistic ritual they practise in this place. They would have captured us if we hadn't been too many for them. What happens here? Who *are* these creatures?'

'To tell the truth,' Johnson replied, 'we know as much about this place as you do. It's a Prison Colony. That's all we really know. And as my companion already pointed out, we are simply Traders. We came last night and we'll be leaving tomorrow. So, if you have anything of interest to show us—'

He spread his hands in invitation.

'We've put it all in a storeroom, come and dry out and then we'll show it to you and we can talk business.'

'We should be keeping an eye on the furniture,' Johnson muttered to The Volunteer.

'Yes,' he agreed. 'You'd better go back and get the porters to bring it in.'

And so, while Johnson returned to carry the Father and the Flame-torch to safety, the ragged strangers led The Volunteer and the complaining girl through the streaming streets to the little cottage with the smoking chimney.

'Is it safe?' asked The Volunteer nervously.

'Oh yes,' replied the strangers, 'they're all safely trussed up.'

'No, I mean the fire. There's a fire inside, isn't there? Is it chained up?'

'Well, yes,' replied their leader in puzzlement. 'It's in a hole in the wall.'

'A hole in the wall?' repeated The Volunteer. 'And that's enough to keep it at bay?'

'Of course,' said the leader, pushing open the door and glancing in confusion at his companions as the two sailors shrank back in alarm.

The Volunteer put on a brave smile.

'We don't have fire in our country,' he tried to explain casually. 'It was wiped out a long time ago. There isn't a single fire left there. We found it was far too costly a creature to maintain.'

The stranger shrugged and entered the cottage with a grimace of amazement at his companions. 'You people keep watch out here,' he ordered. Inside the thick-walled room the air was pungent with the smoke of burning peat that leaked from the fireplace and from flickering tallow-lamps that threw shaking shadows over an interior furnished with nothing but half a dozen bound and gagged women leaning against the peeling white walls.

'We – er – interrogated them,' said the man with a jerk of his head towards the captives as he stretched out his hands to warm at the flames, 'and we eventually discovered that they're some sort of scavenging unit for finding stray human beings that have been washed up on the tide. They take them up to some place in the mountains for a while and then bring them down by river to some Church they've got back there in the plains where they get eaten at some Full Moon Feast.' He shuddered. 'It's horrible! We haven't made up our minds what to do with them. If they didn't look so like humans we'd bash their skulls in. As it is—'

He strode to a door into the adjoining room and threw it open.

'Well,' he said, 'if you're not interested in getting close to the fire we may as well get down to business. The stuff is through here. Technological wealth beyond the dreams of avarice.'

The two sailors moved forward nervously, filled with excitement.

'Step right in,' said the stranger. And then, 'Oh, by the way, we should introduce ourselves. Where we come from my companions and I are called *Barbans*.'

48

Meanwhile, on the bridge of The Admiral's galley, a grim Court Naval was in session. The defendant stood erect, gripping the rail of a tethered basket-kite that floated head-high above the wooden deck and before him stood the two judges, traditionally named Life and Death, who listened to the proceedings with passive formality. The Charges and Substantiating Information had been laid and it remained only for The Admiral to speak in his own defence before judgment was announced. If Life raised its hand and Death remained motionless, the kite would be winched to the deck and its buckled gates thrown open: if Life did nothing and Death raised its hand the restraining ropes would be cut and the kite would drift upwards and away on the swirling high-altitude winds to circle the Earth for an eternity, a skyborne reminder to all who saw it of the wages of sin.

'You speak of *my* crime,' shouted The Admiral emotionally, 'when you yourselves are contemplating an even greater crime!'

He stared down at the faces of Life and Death, the familiar physiognomies of two brother-officers now turned to emotionless masks of ruthless judgment by the Drugs of Justice they had been given. They stood before him, attentive to his every word, yet somehow detached, remote and without interest or compassion.

'I sought to protect the life of one of our own people, one of our shipmates braving new lands on our behalf. That was why I ordered the Beasts unleashed. The decision had to be made instantly and without hesitation. At that moment, as Admiral of The Fleet, I judged it the right thing to do.'

He paused, staring hopelessly round at the ring of hostile or frightened faces, noticing without bitterness that there were those who would clearly like to dispose of him to the skies.

'Alright,' he went on, 'so I was mistaken. He got back to the boats without injury. I admit that. I admit it was a good thing the flagman refused to send my order and that the Beast-Leashers pretended not to hear the shouted signals.' He clenched his fists and punched the air. 'But at the time I was *right*. It looked as though he would be attacked and killed. I'm on trial here for "attempting to cause Unnecessary Death" but, in reality, I was trying to *prevent* Unnecessary Death. And, in the event, you mutinied – all of you. You first countermand an Admiral's Imperative and then have the affrontery to put *me* in the Limbo-basket. This Trial is an excuse to get rid of me so that you can turn this Fleet to what our agents back home call "a more profitable course". I know that. I'm not a fool. I can't argue like this.' He waved his hands in hopeless rejection.

'Cut the ropes,' he said. 'I've had enough.'

There was a long silence and all eyes turned to Life and Death.

Neither made a signal.

The assembled witnesses waited in a silence broken only by the hissing of the boats through the water and the distant mewing of gulls in the clear blue sky.

✱

'You'll have to go on,' a lieutenant suggested gently. 'They haven't decided yet.'

The Admiral gave a sigh of anguish and stared up into the vast azure bowl that cupped the Earth.

'How can I defend myself?' he said. 'I am an Admiral. I acted as an Admiral should act. What can I say? That I am *not* an Admiral? This is ridiculous. This was my last tour of duty.'

He fingered the embroidered rings on his sleeve and began to hum absentmindedly to himself.

The lieutenant cleared his throat and spoke again.

'I'm afraid you'll have to say something more, Sir,' he said. 'Either confess or deny. They can't operate unless you confess or deny.'

The Admiral looked down at him vaguely.

'Confess or deny? Is that what it comes down to?'

The lieutenant nodded uneasily.

'Yes, Sir. You know that, surely.'

'Confess or deny?' repeated the Admiral, voice and temper rising. 'Is that it? Confess or deny to a bunch of mutinous whipper-snappers that were still at school when I was taking out my first fleets? Cut the ropes and be done with it. The world has changed and left me behind. I want no part of it.'

'Is that a confession, Sir?'

'It is blazes a confession! Have you all gone mad? It's an accusation! This navy used to be run on the basis of humanitarian, collective discipline and compassionate good sense. When the State decided we had to find our own finance it didn't reckon on the kind of recruiting changes that would result!' He leaned forward in the basket, his face grave and concerned. 'I can remember a time when all this was paid for by the people back home. Alright. You can smile,' he snapped, seeing derisory amusement flicker across the faces of many listeners. 'You can smile at an old man's claptrap, but it's true. There was a time when we didn't have to spend most of our time scavenging for raw materials and natural phenomena to pay our way. I told them at the time, I said, "If you turn the navy into a selfsupporting unit you'll attract the wrong sort of recruit. A mercenary navy will attract mercenary recruits. Before you know it you'll have mutiny for the sake of profit and discipline will be operated on the basis of greed!" But they ignored my advice and gave me the option of immediate retirement.' He smiled grimly. 'It looks now as though I should have taken that option. Avoided this farce.'

He fingered his rings of service again absentmindedly.

The encircling witnesses waited impatiently.

Life and Death remained motionless.

'Let's just cut the ropes and get it over with,' suggested a voice. 'This has gone on long enough. You all heard him call it a farce. He knows the judges can't operate unless he recognizes the court. He's just trying to stall and hoping he can slide out of it. Cut the ropes!'

'No!' cried the lieutenant. 'If we're going to have a trial let it be a fair one! Some of us even have our doubts about the Admiral of this fleet being on trial at all!'

He stepped up to the hanging basket and pleaded with The Admiral.

'Please, Sir,' he said,. 'Defend yourself. If you don't they may just cut you loose anyway.'

The Admiral seemed not to hear him for a moment but then glanced down with piercing bluc eyes.

'There was a time when we dreamed of all our peoples living in harmony. After the Great Wars we turned away from selfishness and divisiveness and sought to comfort each other with warmth and sharing. But now that is all but forgotten. Now each seeks once more to impose his will on the next. You wait for your leaders to make mistakes and then cut them down, hoping thereby to elevate yourselves to the status of leaders.' He shook his head sadly. 'But that is not the way leadership is learned. True leadership serves others, not itself. I know that it is not Justice that tries me here, but Greed. There are those among this company who would turn this fleet into nothing more than a pack of robbers and pirates. But if the excuse for my death is that I sought to save one of us from death at the point of metal weapons then so be it. I will die willingly for that.'

He stared hard at the faces of Life and Death.

'Decide!' he shouted. 'Cut me loose or bring me down!'

Meanwhile the spirit of Ana, hanging high, at first, above the smoothly skimming fleet, had dropped lower and lower as familiarity bred courage in her curious heart. She had watched the two tiny boats put out for the open shore and had heard in her mind, with sudden astonishment, the tender and supportive confidences of The Partner to her Translator Consort. She had received their images of the two women of her desert tribes and seen them with the strangers' eyes, shocked by the barbarity of their dress and manner, horrified by the bubbling liquor-still with its tortured vegetable hostages, terrified by the sight of fire and metal. At first, responding with the political instincts learned in a lifetime of beleaguered Matriarchy, she delighted in the vulnerability of this alien armada and began to plan the nature of the battle in which she and her reassembled armies would annihilate them, but gradually, the gentle intercourse between the intrepid Translator and his caring Partner aboard the leading galley began to strike harmonies in a heart long-hardened to the subtler and gentler influences of human upon human and she felt shame and sorrow to see her two citizens rise up so brazenly hostile against the blundering innocent. She dropped swiftly down, a cry of soundless anguish upon invisible lips as the scurrying form tripped and fell in his flight and the armed harridans closed upon him. She heaved a breathless sigh of relief as he staggered to his feet, pounded desperately through the sand and scrambled to safety in one of the boats. And as the two craft rowed back to the galley she drew closer to the large ship and witnessed the angry scenes on The Admiral's bridge with puzzlement and anger. Then, hovering unseen, she witnessed the Court Naval with confused alarm and apprehension. Why did this Leader allow himself to be seized so easily by the mutinous crew and charged with these so-called crimes? Why did his guards not strike down the mutineers who had dared to countermand an order so clearly appropriate under battle conditions? Weak he might be, she reasoned, but wrong he was not. She observed the figures of Life and Death with curiosity as they were helped up to the bridge blindfold, and saw that by some strange magic their spirits hung, seemingly lifeless, from the base of their spines and that their spiritless bodies, like fleshed dummies in rigid and stiff-muscled judgment, waited for the proceedings to trigger off emotional responses in their body-cells and brains. She guessed that the robes of black meant death for The Admiral and the robes of white meant life. Curious still and emboldened by her invisibility, she drifted closer to the impassive figures.

Meanwhile, the eyes of the waiting assembly were turned upon the judges. Surely now some judgment could be made.

Surely Death would be moved to respond, having heard the angry call from the lips of the defendant himself.

Surely they would finally be free of this tiresome old Admiral with his archaic notions of command.

But there was a gasp of frustration and anger from those who had sought to overthrow the Admiral and turn the powers of the fleet to their own ends and a cry of relief from those who, like the lieutenant, would have had The Admiral exonerate himself, as white-robed Life haltingly raised a hand.

'Set him free,' said its voice, thick and slurred.

And in the mêlée that followed no one noticed it smile with secret elation.

Nor, as they led the two Justice figures below decks to recuperate did they observe the alert glances that flashed beneath Life's heavy eyelids.

Ana, Queen of the Steriles, Matriarch of the Earth, had found a new body and had taken her first step along the road to renewed power.

49

Meanwhile, back at the Candle Palace, events were beginning to take their toll. The series of blows from earth, sea and sky that had struck the elegant community finally began to loosen social bonds that had held firm for centuries. A Full Moon, A living Man-god, the insect attack, the Volcano and the resulting floods, the appearance of new Man-gods, curling in from the sky upon great white wings to carry off their brother and now the invasion of The Great Hall by the forbidden Desert Tribes, bestial, half-naked and utterly exhausted, bringing with them Tomaly-Somaly, the traitress and yet another Man-god, identical to the first save for his apparent youth – all shook the tranquil composure of the Palace inhabitants until now Amrita herself, blurred with wine and bewildered by the speed of events, screamed, abandoned consciousness and, before anyone could prevent it, fainted away, pitched face forward from The Great Stairs into the oily befouled water in which Rogesse and her ragged tribes stood kneedeep in discomfort.

'Yield!' cried Rogesse, yet again, trapped involuntarily and hysterically in a role of her own choosing, afraid to show ignorance or fear lest she be perceived as a common mortal.

'Yield! Or it will go badly with you!' she cried.

Tomaly-Somaly rushed forward to help Amrita from the water while the rest of the ornately garbed Others stared in mingled rage and fear at the intruders and their captive.

'There am no points in you yelling Yields,' shouted one of the Palace Servants in irritation, appearing from beneath the stairs with a large urn rescued from the waters. 'You am just bawlings in your own ears. Why doesn't you buckle to and helps clears this places up a bit?'

She shouldered through the bewildered women and placed the urn with a pile of salvaged flotsam on The Great Stairs above the waterline. 'You is a long way from the deserts now, so you cans just behave yourself.'

Rogesse turned her impotent anger upon the surly minion and pointed a trembling yet imperious finger.

'Kill her!' she cried. 'Let all learn that the Queen of Women is a force to be reckoned with!'

There was a nervous drawing of swords among the uncertain troops who clearly did not relish the prospect of joining battle within the claustrophobic confines of The Great Hall.

'Ho, ho,' guffawed the servant with bitter irony. 'Me sees it am the sames in the deserts am it am in this Palaces. There am them what gives the orders and there am them what do the works.'

She puts her hands on her hips and stared brazenly at Rogesse. 'Well, lets I tell you, sister, if *me* had somewheres else to be me wouldn't be heres now and that am for sure.'

She looked around at the ragged army who stood perplexed, exhausted and chilled in the slimy flood-debris.

'What am you here for? Am you all crazy? All the elders am dead from the insects, all the foods am underwater. Even The Greats Chapel am broken and finished. What am you running around in the waters on these sides of the mountain for? You am all better off at home, believes I.'

'Kill her! Kill her!' shouted Rogesse furiously. 'Let these bumpkins know the meaning of steel and learn obedience to the Royal Will!'

A powerfully-built soldier, her face streaked with the mud of the passage across the flooded plains turned with a surly countenance to Rogesse.

'We have killed enough for one day,' she said menacingly. 'We are here and The Candle Palace is ours, for what it's worth. Now show us why we came.'

There was a muted murmur of agreement from the dispirited troops and Rogesse suddenly felt the last of her energies drain from her as she realized that this was the moment she had foreseen with terror – her own army demanding 'Why?'

'What good is this ruined Palace to us?' cried another peevishly. 'What can we grow in these waters? Let us return to our homes before the skies send even more rains upon us. What loyalty do we owe to this Queen Who Does Not Grow, this Matriarch of The Leading Nowhere? I say cut her throat and leave her in her precious Candle Palace!'

'Aye,' muttered a weary voice among the crowd. 'Slit her throat and be done with all this foolery.'

There was an ominous movement among the women and they began to edge in upon Rogesse and might have slain her there and then had not Tomaly-Somaly, supporting the sodden Amrita against her shoulder on The Great Stairs, cried,

'No! You must not kill in the Candle Palace! It is against the Law! It means certain death from the Full Moon Gods!'

'Why don't you all clear off and do your killing in your own homes?' shouted one of The Others from the relative security of The Great Stairs. 'You were invited in here to be told what we were prepared to do to secure the safety of our sister, not to start killing each other all over The Great Hall. If you're going to fight among yourselves you'd better do it outside!'

'Oh, Tomaly-Somaly,' sighed Amrita, holding her head in her hands, 'this is all too much for me. Everything has fallen to pieces or turned topsy-turvy.'

'The Whale would know what to do,' suggested Tomaly-Somaly hopefully.

'The Whale is in the catacombs,' replied Amrita tearfully. 'And the catacombs are flooded. There *is* no Whale anymore.'

'And the other sisters?' asked Tomaly-Somaly.

'All gone too,' wailed Amrita. 'Killed by the insects. Trapped in the kitchens. Drowned. There's nobody left but we few and the servants.'

'And the Man-god?'

'Taken away from us. They came from the sky and took him off towards the village. We should have sacrificed him while we had the chance. I realize that now. But he's gone. It's too late.'

Tomaly-Somaly glanced over to where Brother Two stood bound and gagged in the flooded Hall, staring wide-eyed in the confusion around him, and she wondered for a moment whether she should suggest his sacrifice in the stead of the lost Man-god, but something made her hold her tongue.

'Oh Tomaly-Somaly,' wailed Amrita again. 'I just don't know what's happening any more.'

Meanwhile The Others were engaged in heated argument with the ragged army, the former demanding, outraged, that the half-naked unwashed savages go about their grisly business elsewhere, the latter replying with ribald insult and threatening gesture that they would do as they pleased wherever they pleased.

The broken roofing rang with the rising tumult until a Pot-Watcher who had watched the proceedings with growing rage from the shadow of The Great Stairs strode forward angrily, threw up her arms to attract attention and blasted everyone to silence in a voice that had been trained to cut through the din of the bustling kitchens.

'Holds it!' she cried, purple with anger, a large blue vein pulsing visibly across her forehead. 'What am us all doings?' She stared round belligerently.

'Us am got none house! Us am got none foods! Us am up to am knees in water and soon the nights come upon we. Why am us fighting among amselves?'

One of The Others began to protest but the bellowing voice cut her short.

'You shuts up the mouth! Me am talking now.'

She picked out the soldier with the surly countenance who had threatened to slay Rogesse and said,

'You! You am one to make decision. Us in the kitchens am all good workers but us am all finished here. Am there work for to eat in the desert?'

There were cries of 'Traitor' from the stairs, but she took no notice, staring with piercing intensity at the sullen-faced desert farmer.

'The desert feeds all who work it,' she replied cautiously.

'Then take we to the deserts with you. Us will work it and eat,' demanded the Pot-watcher urgently. 'All am finished here. There am none works for we here. Takes we with you where us can works for to eat.'

'And what are we supposed to do?' cried one of The Others angrily. 'For hundreds of years we've taken care of you and provided for your sort, and as soon as things become a little inconvenient it's just drop everything and off to the desert is it?'

'Me said shut your mouths,' snarled the Pot-Watcher, without moving her eyes from the soldier. 'Me am asking a serious question.' She repeated it slowly, a hint of entreaty in her voice now. 'Will you takes we with you? Us will works for you.'

Meanwhile, Rogesse's mind had been racing at the speed of light to avoid the death from which she had so recently been reprieved and at this moment, acting upon an adrenalized moment of inspiration, prepared to try anything to resume control of her mutinous band, cried out,

'Surrender up Yeni, She whom many call the Messiah, She who Bleeds with the Moon, She whom these Others stole from us and spirited away over the desert within a pillar of sand. Give her to us and we will take you with us when we return to our homelands. For until we have Yeni there can be no fruitfulness in the desert, nor any peace between the peoples of the desert, nor any ending to the tribulations of those who live upon the desert.' She turned upon her own army, sensing the confusion in them.

'Have you forgotten why we came?' she cried scornfully. 'Has this short journey so wearied you that you could not remember our purpose?'

She pointed an accusing finger at the huddled Others in their richly-coloured robes.

'There. Those pompous weaklings are they who stole from us our necessary sacrifice in the hopes that our crops would fail, that the algae would desert our shores and that, starving, you could be the more easily beaten into submission. Now they watch in delight as you turn upon the very Queen who led you out of confusion to retrieve what is yours by right. They cast spells upon you and upon your ruler, hold back from you your rightful tribute to the gods, that which will earn the favour of the heavens and without which you have been exposed to the battering tumult of the raging Volcano and the pealing skies!'

'Aye!' cried a voice from the ragged army. 'She speaks the truth! While we had Yeni we were at one with our universe. When we lost her the gods turned their anger against us!'

'Put them to the sword, every one!' shouted Rogesse with bloody glee. 'And then search the Palace. Yeni is hidden somewhere within these walls.'

'Wait,' cried another voice from among the army. 'If it is Yeni we seek there is one among us who must know more of it than any other, for is not our prisoner he who leads the Orphachin packs upon their murderous scavenging and knows all the paths of the desert?'

'Who speaks?' demanded Rogesse impatiently as her troops hesitated before their red-bladed work.

'It is I,' replied one of the soldiers, a small elderly woman wearing the strapped headband of the nether desert region. 'I have seen him with the Orphachin Armies. It is said the Orphachins know all the movements in the desert by day or by night. Ask of him where Yeni was taken and whether she was really stolen from us by these cloth-bound butterflies.'

All eyes turned upon the bemused Brother Two as Rogesse ordered his mouth freed of its muzzle and he stared back wide-eyed and silent, not knowing what was being demanded of him.

'Speak,' ordered Rogesse, 'Tell us of Yeni. Tell us how The Others snatched her away in the desert and brought her here.'

Brother Two stammered uncertainly and tried unsuccessfully to smile.

'Speak!' snapped a soldier at his side. 'Tell us what you know.'

The prisoner licked his dry lips, cleared his throat and tried to speak, but no sound came.

'He knows nothing. As I thought,' snarled Rogesse. 'Go to your work. Kill The Others.'

'Wait,' croaked Brother Two desperately, seeing how the soldiers advanced with naked weapons towards The Great Stairs and Tomaly-Somaly. His mind strove to find some mantra from the texts to assuage the fury of the army and save the gentle goddess with whom he had conversed in the mountains.

'Yeni?' he said. 'Why, I've seen better bags with chips in.'

50

Meanwhile, with powerful, determined strokes, the Orphachin band cut through the floodwaters of the streaming plain towards the Candle Palace like a shower of arrows from a mountain bow. Brother One had long since abandoned the tiring and fruitless effort of calling them to heel and struggled along as best he could with the girl, Yeni, last of the fallen goddesses, less beautiful than some bags in which Brother Two had seen chips yet, in reality, She whom many called The Messiah, Last of those who Bleed with the Moon.

He did not know why the Orphachins had abandoned their tender burden in the waters and redoubled their swimming speed, paying no heed to his angry orders to return, for he could not know of the telepathic communication that his brother had with the urchin army, nor the desperation with which the orphans strove to reach the Candle Palace before it was too late and their selfstyled Goddy-Goddy was slain.

'Tykes! Curs! Deserters!' muttered Brother One bitterly as he struggled to keep the terrified Yeni's head above the water and propel himself through the water at the same time.

'You can rely on me,' chipped in the Snowcamp survivor, supporting She who bled with the Moon by the ankles, swallowing his horror at handling so hideous a travesty of the human form. 'I will not abandon You.'

'Listen,' snapped Brother One through wheezing grunts of effort, 'just try to be a little more help. You're holding him as though you wanted him to drown. Can't you see how badly they've mutilated the poor chap? Show a little consideration for a wounded man and support those legs a little more firmly.'

'Wounded man?' cried The Disciple almost involuntarily. 'Wounded man?'

He struggled through the water in puzzlement for a while, then said,

'That's very charitable of You I'm sure, Lord. You put me to shame. I had thought of her, I mean *him*, as just another of those big devils, but You've opened my eyes. Yes, You're right. Only You would have the Divine Mercy to see it in those terms. And Your Brother of course, not forgetting your brother. Yes, a woman is just a wounded man, I can see that now.'

'What are you babbling about?' grumbled The General, as an errant ripple slapped his face and covered his head with muddy water. 'Why don't you save your breath for swimming and keep his legs up.'

'Yes, Lord,' replied The Disciple, gripping Yeni's limbs with a fearless devotion to his master and a look of new understanding and revelatory zeal in his eyes. 'Anything You say, Lord.'

Meanwhile the Orphachins had arrived at the Candle Palace and stood upon the narrow muddied ledge that separated it from the receding floods, beating their tiny fists impotently against its massive marble walls.

'Goddy, Goddy,' they cried, desperately scurrying this way and that, seeking cracks in the masonry and inserting their little fingers in futile enquiry.

'Goddy, Goddy,' they ranted. 'Goddy, Goddy. Gobbly, Gobbly.'

The voice of the struggling Brother One floated across the liquid plain towards them like the cry of a distant bird.

'Come back, you brats. Come back!'

And inside their heads the voice of Brother Two cried,

'Help me! Save me! They are going to murder me!'

'Goddy, Goddy,' they wailed. 'Goddy Gobbly. Goddy Gobbly.'

Meanwhile, inside the Candle Palace, civilization had been reduced to a form no less chaotic than the volcano's boiling eruption, no more ordered than the downward rush of the melting mountain ice, no more constructive than the tidal wave with which the angry ocean smashed the choking desert, no less confused than the billowing clouds of smoke, steam and volcanic ash that had drifted, burbling and tumbling on the Trade Winds, over the distant horizon.

The Others claimed the Man-god as their rightful sacrifice, the Palace servants sought new masters among the exhausted army who, torn between anger and loyalty, first reviled then cheered their Queen, while Brother Two tried to shout obsequious remarks from the ancient texts over the tumultuous din and The Last Child of Woman Born went,

'Wah!'

No one noticed that from the iron-bound box which carried the faintly-breathing Crone and the body of Ana inhabited by The Crone's spirit came an angry thumping. Some of The Others had ventured into the waters of The Great Hall to cuff the treacherous servants back towards the kitchens, Tomaly-Somaly wrestled with two desert soldiers for the freedom of the Man-god, Rogesse hurled instruction and abuse about her in all directions, partly at her rabbled troops, partly at Amrita, who stood pale, silent and confused at the water's edge upon The Great Stairs and partly at the box that floated, shaking with internal fury, at the level of her knees.

But suddenly, all became aware of a strange turbulence in the waters of The Great Hall as though sharks had suddenly swum, unseen, into the arena. The rugged soldiers felt the ripples of large underwater beasts about their ankles and stared down in terror to see the flash and glint of swiftly-swimming creatures darting through their ranks with terrifying speed. Brother Two fell suddenly on his back as though his feet had been cut from under him and, with a cry of fear, began to float backwards towards The Great Door, weaving between the frozen statued army like a rat through a field of corn. One soldier, bolder than her sisters, reached down into the water but withdrew her hand with a cry of pain and a series of small wounds upon her fingers.

'Orphachins!' she screamed, recognizing the marks of tiny teeth and, with cries of horror and panic, the entire army swept forward as one to take refuge on The Great Stairs, pushing and shouting, rolling up the steps like a tidal wave of flesh, trampling each other in their blind panic, tumbling and falling, racing up the graceful spiral towards the roof and hanging over the curving banisters to gape, open-mouthed and pale of face, at the waters below.

Round and round swirled Brother Two, bumping into walls and floating debris like a gigantic and maddened waterbeetle, crying out in pain, surprise and helpless fear as the underwater Orphachin pilots sought vainly for a way out. Some, sensing the presence of frightened prey, left their brothers and surfaced at the foot of The Great Stairs, staring up at the huddled women with excited eyes and gibbering lips.

'Gobbly, Gobbly,' they chattered, cuffing each other excitedly. And from the corners of their mouths saliva hung in moving threads.

'Destroy them!' cried Rogesse from the second floor. 'They cannot find the door. They cannot escape. Slay them. Every one!' And some of the soldiers, emboldened by panic, fearful of their safety so close to the water, drew their weapons and began to make sweeping cuts at the nearest Orphachins.

But suddenly a wet, bedraggled figure appeared at the door, stooped with exhaustion and streaked with flood-grime. He stared at the chaotic scene with glazed and uncomprehending eyes, taking in with difficulty the packed and crowded stairway, the churning waters, the rapidly revolving figure in the middle of The Great Hall and the rattling chest that drifted close to him. 'Stop!' he cried, angrily beating the water with the flat of his hand. 'How dare you swim off and leave me? I am your General! You take your instruction from me and me alone.' The Orphachins ogling the stairs turned guiltily at the sound of his voice and the submerged pilots, learning of his presence telepathically, rose to the surface one by one until the entire savage band stood shamefaced and waistdeep in the flood.

Meanwhile, Brother Two, bound and floating upon his back, drifted slowly to a halt.

Brother One, turning his head to look at the upsidedown face, gave out a mighty cry of joy that echoed and re-echoed between the walls and flew up the spiral staircase to ring among the highest rafters of The Great Hall.

'Brother!' he shouted in joy and delight. 'Brother! Is it you?' Brother Two squinted backwards with difficulty as Brother One splashed across the few short paces between them.

'It's Brother One!' he muttered, almost inaudible in the echoing Hall. And then, as joy took possession of him, he also gave a great shout of delight,

'It's Brother One!'

What a reunion there was then between the two long-parted brothers as Two's bonds were removed and he stood to embrace and be embraced by his brother.

And what roars of squeaking approval did the Orphachins give out to see their Goddy and their General as alike as two halves of the same shellfish.

And with what savage zeal did the ragged armies cry out from their banistered refuge as The Disciple appeared exhausted in the

Great Doorway with a delicate human burden draped over his sagging shoulders.

'It is Yeni!' they cried. 'She whom many call the Messiah, Last of the fallen goddeses! The Chosen One come to the sacrifice!'

51

Meanwhile, in the wee white fishing village that Brother Two had first spied as he surfaced transcendentally from the exile of the earth's males, the problems of The Volunteer, Johnson, The Girl and The Father were by no means at an end. Discovering that the Barbans had machines of a technological sophistication unparalleled in the history of mankind, the Volunteer's mind had conceived vague plans of enlisting the help of further crew-members to smuggle the machines and the savages on to the galleys.

Now, faced with the finest flowering of the so-called technological master-race, his dreams of vast wealth faded into embarrassing oblivion.

'And this,' the Barban was saying, picking up a length of wood with a large round metal ball on the end, 'is a sleep-machine. It was, at one time, made entirely of metal, but over the years it naturally deteriorated with use and so it was repaired with wood. But it's just as effective as ever.'

'How does it work?' asked The Volunteer almost automatically, pretending with difficulty to be interested.

'I thought you'd ask that,' the Barban replied with an indulgent smile, 'so I'll show you. Along comes an enemy.'

He used two fingers to illustrate a human being strolling along nonchalantly in midair.

'You wait until he's alongside or, preferably, just past you.' He raised the sleep-machine above his head.

'And then you apply the sleep-machine to the skull like this!' The machine fell in a swift and savage imaginary blow, passed through the imaginary enemy and came to an abrupt halt against the Barban's knee.

His lips formed a round O and his eyes closed.

'We'd call that a *club* in our country,' said The Girl, with barely restrained irritation. 'We wouldn't call it a sleep-machine, we'd call it a club.'

The Volunteer frowned in angry warning, shook his head imperceptibly and then with studied politeness examined another machine.

'What's this one?' he asked. 'This looks rather complicated.'

The Barban still stood silently with his lips in an O and his eyes closed so The Volunteer glanced over the machine. It was a long shallow dish on a waisthigh stand with a lid that could be raised or closed by means of large two-handled screws. A drainpipe hung to the floor.

'Fish-crusher,' said the Barban with difficulty, gingerly holding on to his knee and allowing the sleep-machine to slide from his grasp.

'Crushes fish,' he gasped in explanation.

'Oh,' said The Volunteer with a weak smile, 'very interesting.' He glanced once more over the store of primitive tools and implements and said,

'Yes I think we've seen enough.'

'Impressed?' said The Barban, supercilious even through his pain.

'No,' said The Girl.

'Yes,' said The Volunteer loudly. 'Very impressive.'

'So we have a deal?' demanded the Barban. 'All this for a trip home?'

'I'll have to discuss it with my colleagues, but, er, in principle, yes, I suppose we have,' replied The Volunteer edging towards the door. 'Now let's go and see if Johnson has brought the rest of the party in safely.'

'But we do have a deal,' insisted the Barban, suspicion passing across his face. 'Because if you're thinking of backing out—'

'Oh, we're not,' asserted The Volunteer with an ingratiating smile and a conciliatory wave of the hand while backing out through the door.

'A deal is a deal even in our country.'

*

He looked round nervously at the line of gagged and bound women, their eyes turned upon him, and tried to smile and nod casually to them as he crossed the firelit room to the door.

'Wait a minute,' called The Girl, 'We're not going to leave these people trussed up like this are we?'

'We're not?' enquired The Volunteer nervously.

'No,' said The Girl. 'We're not. It's against regulations to curtail the liberty of indigenous populations without good reason.' She began to pull at the cords that bound the nearest prisoner but the Barban bounded forward with a cry of fear.

'No,' he yelled, knocking her hands away. 'Are you crazy? They are devils. They eat human flesh! Release them and we might all die!'

'How do you know they eat human flesh?' demanded The Girl. 'That's what the old man we brought from the Candle Palace claimed, but quite frankly I think it's just superstitious nonsense and anti-feminism taken to the most ridiculous lengths.'

'No!' cried The Barban again, forcibly restraining her from untying the captive. 'We questioned them. They confessed. It's true I tell you.'

'Now, wait a minute,' said The Volunteer uncomfortably and from a distance. 'You can't go about manhandling my fellow-officers like that.'

'Take your hands off me!' shouted The Girl, struggling in the Barban's grasp. 'If it's true, let me talk to them and hear it from their own lips. If I hadn't shouted for help you would have had *me* tied up against this wall by this time.'

She unfastened the gag from the mouth of one of the women and crouched down in front of her.

'Do you speak language?' she enquired solicitously.

'Of course am does,' retorted the woman truculently. 'Unfastens we.'

'These people are afraid that you will attack them.'

'Us am frightened by the many Man-gods. Us wants to go homes. You talks of the Candle Palace. What am happened there? Am all good?'

The Girl shrugged.

'It looks a bit of a mess, but I don't know what it was like before. There were dead insects everywhere. It was flooded and a lot of people had been killed.'

'Oh dears,' wailed the woman, looking with consternation at her companions. 'Peoples killed?'

'I'm afraid so,' said The Girl.

'Careful!' warned the Barban. 'Don't go so close. It will snap at you with its teeth!'

'Oh, please,' said the captive tearfully. 'Don't lets him beats we again. Unties we and lets we go homes to the Palace. Us won't harms no one. Us am only supposed to finds the Man-gods what comes from the sea and takes thems up to the mountain ready for Full Moons. Us am done none harms. Us am eaten nothing. Us am not allowed to eat because us am servants only and not like The Others who am boss at the Palace.'

'It wasn't *us* that curtailed their liberty,' argued The Volunteer. 'We don't have to get involved.'

'Maybe *you* don't,' snapped The Girl. 'But may I draw your attention to the fact that all these prisoners are *females* and all those who want to keep them prisoner are *males*?'

'*Females?*' cried the Barban, staggering back with horror. 'These are *Females*? These are the creatures that drove humanity from Paradise in the old legends?'

'Of course they're females,' replied The Girl angrily. 'What did you think they were? Turtles?'

'Now hold on a minute,' said The Volunteer in a tense and nervous whisper, moving in quickly, 'let's make sure we're not treading on,' he turned his face to The Girl with an expression that pantomimed disaster, '*delicate ground* here. Remember Regulation One Hundred? "never discuss religious matters with unscreened inhabitants".'

'I'm not discussing religious matters,' replied The Girl, beginning to untie the wrists of the ungagged captive who watched the operation with excited glee. 'I'm just setting these women free.'

'Females!' said the Barban again, hyponotized by associations that the word set rolling on the screen of his memory – legends, old tales, horror stories from antiquity, evil and rejection personified.

'I'm just beginning to realize that we may have stumbled on a weird set-up here,' hissed The Volunteer through clenched teeth. 'You were wondering where the men were. There *aren't* any. These guys are strangers. The women talk about "Man-gods" and the men act as though "females" are the most terrifying thing they've ever heard of. Think about it. If we're not careful we may become guilty of the most appalling Culture-damage.' The Girl stopped working on the bulky knots and her face grew pale.

Culture damage! The most serious crime in the Neo-navy's Book!

'But I just said "females" that's all,' she whispered defiantly through her distress. 'Does that make me some sort of criminal?'

'Well *he* was obviously unaware that these people were females,' replied The Volunteer. 'Look at him. He's practically in a state of shock.'

The Barban leaned groggily against the wall staring into unfocussed distance, trembling at the energy that the unlocked realizations had released into his bloodstream, the word 'females' passing over his lips unheard, over and over again.

'We're going to have a problem smoothing this one over,' murmured The Volunteer.

'But you don't have to tell anyone,' whispered The Girl, urgently gripping his arm. 'Nobody need know it was me who used the word first. We can pretend they found out about it before we got here, can't we?'

The Volunteer bit his lips nervously.

'Well,' he said uneasily, disengaging his arm, 'It may not be just as easy as that. I have to think about Johnson, you see. And then there's me too. If we tried to cover for you and it came out we might be implicated.'

The Girl's face hardened although her lips still trembled with fear.

'You selfish swine,' she hissed.

The Volunteer turned to her with an expression that pleaded understanding.

'No,' he said. 'Don't be like that. Look at it from my point of view. Desertion is one thing, so is pilfering and looting, and they're *minor* infringements. But *Culture Damage*!' he swallowed with difficulty as the thought came to him. 'That means the Limbo-Basket!'

'You rotten selfish swine,' The Girl replied, bitterness and resignation mingled in her voice.

'But I'll tell you what I can do,' he said. 'If you stay on the island when Johnson and I go back to the ship we'll say you were killed in an accident. That way you could hide in the hills until the volcano survey is complete and get left behind when The Fleet leaves.' He tried to smile. 'It's not much, but it's better than the Limbo-Basket.'

'You rotten, dirty, filthy, stinking swine,' replied The Girl. Just at that moment the door opened as Johnson helped the limping Father into the shelter of the cottage.

'Everything safe and sound,' he reported. 'How are things at this end?'

'We've got bad news,' replied The Volunteer grimly.

But his reply was interrupted by an apoplectic cry from The Father, who stood rigid with rage and shock in the narrow doorway.

'Barbans!' he cried. 'Barbans! Here of all places! My God! What kind of a universe *is* this? I thought I'd seen the last of you *years* ago!'

The Barban turned his eyes on The Father and uttered no more than a faint whimper at the sight of what he believed to be a dead man's spectre, before slumping to the floor in the innocence of unconsciousness.

'That,' snapped The Girl with vindictive pleasure, 'is what *I* call Culture Damage! That makes all *three* of us guilty now!'

'What's happening?' demanded Johnson, puzzled and alarmed.

'You just put us *all* in the Limbo-Basket,' retorted The Volunteer angrily. 'Now we can *never* go home again. Ever!'

52

Meanwhile, on the bridge of the Neo-navy's leading galley, a lieutenant stood at the right hand of The Admiral gazing out upon the passing shoreline with a curious grief in his eyes as The Watcher read off the effects of the recent cataclysm upon the desert, seeing, on levels beyond the world of mere matter, the plasmic horrors that still haunted the barren and unpeopled wastes.

'Hundreds dead,' said The Watcher in a bored voice. 'Destroyed. First by the volcano, then by the sea and then finally,' she paused in distaste, 'in a great massacre with metal weapons. Injured soldiers put to unnecessary death. All dead. No survivors here. Death, necessary and unnecessary on a vast scale.'

'Are you sure?' asked the Lieutenant, curiously calm. 'No survivors at all?'

'No survivors,' answered The Watcher, nettled. 'That's what I said. If there were survivors they've made themselves very scarce now. There's no one out there.'

The Lieutenant, eyes moist with terrible grief stared out over the passing shoreline and mourned those lost in the cataclysm.

'My Queendom,' he muttered. 'My people – gone.'

He pursed his lips to regain control of the trembling muscles of his face.

'And my body also is gone,' he whispered.

'What's that you're saying?' demanded The Admiral.

'Everything on this island has been destroyed,' replied the spirit of Ana with the quivering lips of the Lieutenant.

'Yes,' agreed the Admiral gruffly, 'but that's bound to happen to every civilization like this, isn't it? Sooner or later.' He shot a glance of curious concern at his subordinate.

'No point in letting it affect you too deeply. It's inevitable. Happens to them all.'

'Yes,' replied Ana quietly. 'To us all.'

And much opportunity did she have as she sailed the Eastern edge of her vanished Empire to reflect on the transitory nature of human power and of life itself from the perspective of a foreign civilization's strange conveyance and in the body of a human sex that she had never before encountered. She perceived many bitter truths of the human condition and of her own part in that drama and as the galley began to round the Southern tip of the island and leave the desert behind, as the cliffs rose up from the sea to buttress the mountain spines of the island, she went below and wept long and silently for herself, for her Empire, for her dreams and her race, loosing tears that she had never been able to shed in her own flesh, a rigid body that had locked all expression of feeling back behind an emotionless and armoured façade.

But, even as she sobbed out her grief in the privacy of the lieutenant's cramped cabin, a figure stepped in unannounced and slammed the door purposefully behind it.

'What is the meaning of this?' snapped Ana angrily, turning away her tear-stained face in shame and straightening her uniform.

'I have come to ask you the same thing,' replied a voice drily. Ana looked up and saw the gleaming eyes of The Watcher upon her, their dreamy clarity seeming to strip away the Lieutenant's flesh and perceive its occupant directly.

'I'm just a little distressed by recent events,' she replied. 'I needed to be alone for a while. Please close the door behind you as you go.'

'I'm afraid that won't work,' replied The Watcher. 'I want to know who you are.'

Ana rose belligerently to her feet.

'I am your superior officer,' she replied brusquely. 'Leave this cabin.'

'That won't work either,' said The Watcher blandly.

And Ana saw the confidence of secret knowledge in her eyes and realized she was discovered.

'How did you know?' she asked.

'Because I can *see*,' came the scornful reply. 'You have a second spirit dangling from your spine! You are a body-thief and a spy!'

'How long have you known? Why did you not denounce me?'

'Because I'm curious,' The Watcher replied, a note of triumph in her voice. 'I noticed you when you first came up on the bridge after the Court Naval. It was you who raised Life's hand at The Admiral's trial. I wanted to know why a spy would want to protect The Admiral. Tell me who you are.'

'Your curiosity means nothing to me,' said Ana with contempt. 'And your manner is offensive. A good servant would have reported my presence immediately. You have betrayed your trust. Get out of my sight.'

The Watcher's face remained as impassive as ever but across her eyes flickered a faint shadow of surprise.

She grasped the handle of the door.

'Very well,' she said crisply, 'if you prefer that I denounce you, so be it.'

Ana made no reply.

The Watcher rattled the handle menacingly.

'Do you hear me? It is still in my power to denounce you. I would prefer you to answer my questions but, if you—'

'Go,' said Ana. 'Do your duty, faithless servant.'

The Watcher flushed angrily.

'I will,' she snapped. 'I will report all I know and with my special sight I see a new trial for The Admiral, but this time there will be a different outcome.'

She opened the door but Ana, stepping quickly across the cabin, closed it with the weight of her shoulder and pushed The Watcher aside.

'A clever move, Sister,' she admitted with an appreciative chuckle. 'I appreciate cunning in an adversary. Come, sit down, let us talk this over.'

She pushed The Watcher roughly on to the bunk and stood over her. 'What do you see now with those strange eyes of yours Watcher?'

'See?' stammered The Watcher. 'I see nothing.'

'Well then I will tell you what is going to happen,' said Ana grimly. 'I am going to cause what you people call Unnecessary Death. Yours.'

'No,' said The Watcher firmly. 'You will not. I am more use to you alive. I can tell you things I didn't tell The Admiral. Things he didn't need to know. The battle in the desert. The tribes travelling through the mountains. The Palace in the plains. You will become my ally. You will not cause Unnecessary Death because I can tell you of all this.'

'Yes, such things are of interest to me,' agreed Ana. 'But I must tell you that they will not save you. Since I have the power to choose between the life of a wretched and treacherous servant and that of your Admiral, your leader and the Rightful Monarch of your nation, I am afraid a few tattle-tale titbits will not protect you nor buy your survival.'

She reached out her hands and grasped The Watcher's throat, but the frightened sailor cried,

'No. Stop. Listen to me there is another way. I care nothing whether The Admiral lives or dies. I came to you with a plan, a plan we can carry out together. I am tired of this wretched life in the Neo-navy. I am weary of being a Seer among the blind. Among my people Watchers are regarded with scorn and derision because of the seeming bleakness and pessimism of their lives. Who could be optimistic about a society plummeting to destruction? But here on this island with so few, men, a Matriarchy could be established with a strong and disciplined army to subjugate the peasant farmers. I see how it can be accomplished! I have seen what has happened on the island and see the disarray into which the people have been thrown. If you tell me all you know of the rules of this land and of the peoples who inhabit it, between us, you and I, together, can swiftly seize power and live out our lives in ease and splendour.'

'Seize power?' repeated Ana with a dry laugh, loosing her grip on The Watcher's throat.

'Yes,' replied The Watcher, nodding eagerly. 'With my Seeing Vision and your detailed knowledge it would be supremely easy! I shall become Queen and you will share my wealth and be my Chief Minister.'

'Oh really?' said Ana. 'Queen indeed?'

She sat down beside The Watcher and placed a comradely arm like a snake across her shoulders.

'Tell me,' she said with a gleaming smile. 'Tell me how you will become Queen of The Earth and Matriarch of The Steriles.'

'First I must know your purpose aboard The Fleet,' said The Watcher suspiciously. 'Before I reveal my plans I must know who you are and to whom you owe your loyalties.'

'A wise precaution,' agreed Ana, 'but unnecessary. You have seen the destruction on the desert and must know that my homeland is destroyed, that I am alone and owe my loyalties to no one. I was the plaything of the Cruel Queen. She took away my limbs when I was no more than a child and had me carried everywhere in a box to taunt and torment whenever she chose. I learned how to travel without my mutilated body, now lost and surely dead somewhere in the desert. I took this body because I saw its rightful occupant deposed by the magic substances of Judgment and I saved the life of The Admiral to win his favour and find a new life for myself among your people.' She lowered her head in seeming sadness to avoid The Watcher's penetrating gaze. 'For I had lost hope of ever being with my own people again.'

'Look at me,' said The watcher. 'Look into my eyes and tell me to whom you owe your loyalties. And do not hope to lie to me.'

'Loyalties?' laughed the Lieutenant, looking fearlessly into The Watcher's liquid stare, his face twisted with bitterness. 'I owe loyalties to no one! The people of the island are traitors, weaklings and simpletons all!'

'And you would not shrink from throwing down the island's Queen?'

'I would do it *gladly!*' answered Ana vehemently. 'She brought nothing but ruin to her people!'

The Watcher peered shrewdly into the Lieutenant's eyes for a moment then her face broke into a delighted smile.

'You are telling the truth,' she exclaimed. 'Good! Good! We have a common purpose. I had intended to keep silent and return to this island with hired soldiers and capture it by force. But with your help it can be done quickly and by stealth without the need for mercenaries and their greed.'

'The island will fall so easily?' enquired Ana in surprise. 'How is that possible?'

'With your help,' replied The Watcher eagerly, 'we can spread herbs and potions among the existing powers upon the island that will incapacitate them and bend their will to ours. It is swift, sure and simple.'

'But upon the bridge you said that none survived,' argued Ana. 'Are they not all destroyed by the Volcano?'

'Many are destroyed, it is true,' agreed The Watcher, 'but many have survived and move across the mountains in winding armies. This I kept from The Admiral for fear he would send in the Plague-Dogs and destroy the very peoples whom I hope to make subject to me.'

'Tell me what you saw,' Ana urged gently, squeezing her companion's shoulder with the snake-like arm.

The Watcher snorted in near-contempt.

'Oh, a classic case of terminal breakdown in society,' she replied. 'It probably doesn't mean much to you but to a student of supernova cultures like myself it's very interesting. Having seen one or two elements of it I can easily conjecture what the rest will be.'

'You must have great wisdom,' murmured Ana with eyes of wonder, 'to know so much having seen so little.'

'That's the secret of a Watcher's Art,' was the proud reply. 'To know an object in the round having seen only one side.'

'And what did you see of the island?' Ana pressed her. 'Tell me what you have seen and I will confirm the accuracy of your vision.'

'I saw the collapse of a military dictatorship in the desert, for one thing,' replied The Watcher readily. 'And since so many soldiers had been massacred one can assume that it was a popular uprising. No doubt those who lived upon the desert were simple people, surviving through toil upon a barren land and therefore gullible, easily manipulated by superstition and by the fear of soldiers. Am I right?'

'Yes,' replied Ana. 'The Queen did indeed exert absolute control by the cunning use of religion and force.'

'Not too difficult a job for the right person,' remarked The Watcher with a dismissive gesture. 'Such a Queen would be one with so inflated a sense of self that she could subjugate others simply by concentrating her distorted will-power upon them. Am I right? Look what she did to you! That's typical of a demagogue as sick as she.'

Ana made no reply save for a stiffnecked, tight-mouthed nod of agreement.

'And she would be totally paranoid,' The Watcher continued. 'Distrustful, unable to delegate power and therefore unable to establish a successor in the event of her death. A classic case of sickness masquerading as leadership. Right?'

'Right,' agreed Ana icily, swallowing her anger.

'Anyway, there are only three things that happen to people who take the totalitarianism implicit in the structure of a State to its logical, extreme and ultimately absurd conclusions – they're either betrayed from within by jealous rivals, destroyed from without by the superstitious peasantry upon some messianic crusade, or else they die of cancer.' She grinned ruefully. 'And judging by the number of butchered spirits that still hang over that desert I think the last alternative unlikely.'

'There are people called The Others who live in the Palace of which you spoke in the plains to the West of the mountains,' said Ana, 'Was it not their treachery and malice that overthrew the Queen?'

'Oh no,' answered the Watcher with a contemptuous laugh. 'They're even sillier than this Matriach we shall replace. They're just a classic example of decadent aristocracy, inherited title, form without content, probably retaining *some* links with the time when the society was a burgeoning, living entity, but only in a ritualized form, probably with monstrous misunderstandings and distortions that prevented any development that might still have been possible. That's my guess, anyway. I could be wrong. But wherever you find a military dictatorship you'll always find a decayed gentry that pretends it hasn't happened. Now that their lands are ruined by the floods they'll just wither away and die or become desert farmers like their ancestors.'

'And the Orphachins,' demanded Ana grimly. 'What of them? Was it they who overthrew the Queen and slew her troops?'

'Unlikely,' said The Watcher, 'though I have to admit I haven't seen much about them yet. But I don't see how they could present us with much of a problem. Like any isolated minority they will have developed a secret language and mores quite distinct from the group that threw them out. But, being a tight-knit group, they will easily be manipulable by a semblance of superior power, divinity for instance, or else they can be wiped out. We can decide later which is the more convenient. Am I right?'

She turned to find Ana staring at her strangely. 'What is it?' she asked nervously. 'Why are you looking at me like that?'

'All my life,' Ana replied slowly, 'I believed that this island was the whole world, that there were no lands beyond these shores, that the horizon was the edge of the world. I believed that right and wrong were decided by what one could or could not accomplish. I see differently now. I still know not what right and wrong are but I will find out.'

'But you were right!' exclaimed The Watcher. 'Morality *is* power!'

'No,' said Ana dreamily. 'I have been The Queen of The Steriles, Matriarch of The Whole Earth. I know that you are mistaken.'

'A Watcher is *never* mistaken,' replied the woman haughtily. 'You will come to learn that in time.'

'Perhaps,' said Ana, a cold, cruel gleam in her eyes, her hands snaking forward to The Watcher's throat. 'But first I will teach *you* something.'

53

*And let the name Ana ring through Time and Space to the ends of the
Universe, that every intelligence, even to the furthest uncaring star shall
hear her scream and know my name!*

from *The Boy's Book of Empty Threats* by Madame Lottie Eucharist

Meanwhile time had finally run out for the divided society upon the
battered island.

It has been said that Nature abhors a vacuum; but for unresolved
opposites Nature has an even keener hatred. In all but the purest
cultures the male and female components of humanity are held apart
by some form of social stricture or taboo. As an inevitable consequence disease, sickness, war and death crackle like static electricity
between the pages of history as Nature Denied releases its negatively
charged potential along complex genetic pathways, burning out
archaic structures, destroying civilizations, erasing Time itself.

On the island of Scarabim for hundreds of years the naturally
valent halves of mankind's internal Universe had been separated by
an artificial barrier of false creed and unthinking ritual, by the wor-
shipping of men as gods, by cloning and by secular parthenogenesis.
And over the island had gathered centuries of Nature's dreadful
hatred, held back, pent up as though by curious and mischievous
gods, until no force in the universe could have contained it.

At that moment came the ultimate blasphemy.

At that moment the selfstyled Matriarch of The Steriles swore
to the heavens to take the life of Yeni, Last of Those Who
Bleed with the Moon, last of Nature's true children. 'And let the
name *Ana* ring through Time and Space to the ends of the universe,
that every intelligence, even to the furthest uncaring star shall hear
her scream and know *my* name! *Ana!*' A foolish and dreadful oath
that finally earthed the accumulated anger of the heavens upon the
island's blasphemy, a discharge heralded by a silence in which the
Earth did not turn, nor the moon revolve around it, nor the planets
flame their dreadful orbits, when Time itself stood still and with a
noiseless scream, began to reverse itself, slow and ponderous at first,
but gathering pace as it recoiled diagonally across centuries of

centuries, unwinding history as easily as it had been ravelled up, a self-cancelling vortex, a collapsing spiral, a mirror negation of all that had ever been.

Nature's revenge!

Insect life turned upon humanity, the earth burned, the sky opened, the seas punished the people.

Yet those who survived heeded not, clung ever more strongly to their sterile dogmas, battled and bickered among themselves, scrabbling and squabbling to piece together the ruins of their respective civilizations, hollow copies of the social structures that had been so thoroughly destroyed, plotted for power on the very principle that had induced the holocaust.

As the sun dipped more swiftly to the Western edge of the turning world, the last curling streams of vapour leaked skywards from the volcano's spattered lips, the Earth began once more to knit up its wounds and the citizens of the soil crept from their hiding places and went about their tiny business, scavenging here, burrowing there, weaving together again the broken filaments of an ecological net that had been damaged by the disaster.

Not so humanity.

False Queens bawled their sovereignty, soi-disant Generals pulled rank, the enslaved sought masters and traditional antipathies loomed larger than common sufferings.

Oh, foolish mortals! Beware hubris!

Over centuries the genetic helix had become brittle with misuse until even regeneration of The Whales had ceased. The Whale, last of those who spontaneously and immaculately conceived, was gone, drowned in her subterranean exile. And for Yeni, Last of Those who Bleed with the Moon, last fragile link with Life's mainstream, last of those who could propagate the benighted species, life hung in the balance as the angry rabble thronging upon The Great Stairs called for her death to propitiate imaginary gods, unwittingly crying for the destruction of the genetic spiral itself, messenger of life, human history incarnate in a simple twist of fate, carrier of their own destiny.

Their cry was answered.

The spiral snapped.

But with the familiar irony of a comic universe, it was not their victim who perished, but they themselves.

The structure of the Candle Palace, weakened by flood and fire, could no longer support the weight of the hundreds who crowded angry and violent upon The Great Stairs. Unheard over the tumult of their voices, the structure of the helical stairway began to creak and crack, its weakest members snapping one by one as it tottered imperceptibly, groaning like a live creature in unutterable pain, whining with terrible agonies, sagging and bending beneath forces far greater than those which it had been designed to withstand until, suddenly, with a roar as frightening as the volcano's dreadful rumbling, as terrifying as the thundering skies, as awful as the angry wind and the maddened boiling sea, it fell, coiled, collapsing in upon itself, its monstrous mass turning downwards, swallowing up its fragile burdens, crushing them instantly between massive marbled teeth with a speed and sureness that bordered on the absurd.

Some few escaped.

Those who stood at the water's edge were blown forward into the floods by the exhaled wind of that collapsing lung. Those who stood in the water were washed away by the waves that sprang from beneath the marble cataract as though they were motes of dust in a cannon mouth. Those who stood by The Great Doorway were blasted out into the flooded plains by the sweeping wall of water.

And as the survivors fought against shock and fear, forcing their bodies through the angry swirling torrents to escape from the flesh-devouring masonry, the outer walls of the Palace, deprived of their principal support, fell slowly inwards, screaming under stress, tearing and snapping beneath their own weight, toppling in slabs and pillars upon the flattened helix that had sustained the structure for a millenium. And as the outer walls crashed in upon the vanished centre, the honeycombed cellars sagged and crumbled, collapsed in upon themselves like a crushed heart and sank beneath the plains, weighed down by a marble sarcophagus, sliding reluctantly but inexorably into the earth, bubbling and screaming, the voice of stones in agony piercing the evening air like birds of prey crying for the kill, until all sank into the plains and the impassive floodwaters covered the debris with a skin of glass and to the shocked and incredulous watchers it seemed as though the Candle Palace had never stood upon the plains, nor raised its proud turrets nobly to the sky, nor hummed with music, nor burned so bright with flames and candles that it seemed to shine, translucent from within as the wing of a gullhawk against the sun, nor glowed like a pale rosewater moonstone in the purple darkness.

At first some cried out in astonishment or grief, but in time there was no sound but the bubbling air escaping from the underwater tomb and the turbulence of water crushed from the sinking stones.

And within the hour, as the sun sank, slowly dimming, towards the horizon, even this movement ceased, the floods grew tranquil in the waning, blood-red light and the survivors stared out over a liquid and utterly featureless plain. The Candle Palace had vanished.

In the shocked silence that followed, Brother Two turned to Tomaly-Somaly who stood beside him, The Last Child of Woman Born clutched in her arms and, choosing his words with great formality, said.

'I've heard of shooting your wad, but that's ridiculous!'

54

The Candle Palace, repository and shrine of Female Wisdom, Temple of Parthenogenesis, riddled and rotted through by rusted ritual until its Priestesses were chosen only from the sterile and therefore became itself sterile, finally, had been utterly destroyed. Yet miraculously, and not for the first time, Mankind slipped through some loophole in evolutionary logic and survived to betray itself again.

Look, see how even now the survivors string out in a weary line beneath the darkening stars, travelling Westwards through the night, going they know not where and all for different reasons.

The Orphachins follow their Goddy and their General, indistinguishable save that one shouts with his mouth and the other whispers with his mind; Goddy and General, Brothers One and Two, following the tracks of their father, source of their cells, image of their old age; the first Man-god to enter the Parthenogenetic Temple and live; behind them come The Disciple and Tomaly-Somaly, she with The Last Child of Woman Born in her arms, he with the delirious Yeni over his shoulders; and in the rear comes Amrita ripped from her pampered world and forced to follow, destitute, or remain behind to die alone, paying for her passage by dragging the floating iron-bound body-box.

Meanwhile, in the sunken Candle Palace, the disparate elements of a decayed aeon are crushed together in the starless blackness, pulped for recycling, slowly separating into constituent salts, dissolving back into the earth from whence they came, Nature cutting its losses, salvaging its investments, going about its work without the irksome nuisance of the human will to pervert its processes; The Others, their servants, their enemies, their Mothers and their mythology mingling and melted away.

But what of the survivors? What further chaos were they destined to cause in the explosive mix of cultures that seethed and struggled in the wee white fishing village towards which they waded over the flooded plains? For all its other faults, there is, perhaps, no clearer account of the events that followed that night than Brother One's autobiographical story of life with the Orphachins, 'The Good Die Young'. Although, as stated earlier, doubt has been thrown on the accuracy of much of this work, the section dealing with that dreadful journey is of more than passing interest to the student of supernova cultures.

(This extract appears by kind permission of *The Military Press*.)

It had been a tough day with very heavy losses, but as night fell there was still much to do. There was no dry land to be found near the sunken Palace, even though the floodwater was falling rapidly and so we had but two alternatives:

a) to withdraw to the higher ground of the mountains

b) to push on in the direction we learned The Father had been carried by the mysterious winged strangers.

Learning that there was a possibility of finding shelter in an ancient village on the Western shore we took the latter course of action, a choice that subsequently proved correct.

All personnel were severely shocked by the unexpected disaster of the collapsing Palace, but, with the exception of the fellow I had encountered in the mountain pass, who whined incessantly about having to carry the wounded chap on the Westward march, everyone bore up with remarkable courage and fortitude. Exhausted though I was, nothing could have prevented me from performing the happy duty of recounting my adventures to Brother Two and he from relating his to me. It was at this time that I first learned of his peculiar ability to communicate telepathically with my Orphachins, although I must admit that at first I treated his claim with a certain scepticism. He reminded me that I had been sceptical also of his belief that there existed a world other than our submarine civilization where lived a race of angels with whom it had been our privilege to live in harmony and ecstasy, and yet, as he pointed out, here I was in that very world. I replied that my scepticism was not without some justification since, in the days spent among these women, I had seen not a single trace of ecstasy or harmony but, on the contrary, witnessed much unpleasantness and discord. I needed to refer only to the conduct of those who had so recently met their end in the fallen Palace to win a grudging agreement from my Brother on this point. However I conceded that his beliefs concerning the ancient manuscripts and the Mandaladies may not have been as wild as first I thought, although how much the recitation of 'Suck leather, Sister. Suck leather, Sister,' was responsible for my salvation is impossible to say. I expressed surprise that he still clung to the bulk of his old beliefs in the face of the reality he was experiencing, but he pointed out that the 'angels', as he insisted on calling them still, may have merely forgotten their cultural heritage just as we might have forgotten ours had it not been for The Teachings. 'I have not given up hope,' I can remember him passionately declaring, 'of finding an angel who will respond to the sacred texts.'

But then, he always was rather smug.

He even sought to criticize my leadership of the Orphachins, maintaining that I should have dissuaded them from the practice of cannibalism (as he perversely chose to describe it) but, as I have stated elsewhere in this volume, it is difficult to see how they might otherwise have survived. And, in answer to his rather intemperate comments on the practice of eating 'angels' I was forced to be fairly stern with him, pointing out that every living creature eats, that it is universal and therefore entirely natural. The purpose to which he proposed to put these 'angels', on the other hand, this ridiculous notion of 'mating', was *neither* universal *nor* natural. I informed him that it was rather smug to criticize my activities when his own were a good deal more questionable.

But, despite these minor differences of opinion, we were greatly delighted to see each other once more, having each believed the other lost for ever, and our intercourse helped speed the weary hours of that blundering struggle over the darkened, flooded plains. Often we were forced to halt in order that the two surviving women of the Palace with the strange box and the tiny Orphachin would catch up with us, for their progress was much hampered by the folds of cloth festooning their bodies and we were no less delayed by the slow progress of the toady who carried the human being that I had rescued in the desert the previous night. Brother Two claimed and, in fact, still holds to the claim, that this creature is a women. But I had reason to believe otherwise, having seen the fresh wounds that had been inflicted upon him and, to this day, have great reservations on the matter.

Slow and halting though our progress was, we were able to reach the Western coast where, on the firmer footing of the sandy beaches, we made our way to a village that Brother Two had encountered when he first emerged from the sea many months before. The Candle Palace women were at first reluctant to approach it, claiming it was taboo to all but chosen initiates among their servants, who made up some form of religious community, to prepare the rituals in which, we were led to understand, The Father had at one time been destined to play a part. But a few admonitory nips around the ankle from the Orphachins soon persuaded them that their wisest course was to remain with the main body of the party.

We finally reached the village and, weary as we were, we made camp immediately in the first dry buildings we could find while some of the Orphachins sortied out in search of supplies. They had not eaten during the whole day of forced marches and it was only with great difficulty that I could restrain them from menacing our Candle Palace refugees or the whining toady whom my brother had rescued from the Snowcamp. And although we found supplies of peat and faggots which enabled us to light a large fire to warm ourselves and dry our clothes, I realized that, unless they could obtain food, all our lives would soon be in danger. However, knowing the opposition that would be encountered if I sent the Orphachins out hunting for females, I waited until everyone had fallen asleep before giving the order,

'Fetchy, Gobbly. Fetchy, Gobbly.'

Before long the brightest of them had returned with small morsels of flesh plucked from a kill which I devoured with great enthusiasm, having myself eaten nothing since the previous day. I supposed that the Orphachins had discovered some straggler, perhaps part of the religious order that lived in the village, and that they had divided her up amongst themselves somewhere. I sat before the fire, eating my fill and feeling my strength returning, regretting only that the others could not, (or would not) share my good fortune until my brother, who had been tossing and turning restlessly in sleep, woke himself with a loud cry and came over to the fireside to tell me, in desperate tones, of a terrible dream about the Orphachins that had disturbed his slumbers, whereupon I admitted that I had sent them out scavenging for food and his dream probably resulted from the telepathic empathy that he claimed to enjoy.

He grew pale and asked if I realized what I had done. Thinking that he was opening up needlessly the debate on the morality of cannibalism, I

251

made no reply, but turned to accept a gift from another Orphachin who sought to curry my favour.

It was an arm and a hand.

Not the tastiest of morsels by any means, but welcome enough under the circumstances except for one thing.

Across the back of the hand was a deep scar.

'The Father!' my brother screamed angrily, snatching the limb away from me. 'You're eating The Father!'

55

'They are the scum of the sea-bed,' whispered The Father fervently. 'I should know. I lived with them for years and then they sentenced me to death.'

'I don't want to interrupt,' interrupted Johnson uneasily, 'but could you perhaps keep your voice down a little? If they're as nasty as you say, then things might become a bit difficult if they overhear.'

'They're even *nastier* than I say!' exclaimed The Father in a hoarse undertone. 'It was deliberately bred into them by the selection of genes. Even hundreds of years ago their ancestors wanted to take over the political structure. So they bred selectively to produce offspring that were especially stubborn, selfish and untrustworthy until they developed the perfect political animal. And they've been duplicating it ever since and have gained almost total political control of our civilization. They even started getting rid of their opponents with all kinds of sneaky tricks. For instance, in my case, they passed a law that made it illegal to clone two offspring at once – twins – which is something I'd managed to do fifteen years earlier. And then they tried me in the Council Cave, found me retrospectively guilty, sentenced me to death and shoved me out through The Tubes.' He shook his head in dismay. 'They're *evil*, I tell you. The scum of the sea-bed!'

Johnson nodded his sympathy but with a puzzled frown.

'That's terrible,' he agreed. 'But what's cloning?'

'You don't know what cloning is?' demanded The Father in surprise. 'How do you suppose *you* came into existence?'

'Oh, I see,' blushed Johnson with an embarrassed grin, 'we have a different name for it where I come from.'

'The point is that they're vicious and dangerous people. We can't trust them even while we're looking at them. Their first thought when they pull themselves together will be how to get the better of us. I warn you. Before you know it they'll have set up all kinds of rules and regulations which will mean we have to start paying fines or being locked up or saying we're sorry all the time. Whatever we find to eat, they'll make laws that say we have to give them half of it and they'll always be thinking up new ways of getting the rest off us. Why, I wouldn't be surprised if they end up forming us into two sides and make us fight each other.'

'That sounds terrible,' replied Johnson.

'And as for those other creatures,' The Father continued, covertly pointing to the door behind which the women held them captive, 'they're just as bad in their way. They eat people. I should know. They tried to eat *me*. They kept me in this Snowcamp up in the—'

'Yes, I know,' said Johnson hurriedly, a nauseated smile flickering over his lips. 'You've already been through all that. Twice.'

'Well, then you understand the difficult spot we're in.'

'Of course I do. But it doesn't help to keep going over it again and again, does it? We're trapped here for good unless we can persuade the women to let us go, so instead of continually pointing out how tough the situation is, why don't you try to think of some way we can get out of it?'

'I just want to be sure you'll take me with you when you go,' replied The Father. 'I just want you to understand that I can't stay here with these awful creatures.'

'We're not going anywhere,' said Johnson gloomily. 'We're all stuck here now. I know we told the Barbans we'd take them home but things have changed. We thought that they'd come from some other continent like us. We didn't realize that all you males had been forced to live under the sea for all these years. Even if we could go home ourselves we wouldn't be allowed to take you people because you're all criminals.'

'Who is?'

'You are.'

'Me?'

'All of you.'

'Why?'

'I don't know,' replied Johnson unhappily. 'You just are. This is a prison island and has been for more than a thousand years. We're not allowed to take you back because you and your kind are supposed to be in quarantine until you die out so that we don't get infected with your illegal mental attitudes.'

'What illegal mental attitudes?'

Johnson shifted uncomfortably on the wooden floor.

'Well,' he shrugged diffidently, 'an unhealthy preoccupation with machines and stuff like that. Machines are illegal in our country. Have been for hundreds and hundreds of years. They make people immoral.'

'But I thought you were looking for machines,' replied The Father, puzzled. 'At the Candle Palace you wanted a Flame-torch. I remember.'

'Well,' explained Johnson, 'that was just – er,' he tried to find a plausible excuse, but failed. His face took on an expression of whimsical amusement and he shook his head sadly.

'Greed,' he said. 'That was just greed.'

A Barban tiptoed over from the door and held out a sleep-machine.

'Your turn to keep watch,' he told Johnson. 'I've been listening through the door and they're still talking, but I can't hear what they're saying.'

'Alright,' agreed Johnson, taking the weapon and climbing stiffly to his feet. 'Though I'm not sure I could use this thing if it came down to it.'

He crept soundlessly to the doorway and, pressing his ear to the woodwork, strained anxiously to hear the conversation in the next room where The Volunteer was desperately bargaining for their freedom. Unable to hear the words, he listened disconsolately to the angry buzz of argument and then huddled up on the floor to wait, the sleep-machine cradled in his arms.

'Listen,' The Volunteer was saying, 'I *know* you outnumber us. You don't have to keep harping on the fact. It's obvious. There are six Barbans, the old man, Johnson and me in there and ten women and you in here.'

'I'm a woman too,' snapped The Girl 'That makes eleven women.'

'Yes, I know you're a woman,' he said throwing up his hands in despair. 'I'm not arguing with that. I'm saying that just because there are eleven of you and only nine of us it doesn't mean we have to behave like this.'

'Winners' Rules,' retorted The Girl coldly 'That's what I said right from the beginning.'

'But it's just not *fair*,' whined The Volunteer. 'What do I have to say to convince you we shouldn't be behaving like this? Listen—'

'No,' interrupted The Girl, '*you* listen. We're stuck on this island now, all of us, for good. Each of us has to survive as best we can. My best chance of survival is with people of my own sex. That's become abundantly clear to me, I'm sorry to say. I'm a woman and when the chips are down that's where my loyalties lie. We want you to hand over the Barbans and the old man to use in the Full Moon rituals and we want them *now*. Nobody is leaving this village until we get them. You've got weapons in there so we can't take you by force, but we can wait you out and wear you down and we'll get you in the end.'

She smiled cruelly

'That's a woman's strength, you know, endurance. You men may be pretty impressive when it comes to short bursts of intense effort and shows of strength. But when it comes to perseverance through time we women will take you on any day.'

'It's brutal and beastly and immoral. It's unnecessary death and you know it.'

'It's not immoral *here*,' snapped The Girl. 'And if it keeps the culture alive then it's not unnecessary death either. So hand them over? What's it to you? You and Johnson are free to go.'

'Until you run out of sacrificial lambs,' retorted The Volunteer bluntly, 'and then it will be our turn. In nine months you'll be hunting us down like a pack of Plague-Dogs.'

The Girl winced nervously at the mention of the lethal Beasts.

'Nine months is better than half an hour,' she replied. 'If you keep us waiting here much longer you'll be easy meat for The Dogs when they're unleashed on the island at dawn.'

The Volunteer shrank back and studied The Girl's face with horrified reappraisal.

'You wouldn't let that happen!' he murmured. 'You wouldn't expose us to The Dogs!'

She sniffed and blinked rapidly.

'I might,' she said evasively, doodling on her knee with a slender forefinger, 'if I have to.'

'But I—' The Volunteer blurted out but hurriedly bit off the sentence.

'What?'

'I'd somehow thought that—'

He stopped again.

'Thought what?'

'I'd somehow thought that – well – if we were going to be – that is – if we have to stay on this island for the rest of our lives, I had sort of assumed that we, that is to say, you and I might perhaps be—'

He ground to a halt.

The Girl frowned impatiently.

'Might be what?' she snapped.

The Volunteer looked at her in empty despair for a long moment and then, in a miserable voice, said,

'I love you.'

She sneered and turned her face away to look in the fire. Then looked back at him with curiosity.

Frowning.

'That's a rather absurd thing to say under the circumstances.'

'I know,' he replied. 'But at least I've said it. I won't get the chance again. I just want you to know. I've never said it before for just that reason – it's absurd.'

'Why?' demanded The Girl with a hint of irritation in her voice. 'What's so absurd about it?'

'Well, two career officers in the Navy. It's just a little impractical.'

'And it's not impractical now?'

The Volunteer shrugged.

'Forget it,' he said. 'You're right. Wrong time, wrong place. It's absurd.'

'Is it?' demanded The Girl.

To Johnson, half-dozing, half-listening on the other side of the door, it seemed as though talks had broken down and the sudden silence that brought him to full alert grew more ominous as it grew longer.

But, if truth be told, he could not have been more mistaken. For a millenium the naturally valent halves of man's internal universe had been held apart, until Nature itself seethed with rage at the Cosmic Crime. Now, at least, upon the island, humanity was beginning to weave together again the broken filaments of an ecological net that had been damaged by the long-perpetuated blasphemy as The Volunteer and The Girl held each other in a silent and grateful embrace.

The women huddled together in the little room looked on aghast, as though seeing a holy apparition come amongst them, as though witnessing a natural phenomenon of incredible magnitude and brilliance, as though observing their own death and rebirth.

'I can hear music,' whispered The Volunteer drunkenly.

'I can hear singing,' murmured The Girl gently.

'I can't *hear* anything,' croaked Johnson fearfully.

'Me hears noises,' muttered one of the women suddenly.

The others listened.

It was true.

Peculiar, tiny ululations filtered into the smoke-filled room from the dark night outside the shutters.

The couple reluctantly drew apart, trying to identify the approaching sounds.

'Oh no!' whispered The Girl. 'It can't be The Dogs. He wasn't going to unleash The Dogs until dawn!'

'Those aren't Dogs,' replied The Volunteer. 'I don't know what they are, but they're not Dogs.'

There was a scrabbling on the cobbled streets outside the cottage and then came an inquisitive scratching and sniffing at the shutters.

An excited sing-song voce began to mutter ominously. It said,

'Gobbly, Gobbly. Gobbly, Gobbly.'

56

Meanwhile, upon the galleys anchored not far off the Western shore, the silence of the night lay heavy and treacle-thick. Still now were the long and slender oars, folded away the kites of the Watchmen and no lights gleamed from the shuttered portholes of the somnolent fleet.

Only on The Admiral's bridge could life be seen, staring up at the heavens with motionless concentration.

'There it goes again,' said The Admiral, pointing to a faint speck of light speeding across the star-spattered sky. 'See it?'

'Where, Sir?' replied the lieutenant of the watch. 'I can't—'

'It's gone now,' said The Admiral.

He continued the stare up into the weighty blackness of infinite distance with the curiosity and joy of a child upon his face. 'I wonder where it was going,' he murmured. 'I wonder where it was off to.'

He turned to look at their companion ships shifting gently on glass-calm waters and sniffed the cold, clean air moving in from the open sea.

'I shall miss all this,' he said quietly.

'Sir?'

'The space. The peace. The silence. I shall miss it,' he repeated.

'I beg your pardon, Sir.'

'I'm retiring. This is my last trip. I've decided.'

The lieutenant made no comment for a long time and then mumbled.

'Pity to send in the Plague-Dogs on your last trip, isn't it, Sir? Sort of going out with a whimper, wouldn't you say?'

'Better safe than sorry.' replied The Admiral curtly.

The lieutenant sniffed disparagingly.

'There's not many on board would be sorry to go ashore tomorrow. Seems a waste. Should be plenty of worthwhile pickings on that place.'

'Perhaps there would be under another Admiral, but not this one. Subject closed.'

There was a whistle from the Speaking Tubes and the lieutenant took up the mouthpiece.

'Bridge,' he said firmly.

But as he listened his face grew pale in the moonlight.

He replaced the instrument slowly and turned, shaken, to The Admiral.

'That was Willis, Sir. Trying to find The Watcher for you. He found her, Sir. She's—' he steadied himself against the wooden railings. 'She's dead, sir.'

*

The Admiral did not turn his head from the contemplation of the heavens but his shoulders stiffened at the word.

'Dead?' he repeated uncomprehending. 'The Watcher? Dead?'

'Willis says it looks as though she's been strangled, Sir.'

The Admiral removed his hand from the pocket of his coat and rubbed his forehead gently with trembling fingers.

'I knew it,' he said softly. 'I knew there was something strange about this island. A kind of malevolence, a sense of foreboding and doom.'

'It wasn't the island that did it,' replied the lieutenant. 'It was Lieutenant Parks, Sir. The Watcher was in his cabin. Willis is holding him until you get down there.'

'Thankyou,' said The Admiral numbly, moving towards the steps. 'I'll go and talk to Lieutenant Parks.'

He stopped with only his head showing above the deck as he descended the ladder.

'After this,' he said grimly, 'whatever doubt I might have had about The Dogs is gone. Nobody, and I repeat, nobody is going to set foot on that island while I'm in command of this fleet. It's poisoned, I tell you. The Watcher spent the whole day watching it and look what's happened to her now. We're not even going to wait to look for those three fools who went ashore this morning. There's something evil about that place and none of the sailors in my care are going to be exposed to it.'

Meanwhile, Lieutenants Willis and Parks sat facing each other across the narrow cabin, lit eerily from below by a small firefly lantern.

Willis was rigid with horror and disgust, terrified of The Watcher's corpse that grinned up maniacally from the floor, the eyes staring emotionlessly into infinite distance almost as though they were still at work.

Parks slumped numbly on his bunk, head in hands, sobbing quietly.

'In all my years,' Willis murmured for the hundredth time. 'In all my years. In all my years.'

Neither of them moved as The Admiral entered save that Willis nodded when The Admiral asked,

'Is she dead?'

He stooped to place his fingers on the artery at the side of her neck and grimaced with distaste to feel no pulse.

'Detail two sailors to remove the body. Women. It will be easier for them to take.'

'He strangled her,' said Willis with difficulty. 'Deliberate Unnecessary Death. I'm not sure you're safe alone with him, Sir.'

The Admiral held open the door in reply. Willis went out shaking his head.

'Well?' said The Admiral, after looking silently down at Parks for a long moment.

'No,' mumbled the Lieutenant through his tears.

'No what?'

'I couldn't have. I mean – why?'

'Who did?'

'I don't know. Me perhaps! But I wouldn't! I just don't remember anything! I just felt someone shaking me awake and it was Willis, then he pointed at the floor and I looked and—' he burst into fresh floods of tears. 'I just *couldn't* have!'

'What's the last thing you remember?'

'The Justice Drugs,' replied Parks. 'I remember being given the Justice Drugs. Nothing after that. Until this!'

The Admiral watched his face carefully in the glow of the fizzling firefly lantern.

'Do you remember the trial?'

'No,' replied Parks, near to hysteria. 'Nothing! I remember nothing!'

'You were up on the bridge earlier today. Do you remember that?'

'Nothing! I told you Nothing!'

'We talked of death and melancholy, don't you recall?'

'I don't even know who Mel Ankoli is!' answered Parks desperately. 'I tell you it's a blank. I don't remember anything!'

The Admiral let the air slowly out of his lungs in a long sigh of understanding.

'I knew it,' he said. 'This place is bewitched. Even when you were up on the bridge it seemed as though I was talking to some bitter, withered spirit, some ancient, cynical creature with three times your handful of years.'

*

He placed a firm reassuring hand on Parks' shoulder. 'Bear up, lad,' he said. 'You've been the victim of some strange devil from the island. It must have entered you while you were emptied out by the Justice Drugs.' His voice trailed off as he was about to say 'after you judged me innocent and had me brought down.'

And he frowned in puzzlement.

'I wonder if—' he muttered, almost to himself, 'Could it be that—' he smiled a bitter smile, 'Perhaps I owe my life to that grim parasite.'

Footsteps clattered along the corridor and he stood up determinedly.

'Parks, you'd better get some rest. Take my cabin until we get everything cleared up in here. Try not to blame yourself. Perhaps others will, but it will all blow over in time.' And then, turning to Willis who had arrived with two sailors, he snapped,

'Go below and wake the Beast-Leashers. *All* of them.'

'All of them, Sir!' cried Willis aghast. 'Why on earth should we—'

'*All* of them,' repeated The Admiral. 'At dawn we're going to put every Dog we've got onto that island and clear the place up once and for all. Now jump to it. It will be light soon.'

Meanwhile, The Killer, The Phantom Strangler, The Body Snatcher, The Once-Great Queen of The Steriles, She who had thought herself Matriarch of The Whole World, drifted in from the sky, invisible against the stars, tracking, with barely understood senses, the whereabouts of her material form, puzzled to discover herself drawn, not to the desert as she had presupposed, but towards the wee white fishing village that stared imperturbably out towards the Western horizon and she marvelled at the magic that could have transported her body across the world in a single day.

And more bewildered did she become, as closer to the stone-rooved houses she flew, to perceive scurrying forms in the darkness of the narrow, cobbled streets. But greater still was her astonishment to find herself drawn into a scene the like of which she had never before witnessed. A tiny, smoke-filled room, a peat fire, huddled creatures, some in the clothes of The Others, some in the bodies of men that she had learned to recognize from her own ordeal inside one and, in the corner, the iron-bound box in which she had imprisoned The Crone throughout her persecuted existence.

*

She paused in wonderment but then, remembering her purpose, she entered the box, her immaterial body sliding into the hollow darkness as though there had been no impediment.

'So,' she said to The Crone in severe tones. 'I have found you again.'

There was a gasp of surprise in the darkness.

'Ana!' croaked The Crone, waking from an uneasy and restless slumber. 'Ana, is that you?'

'Aye,' replied Ana. 'Who else would waste their time talking to the likes of you?'

'I am weak, Ana,' said The Crone. 'I have no stomach for your bitterness. Leave me in peace. I borrowed your body but it has imprisoned me. I cannot extricate myself and it is dying.'

'Everything dies, Bearded One, except you whom I have many times wounded mortally to no avail.'

'Oh, that was then,' replied The Crone. 'I clung to life to see myself revenged upon you, Oh Sterile One, but I have seen disaster come upon your Royal House and upon your peoples until I am sickened with it. I have seen enough. I am finished. The moment of my death is soon upon me. I have always known it would be like this. Listen. Do you hear the voice of a tiny child?'

In the silence of the room The Last Child of Woman Born lay awake, gurgling peaceably at the flickering shadows of the firelight.

'I hear it,' replied Ana.

'That sound has always been in my dreams of death. New life replacing the old.'

The breath of Ana's body rattled drily in her throat as The Crone struggled to speak.

'I hear it now and welcome it. I long to be free of this prison world. Do what you will, Vicious One. At last you may have the satisfaction of taking my life, even though it be wrapped up in your own body.'

'I have taken lives enough,' replied Ana. 'I am done with dreams of power and am saddened to find you so weak in spirit. I have seen much and learned much since we waited together in the desert tents for the approach of the armies with the intended sacrifice.'

'I hope they were bitter lessons for you, Wicked One,' rattled The Crone through Ana's lips, forcing a mocking laugh. 'You are utterly destroyed, Sterile Tyrant, your people are gone, your desert is carpeted in ash and your body is broken. If you have tears to shed, shed them now and may they choke you!'

'Ah, Brainless One,' replied Ana with delight. 'I see there is still some fire left in my playmate. Good. I had been afraid I would have lost you and never again enjoyed your smooth and charming repartee.'

'What devil drives you that you come to mock me even at the moment of my death?' whined The Crone angrily. 'Is there no end to your vicious malice, Ana?'

'I have not come to mock,' replied Ana, suddenly gentle, the words trembling as they passed from mind to mind. 'I have come to take you with me. We were children together once, you and I, playing as children play in the Palace Gardens. Then I became Queen and you became a stump. From that moment we were children no longer, but rather pawns in some brutal game that the heavens sought to play. Come, fly with me now. Let us find once more, together, our lost innocence and explore the gardens of the world. Let us be once more as tiny children to whom all is new and fresh and wonderful. In Life it was a strange bond of Hatred that yoked us together. Come, leave that worthless body and we will soar the skies, bound by Friendship – for in all those years of my blind and foolish sovereignty it was always to you I turned in desperation or fear. Do not leave me now to face the universe alone.'

'Fly with *you*?' came The Crone's icy reply. 'I would as soon fly with The Beast of Unreason.'

For a long moment there was a silence, then The Crone coughed once and the rattling breath in Ana's throat suddenly ceased.

'No!' cried Ana desperately. 'Do not leave me! Please! No! I dare not be alone! Crone! Old Companion! Do not desert me now!'

But all life had ceased in the withered frame as cold it grew in the grip of death.

'Please!' whispered Ana, beside herself with grief and loss. 'Please don't desert me now.'

But there was no reply from the inert body.

'Now are you revenged, Ancient One,' she muttered in anguish. 'Now am I doomed to an eternity of bleak solitude.'

And she was just about to hurl herself despairing into the beyond when a sharp voice crackled out beside her in the box.

'Well alright, Frightened One,' came the familiar tones of The Crone. 'I'll try for a while. It might not be such a bad idea. But this time *I* want to be called the Queen and I want *you* to be The Crone. Is it agreed? Say it. Call me "Your Majesty".'

'Very well,' replied Ana in relief and delight. 'Very well,' she almost choked on the words but forcing them out, said. 'Very well, Your Majesty.'

57

Meanwhile, elsewhere in the darkened village, there had been a tragic accident. The Disciple, having seen Brother One give his covert instructions to the Orphachins and pretend to fall asleep, slipped from the cottage where the weary group had taken shelter and waddled, as best he could on water-numbed feet, in search of the scavengers.

'Don't see why they should get to do The Lord's bidding and not me,' he muttered as he squinted into the moon-shadowed blackness, trying to detect the tiny scurrying forms skulking in the sidestreets.

'And besides,' he grunted to himself, 'they're sure to have gone off looking for something to eat. Why shouldn't *all* of us acolytes get fed?'

He blundered on over the cobbled streets from which the flood waters had almost drained away and chanced a few tentative calls into the darkness.

'Gobbly, Gobbly,' he cooed. 'Gobbly, Gobbly.'

That should fetch them, he thought. That's what they say to each other. Easy when you know the lingo.

'Gobbly, Gobbly. Gobbly, Gobbly.'

Suddenly he stopped in surprise to see the silhouette of smoke rising up against the sky.

'Lost my way,' he muttered. 'Gone full circle. Back to square one!'

But just then he heard the soft gobbling of the Orphachins in the shadows at the base of the cottages and crept eagerly forward. It's not the same place, he thought. They've found food! They're all twittering.

It was true.

As he drew closer he could see them scratching at the shutters of the cottage with the smoking chimney, a cottage that must contain eatables, for the Orphachins gobbled hysterically, crawling upon each other's backs in their excitement and being crawled upon.

'Gobbly, Gobbly,' he called softly. 'Gobbly, Gobbly.'

They turned towards him and a shaft of light squeezing through the cracked shutter picked up several pairs of bright eyes.

'Gobbly. Gobbly,' said spotlit, sharp-toothed jaws in reply, and from the corners of their mouths saliva hung in moving threads.

'Gobbly, Gobbly,' he agreed, nodding. 'Fetchy, Fetchy. Gobbly, Gobbly.'

These were the last distinct words The Disciple ever uttered.

The Orphachins swarmed across the cobbles and fell upon him.

Ravenous.

One or two shrill screams pierced the darkness but they were cut short even before the echoes had returned from the narrow alleyways of the village as the cannibal army acted upon his nodded consent to Gobbly Gobbly.

So hungry were the Orphachin pack that most forgot they had been sent out to scavenge food for their General, although one or two slipped away with a few small pieces. For the rest it was simply a matter of catch-as-catch-can, sinking in their teeth wherever they could, tearing away limbs and scrapping about the streets with them, fighting each other for the prizes, trying to drag away chunks to eat in privacy. And it was with great difficulty that one loyal Orphachin escaped with an arm and hand, running through the back streets, hotly pursued by half a dozen starving brethren, able to give them the slip only after a long and tortuous chase. He failed to notice that the hand bore the scar of a Snowcamp survivor and could not have understood why, on delivering his gift to The General, The Goddy should have become so angry in the head, ripped it from The General's hands and made all the Orphachin minds go blank with rage and grief.

Even as they stood over the bones of The Disciple the thoughts came to them and filled them with a sense of dreadful anguish and terrible loss, so that they covered their ears with their little hands and cowered against the wet ground.

'Goddy, Goddy,' they whimpered anxiously, feeling his loathing and revulsion wash over them. And so strong did their hatred for the act they had so recently perpetrated become that they began to cuff each other involuntarily over the head and spit upon themselves contemptuously.

'Goddy, Goddy,' they wailed, accentuating each word with a blow to some other Orphachin, 'Goddy, Goddy. Naughty, Naughty. Goddy say Naughty, Goddy say Naughty.'

And as Brother Two's raging anger built up to a crescendo inside their little heads, they became traumatized by the savagery of the emotion, their collective consciousness seared and torn by the white-hot waves of hostility and horror for each other that flooded over them, washing their sense of self away until they stood, glazed, shaking, trembling and weeping in self-disgust, unable to understand anything except that they had committed the most dreadful crime in their Goddy's Universe.

From that moment to this no Orphachin has laid a single tooth upon human flesh and even thoughts of so doing produce a blinding mental agony that reminds them of that awful traumatic night. And so, perhaps, The Disciple did not live and die in vain, for his passing marked the end of an era for the Orphachins, an end to their parasitical existence, freeing them from the curse of centuries, healing up the short-circuit of their destinies that had caused them to die at puberty, opening up, in one white-hot moment of terrible selfdoubt, the perhaps equally painful road through full manhood.

And upon the spot where he fell, to die horribly between a hundred teeth, was erected a magnificent monument to his death – The Tomb of The Fallen Disciple – marking not only the evolutionary change of course for the Orphachins, but also the place at which the survivors upon the island first came together.

For, as the horrorstricken brothers and their frightened companions rushed to the tragedy, the door of the cottage burst open and out ran The Father, The Barbans and the women of the religious sect that served the Candle Palace, all armed, somewhat clumsily, with the primitive weapons of the submarine civilizations.

They converged on the spot, expecting to witness a terrible butch-

266

ery, but instead stood thunderstruck to see each other appearing from the darkness of the night.

The Candle Palace servants recognized Amrita and Tomaly-Somaly with cries of relief, delighted that two of their mistresses had come to lead them out of the terrors of their frightened confusion.

And The Brothers recognized The Father, wrinkled mirror-self, source of their genes, and cried out in joy, shouted in glee, seizing him and each other with eager arms and dancing round and round in a hysterical ecstatic circle, jigging up and down the cobbled street, wheeling and spinning, hugging and pushing and cavorting until their throats were hoarse, their feet were sore and their chests ached from laughing and singing.

The Orphachins, bleached pure by the searing red-hot telepathic rage of Brother Two, now found themselves carried away in turn by waves of joy and laughter, clasping each other in like fashion and jumping round and round with manic, hysterical and uncontrollable glee, whirling between the empty echoing cottages with shrill peals of sweet relief and mad-cap fun. And who could have stood sourly by to see such celebrations flare out so suddenly and brightly in the darkness of a dread-filled night?

And who could not have been swept up in a joyful release of long pent-up tension?

Who could not have seized the nearest partner and plunged head-long into that same bacchanalian frenzy?

Barbans danced with Barbans, The Women danced with The Women, The Orphachins danced with The Brothers and Their Father, Tomaly-Somaly and Amrita danced with Barbans who danced with The Women, who danced with the Orphachins, who danced and danced and laughed and danced and sang and humanity dissolved from its separate shells and mingled indiscriminately in the hysterical mêlée, all celebrating the joy of all in one all-consuming, salving and purifying, moon-swayed madness, while high in the sky The Queen and The Crone spun, twisting and whirling across the sky, shadow against the stars, tumbling and wheeling over the moon-snowed rooftops, laughing in guileless glee to see such innocent joy.

Meanwhile Yeni and The Last Child of Woman Born slept sweetly before the flickering warmth of the fading fire.

*

Meanwhile three hunched figures crept, terrified, towards the sea.

'Anything!' The Volunteer grunted as they stumbled down towards the stone quaysides, 'We should try *anything* rather than stay with these people! They're crazy! All of them.'

'We could say they attacked us,' wheezed Johnson, running as though the Wolves of Hell were on his heels.

'The Limbo-Basket would be a better way to go,' agreed The Girl, holding tightly to The Volunteer's hand to steady herself in their wild descent to the water's edge.

Meanwhile, on the far side of the island, night gave way gracefully to the red-eyed dawn.

The sun, peeking over the horizon, bent its weak and nearly horizontal rays across the sea, sliding its warming fingers over the desert, turning the twin-spined mountain range to pearl and coral. Slowly rolled the Earth, basting itself, perpetually turning its cold and benighted blindness towards its burning God. And the edge of Dawn, a red and softened line of light, rippled, static, over the revolving ocean, waking the sun animals from their dreams and filling the creatures of the dark with sleep. And the heavy-lidded Watchmen, snapping out of slumber with the precision of a lifetime's practise, sang the familiar call,

'Dawn. Up on deck. Dawn. Up on deck.'

But for The Admiral there was no joy in the softly changing colours of the sky or the dissolution of the darkness in the soft warmth of morning. He stood alone upon the bridge, all officers sent below lest they attempt to sway his grim purpose, dissuade him from the grisly duty he had vowed to perform. He took the Speaking Tube in his hand, breathing deeply to calm himself. He did not want his voice to shake when the order came.

'Cox!' he snapped brusquely into the mouthpiece.

'Sir?' came the surly, resentful, knowing reply.

'Are all Beast-Leashers standing by?'

'Standing by, Sir,' came the reluctant confirmation.

'All Plague-Dogs aboard the boats?'

'All Plague-Dogs aboard the boats,' came the distressed monotone.

'Beast-Leashers to the boats,' ordered The Admiral, forcing all emotion from his voice, speaking in the dry clear tones of impersonal Fate. There was a long moment of dreadful, heavy silence and then,

'All Beast-Leashers aboard the boats, Sir.'

The Admiral shakily replaced the Speaking Tube in its cradle, turned away from the island and stood looking out over the ocean, hands gripping the wooden rail so tightly that he could feel the shape of his fingernails pulsing with blood-filled pain.

'Steady, Admiral,' he whispered.

He turned to the island, shrouded in a faint morning mist as the sun trickled through the mountains and spread its warmth over the streaming plains, then, closing his eyes, he reached for the Tube again.

'Cox?'

'Sir?'

He felt a trembling shudder rise up inside him and heard it break from his mouth in a single anguished sob.

'Pardon Sir?' queried the tiny, distant voice. 'I didn't catch that.'

The Admiral drew himself stiffly erect, covered his mouth with his hand and, bracing himself for a final effort, spoke with firm clear tones into the mouthpiece.

'I said all boats away.'

Ten seconds passed like hours before the reply came, muffled and anguished.

'All boats away, Sir. All the damn boats are on their bloody way.'

58

The graceful boats slipped from their kennels and bounded over the tranquil sea. From the rails of every galley the crews silently watched the lethal loads scything through the water towards the island's shores. The whining and screaming of the shrouded baskets mingled with the wheeling shrieks of the curling gull-hawks to fill the morning with penetrating and mournful discord, while the rowers reluctantly plied their oars and The Beast-Leashers stared back, white-faced, at their companions aboard ship. No words were exchanged in that dreadful creaking silence as the flotilla of doom carried their diseased weapons across the narrow breadth of water. The Dogs, The Ecological Destroyers, the Ultimate Weapon in the Neo-navy's arsenal, yapped and slavered in their headbags, maddened by the shifting foothold of their basketwork cages, sensing the wild free-run killing that was to come. They screamed and strained against their leashes, frothing and churning, formenting in the fury of the drugs-roots that turned them from powerful, loyal and obedient hounds to rabid, implacable killers, known to attack even though their limbs were half-severed, driven beyond the credible limits of a living organism by the crazy power of their curdled minds. Once a Plague-Dog had slipped the leash it would kill and kill until its legs could no longer carry it, would then attack the very ground on which it lay, the very legs that had crumpled in exhaustion, rip out its own belly in hysterical frenzy, sinking its diseased teeth hungrily into its own flanks over and over again until the vital organs gave out and it lay, even in death, twitching and snapping uncontrollably with lifeless jaws. Nothing could stand against a Plague-Dog. The smallest nip from its monstrous teeth would mean, sooner or later, inevitably, a horrible lingering and tormented death in the grip of the terrible virus they carried within them.

The Admiral moved to the signal mast, unsleeved the black flag which would order the Dogs released and watched as the tiny boats closed up to the stone jetties of the fishing village. None would dare disobey a signal flag and this time there was no mutinous Flagman to subvert his command.

Clear and calm now, with the cold resolve of the mass-killer, unreflective, determined, resentful, he released the slender ropes to send the flag sailing up the mast on its counter-weight, unfurling into the onshore breeze, billowing out, dark and deadly, against the dawn sky.

It was done.

The order was given.

To all in the Neo-navy that flag had but a single meaning. 'Unleash the Beasts!'

The Beast-Leashers watched it open up in the wind and stared at each other without expression, emotionless, distressed, until a grey-haired old man amongst them rose to his feet crying, 'Come on! If we're going to do it let's get it over with. But hear this—'

There was a reluctant proprietary pride in his voice as he laid a trembling hand upon his Beast's covered cage.

'I've had this Beast twelve years without once unleashing her. This was our last trip and I know she'll not come back.' He stared round belligerently.

'So Pluggo goes first! Understand? It's her *right*.'

The Volunteer, The Girl and Johnson also saw the black flag unfurl upon the masthead of The Admiral's galley as they ran along the quayside hailing the boats. They had seen the grim cages and knew the dreadful creatures they contained, but their voices would not carry to the Beast-Leashers over the furious rabid yapping of the slavering charges and they flew desperately, on wings of terror, knowing full well their lives depended on it, shouting and waving maniacally.

'Alright,' agreed The Captain of Leashers, 'Pluggo goes first, but we can't give her more than a few seconds. It's too dangerous while we're so close to shore. Ready with your balls, men!'

Each Beast-Leasher took a coloured ball from the pouch at his waist and held it in readiness. The Dogs had been trained to follow their own special ball on first leaving their cages. By the time the balls had been bitten to pieces and the lunatic hounds turned in search of new quarry the boats would already be halfway back to the ship and safely out of reach.

'Uncover cages,' ordered The Leasher Captain.

The Volunteer and his desperate companions were now in sight, stumbling and flailing, exhausted, along the quay and shouting as though they intended never to use their throats again. But all attention was fixed upon the Dogs, screaming and snarling with ever wilder fury as the morning light fell upon their bloodshot, rolling eyes. Once the cages were opened they would be ashore in a single bound and forever beyond recall.

'No! Wait! We're here!' screamed Johnson and The Girl.

'Please God! No!' shouted The Volunteer. 'Wait! We'll never make it in time. Turn back! We'll never make it!'

'Take your lanyards,' bawled The Leasher Captain and each man took firmly in his hands the thong that would open the dreadful cages. There could be no mistakes without appalling fatalities. Every nerve stretched tight as a bow-string.

'Stop! No! We're here!' shouted the running sailors.

'Pluggo first,' The Leasher Captain reminded them, roaring hoarsely over the cacophony of the Dogs. 'On the count of three.'

'No! For God's sake stop!'

271

'One!'

'Don't let them loose! We're here. Stop! Stop!'

'Two!'

'Look! Stop! No! Please! No!'

'What's that noise?'

'Look, Sir! There, Sir! People running! It's Johnson and the others! They're alive! They made it back!'

'Stand down Leashers! Cover your cages!'

There was pure pleasure in the Leasher Captain's voice, the delight of giving commands that expressed every man's heartfelt wish.

'Balls away!' he ordered.

And as the three exhausted sailors flung themselves gratefully into the boats a spontaneous cheer broke out.

'Back to the fleet,' ordered The Captain readily, and the oarsmen pulled swiftly and willingly away from the shore, more light of heart than any drug could have rendered them, while the crews of the galleys gave a rousing cry of joy to see the boats returning with their baskets still loaded.

Even The Admiral gave a grim smile along on his bridge.

'Well,' he breathed with a long sigh, 'I did what I could. Sod them all. Now they'll break loose, take discipline into their own hands, go ashore looting.' He shook his head in resignation. 'And put me in the Limbo-Basket, I shouldn't wonder.'

But his spirits lifted as the boats drew nearer and he saw they carried the three ragged deserters.

'Send those three scoundrels up to the bridge when they come aboard,' he ordered down the Speaking Tube.

'Yessir,' came the elated voice of The Cox. 'Shall I hold the boats, Sir?'

'Yes, Cox.' replied The Admiral. 'Hold the boats for further orders.'

He glanced up at the black banner flying in the wind and shuddered.

'Perhaps it's just as well,' he muttered, winching it slowly down the mast. 'Perhaps it's just as well.'

The three survivors clambered wearily but happily aboard the galley and ran the gauntlet of their cheering comrades to scale the ladder to the bridge, where The Volunteer poured out their hurriedly-prepared story with confused haste.

272

'Terrible place – strange demons, Sir – no people – just invisible creatures – flew over the whole island – volcano dormant again – evil influences – utterly barren – no sign of civilization – horrid ghosts – wailing banshees – perpetual terror – fear for the safety of the fleet – suggest we turn for home without delay – Plague-Dogs no use against invisible enemy – not a moment to lose – too risky to send a survey team – we escaped only by skin of teeth – unbelievable horrors – never encountered anything like it – hear they came on board and caused The Watcher unnecessary death – dangerous to stay.'

'Stop, stop, stop,' complained The Admiral gently, holding up his hands defensively. 'It's as I suspected. The island is inhabited by invisible spirits. I suppose we should have expected the unexpected from a technological civilization. Go below and make your report to The Narrator; he'll take it down verbatim and we'll sift through it later. In the meantime, consider yourselves reprimanded for contravening orders—'

'But, Sir!' protested The Volunteer. 'We were only trying to save you having to unleash the—'

The Admiral stopped him once more with upraised hands.

'Consider yourselves reprimanded,' he repeated, 'and welcome back aboard. You'll be relieved of duties for twenty-four hours to give you a chance to rest. You look pretty worn out. Dismiss.'

'Is that all, Sir?' asked Johnson in surprise and relief.

'What else did you expect?' said The Admiral suspiciously.

'Oh, nothing, Sir,' replied The Girl quickly, putting all her weight on Johnson's foot. 'Are we turning for home, Sir?'

The Admiral looked out over the island, its mountain ranges silhouetted against the rising sun, and looked back at her.

'You're very anxious to get away,' he remarked drily, 'considering how anxious you were to go ashore this time yesterday.'

'We're concerned for the safety of The Fleet,' replied The Girl. 'That's all, Sir.'

The Admiral examined their faces closely one by one, observing the flicker of guilt in their eyes and the tense, unnatural posture of their bodies.

'Whose idea was it to go ashore?' he demanded with sudden severity.

They shuffled uneasily and made no reply.

'Johnson. Was it you?'

'No, Sir.'

He turned to The Girl.

'Was it you?'

'No Sir,' replied The Girl uncomfortably.

The Admiral stood before The Volunteer, his face only inches away and said,

'I'm going to teach you a lesson that you'll never forget. You're going to learn the meaning of discipline in the hardest possible way.' He glared with vindictive savagery. 'I'm going to recommend you for *Admiral*.'

The Volunteer's jaw dropped in surprise.

'And one day,' The Admiral continued, 'when you retire, as I am about to do, perhaps you'll drop by and tell me just what happened on that island. Will you promise me that, Lieutenant?'

'Yes. Sir,' stammered The Volunteer.

'Good,' replied The Admiral, nodding his satisfaction. 'Now go below and get your story straight before you speak to The Narrator. We don't want some Desk-Dog dragging all this out of the archives for an enquiry in twenty years time. Dismiss.' He watched the relieved sailors disappear down the ladder and smiled to himself.

It's almost as though they had 'Culture-Damage' branded on their foreheads, he thought. But how much can a retiring Admiral be expected to do in one day? If I could cope with all this I wouldn't be quitting.

He reached for the Speaking Tube again.

'Cox?'

'Yessir?'

'Bring in the boats. Beast-Leashers stand down. Man the oar-decks.'

'Does that mean we're going home, Sir?' came the delighted reply.

'Any objections, Cox?'

'No, Sir. Sorry, Sir. Right away.'

The galleys clattered with life as shrill whistles sent the crews scattering to their stations and The Admiral breathed a sigh of relief to find the others as anxious as he to be gone. The Lieutenant of The Watch appeared on the ladders.

'Alright to come on duty now, Sir?'

'Yes, Lieutenant. I'm going below to get some rest. You take over for a while.'

'What instructions, Sir?' asked the Lieutenant warily and the Admiral smiled.

'Instructions? Instructions?' he said softly. 'Why, take it home, Lieutenant. Just take it home.'

59

Suddenly I was back in the boathouse, the familiar rough wooden boards against my cheek, the same river lapping against the structural piles, the same fetid darkness broken only by a chink of light in one of the wooden walls.

I jerked fully awake.

It wasn't possible!

A dream?

The torments of the snowcamp, the volcano, the forced march across the flooded plains, the collapse of the Candle Palace, reunion with my brother and my father, all a ghastly dream? It seemed impossible and yet – I stiffened with fear as I heard an inquisitive scratching at the chink of light and, somewhere in the background, very softly whispered, the words,

'Gobbly, Gobbly.'

For a moment I was filled with a despair so terrible that I was almost overwhelmed.

I could hardly believe that my imagination would play so cruelly with my tortured heart.

But then my courage returned and I sat grimly in the darkness, realizing I must face whatever reality chose to bring me and deal with it as best I could.

I crawled over to the hatch to check that my battening was secure, moving as slowly and quietly as my wretchedly desperate body would allow, feeling around in the darkness for the familiar shape as the scratching at the walls grew to a loud and forceful banging. I had lost my bearings and scrabbled across the floor in confusion, sweeping the rough boards with my hands in wide arcs, disconcerted, lost and blind.

Suddenly a great hole blew open in the wall, my cell filled with light, the sunshine blazed in, my senses staggered and I gave out a mighty cry of rage and fear.

There at the window stood Timbley-Mumbley!

I shook my head in disbelief once more.

This was no boathouse!

This was a cottage in the little fishing village. The sound of the river was the draining floods bouncing down the gutters of the cobbled street. The voices of Orphachins filtered out from some game they were playing nearby.

It had been no dream!

It was real!

'I'm sorry if I startled you,' said Turley-Surley, startled. 'I couldn't open the shutter. It was stuck so I thumped it in from the outside. I thought you would like to wake up before the afternoon is all spent.'

'It wasn't a dream,' I mumbled inarticulately. 'You're real!'

'The Orphachins found a stag that drowned in the floods. The Barbans have built a fire to roast it. My women are preparing it. You must come.'

'I have to talk with you, Timbley-Mumbley,' I said seriously. 'Please come inside.'

'Tomaly-Somaly,' she corrected then, reappearing at the door, said, 'We must go to The Feast. I would not like to be late for The Feast.'

'Just for a moment,' I said. 'Please. There's something very important I have to ask you.'

She entered gracefully and sat down in front of me, arranging tattered robes about her feet.

'What is it you wish to ask?' she enquired, gazing up at me with her frank, blue eyes.

'I wanted to ask you if you would like a yard of this up your passage,' I replied earnestly.

'A yard of what, Brother Two?'

I pondered for a moment, puzzled.

Surely this was not the appropriate response.

I tried again.

'How about a good time, cheesecake?'

'Very well,' she replied with a shrug. 'Let's go to The Feast.'

'No, you misunderstand. Listen carefully.' I searched my mind for anything that might trigger off the 'mating behaviour' I had been led to expect.

'How about a bit of nookie, slap and tickle, how's yer father, baby's arm with an apple in its fist, you know-what, hanky-panky, doctors and nurses, your place or mine, Long John Thomas, Tricky Dicky, Whey-hey-hey, whadya say baby, two-backed beasts, naughty negligees, quick bunk-ups, leg-overs, do you smoke afterwards I don't know I've never looked?'

Her face remained impassive.

'Well?' I insisted.

'Well what?' she asked blankly.

'What about it?'

'What about what?'

'Any of it!' I exclaimed in frustration. 'Don't you have any response at all?'

She shrugged and looked thoughtful.

'Babies can't eat apples. They don't have any teeth,' she replied.

I closed my eyes in defeat and let my head fall.

'You are unhappy?' she enquired with concern. 'Have I done something to upset you?'

I shook my head wearily.

'Nothing,' I replied. 'It's just I thought that perhaps – but then I must have been mistaken. I suppose it was too much to hope for. That's always been my trouble, Tibley-Bobley, optimism.'

'Tomaly-Somaly,' she corrected. 'What is it you hoped for?'

Before I could choke it back, a bitter and ironic laugh escaped from me.

'Angels,' I replied bluntly. 'I suppose I expected angels and goddesses.'

'Why do you seek goddesses?' she asked suspiciously. 'Do you hope to catch and eat them?'

'No. Not exactly.'

It was the open innocence in her eyes that made me decide to explain.

'You see, Tummy-Dummy—'

'Tomaly-Somaly.'

'Oh yes, sorry. You see I had this belief that at one time men and women lived together on the earth in total harmony and continual

277

ecstasy. Where I come from, at the bottom of the sea, certain ancient manuscripts have been preserved in the libraries that seemed to tell of such a time and even describe how the two races related to each other. I had hoped that by learning the language and coming up out of the water I could re-establish the old contact and communion and restore the ancient balance of nature. When I say things like, "fancy a quick one behind the gardenias?" you're supposed to become very excited and say something like, "I've been hot for it ever since you walked in" or "I won't tell your wife if you don't tell my husband." And then—'

'What does that mean?' she asked.

'I don't know,' I replied uncomfortably. 'But that's what happens in the ancient Teachings and I was hoping to find out.' I realized from her face that she was just as puzzled as me.

'I suppose the language must have died out,' I said mournfully. 'No more angels. No more goddesses.'

'There is *one* goddess left,' suggested Turbley-Durbley helpfully, 'but she doesn't speak at all. She is the last of the Wandering Menstrals.'

'Who are they?' I asked with a glimmer of hope.

'Oh, they are just young whales that didn't conceive. They bleed with the moon and so are initiated into the secrets of The Mothering, but when they do not become with child their tongues are cut out and they are expelled from the Candle Palace to wander wherever the wind blows until the Man-gods take them to the sky.'

She stopped in alarm and covered her mouth with her hand. 'Oh, I suppose I shouldn't say that any more. But that's what we were all told.'

'Yes,' I said excitedly. 'In the ancient texts there is much talk of not having children, which means that the goddesses must have been *capable* of having children, even though they never did!'

I was filled with renewed zeal.

'Who is this goddess? Where is she?'

'She is Yeni, Last of the Fallen Goddesses, Last of Those Who Bleed with the Moon. She was to have been sacrificed by the desert tribes to bring fertility to their barren lands as many of The Wandering Menstrals met their end, but your brother took her from them. She is with us.'

She suddenly frowned.

'But I must warn you against too much hope. The Wandering Menstrals are tragic mutants, they are neither women nor whales,

278

they bleed but do not breed. What use are they to anyone?'

'There's a slim chance that some of the ancient Teachings may survive through her,' I replied enthusiastically. 'And I can't give up hope until I've spoke to her.'

'Then let us go to The Feast,' replied Turbley-Burbley brusquely, 'for that is where you will find the sad creature.'

And what a feast there was!

The women had brought vegetables from their storehouse in the village to garnish the roasting venison and later, nervously, produced great jugs of carrot whisky, the source of which they refused to disclose even though Amrita accused them of trading illegally with the desert tribes. And all were elated to find food and friendship after the dark hours of despair that had threatened to annihilate us. And all were fit and well-rested, having collapsed, exhausted, by the wild, jubilant dancing of our first meeting and slept soundly for the whole day.

And as night fell we gathered closer around the crackling bonfire built by the Barbans in the tiny cobbled square and toasted our survival and our success, our past, present and future, with many a warming draught from the fast-circling liquor-jugs. We laughed and talked and drank and ate, learning much of our different worlds, now united in camaraderie around the cheering blaze, told all, forgave all and pledged all in a common resolve to live at peace together upon the tattered island as best we could, until sleep began to thin out our gathering with its gentle hand and the Orphachins, much affected by the whisky, broke off their good-natured brawling and staggered off to sleep, leaving the rest of us to stare into the fading firelight or lie back contentedly and gaze up at the stars.

Yeni sat with us, as silent as ever, but I did not venture to speak privately with her there, for my brother's tongue, loosened by the whisky, had made mock of me more than once that night for my 'fantasies of heaven', as he called them, and he guarded his 'rescued chap' with a jealous eye.

'One thing that's been puzzling me,' The Father said, after gazing reflectively into the fire for a long time, 'is where those people in the strange uniforms went. They just seemed to disappear.'

'They came from the sky,' Tumbley-Bumbley said. 'Perhaps they vanished in the same way.'

'Yes,' agreed Amrita. 'I saw strange apparitions over the rooftops when first we met over the bones of The Eaten One. I am sure they have flown back to their home in the moon.'

'More likely got polished off by my Orphachins,' boasted Brother One with a wobbling head. 'Good lads. Just went a bit astray. Seem to have lost control of them now, though. I wonder if—' He trailed off into a loose-lipped, drunken reverie.

'Orphachins am not eaten they,' replied one of the women with deep conviction. 'Them am the gods come to save we all. Mans-gods and Woman-gods come to reveal to we the ways.'

'What ways?' demanded The Father. 'All they revealed to *me* was how to tie someone to a table!'

'Them am comes to says none more eating mans,' replied the woman. 'Them am comes to tell we the news rituals so us can live in the new worlds without the killings.'

'New rituals?' said Amrita in surprise. 'All they told *me* was that the Candle Palace was in a terrible mess!'

'Them am showed *we*,' replied another of the women proudly. 'Us am them as have received the new teachings. And after us had been showed – pouf!' she threw her arms gracefully towards the stars, 'all am disappeared!'

'What did they show you?' demanded a Barban truculently. 'They told *us* they were Traders and would take us home. We made a deal and they broke it. What does that show?'

'That shows that them am not confidents that you am the right peoples to be the Chosen Ones like us am. Justs before the dawns the Man-god and the Womans-god puts the arms around their selves like these.'

She arranged the Barban's arms around her and placed her own around him. 'And then looks at each others likes this.' She forced the Barban to stare into her eyes for a long moment. 'After thats,' she said, breaking the embrace and reaching out for the liquor-jug proffered by her neighbour, 'every things come suddenly right. Us am cured from the Orphachins, us am stopped with the fightings, us dances, us laughs and sings, us rests, eat, drink and is happy. Before that – boom – every things is back and dyings. The gods am been sents to saves we at the nicks of time and shows the way us must keeps peace with they from now on.'

'Seaweed!' replied one of the Barbans contemptuously. 'Stinking seaweed!'

'Oh, I don't know,' put in The Father quickly, his eyes gleaming shrewdly even through an alcoholic glaze, 'I think they might be on to something.'

He nodded sagely.

'If we're going to live on this island then we're going to have to propitiate the island's gods and I think these good women would know far more about that than we do. After all,' he went on expansively, 'we're virtually *strangers* here. I think we would be very wise to go along with this.'

The women nodded their stern agreement with these sentiments.

'I think you Barbans should be on hand to perform these rituals every morning just before dawn.'

He grinned at The Barbans in mischievous triumph.

'That way we'll be able to keep an eye on each other and keep the gods on our side at the same time.'

'What kind of trick are you trying to pull?' snapped a Barban angrily.

But he was cut short by one of the women who slid her arms around him with grip of iron.

'Me takes this one. Same one every day. That way no persons forget.' She glared at him coldly. 'There am none choice where the gods am concerned. You fulfil the news ritual or else us eats you in the old one.'

The Father chortled in glee.

'A fine notion. Couldn't work out better! What do you say?'

He turned to Brother One, but the only reply from the unconscious form upon the cobbles was a gentle snoring.

'Brother One says yes,' giggled The Father.

I had waited anxiously for this opportunity all night and seized it immediately.

I slid over to Yeni, who watched the proceedings with aloof interest.

'Hey,' I said softly 'Why don't we go back to my place and get to know each other a little better?'

She turned to me and smiled.

A response!

I stood up offering my hand and, to my delight, she took it and rose to her feet.

With wildly beating heart I led her from the firelight and through the narrow darkened streets away from the square. Now, at last, I was to destruction-test my dreams!

60

Hand in hand, the goddess and I climbed the steep, cobbled streets until the buzz of argument around the crackling bonfire no longer reached us through the tranquil night. I looked around for a suitable cottage in which to talk with her and chose a building much larger than the others with a stout square tower and massive wooden doors opening on to a long hall supported by columns of crumbled stone.

Through a tall and elegant window moonlight flooded in, bathing the stark building with a soft luminescence.

'Come on in,' I said, watching her face closely for the slightest spark of responsive understanding, excitement, love or lust. 'Make yourself comfortable while I fix us a nightcap.' She was listening to me, but her gaze wandered round our eerie hiding-place; she stared long and hard into the shadows before satisfying herself we were alone and sitting down on a low step in the brightest patch of moonlight.

'Timbley-Bumbley tells me you're a goddess,' I said. And in reply she nodded sadly, drew a cross on her belly, a cross upon her mouth, shrugged and hung her head.

'I came from another world looking for you,' I blurted out in a clumsy attempt to comfort her. '*I* don't think you're a mutant. I think you're rather beautiful.'

She made no reply, not even raising her head, and then I saw a single tear drop gleaming through the moonlight.

Blew it again, I thought. Why do I keep forgetting that I've got to stick to the language of the Teachings?

'Jeepers creepers, take a look at those peepers,' I said sympathetically. 'What's a swell dame like you doing in a place like this?'

She looked up at me and tried to smile.

At last I thought, spirits rising, I might be getting somewhere.

I pressed home my advantage.

'First time I saw you I thought I was married to a guy!' I said. 'What time do you get off work, Doll-face? Are those jugs real or have you got cancer?'

I laboured on under her inscrutable stare.

'Excuse me, but I'm a stranger in town, could you direct me to your house? I'm loaded in more ways than meet the eye unless you look carefully. Stick with me, baby, and I'll make you a star!'

I had her attention still, but seemed to have made some sort of mistake, for the shadow of a frown flickered across her forehead.

I pressed on desperately.

'Hey Toro! Go for your gun, you swamp-rat. I used to be a seven stone weakling. Don't worry Olive, I'll save you. Any more at home like you, Sister? Who's this guy in the wardrobe? Won't you wear my ring around your neck? Who needs contraceptives at a time like this? The guys tell me you come across. Why don't we climb in the back?'

I began to recognize the expression on her face as one of incomprehension and redoubled my efforts to communicate. 'Nobody looks at the mantel piece when they're stoking the fire. She'll be alright with a bag over her head. Either treat me nice or you can walk back to town.'

I dried up in discouragement as she turned to stare at the moon framed in the arched window.

The light fell across her hair and shoulders as lightly as a caress.

'I got the hots,' I muttered at random, running out of memorized phrases fast, pacing urgently around the hall to aid my concentration and applying myself once more to the task.

'What do you say to a hundred dollars, fruitcake? Darling I'd like you to marry me. Do as I say or I'll scar you for life. I can do it eight times a night. What kind of massage do you do? We ought to find out whether we're sexually compatible before we get involved in anything deep and meaningful, don't you think? Has anyone ever told you that you have the most exquisite hands? It's just I have this sneaking fear that I'm a homosexual, what do *you* think? If I say I'm sorry will you let me do it again? Down the hatch, Honey. A frank exchange of sexual fantasies is always healthy, don't you agree? Okay, games over, get 'em off. You wait here while I get the room key. Because it said "no clothes" on the invitation that's why.'

I could tell I was getting nowhere.

I had made three full circuits of the room, raking up everything I could think of, but to no avail.

Sometimes I would look up to see her watching me with puzzled interest, at other times she would be gazing out of the window, staring into the shadows or playing with her fingers.

'Hey, Nurse!' I called to her without conviction, 'What's your treatment for hot nuts?'

She didn't even look round.

It was no good.

I had to admit I was beaten.

Brother One had been right. This wasn't heaven. There were no angels.

'All the goddesses are dead,' I murmured to myself bitterly.

'We're all just men and women now. Just ordinary men and women.'

I walked over to her sadly and held out my hand.

'Let's go to the others, Yeni,' I said. 'You must be getting very cold in here.'

For a moment she seemed not to have heard me, staring out at the night sky with a curious concentration. Then, to my surprise, she looked up, took my hand and pulled me down beside her with a shy smile.

'What is it, Yeni?' I asked. 'What's the matter?'

She pointed out through the window eagerly and I saw a soft change in the colour of the sky, a melting blue spreading up through the blackness of the Eastern night.

Very gently she took my arms and placed them round her and, after pointing once more at the approaching dawn, placed her own around me, turned my face towards her with delicate fingers and stared into my eyes.

'Oh, the dawn,' I said, suddenly understanding.

I laughed.

'Yeni, I don't think we have to take that too seriously. That's just some crazy misunderstanding the women got into their heads.'

Even as I spoke the light reflecting in her eyes changed from the dark blue of night to the violet of dawn.

'And The Father went along with it because he—'

I felt the warmth of her skin for the first time.

'And he went along with it because the Barbans and he—' It seemed as though an unseen ray of light joined us together.

'And he—'

There were enormous depths in her eyes. Humour, passion, sadness, wisdom, warmth. I tried to speak but found no words.

No words that could have any meaning over the powerfully charged understanding that grew between us. For a long moment it seemed as though I perceived all humanity within her, all the intelligent and magical symmetry of the universe in complex and myriad beauty and within myself I experienced an intensity I had never known, a joy, a power, a clarity I could never have dreamed possible. It was as though my entire being were passing into her through hands and eyes and being returned to me, subtly transmuted and recharged a hundredfold, only to pass into her again and be returned until we became a single organism within whom a magical energy spiralled upwards, doubling and redoubling, drawing every sensate atom of our bodies into its accelerating climb, inhaling the earth and sky, consuming the universe itself as it narrowed into a blinding point of incandescent energy.

The bonds of Time and Space snapped apart and fell away, eternity existed for a single instant and the moment lasted for ever, everywhere, for we were the future and the history of the universe in cypher and, for that instant, on levels beyond thought and feeling, we understood the meaning of that cypher within ourselves and, in that instant, were gods.

The hidden mysteries of blinding splendour expressed in purest simplicity.

Revelation.

The moment faded.

We became aware of our new awareness.

Became once more a part of the universe instead of containing it.

The structures of Time and Space reappeared around us.

We shrank to the stature of human beings, limbs intertwined, sitting awkwardly on a cold stone floor in the pearly sunlight of a chill dawn.

We had not moved.

But we were not as before.

Nor ever would be as before.

We smiled into each other's hearts and slowly drew apart, breathing a shared sigh of wonderment and awe.

'I think we might have stumbled upon something here,' I tried to say. But, once more, words were too coarse an instrument to separate the delicate elements of our shared rebirth, ringing flat and hollow in the empty air.

'I think I'll let you do the talking,' I whispered.

*

Meanwhile the dawn comes, seeping on to the tiny island crucible, working once more its cyclic magic upon earth, sea and sky in the revolving drama of birth, death and resurrection. The Orphachins blink awake, startled and inspired by their mutually shared dream of a universe within and the dissolution of Time and Space, sharing the essence of the revelation in the hilltop shrine. The Barbans submit with ill-grace to the perfunctory embrace of the new apostles and yet are not unduly displeased. The Last Child of Woman Born, destined to lose his title to a sibling, gazes at the changing patterns on his unfocussed eyes with the complete wisdom of tranquil innocence and says,

'Wah,'

To the sunshine.

Tomaly-Somaly and Amrita lie dreaming in each other's arms, sharing at least some of heaven's beauty in their reflected selves while The Father and Brother One snore out the carrot whisky beside the dying embers of the night.

And, somewhere between the earth and stars, Ana and The Crone, youth and folly restored, observe with keen and penetrating joy how a silence has fallen upon the earth, a silence that the world has known but once; a silence in which even the Earth does not turn, nor the Moon revolve around it, nor the planets flame their dreadful orbits, when Time itself stands still and with a noiseless scream reverses itself once more, slow and ponderous at first, but gathering pace as it recoils helically through centuries of centuries, knitting up history as easily as it had been unravelled, a self-perpetuating radiance, a re-affirmation of everything that has ever been.

Meanwhile, watched only by the rising sun and the fading moon, with the passion of purity and the purity of innocence, Yeni and Brother Two consummate their dreams in a divine manifestation of the real.

Now read on.

Gabriel García Márquez
One Hundred Years of Solitude £1.25

A band of adventurers establish a town in the heart of the South American jungle. The occasion marks the beginning: of the world, of a great family, of a century of extraordinary events, and of an extraordinary novel.

'Sweeping, chaotic brilliance, often more poetry than prose ... one vast and musical saga' THE TIMES

'A classic on the grandest scale ... Márquez is a spellbinder' SPECTATOR

Caroline Blackwood
Great Granny Webster 80p

Great Granny Webster, silent and impassive in her straight-backed chair, is the rigid embodiment of all that is 'correct', as she ekes out her joyless and respectable existence. But her effect on succeeding generations of her aristocratic family is insidious and far-reaching ...

'A wicked black humour' GEORGE MELLY, OBSERVER

'A writer of such unusual subtlety and penetration' TIMES LITERARY SUPPLEMENT

Elias Canetti
Auto Da Fé £1.75

This extraordinary novel, set in Germany between the wars, tells of a distinguished scholar, Peter Kien, whose eccentric temperament leads him to destruction at the hands of a grotesque society. On one side stands his illiterate and grasping housekeeper who tricks him into marriage; on the other, a brutish concierge – and typical Nazi material. Kien is forced out into the underworld of the city, a purgatory where his guide is a chess-playing dwarf of evil propensities. Eventually restored to his home, he is visited by his brother, an eminent psychiatrist who, by an error of diagnosis, precipitates the final crisis ...

'A novel of terrible power' C. DAY LEWIS

'Disturbing ... terrifying ... ferociously funny' WALTER ALLEN

Ann Charters
Kerouac £1.25

'Kerouac conjured up a modern style hero in *On the Road*, invented the Beat Generation, fathered a life style and a writing style ... my generation weep over his loss' STANLEY REYNOLDS, GUARDIAN

'Behind the "crazy rebel" of the novels ... lay a life of insecurity and wretched loneliness ... a duality perceptively illustrated by Ann Charters in her lucid, well-researched biography' SUNDAY TELEGRAPH

'This exuberant, chaotic, and latterly wretched life ... an immensely readable story' TIMES LITERARY SUPPLEMENT

Colin Wilson
The Outsider £1.50

The classic study of alienation, creativity and the mind of modern man ... In a new introductory essay – written specially for this Picador edition – Wilson says of the book: 'It still produces in me the same feeling of excitement and impatience that I experienced as I sketched the outline plan on that Christmas Day of 1954 ... a feeling like leaving harbour.' This famous bestseller for the thinking man surveys the iconoclasts, from Barbusse to Camus, looking back to Dostoevsky and Tolstoy, to Blake and Nietzsche ...

'Astonishing' EDITH SITWELL

'Extraordinary' CYRIL CONNOLLY

'Staggeringly erudite ... a brilliant and unusual analysis of the pessimistic tradition in civilized thought' TIME MAGAZINE

You can buy these and other Picador Books from booksellers and newsagents; or direct from the following address:
Pan Books, Sales Office, Cavaye Place, London SW10 9PG
Send purchase price plus 20p for the first book and 10p for each additional book, to allow for postage and packing
Prices quoted are applicable in the UK

While every effort is made to keep prices low, it is sometimes necessary to increase prices at short notice. Pan Books reserve the right to show on covers and charge new retail prices which may differ from those advertised in the text or elsewhere